All the Hidden Truths

CLAIRE ASKEW

All the Hidden Truths

HODDER &
STOUGHTON

First published in Great Britain in 2018 by Hodder & Stoughton
An Hachette UK company

1

A CIP catalogue record for this title is available from the British Library

Hardback ISBN 978 1 473 67302 1
Trade Paperback ISBN 978 1 473 67303 8
eBook ISBN 978 1 473 67305 2

Typeset in Plantin Light by Hewer Text UK Ltd, Edinburgh
Printed and bound in Great Britain by Clays Ltd, Elcograf S.p.A.

Hodder & Stoughton policy is to use papers that are natural, renewable
and recyclable products and made from wood grown in sustainable
forests. The logging and manufacturing processes are expected to
conform to the environmental regulations of the country of origin.

Hodder & Stoughton Ltd
Carmelite House
50 Victoria Embankment
London EC4Y 0DZ

www.hodder.co.uk

For all the students I worked with at Edinburgh College.
You taught me way more than I ever taught you.

The day before

13 May, 12.30 p.m.

Moira Summers was on the top deck of the number 23 bus, her face turned up to the sun like a cat – it was the first day that year that could really have been called *hot*. She felt the bus pitch and begin to chug up the Mound. She'd always loved this view from the 23: on the right, the Castle, black and hewn, seeming to rise up out of Princes Street Gardens' seething trees. On the left, the whole of the New Town laid out in its smart grid. In the sunshine, Jenners department store and the Balmoral Hotel looked like gilded chocolate boxes, and the Scott Monument was Meccano-model-like, unreal.

She forced herself to press the bell and shuffle out of her seat, down the aisle and then the stairs of the swaying bus. She alighted outside the National Library of Scotland, whose double doors were mobbed by a gang of school kids. Moira felt herself tense. She'd come to sit in peace and do some studying for her OU degree, but the thought of being holed up in the dark, oppressive reading room on a day like this had already put a sullen feeling in her chest. A school-trip group clattering about the place practically guaranteed that she'd get nothing done.

'I want you in pairs!' A young, blonde woman was standing at the top of the steps inside the library entrance. 'In *pairs*, in *pairs*,' she chimed at the teens, but they paid no attention. Moira guessed they were maybe thirteen or so, but she'd become increasingly bad at guessing the ages of children. She always guessed too young – her own son, Ryan, was twenty, and although he looked like a man, she felt sure he could really only be ten at the most. Surely. Had time gone by so fast?

'*Pairs*,' the teacher said again. She looked young, too. Out of nowhere, Moira thought of her husband, Jackie: he'd been a teacher when she first met him. He'd taught PE to kids this age for decades, and she could imagine him making the same sing-song chant as this young woman. She tried to picture him: the young, lean man he'd been when they met, and found that she couldn't. *It hasn't even been that long*, she thought. *I can't lose him yet.*

As Moira blinked away her tears' warning sting, she realised the young, blonde teacher was speaking about her. She pointed down the steps at Moira – the pointing hand weighed down by a massive, turquoise-coloured ring. 'Kids, this lady wants to come in.'

Moira flinched.

'Oh no, I don't,' she sang over the heads of the children. Then she laughed, because it was true. But the mob did begin to trickle over to one side of the steps, and form a vague line.

Moira dithered. The ring on the teacher's hand looked like the lurid, sugary gobstoppers Ryan used to whine for in the corner shop, back when he really *was* ten years old. The children in front of her seemed to bear no resemblance to him, though – to the kids he'd been in school with. Children – and especially older children – seemed so much tougher, more streetwise, these days. The girls lounging on the steps before her all wore the same black, elasticated leggings, tiny skirts stretched over them so tight that Moira could see which girl was wearing lacy lingerie, and which was wearing piped cotton. She blinked and blushed, feeling like a pervert and a pearl-clutching granny all at once.

'Come on in,' the teacher called, over the heads of the chattering line.

But the boys at the top of the mock-marble steps were shoving and elbowing. Moira watched one of them take a slow, calculated look over his shoulder, and then swing out backwards, slamming his weight into a smaller boy on the step below. The big kid kept his hand firmly on the banister, making sure that he didn't fall – but his victim careened sideways into empty space, landing with a clatter and smack on the hard staircase.

'Jason!' The young teacher barked out the name in a way that sounded well practised. Moira winced, looking at the young man now sprawled on the steps. *Another Jason*, she thought. *The bad ones are always called Jason* – something Jackie used to say.

She turned away from the steps and the library, walking quickly until she had left behind the snickers of the tight-skirted girls. Moira thought of that boy's mother – how later, her kid would likely come slamming home morose, silent, and pound up the stairs without looking at her. Had that mother also given up asking what happened? Had she too begun to assume that this was just the man her son was growing into? And did she also, in moments of barefaced honesty, suspect that her own behaviour might be to blame?

Again, Moira blinked the sting from her eyes: *stop it*. She'd essentially just bunked off school, and it was a beautiful day. *Don't waste this*.

Across the street was an orange-fronted sandwich shop, not much more than a fridge and a space where two or three people could stand. Moira ordered a BLT with mayo – old-fashioned, she thought, scanning the fridge's display of quinoa, hummus and pomegranate seeds – and swung the meal in its brown paper bag as she paced up the ramp into Greyfriars Kirkyard.

This was a popular picnic spot: office workers in smart clothes sat in ones and twos on the grass, some with their shoes kicked off. A knot of people took it in turns to snap photos at the grave of Greyfriars Bobby, and to add to the pile of sticks left as presents for his canine ghost. Moira veered away from the kirk itself, heading downhill along the pea-gravel path. Her breath caught in her chest. A slim, vigorous laburnum tree blazed over the path in front of her: its vivid yellow blooms hung so thick that they bent the branches groundward in graceful arcs. She couldn't believe no one was down here, photographing *this*. She fished out her mobile, and thumbed a couple of photos of her own. They didn't do it justice.

Clutching her lunch, Moira ducked under the laburnum's branches and settled herself on the grass at its foot, leaning back against the trunk. It wasn't a comfortable seat, but the sunlight filtering through the tree's canary-coloured blooms made her feel warm and safe. Like sitting in her own miniature cathedral, or – Moira smiled – one of those plastic snow globes filled with glitter instead of snow. She chewed on her sandwich and looked out across the kirkyard. Many of the headstones were disintegrating now, having borne centuries of Edinburgh's famous sideways rain. Some had fallen face down on top of their graves. But in sheltered spots, there were still a few intricately carved gargoyles, winged and grinning skulls, hourglasses . . . even the occasional angel. The fancier Edinburgh families had crypts, sunk into the grass – iron-work grilles protecting underground rooms where no one living had set foot in years.

A peal of laughter clattered across the kirkyard, and Moira looked up. A boy of about Ryan's age was sitting on the roof of one of the crypts, swinging his legs off the lip of the doorway. Across from him, a girl with pale-coloured hair balanced atop a headstone, her back turned to Moira. She'd stretched over the pathway to pass the boy something, and it had dropped onto the gravel below. The graveyard rang with their laughter: the laughter of two people who were very drunk, or perhaps high on some substance or other. Moira watched as the boy climbed gingerly down from his vantage point – his tender dance on the gravel below made her realise he wasn't wearing shoes. The thing he retrieved was white, and he cradled it in both hands like a kitten. It was, Moira realised, a half-wrapped fish supper. He picked his way across the path, and handed it up to his girlfriend, waving away what seemed to be an offer to share. They looked radiant, the two of them: lit up in the sunshine, framed by shifting yellow blossoms, and young, so impossibly young. The boy stood at the base of the headstone, rubbing his girlfriend's feet as she ate – even at this distance, Moira could see that apart from his bare feet, the boy was well dressed, smart. Sunlight flashed off his glasses. The girl's kicked-off flip-flops were splayed on the grass below, near where the meal had fallen. Moira quietly gave thanks for her steady hands, holding the sandwich in its clean, brown paper.

She wandered out of the kirkyard dazed, everything a little too bright outside the laburnum's golden cocoon. She turned right, passing shop-fronts with their windows dressed for summer: sunhats, gauze scarves, sandals with rainbow-jewelled T-bars. *I'm walking to work*, Moira thought. But it was nearly a year since she had taken early retirement – two years since Jackie had died and his life insurance had allowed her to – and far longer since she'd worked *here*. And of course, when she turned the corner, the old Royal Infirmary looked nothing like it had when she'd walked here every day as a young staff nurse. Behind the original sandstone hospital buildings, the developers had stacked up blocks of flats that looked to be made entirely from glass. On the lower floors, twenty-foot blinds hung from the ceilings to keep out prying eyes. But the topmost floors seemed to have no curtains or blinds at all: they were transparent boxes, open to the sky. Moira sighed. She was glad that her old workplace was being put to good use, now that the new, state-of-the-art hospital had become established in the suburbs of Little France. She just wished it had been turned into something more accessible: a brief internet search had told her a while back that even a studio in the development would cost nearly a quarter of a million.

Moira crossed the street, and stepped into the patched shade of the sycamores at the entrance to the Meadows. There were no gates here, but there was a sandstone monument built to mark the entrance: tall as a bungalow, a stone unicorn carved at the top. Moira gave the unicorn a very slight nod, as she always had, walking to and from the Infirmary each day. She remembered Jackie again – little scraps of him seemed to be everywhere today – standing in the shadow of that monument, waiting for her to come out of work so they could go to the pictures, or walk through the park to the ice-cream parlour. She could pick out his tall, wiry figure a mile off, even in the dark, with the orange streetlight slanting over his shoulder and hiding his face in shadow. That was the way she saw him now: half obscured by time's fallen curtain. She thought she'd been so careful, too – trying to preserve every memory.

She idled down the hill a little troubled, passing through the park, along the east side of the old Infirmary site. She stepped into a little flagged courtyard, with saplings planted in square beds, and angular, dark-coloured marble benches. This both was and was not a place Moira recognised. A lot of the so-called modern buildings that had made up the hospital had been torn down: only the listed sandstone remained. She sank onto one of the hard benches, tipping her face upwards as though trying to *hear* the memory that was forming. She thought about the night shifts she used to do in summer, coming on in the evening – finding herself climbing the stairs yet again because the lift was full or broken or just too slow – and stopping for a moment on a high landing. Those long summer evenings, the last of the light would stream in off the park, slightly green, and dust from the hospital's bodies and blankets would swim in shimmering eddies up and down the stairs. She'd treasured those small, still moments in the midst of a chaotic shift. She wondered now if she'd lost the ability to feel things as keenly as she used to as a young woman: that perhaps it was age that kept her from properly remembering Jackie, from properly committing to her OU course, or from talking to Ryan about why he was so moody these days. Even now, lounging on a bench in a pretty courtyard, on a beautiful late spring day with absolutely nothing in the world that she needed to do, Moira still didn't feel as calm and whole as she once had, pausing mid-shift in that stairwell.

She could hear an ambulance somewhere. At first, she wondered if the sound was inside the memory; ambulance sirens had been a big part of the general background noise in this place. Perhaps it was a ghost ambulance, hanging around the old building where it had drawn up so often. But no – Moira's more logical mind kicked back in. It was somewhere behind her, held up at the Tollcross junction, perhaps, and moving closer.

The siren grew louder until it felt like the vehicle must be almost on top of her. Moira half expected it to screech round the corner and into the little sheltered square. She could hear the engine now, as well as the siren – it could be only metres away. She'd learned as a nurse that there was nothing quite like the sound of a siren to grab the attention of passers-by – that there's something in human beings that is drawn to screams and spatter and tragedy. People *want* to see what will be wheeled out of the back of an ambulance. They want to see it happen to someone else, because if it's happening to someone else, it isn't happening to them. But even as she had this thought, Moira found herself rising, and walking towards the sound.

As she rounded the corner, the siren was shut off, and the back doors of the vehicle were being banged open. Three young men in fluoro vests and hard hats were shouting at the paramedics, telling them to hurry, gesticulating with wide-open arms. They all looked very young, Moira thought. She loitered at the corner of a building, trusting that her middle-aged-woman status would keep her from being seen. The workmen all had tool-belts strapped to their waists, and as they hustled the paramedics and stretcher into the building site, the D-rings and instruments jingled like chunky chatelaines.

I should leave, Moira thought. A couple of other people had stopped to gawk, and she realised how distasteful it looked. But she didn't move. She looked up, past the hoarding, at the visible bits of the building site sticking up above. There was a huge piledriver, bright yellow and oddly gallows-like with its supporting struts. A massive crane swung in the air, visible only in bits between the buildings. She could see part of its latticed central mast, and the ladder inside, which a man was now slowly climbing down. Clearly, all work had stopped. This crane operator looked tiny – the drop, if he fell, was massive. Moira felt a prickle of fear: there were so many horrible ways to be hurt in a place like this. Did she really want to see what might be brought out to this ambulance?

It was too late to move. The paramedics came rattling back into view, trailing their patient on a stretcher. For a moment, she forgot how to breathe. On the stretcher was a dark-haired young man – same fluoro vest, same tool-belt – the upper right corner of his body impaled by an iron-coloured rod.

'Ryan,' she heard herself say. It wasn't – the boy didn't even look that much like her son. But he was about the same age, the same build, and just for a second her imagination superimposed her son's face over the face of this stranger. His teeth were gritted hard, she could see. Even with a starter bar jammed through his shoulder, he was determined not to cry out. To be brave.

'Wait, you know that kid?' Another of the rubberneckers – a young woman with blonde hair, young enough to be a student nurse – appeared at Moira's elbow.

'No,' Moira said, unable to pull her eyes from the stretcher, 'no, I just—'

But the girl had already started towards the ambulance, waving an arm to get the paramedics' attention.

'Hey!' she was shouting. 'Hey! There's a woman here who knows this guy!'

The two men were bumping the stretcher into the ambulance. The one at the back, still out in the open air of the site, poked his head round the vehicle's open door. Moira flinched. She ran after the girl, the two of them arriving by the ambulance at the same time.

'Listen,' Moira said, 'I'm sorry.'

'You know this man?' The paramedic looked exhausted, but then, she thought, they always did.

'No,' Moira replied, unable to meet his eye. She made the mistake of looking into the ambulance instead, where the young man – now sheltered from the collective gaze of his workmates – had begun to hiss in pain, pulling quick, ragged breaths through his teeth.

'She's mistaken,' Moira said. She looked hard at the girl – perhaps too hard, because she shrank away behind the open door of the ambulance, and out of sight.

'I – I'm a nurse.' Moira's face burned. As if this information could do anything to explain the last thirty seconds.

The paramedic raised his eyes heavenwards. She wanted to apologise to him – she wanted to apologise over and over, to grovel – but she couldn't form the words.

'Sorry, love,' he said, 'but I think we've got this covered. I need you to stand clear *right now*.'

He swung himself up into the ambulance, and slammed the door. Moira leapt back as the siren started up again, clanging in her ears. The driver turned the vehicle neatly around and then it sped off, kicking up a brown haze of building-site dust.

Moira stood listening to the siren as it moved off through the city. To stave off the crushing embarrassment she felt, she tried to imagine the route it might be taking to get the boy to Little France. She listened as it looped round the far end of the Quartermile, and then onto the long drag of Lauriston Place, where it could pick up speed. But beyond that, she lost the thread of the journey, and could only listen as the wah-wah-wah got slowly quieter, swallowed by traffic noise.

Looking up, she saw that the trio of workmen had returned, and were doing the same as she was – standing still and quiet with their heads cocked, listening. She tried to imagine what she must look like to them, with her mousy wash-and-go hair and the same faded jeans she'd worn while she'd been pregnant with Ryan. *They'll just think I look like someone's mum*, she thought. *Someone's mum, someone's wife*: nothing to identify her but the wedding ring her dead husband had given her. Moira cursed herself for having said her son's name at that crucial moment, for pulling the attention of the paramedic towards her, and away from the suffering boy. She imagined *his* mother, probably hard at work somewhere right now – tapping away at a laptop, or chairing a meeting. That woman had no idea, but she was about to get a terrible phone call. Then Moira remembered the boy from earlier – the little boy, who'd been pushed down onto those hard stone steps. She straightened, giving her head a shake to dislodge the last of her embarrassment. She turned to walk back the way she had come, now with a purpose for the rest of the day: whether he liked it or not, it was time. She'd left it too long, but no longer. She was going home to talk to her son.

13 May, 4.55 p.m.

When Helen Birch finally arrived at Gayfield Square, Banjo Robin was standing out front, as though waiting for her. She'd hoped the dappled shade thrown by the square's trees might turn her into just another anonymous pedestrian, but as she approached she realised he'd clocked her. She pulled in a long breath and steeled herself for the verbal barrage, which she guessed would begin when she was about twenty paces away.

'Don't start, Robin,' she said, as she reached his earshot. 'I don't work here any more, okay?'

She might as well not have bothered.

'Ken what, hen? This time youse've really fucked me over. Like *pure* fucked me over.'

Banjo Robin was a local pain in the ass. He was somewhere in his early sixties, and ran with a crowd of similarly aged folk musicians who were what the official documentation would call *vulnerably housed*. They weren't homeless as such – Robin had a girlfriend in every postcode district, and lived with whichever one he hadn't yet punched that week – but they were of no fixed address. On the rare occasions when he was sober, Robin was startlingly adept at the banjo. Problem was, he liked to top up his busking money by slinging illicit substances. They were usually dubious in quality and minuscule in quantity, which was how he'd managed, thus far, to avoid the jail. But he was a regular visitor to the drunk tank. When a call went out about a sixty-something man urinating in the street, loitering suspiciously around parked cars or shouting obscenities at some woman's lit window in the small hours, it was highly likely that the attending panda car would return from its drive-by with Banjo Robin in the back seat.

Unsurprisingly, he knew all the officers at the Gayfield Square and St Leonard's stations by name.

Right now, he was babbling. Birch drew level with him and held up one hand, palm flat, as though trying to stop traffic.

'I mean it,' she said. 'Don't tell *me*, I don't work here any more. If you want to talk to someone, you can come inside.'

He made a huffing sound.

'Been inside,' he said. 'Cunts willnae dae anything.'

He began patting himself down, and with shaking hands fished a tobacco pouch and rolling papers from somewhere about his person.

'Am I right in thinking,' Birch said, as he began pinching little hairs of tobacco into a meagre cigarette, 'that my colleagues in there have asked you to leave?'

'Naw.' Robin put out a thin, grey tongue to damp down the cigarette's long edge. 'Well, aye, but that's no fucking fair, I mean, is it? I mean is that even fucking . . . *professional?*'

Birch couldn't help it: she rolled her eyes.

'Okay. Well, if they've refused to help you in there, and they've asked you to leave, then there's really nothing I can do. You should go home now, Robin.'

'See that's the hale fucking problem,' Robin replied. He paused, and tried in vain to light his cigarette: the lighter sparked and sparked and sparked. 'I dinnae have a hame. Bee fucking threw me out, for nae *fucking* reason, and then called you lot on me.'

Birch shook her head. She'd met Bee, the Tollcross girlfriend, a couple of times years back, attending Robin's domestic disputes. She'd seemed a nice, gentle sort of woman. She had a pretty north-west-coast accent, hennaed hair and several cats. Why she put up with this bozo time and again was anyone's guess.

'I'm going in now,' Birch said. 'I'd advise you not to follow me.'

The lighter finally caught. He grunted at her as she moved past him.

'Good luck, Robin,' she said. *Funny*, she thought. *I might even miss him.*

The lobby was dim, though strip-lit. The station was a low, modern-ish building that had been wedged in between rows of tall, old tenements. Those big trees out in the square didn't help. The only natural light that got in was thrown in odd oblongs over the floor, reflecting off the hi-vis police vehicles parked up outside.

'Arright, chuck.'

Birch turned.

'Hello, Sergeant,' she said.

Al Lonsdale had known Birch longer than anyone else here. He was one of the custody sergeants, and right now he was standing to the extreme left of the lobby's glass doors and peering out through them – sideways, like a kid playing hide-and-seek.

'Keeping an eye on Banjo?' Birch asked.

Al nodded.

'Just want to make sure he goes his merry way, the slack bugger.'

Birch smiled. Al was from Wakefield, but decades of living away from that city had failed to knock the edges off his accent.

'We checked him in to his usual suite last night,' Al went on. 'Just your regular Banjo shenanigans – he'd had a skinful, of course. We ought to set him up with a loyalty card, he's here that much.'

Al shuffled away from the door, and as he passed Birch, he looked into her face, twisting his head like an inquisitive bird.

'You all right, love? You look a bit . . . off.'

Birch smiled and opened her mouth to speak, but Al rarely required a response.

'Of course,' he was saying, 'I should be moderating my tone around you now, shouldn't I? Now you've got your pips, and all that. I should be calling you *Marm*.'

Birch laughed. On Al's tongue the word had no *r* in it – he sounded a little like a sheep, bleating.

'Maa-m?' she mimicked. 'I'd rather you didn't.'

Al grinned widely.

'All right, Detective Inspector Fancyknickers,' he said. 'No need to take the piss.'

He made to slip behind the lobby's desk, but Birch caught him by the arm.

'I'll miss you,' she said. 'I'm going to miss this old place a lot.'

They stood looking at one another for a second, Birch still holding on to his forearm. Then Al reached down and pulled her into a bear hug. She sniffed.

'Arright, arright,' he said, his voice muffled against her hair, 'no need to get all soft about it.'

Over his shoulder, Birch noticed the pile of boxes she'd asked to be brought down for her.

'That's enough now,' Al said, opening his arms. 'Any longer and I could have you for sexual harassment. And me old enough to be your dad.'

Birch's face hurt from smiling while trying not to cry.

'That's not super politically correct of you, Al,' she said.

He shrugged.

'Well, you know – all this equalities legislation. It changes too often for us old-timers to keep up. Speaking of which, let me summon up some burly young man to help you with those boxes.'

Birch grinned.

'I'll be fine,' she said. 'The car's not far.'

Al got in behind the desk.

'You take what you can get now, missy,' he said. 'It'll not be like this working at headquarters, you know. There's no one'll give you the time of day over there.'

Birch shook her head.

'Hey, *Sergeant*,' she said. 'For a start, they don't call it headquarters any more – we're all equals now, remember? And secondly, it's fine. They're fine. They've given me a very nice welcome so far.'

Al gave one, sharp nod.

'Aye, well, see that it continues. I don't want to have to come down there and have a word with that chief inspector of yours.'

For a moment, Birch allowed herself to imagine Al storming into DCI McLeod's office, sworn to defend her honour. She was still smiling, but the smile was weak. Al was right. The new place did feel impersonal. *Shit. Have I done the right thing?*

But Al had the phone receiver lodged between ear and shoulder.

'You just stand there and look decorative,' he said to Birch. 'I'll have a dashing young constable down here in a jiffy. Least we can do on your final visit, eh?'

The boxes were filled with stuff that needed sorting out – had needed sorting out for years. She'd collected them last because she'd been putting it off. Now they were slung in the back of her car, the seats pulled down to accommodate them. The last tie she'd had to the station at Gayfield Square was loosed.

Al had got a janitor, in the end, to help her with the boxes. The poor guy had made the mistake of wandering into the lobby, and Al had exclaimed, 'Just the man!' He may have been right: the janitor had found an old moving trolley, which – though it gave him some difficulty outside on the cobbles – did make for a quick job.

'You hear about that kid?' the janitor had asked in the space between hefting one box into the car and lifting another. 'The one who got impaled?'

Birch blinked.

'Impaled?'

'Aye. Got the radio on in my office and they said, wee gadge working on a building site up town falls ten feet off, I don't know, something. Ends up with a starter bar running right through him.'

'Ouch,' Birch said, and then, after a pause, 'What's a starter bar when it's at home?'

The janitor made a gesture in the air.

'They stick up about *so* long, out of foundations on buildings. They're sort of twisty. Like an old-fashioned butterscotch cane, ken? Maybe you're too young to remember those.'

Birch was plenty old enough, but didn't say so.

'Oh okay, I know what a starter bar is. Poor kid.'

'Aye.' The janitor looked at her with what might have been suspicion. 'Surprised you didn't hear about it, on your police radio or whatever.'

'Oh,' Birch said. 'I've not been very gettable today. But it's likely someone from this place did attend.' She nodded backwards towards the station. A thought struck her.

'Is the boy dead?' she asked.

The janitor hauled another box off the trolley, and planted it with a rattle in the back of the car.

'Not yet,' he said.

Now, as she drove home, Birch had no difficulty keeping her mind off the boxes – the impaled boy loomed large in her imagination.

Please don't let that come across my desk, she thought – and the thought came back over and over, like a mantra. *Sounds like a potential nightmare.*

But she was also thinking about what the accident must have felt like for that boy. A quick Google on her phone before she'd started the engine had told her he was only twenty. *My brother's age*, she thought, though it wasn't true. In her mind, her brother Charlie was forever twenty. In fact, he'd have celebrated his thirty-fourth birthday that year, had he still been around. She imagined the building-site boy framed inside scaffolding, his back to the terrible drop, working away on something, thinking his own private, mundane thoughts. In her mind he was handsome, as all twenty-year-old boys are – in a gangly way that they themselves have never noticed. She imagined he had Charlie's face. And then she imagined him falling. Flying backwards as though pushed, eyes wide, hands grabbing at nothing. *How long does it take to fall ten feet?* Probably half a second, if that, she decided. Barely long enough to register what's happening to you. The sort of fall that a person could potentially walk away from with nothing more than an impressive bruise or two. But not this time. She remembered saying 'ouch' to the janitor. *I can't believe that was my reaction*, she thought.

Traffic on Leith Walk was heavy. Birch trundled along past the Polish food markets and the phone-unlocking shops; past the artisan doughnut bakery and the Sikh women's food co-op. At one particularly stubborn set of traffic lights, she sat admiring a rainbow of shimmering saris behind the plate-glass window of a small boutique. She tried to crowd the injured boy out of her imagination, and found herself thinking again about Charlie. He'd been gone for so long now. *How does a person just go missing*, she thought, *without a trace, in this day and age?* It was such a well-worn thought that it occurred to her without emotion attached – only nagging annoyance at the lack of an answer. She'd spent fourteen years keeping Charlie in the back of her mind, and she filed him away there now, his twenty-year-old face like an old photograph gone soft at the folds.

Were the roads always busy on a sunny day? It seemed illogical – surely people would be keener to walk when the weather was beautiful. Or maybe it just *seemed* busier when the weather was hot, because she was so keen to get home and take off her shoes. Salamander Street and Seafield Road were like car parks at this time of the day, no matter where you joined them. Birch rolled past the cemetery at walking pace, watching cyclists zip and weave through the standing traffic. The scent of hot grease from a McDonald's Drive-Thru mingled with the sweet death-stink of the Seafield sewage treatment works, the hundreds of idling engines chucking their fumes out behind them. *This is the Edinburgh the tourists don't see*, Birch thought, cursing the cocked-up traffic-light sequences no one had put right for years. But soon enough she was past them, and got up the speed to kick into fourth gear as the sea – blue as a travel agent's catalogue – blurred between the buildings.

A secret she hadn't told anyone: Birch had always wanted to live on the Portobello prom. Ever since she was a little girl, brought there with her little brother for donkey rides and ice cream, she'd longed to set up home in one of the little villas that faced out to sea. The dream had become a plan, and then – only two months ago – the plan had become a reality. A mid-terrace villa had come up near the Joppa end of the beach, at a reasonable price because of its state of disrepair. Birch had moved in the day her promotion to DI was announced. Most things were still in boxes. Driving along Portobello High Street, she felt a thrill that hadn't yet worn off: *I'm going home.*

She parallel parked on the side of the street. Her new house had a garage, down a narrow, cobbled lane at the back, but it was still full of the previous owner's stuff. He'd died, the old man who'd lived here before, and while his kids had been willing to come up from London to empty the house, they'd balked at a tumbledown garage filled almost to the roof with tea chests. Birch had too, if she was honest – she still didn't know what was in most of them. She decided there was enough room left in the garage for the boxes she'd just hauled from Gayfield Square – they could wait until some weekend when she'd time to sort the whole lot out. *Yes,* she thought, *I'll do that,* knowing already that it wouldn't happen.

She walked round the front of the China Express – a cheap hole-in-the-wall takeaway that occupied what had once been the cafe at the tail end of the prom – and along the seafront. To her right, the tide was out. Children, tiny as bugs from this distance, jumped and splashed in the waves. Bikes zoomed up and down the prom, and there were dogs everywhere: dogs proudly carrying driftwood in their mouths, dogs running away from the water to shake a fine, salty spray onto passers-by. To her left was the neat row of front gardens that the prom-dwellers kept. In some of them, her neighbours sat out on shady camping chairs, wind-up radios murmuring in the warm air. Birch called out her hellos, and waved. Her own garden was the only unkempt one in the row.

She reached it now. The wooden front gate needed painting, and up the side of the brick path two hollyhock bushes grew rampant, pushing their ten-foot blossom towers into the air. The garden had been cared for once: the plants here weren't wind-sown weeds, just woody and overgrown versions of their former, well-kept selves. Birch was loath to clear them. The garden was ugly, but it was old, and she felt that was worthy of respect. It also smelled wonderful, thanks to a dusty, pale yellow rose whose creeping fingers had long since turned its supporting trellis to matchwood. Around the living-room window, honeysuckle was preparing to flower. The plant was so thick that if Birch had plunged her hand into it, her arm would be sunk elbow-deep in foliage before her fingers could touch the wall.

Before she unlocked the peeling front door, she stood with her back to the house, looking out. From here, she could see North Berwick Law, out where East Lothian curved round into the Forth. Along the horizon she could see the huge freighters crawling through their shipping lane. Beyond them, a grey-green smudge that lit up at dusk with a string of pin-prick lights, was Fife.

A woman in a hot pink shirt walked by, a portly old chocolate Labrador plodding beside her.

'Beautiful evening!' The woman raised one hand in greeting, and then tilted it towards Birch. 'Something in your garden smells de*light*ful.'

Birch grinned.

'The roses,' she called back from the path. 'They're enjoying this sunshine.'

The woman hadn't stopped, but her voice trailed back to Birch as she moved beyond the hollyhocks – a hot pink backdrop between their leaves.

'Long may it last,' she said. 'Cheerie-bye!'

Birch turned to the door smiling, keys in hand.

She'd quite forgotten about the injured boy. It wasn't until she was truly settled in for the evening that he came back to her. She'd kicked off her shoes, changed into her yoga pants, and uncorked some wine. The house faced roughly east and, deciding she needed a little sun on her bones, she headed out to the back garden, where some of the day's heat still lingered. The only bit of garden she'd cleared so far was the slate-coloured patio: a few flags wide but big enough to accommodate a garden bench, which, like everything here, had seen better days. Birch had dragged an IKEA coffee table out – she'd only paid £15 for it, so a little rain-damage wouldn't hurt – and now she was looking at a wavering red spotlight on its surface as the late sun shone through her half-filled glass.

Oh God, she thought, remembering the boy. *Please don't let that come across my desk.*

She closed her eyes, tried to focus on the sun's heat, the sound of the waves as the tide crept back towards the house. Beyond the garden wall, cars buzzed by at intervals, like bees. Somewhere, someone had a barbecue going – the smell of smoke drifted over the rooftops from the twilit beach.

I've got enough to think about right now, Birch thought, opening her eyes again. As if on cue – somewhere far off in the blue evening's calm – came the panicky call of a siren.

13 May, 8.59 p.m.

Above the matte Astroturf of the high-school playing fields, and above the ponytailed heads of the girl footballers, moths and midges birled and hung. At this distance, they looked like flecks of glitter swimming through liquid. Swifts dived in and out of the floodlights' glare, their calls carrying over the car park in the warm evening. Ishbel Hodgekiss zipped up the electric windows of her Nissan Qashqai. She wouldn't risk a midge bite, even at this distance.

The dashboard clock read 20:59, so she flicked on the car stereo to catch the headlines. She'd expected the Radio 2 announcer, but instead she was treated to a blast of cheesy jingle: Abigail had tuned the stereo over to local radio again.

Questions are being asked, said the newsreader, *about an industrial accident that happened earlier today in the centre of Edinburgh.*

Ishbel bent over the steering wheel, trying to see how to retune the station, the newsreader's bouncy speech pattern grating in her ears.

The site developers claim, he was saying, *that the man was not following correct safety procedures when he fell ten feet into the building's foundations. Our correspondent Jenna Buckie has more …*

Somehow, Ishbel found the right button, and flicked through stations until she heard a voice she recognised. She settled back to listen, and began to scan the football fields for any sign of Abigail. Practice had just finished – she'd heard the full-time whistle – so any minute now her daughter should come sauntering out through the gate in the tall, green chain-link fence, and over to the car.

Ishbel didn't entirely approve of her daughter's continued interest in football. After-school clubs were all very well, but now Abigail was in college, her mother felt that any extra-curricular activities ought to be more academic in nature. The fact that Abigail still lived at home brought Ishbel a quiet, if guilty, joy: it was perhaps the only silver lining to her daughter deciding against attending proper university. But she couldn't help but feel that this weekly return to high school – to practise for an under-25s team that included girls far younger than her – was doing Abigail no favours.

'You can't put football practice on your CV, you know,' Ishbel had said, more than once.

'You can, Mum,' her daughter would reply. 'It shows you're a team player.'

Ishbel still hadn't come up with a suitable response to this.

Girls began to trail out of the long, low buildings and back across the Astroturf to be met by their lifts. The younger ones climbed into cars like Ishbel's: family saloons and people-carriers manned by parental taxi-drivers. But older girls, the ones more Abigail's age, tended to walk up to empty cars – tiny Ford Kas and rusted Citroën hatchbacks – slinging their gym bags into the passenger seat and driving away on their own. Abigail hadn't yet passed her driving test, though the constant switching of the radio station was testament to her practising. Every week there were a couple of girls who were picked up by unsuitable-looking boyfriends. These young men would sit in their decked-out Imprezas – engines running, music shuddering through the tarmac – and then peel out with a hiss of air from their full sequential gearboxes. Ishbel shuddered.

'There's a boy,' Aidan had said to her one night, about a week ago. He'd said it in a breathless voice that Ishbel remembered girls at school using to divulge information while swapping lipstick in the French-block loos. He said it as though he were a co-conspirator – there was no trace of paternal concern.

'What do you mean, *there's a boy*?' She'd known exactly what he meant – she just didn't want to admit it.

'I mean,' he said, 'I think our daughter may have a boyfriend.'

Ishbel went quiet. Abigail had had boyfriends before, of course, but that was in high school – back when Ishbel could reasonably lay down rules and curfews and ask Aidan to help her enforce them. Now, Abigail was nineteen. In her head, Ishbel heard her own voice saying *no, no, no, no*.

'How do you know that?'

Aidan had smirked at her. He'd been standing in front of the dressing table, shrugging on a clean shirt, and in the wrap-around vanity mirror, Ishbel had watched his three-times-reflected torso disappear into the fabric. For some reason it had occurred to her then – for the first time in what must have been years – what an attractive man he was. Still was. A spike of some old anxiety bothered at her.

'She *told* me,' he'd said. 'She talks to me, you know.'

Ishbel had been folding laundry. She remembered looking down at the white cotton T-shirt in her hands and seeing it turn pink as anger clouded her vision. She was angry with Aidan a lot lately – they were angry with each other. She'd had that thought and then verbalised it, almost without meaning to.

'Aren't you angry?' The words had come out sharp, an elastic band snapping.

'Angry?' She'd amused him, it seemed. She pulled in a breath. *Is he just making this up*, she wondered, *to rile me?*

'I just . . . In the past, you've been one of those "no one's good enough for my baby"-type dads. You've hated her boyfriends. We used to *joke* about it.'

He looked away from her, and pulled his hands down the front of the shirt to smooth it.

'Sure,' he said. 'And you know as well as I do that if this young man decides to break her heart, then I'll go for his knees.'

Ishbel had rolled her eyes. As a young woman, she'd loved his gallusness, his masculine swagger. Now she found it grating, and he knew that. He was still speaking.

'But she's an adult now. Protective dad needs to know when to take a step back.'

He'd paused, and shot a glance back at her. 'Neurotic mum could learn to calm down a bit, too.'

Ishbel had closed her eyes. These small barbs were part of the daily routine these days, the double-act shtick the two of them seemed to have established. *Why do I stay?* she'd wondered to herself, more than once. *Abigail,* was the answer. *Abigail, who adores her dad. She'd never forgive you.*

A long silence opened out between them. That old anxiety swished around inside Ishbel like dirty water, until she'd felt like she had to speak.

'She talks to *me*, too.'

Aidan had made a *maybe* face at her. Not for the first time, her palm itched with the desire to slap the expression away.

'Sure,' he said. 'But you've been pretty distracted lately.'

Ishbel shook herself out of the memory. Across the road, Inverleith Park was blurring into a dark mass under its trees. If she looked in the rear-view mirror, she could see the spiked turrets of Fettes School silhouetted against the dimming sky. It wouldn't be properly dark until after ten, but beyond the football field and its ring of artificial light, the city was an indistinct jumble of gables and spires. Streetlights began to flick on. The clouds turned pink: another fine day tomorrow, Ishbel thought.

Aidan was right. The Telford case – the biggest complaint she'd ever dealt with at work – had thrown her totally off balance. Even now it was all over, nearly three years since the initial complaint, she was finding it hard to get back into her old work-life flow. She *had* been distracted. So distracted that she'd let a week go by since that conversation with her husband, and she still hadn't spoken to Abigail about the whole *boyfriend* issue. Aidan had told her that this boy was on Abigail's course at college, and he had his own car and some sort of job. 'He seems to come from a *nice family,*' Aidan had said, twisting his voice into a parody of Ishbel's own. 'I know that sort of thing is important to you.' She'd shrugged off that particular jab – she picked her battles carefully these days. But she'd allowed herself a small eye-roll. Her husband always accused her of being too status conscious, yet she found *his* endless positioning and repositioning of himself almost too tiring to keep up with. 'Now there's a *real* man,' he'd say, about some athlete or celebrity he approved of. For years, she'd found it charming

– sexy, even. Exciting. Now, she was relieved they'd had a daughter, not a son . . . but she was also worried about what Aidan's enthusiasm for this new boyfriend *meant*. She'd pressed for more information, but Aidan claimed that was all he knew.

'I've seen a photo, though,' he'd said, puffing out his chest, an *I know something you don't know* gesture. 'He's the tall, dark and handsome type. And he's got a twinkle in his eye.' Aidan had grabbed his keys: heading out once again to some rendezvous Ishbel didn't quite know the details of. 'You should be worried,' he'd said.

Around Ishbel, the car park emptied. The football coach walked back out onto the pitch in her coat to patrol for litter, for jumpers or mobile phones left behind. Ishbel watched her: a small, compact figure pacing the perimeter. Soon the floodlights would be damped out, and the feeding swifts would be replaced by bats. Abigail had not come out. Ishbel's was the last remaining car.

The clock now read 21:19. Ishbel made a clucking sound in her throat as she pulled her phone from her handbag, and dialled her daughter's number. The phone rang through to voicemail. Ishbel could have predicted this – if Abigail was rushing to change her clothes and saw her mother calling, she'd surely ignore it. She'd know the call was a tacit nag: *get out here already*. Ishbel caught a glimpse of her own reflection in the driver's side mirror. She looked pale, her short dark hair – dyed, these days – a little mussed. *God, I look old*, she thought. In her head, she was still Abigail's age, and she always got something of a surprise, looking at her reflection and seeing the thinning lips and crow's feet of an older woman.

Ishbel was seized by the impulse to leave a voicemail.

'Abigail,' she said, 'this is your mother. Remember me? I have half a report to write tonight and I'd hoped to be home getting on with it by now. Whatever you're doing, please get a move on, okay?'

She flicked the display to end the call, and felt thwarted. The cruelty of smartphones: you didn't get the satisfaction of slamming a receiver down.

Ishbel didn't return the phone to her bag, but propped it on the dashboard, just in case it rang. As she looked up from its glowing screen, her eye was caught by a far-off movement, a quick swim of light. A block away down the hill, Comely Bank Road ran parallel to the car park: from her vantage point in the car, Ishbel could make out the lit canopy of a newsagent's, and the odd car rattling past the crossroads.

What had caught her eye was a city bus – a single-decker with big plate windows, lit up from inside. Some glitch in traffic had caused it to stop across the junction, idling in the yellow box until someone blew their horn. Standing, hanging on to the bus's overhead rail, was Abigail. Ishbel was a long way off, and the bus moved on almost as soon as it had stopped, but she'd recognise her daughter's profile anywhere. Unsure of her next move, she sat in the car, her hands on the steering wheel at two and ten, scrolling through a cycle of silent questions. Why would Abigail be on a city bus? Hadn't she been at practice? If not, then why? And where *had* she been?

There must be some reason, Ishbel thought. *Come on.* But she could think of none.

It took about a minute for her daughter's small figure to round the corner at the bottom of the block. The twilight made the vision indistinct, but Ishbel knew it was her. The pale cloud of hair, the shoulders hooked inwards – no matter how often Ishbel nipped at her to *stand up straight* – the striped, drawstring gym bag slung on one hip. The figure she was sure was Abigail slipped into the grounds of the school through a side gate, and disappeared.

Ishbel's phone buzzed, but the text was not from her daughter. It was Aidan.

Assume you picked up Baby okay? If you're at shop, pls get dishwasher tablets. A.

Baby was a pet name Abigail hated – or she hated it when it came out of Ishbel's mouth. For some reason, from Aidan it was allowed. When Abigail was born the two of them had struggled to name her. Back then, you weren't told the gender of your baby ahead of time, but Aidan's mother believed in all sorts of old wives' tales and convinced Ishbel she was carrying a boy. When Abigail arrived – the most feminine baby ever, her long blonde lashes already fully formed – they were caught unawares, unable to use Nathan or Jackson, the names they'd prepared. So, for a long few days they called her Baby, and Aidan had never really stopped.

Baby late out. Back soon. I. Ishbel thought about adding an *x* to the end of the text, but the corners of her mouth turned down at the very idea. She hit *send.*

She watched Abigail open the door onto the pitch and step out into the floodlights' yawn. As she got about halfway over, they blinked out, plunging the practice fields into darkness. Instinct caused Ishbel's heart to miss a beat, but her eyes became accustomed to the new dimness in only a second or two. Abigail was still trudging towards the car, the striped bag thumping against her side.

'Sorry, Mum,' she said, swinging open the passenger door. 'I got chatting with Ms Lessenger.'

Emily Lessenger was the coach Ishbel had just seen patrolling the empty pitch. She flinched at her daughter's smooth lie.

'No you didn't,' she replied. 'Ms Lessenger's been out *here*, checking the pitches. I saw her. She was on her own.'

Abigail ditched the striped bag in the footwell, and slammed the car door.

'When, just now?' The girl's face was placid, moon-eyed: butter-wouldn't-melt.

'Five minutes ago,' Ishbel said. 'Or so.'

Abigail tossed her head, shaking her hair off one shoulder and onto the other.

'Oh,' she said. 'Before that, then. I talked to her and then got changed. Sorry. I didn't realise the time.'

Ishbel studied her daughter. Believing her would be easy: it had been some other girl on the bus, some other girl who snuck across the street and through the school to the pitch. Just another girl with blonde hair and a stripy bag. *Believe it.* She could feel her daughter willing her to.

'I phoned you,' Ishbel said. She decided she ought to start the engine: the dash clock read 21:26. As Abigail rummaged in the gym bag for her phone, Ishbel reversed out into the road, and pulled away.

'Oh yeah,' Abigail said, lighting up the smartphone. 'One missed call. Sorry.'

Ishbel made a left, and then an immediate right. She liked to drive along the park, past the Inverleith mansions with their oriel windows and electronic gates.

'I've got a text from Dad as well,' Abigail added, looking down at her phone – the pose Ishbel saw her in most often these days. 'He says to say to you: dishwasher tablets.'

They paused at the 'give way' sign on Inverleith Row, waiting for another city bus to pass: the double-decker 23 to Trinity. *Going my way*, Ishbel thought. *Typical*. Now she'd have to follow in its chugging wake.

'We don't have time for dishwasher tablets,' Ishbel said. 'I've got to work on this report tonight, it's due back to the complainant tomorrow. It's late enough as it is. Text him to wash up by hand for once. It won't kill him.'

Abigail snorted, but began thumbing out the text.

'You know he'll leave it for *me* to do when we get in,' she said.

'Yeah? Well it wouldn't kill you, either.'

They drove on in silence. The 23 pulled up at a stop beside a row of takeaways: pizza, curry, Chinese. Ishbel glanced in the rear-view mirror, then nipped out past the bus and into the right-turn lane for Ferry Road. A cab driver pipped his horn as he let her go by. 'Screw you,' Ishbel hissed.

Abigail glanced up.

'Jesus, Mother.' She laughed. 'You're cranky this evening.'

Ishbel pressed her back teeth together. She steered off Ferry Road and into Trinity. They'd be home soon: only a few more streets. She had to say *something*.

'Where were you really, Abigail?'

Her daughter's head snapped up.

'What do you mean?' That moon-eyed face again.

'Tonight,' Ishbel said, pushing her voice into an even line. 'Instead of going to practice. Where were you?'

Abigail laughed again. It was a confident laugh, there were no cracks in it – but there was something else. A little edge of nastiness.

'I don't know what you mean. I *went* to practice. You dropped me off. You saw me walk in. You just saw me walk out again.'

Ishbel soothed the car down to a lower speed.

'No,' she said. 'What I saw was you getting off a bus on Comely Bank Road just now. What I saw was you sneaking in the side door of the school. *Then* I saw you walk out.'

'*What?*'

There it is, Ishbel thought. There's the crack in the veneer.

'I *saw* you, Abigail. You got off the bus, you sneaked in the side door, and then you walked out over the pitch to make it look like you'd been at practice the whole time.'

Abigail said nothing. Her phone rested in her hands, its screen dark. She didn't look down at it, just stared ahead through the windscreen.

'Is it this boy?' Ishbel kept her voice light, even as she tried to push out of her head the image of her daughter being bundled into some dim bedroom: some pungent male space full of pizza boxes, *Playboy* posters on the walls. 'Dad told me you . . . might have a boyfriend.'

Abigail rolled her eyes.

'*Dad* can't keep his mouth shut.'

It was true, then: Abigail had sought her father's confidence, but had deliberately kept this fact from Ishbel. Had Aidan always been so smug about things? She couldn't, right then, remember.

'Is it anyone I know?' As she said it, Ishbel realised that she didn't really know who Abigail socialised with these days. She knew of only one other person from the same high-school year who attended Three Rivers College – and he was a dark-haired boy.

'Is it Ryan?' she asked.

Abigail still wasn't looking at her.

'Ryan?'

There was a pause. Abigail wrinkled her nose.

'Wait – you mean Ryan *Summers*? From *high school*?'

'Summers,' Ishbel said. 'That's it – that's his name.'

'Jesus,' Abigail said. 'Absolutely not. I mean – *ew*. Ryan Summers is a total creeper. I wouldn't go out with him if he was the last straight man on this planet.'

'Okay!' Ishbel lifted her hands from the steering wheel for a second, then imagined the driver in front seeing the two white stars of her palms flashing in their rear-view. 'I just wondered. You can't blame me for being interested in this boy . . . especially if he's good enough to miss football practice for.'

She was trying to sound jokey, throwaway. It wasn't working.

'His name, for your infor*ma*tion, is Jack. I'm surprised you don't know that already, since Dad's been blabbing. But I didn't miss practice for him – I didn't. I haven't been anywhere *near* him tonight, okay?'

'I wouldn't mind if you told me you wanted to miss practice sometimes. I wouldn't mind if you wanted to go to . . .' Ishbel swallowed, and tasted acid. 'To a friend's, or something. But *tell* me. Just tell me, Abigail.'

They'd reached the road-end for Primrose Bank: *home*, Ishbel thought. She turned right. Abigail was still staring straight ahead, but Ishbel could practically hear her daughter's mental gears shifting.

'I just want to make sure you're . . . being careful,' Ishbel said.

Her daughter drew in a breath, as though to speak. As she pulled the car into the front drive, Ishbel thought maybe Abigail was about to own up – to admit what she'd been doing, and apologise.

'Mother,' she said instead, 'you're on fucking crack.'

Ishbel blinked hard. A shudder ran through her. She'd never heard Abigail speak like that – not once, in almost twenty years. The engine was still running, and her foot was still on the brake, keeping the car from rolling back out of the drive and into the road. But Abigail grabbed the bag at her feet and shoved open the passenger door.

'Don't you think you can speak to me like that,' Ishbel heard herself say. Abigail slammed the door on her words, and stomped around the front of the car. As she passed, the car's headlights lit up the backs of her legs. There were grass-stains on her acid-wash jeans.

Ishbel wrenched the handbrake on and turned the key in the ignition. Abigail had unlocked the front door and stormed through it – now it slammed behind her. Ishbel grabbed her bag and climbed down out of the car. When she reached the front door, she found that her daughter had slipped the security chain on, so she couldn't get in.

'We're going to have serious words, madam!' Ishbel yelled through the three-inch gap the chain allowed. She put her finger on the doorbell and left it there, listening as the non-stop trill filled up the house.

'Darling.' Aidan's face appeared. '*Please.*'

Ishbel let go of the bell, and the door handle, which she'd been clutching so hard that the lines of its brass octagon had sunk into her palm. She listened as Aidan fumbled the chain off from the other side. He let her in.

'I don't know what's going on,' he said, 'but can we think of the neighbours?'

Ishbel dropped her handbag onto the stripped wooden floor of the hallway.

'Never mind the neighbours, Aidan. Where has she *gone*?'

Her husband put a hand on her shoulder.

'Bel. What happened?'

She flinched the hand away.

'She's been sneaking around somewhere. She was late getting out of football, then just after I texted you, I saw her get off a bus at Comely Bank. She let herself into the school and walked out again to make it look like she'd been there all along. She thinks I was born yesterday.' Aidan opened his mouth to speak, but Ishbel went on: 'Then she gets in the car and lies about it, to my face. Right to my face, Aidan. Smooth as anything.'

Ishbel realised she was shaking. What was it – shock? Anger? Worry, she thought. But her husband was smiling at her.

'That's all?'

Her eyes widened.

'What do you mean, *that's all?* Where has she *been*? Why is she lying to me? Why didn't she *tell* me she's got a boyfriend?'

Aidan chuckled.

'Come on, Bel. Did you never have secrets from your parents?' He made that slap-worthy face again, and then added, 'I mean, from your mother?'

Ishbel paused, then waved her husband aside and stepped past him.

'I can't believe you're saying this to me.'

She started up the stairs. Behind her in the hall, Aidan was still talking.

'Did you never sneak off anywhere on your own? Did you never want to have something that was just for you?'

Ishbel whirled around, hand on the banister.

'Do you know something else?' she asked. 'What else has she told you? Do you know what this is about?'

Her husband frowned.

'No,' he said, and she could see he was telling the truth. *Damn.* Him being party to something else that she wasn't would have stung, but at least she'd have had a chance at winkling it out of him. 'I told you everything last week. But Bel, she's nearly twenty years old. She's an adult. What she does and where she goes isn't really our business any more.'

Ishbel smacked the flat of her hand off the banister. It hurt.

'For Christ's sake, Aidan,' she said. 'You *know* why I'm upset about this. It's not the doing and the going – it's the lying. I mean, why lie to me? Why swear at me, why be abusive? She's not just coming and going as she pleases. There's something going *on* here.'

Her husband threw up his hands: a *whatever, you win* gesture. It irritated her. Why wasn't he angry, too? What *was* this?

'No.' She brought her hand down again. 'You don't get to just surrender! For once, just for once, Aidan, I need you to be on my side. I need you to feel the way I feel, or at least acknowledge it. She still lives under our roof, she still eats our food, I still sit in that godforsaken car park every week waiting for her to come out of football. When none of those things are true any more, *then* she can come and go as she pleases. When I'm no longer washing her jeans for her, *then* she can roll them around in the dirt. But while she lives here I have the right to know what the hell's going on!'

In the quiet that followed, Ishbel realised she was breathing hard. The staircase and its landings rang with the harmonics of her outburst. But she didn't feel any better. Something was still pent up inside her.

'You hear that, missy?' She tilted her head up, sending the yell in the vague direction of her daughter's bedroom. Her voice was beginning to get hoarse. 'We're not done here, you know. You're not going to lie to my face and get away with it, not while you live in this house!'

There was no answer. No sound came from above her head. Ishbel wondered if her daughter had even heard her – she could have put on her noise-cancelling headphones. She could be watching a TV show right now, oblivious. Down in the hall, Aidan's hands were still in the air, as though someone were pointing a gun at him. Ishbel could see him on the edge of her vision. She felt as though all the life were ebbing out of her.

'Well,' Aidan brought his arms down by his sides. 'Now that we've all had chapter and verse, can you please calm down?'

Ishbel glared at him, but the fight in her was dying.

'I don't know what's going on with you, Aidan,' she said. 'This really isn't like you at all.'

He shrugged.

'You're just being melodramatic,' he said. 'And I think you know that.'

They stood looking at one another for a long time. Aidan in the hall, his shirtsleeves rolled up, a hole in one sock. Ishbel five stairs above him, her feet sore in her high-heeled shoes, and her heart thudding in her ears. *Of course*, she thought. *He wouldn't care about our daughter disappearing at all hours of the day and night. He does it himself, all the time.* She tried to push the thought away.

'Did you *buy* dishwasher tablets?' Aidan said.

Ishbel brought both hands to her face, to shut him out.

'I'm going to bed,' she said, speaking into her own palms. When Aidan said nothing, she added, 'In the spare room.'

But a moment later, when she dropped her hands, he'd already walked away.

THREE RIVERS COLLEGE SHOOTING

From Wikipedia, the free encyclopedia
(Redirected from Ryan Summers)

Location	Three Rivers College, UK
Date	14 May c.8.30–9.00 a.m. (GMT)
Target	Students at Three Rivers College
Attack type	School shooting, murder-suicide, mass murder, spree shooting
Weapons	Bruni Olympic .380 BBM modified blank firing revolver (x3)
Deaths	14 (including perpetrator)
Non-fatal injuries	2
Perpetrator	Ryan Andrew Summers

The Three Rivers College shooting occurred at the Tweed Campus at Three Rivers College, a further- and higher-education college. 20-year-old gunman Ryan Summers fatally shot 13 fellow students, all female [1][2][10][37], and then committed suicide at the scene [1][10]. This incident joins the 1987 Hungerford massacre, the 1989 Monkseaton shootings, the 1996 Dunblane school massacre and the 2010 Cumbria shootings as one of the deadliest criminal acts involving firearms in the history of the United Kingdom.

The shooting has prompted debate over gun control laws in the United Kingdom [3], where firearms ownership is already strictly regulated [4]. Following the Dunblane school massacre, the Firearms (Amendment) Act 1997 and the Firearms (Amendment) (No. 2) Act 1997 were enacted, effectively making private ownership of handguns illegal in the United Kingdom. Following the incident, the UK police launched a public safety campaign detailing the dangers of gun modification [48]. The shooting also led to the publication of new police guidelines on the most effective ways to contact emergency services [22].

Background

At the time the shooting took place, there were 26,708 fully matricu-lated students enrolled at <u>Three Rivers College</u>, though some of these were enrolled as online or <u>distance-learning</u> students [5]. The college consists of three separate campuses: the main Tweed Campus, the Esk Campus and the Forth Campus.

That day

14 May, 8.20 a.m.

'All right, Sarge. Looking gorgeous today, as ever.'

Birch blinked. She'd been staring down into the chiller cabinet, trying to decide if she wanted fruit toast – a good start to the week – or a cinnamon swirl, decidedly bad. With breakfast less than half an hour behind her, she wasn't at all hungry, but it seemed to be station policy that everyone arrived with a pastry. She had to at least try and fit in.

'Sorry, Danny. I was miles away.'

Around her, the coffee shop crashed and rang. It was nearing eight thirty, and every commuter in town was cramming into their favourite warm, well-lit queue. Birch was brand loyal – she'd been coming to this little place just off Leith Walk for years, and was determined to carry on, new station or no new station. Danny was her favourite barista. He was maybe seventeen, a recent college dropout, clearly thrilled by his ability to make money that belonged to him alone. That early work-life excitement: if she tried hard, she could just about remember it. She always tipped him well.

'Just paying you a compliment, Sarge,' Danny winked, already scribbling her usual order onto the side of a cardboard cup. 'It's only a matter of life and death.'

Birch swallowed. She'd been putting off telling people – afraid it might seem like a brag – but watching Danny ink *Sgt Birch* in marker pen felt like being demoted.

'Actually,' she said, 'it isn't Sarge any more.'

'Shit.' Danny flipped the cup over his shoulder, not looking: knowing it would be deftly caught by his colleague at the coffee machine. 'You been fired?'

He'd said it to make her laugh: her station lanyard was clearly visible at the neck of her blouse. She obliged, showing him her teeth, and he beamed back.

'Don't be silly, Danny.' She was flirting with him – flirting in that safe, meaningless way that's allowed when the man is twenty years your junior. 'No, I got myself promoted. These days I'm a DI. Detective inspector, if you can believe it.'

'I believe it fine.' Danny put out his hand for the money she owed. 'Just want to know what took them so long, really.'

As she slid a ten-pound note from her purse and watched him count out the change, Birch realised she felt proud of herself for the very first time. In the weeks since she'd heard, her primary feeling had been dread: at leaving Gayfield Square and her team, at moving to Fettes, working right under the DCI's nose. At being the only woman all over again. But Danny admired her – she could see it in his face as he palmed the cap over the coffee and passed it across the counter with both hands. The work she did was admirable.

'Oh, and a cinnamon swirl,' she said. 'To go. You keep the change.'

Outside, the last of the night's chill was starting to lift. A few bolts of purple cloud hung above the Leith tenements, the sky a kind of Disney princess pink. *Red sky in the morning*, Birch thought, and shivered. A warning. She'd parked the big, black Mondeo, her new CID car, across a road that was suddenly stacked with buses. She waited for the crossing in the chug of exhaust, enjoying the hot bite of the cup in her hand, catching its burned-sugar smell.

As she unlocked the car, she could hear the police radio talking to itself inside. A male dispatcher: a voice she didn't know. She plopped the coffee cup into its holder, her brain racing to catch up with the chatter. The guy sounded frazzled. *Bit early for that*, she thought.

Then she heard him say 'college shooting'.

She found the receiver in her hand almost before the thought was fully complete.

'Charlie Alpha, this is CA38, DI Birch. Did I hear you right just then? A college shooting, over.'

The line crackled.

'This is Charlie Alpha. You did, ma'am.' He hadn't expected her and she practically heard him flinch. 'Shots reportedly fired at a campus of Three Rivers College, but we believe it's a hoax. Two units have been dispatched to the scene, over.'

'Who's decided it's a hoax? This should be strategic command tier, shouldn't it? Over.'

Birch could have sworn she heard the dispatcher sigh.

'Our SO isn't in yet, so we're not talking about Gold command. It's some teenager's phoned it in. With a mass shooting, we'd expect a second call.' He made a kind of snorting sound. 'We'd expect a hundred calls, over.'

Birch looked at her watch. Eight forty.

'The two units, are they armed? Over.'

'No ma'am, over.'

Fear began to rise from somewhere inside her. It started in the diaphragm, and seemed to seep up through her throat, like swallowing hot liquid in reverse.

'Are they CID units? Unmarked cars, yes? Over.'

'No ma'am.' By now, she could tell the dispatcher was annoyed. He wanted rid of her, and to get on with his day. 'Both cars were in the area. I'm expecting the report any minute, over.'

Birch fired up the Mondeo.

'Give me the location, please. Over.'

The Tweed Campus was a way out of town. Birch had been there once, for some work event or other: in summer, while the students were away, they hired the place out as a conference venue. It was pretty swish, fairly new-built. She remembered a lot of glass, a lot of steel. A cafeteria with bright red walls.

The morning traffic had already peaked, but Birch found herself held up in a queue behind a bin lorry. She set up a mental abacus of regret: flirting with Danny, snapping at the dispatcher. Saying she'd go out to a crime scene that probably wasn't a crime scene. As she fretted, she kept one ear out for the radio, chattering away between the static. What would she say to DCI McLeod? 'I just wanted to check it out'? She'd be an hour late now, at least.

'Charlie Alpha, this is CA19, Park.'

Birch's senses sharpened: the voice belonged to a PC she'd worked with a while back. Nice girl. Green, when they'd known each other, but showing potential.

'I'm at the Tweed Campus of Three Rivers College and I can confirm that shots have been fired; I repeat, shots have been fired, over.'

Without waiting for the dispatcher's reply, Birch flicked on her siren. As often happened, the guy in front slammed on his brakes in surprise – a move that once upon a time might have resulted in the unmarked car going nowhere but the bodyshop. But this wasn't her first emergency response rodeo.

'Thanks, mate,' she said aloud, flicking the car's nose out into the road and punching up through the gears. The traffic peeled back like a pulled tarp: a sight she never tired of. On Park's channel, the dispatcher was faltering.

'What do I do?' she heard Park asking. The girl's voice was spiky with fear. 'What do I do, over?'

'PC Park, this is DI Birch,' she said. 'CA38. I'm on my way to the scene, over.'

A strange calm settled over her. She felt as though the car were driving itself: speedo hitting 60 and rising, tangle of cars whipping by like a film playing out. Even the siren seemed distant – the sound coming to her as if through a fog.

'Ma'am.' Birch coming onto the channel hadn't done much to settle Park. 'He went inside. He went inside, and I heard shots, over.'

'Who went inside? Over.'

Park didn't reply, but Birch could hear her speaking. Someone else was there, then. Good.

'Charlie Alpha, this is Birch. If you haven't already, you need to go to Gold command: repeat, Gold. Go to Gold, over.'

'This is Charlie Alpha.' His voice cracked. She imagined the panic there: they'd had to call it, and they'd called it wrong.

'I'm sorry, ma'am,' the dispatcher was saying. 'But do you have the jurisdiction . . .'

'Oh, *now* you're following the rule book.' It was cruel, but she'd said it before she could stop herself. 'We have a confirmed shooting, and unarmed officers at the scene. This is a strategic command incident. Go to Gold. Over.'

As she approached the campus, Birch realised hers was the only siren she could hear. *Fucking dispatch*, she thought. She'd hoped that by the time she arrived, an armed response team would be there to wave her away: she'd heard the call go out. She flipped the siren off. If the gunman was still at large, she'd rather not become an obvious, noisy target – or worse, have him freak out at the sound and shoot a bunch more people. She calmed the car back to a normal speed, and eased into the campus car park.

The sight that greeted her was an embarrassing government inquiry waiting to happen. Students were streaming out of every building: most from the main reception doors, trampling over one another like cattle, many of them screaming. Others were appearing from fire escapes and side doors, with no effort being made to corral them. Some were running for the safety of undergrowth at the campus perimeter, stupidly crossing open stretches of tarmac and grass where they could have been picked off by sniper fire. Worse: many more were milling around close to the buildings, and staring open-mouthed at the upper floors. As Birch pushed open the door, the car filled with the shrill pinging of the college fire alarm: a sound seemingly designed to incite chaos.

A few metres away, Park and two male uniformed officers were crouching in the shadow of a police panda car. Park was talking on the radio: Birch could hear her voice. *There should be four of them*, she thought. That was who Park had meant when she said someone had gone inside: her partner.

'Christ,' Birch hissed.

She pushed her driver's door out to its widest point, and stepped from the car in a crouch. The door wouldn't do much to protect her from a bullet, depending on the type of gun, but being behind it felt better than nothing.

'PC Park.' Birch had to shout over the fire alarm and the general student cacophony. The girl looked up, her face a mask of terror. 'It's DI Birch. How long since the last shot was fired?'

There was a pause.

'I don't know, ma'am,' the girl yelled. 'I'm sorry. I think it's . . . it might be a good fifteen minutes now.'

'Okay.' The car was alive with chatter: voices on every channel, dispatch communicating with ambulances, fire, and those all-important guys with guns. Birch reached behind her.

'Charlie Alpha, this is Birch,' she said. 'I'm at the scene. Where the hell's this armed response unit?'

A female dispatcher replied: it seemed all hands had been brought on deck, and in the midst of her panic, Birch felt glad the smarmy male voice was gone.

'This is Charlie Alpha. DI Birch, are you the commanding officer at the scene, over?'

Birch crouched behind the scant cover of her car door. A male student whipped past, heading for a patch of trees.

'Oh my God,' the boy said, apparently to her. 'I think Liz is dead. I think she's dead.'

She watched him until he made it to a decent hiding place, then turned back to look at Park and the two constables. One of the men had begun to cry, though he was trying to hide it.

'Oh Jesus, Charlie Alpha,' Birch said. 'I think I must be.'

14 May, 8.20 a.m.

Ishbel's employer had their local offices in one refurbished quarter of what had been an old mill. Walking across the courtyard in the still-thin morning light, Ishbel let herself imagine a possible former life: that of a young mill-working woman, dressed in long skirts, coming to begin a punishing, physical day. The many windows in the buildings' upper floors were caught by the early sun, and cast quivering rhombuses of light down into Ishbel's path. Once upon a time there would have been no electricity, no heating, and certainly no water cooler or coffee room for the workers here. Walking in to clock on must have been a little harder with every passing day.

See, Ishbel thought. *You don't have it so bad.* But she didn't feel convinced.

As she reached the main door, someone called out to her.

'That one's not open yet.'

She turned. Joan, one of the mill complex's cleaners, was standing in the building's navy blue shadow, camouflaged in her navy blue uniform.

'I havnae opened the main doors yet,' she said, as Ishbel approached. Thick, white smoke curled from her mouth along with the words, and Ishbel smelled the strawberry tang of her chosen vape. 'You're fair early, hen.'

Ishbel smiled.

'Didn't do my homework last night,' she said.

Joan nodded.

'Ach, well, say no more. Side fire door's open. Just leave it propped, hen – I'll be in right after ye.'

Once upstairs, Ishbel dumped her handbag and armful of files onto her desk. The office had a hot-desk policy that everyone ignored: each of the little cubbies was personal territory, marked by photos and keepsakes. Two desks along, Ishbel's colleague Dave still had a string of red tinsel Blu-Tacked along the top of his monitor. *May as well leave it up for next year*, he'd begun saying.

Ishbel's own desk had no desk-tidy: she stored her pens, stapler, rubber bands and other random office bits in a series of coffee mugs, most of them lifted from company display tables at conferences and training days. She also had an ancient foam mouse mat – defunct now, but still there on the desk – emblazoned with the words *My Mummy Is a Superhero*, and a scribbled drawing *by Abigail H, age 4*. Aidan had had it printed for her one Christmas – a fact that Ishbel now found mind-boggling. They hadn't exchanged Christmas gifts at all in the past few years. Rather, they'd agreed to spend the extra money on Abigail, and then tried to out-invest each other, like two lab scientists competing over a shared project. Feeling a spike of anger, Ishbel flipped the mouse mat over. Its black underside was perishing: the mat threw a scatter of little black shreds across the desk.

In the coffee room, she watched the miserable drip-drip of the machine and tried to dissolve her anger. *Admit it*, she thought. *You didn't need to come in this early*. She pulled in a long breath, trying to make a pre-emptive caffeine hit out of the room's coffee smell. She had absolutely no stomach for the half-finished report. If she was honest, she could have made up some excuse and given the complainant an adjusted deadline. *I just didn't want to be there when Abigail woke up. I'm sick of always being the one who apologises.* Ishbel clattered her favourite mug out of the dishwasher. *Let her stew in it for a day, it won't kill her.*

The coffee was bitter, but it was hot and strong, and it would do.

Back at her desk, Ishbel listened to her PC click and whir as it booted up, and thought about Abigail. She couldn't help it. It was nearing eight thirty – if she'd got herself out of bed on time, her daughter should be arriving at the college right about now. Though her first class wasn't until nine, she liked to get there a little early. Ishbel had always put this down to studiousness, a desire to be properly prepared for a good day's learning. But now the early starts seemed suspicious. Was Abigail really going to college early, or was she making some detour on the way? Was she even – Ishbel shuddered – was Abigail attending college at all? She realised that there was very little evidence, beyond her daughter's weekday routine, to confirm that she was in fact showing up for her HND classes. Abigail's chosen subject was Acting and Performance – a choice that, when it had first been made, Ishbel was sure had been designed as a personal slight. She'd done her best to make peace with it and not say anything, though she suspected Abigail knew of her reservations. She perhaps also suspected that Ishbel was secretly praying for a change of heart, a switch to a more cerebral subject, which was true. Now Ishbel cursed the Acting and Performance course anew. Any other subject would produce essays. Worksheets. Paperwork. Abigail was adept at leaving things lying around the house, yet Ishbel found herself wracking her brain for the last time she'd seen anything even vaguely college-related discarded on the kitchen worktop. *I really have been distracted*, she thought. How could you live in the same house with someone and not have any real sense of their daily movements? She knew even less about what Aidan did with his time.

This evening they'd need to talk. All three of them, ideally, but she and Abigail at least. Ishbel began to rehearse a speech in her head. *I know you don't like this, but I have to ask. If you're lying to me about attending football practice, how am I to know you're not lying about other things?*

The PC played its little start-up jingle, and then Dave walked into the office.

'Shit.'

Ishbel looked up at him.

'Good morning to you too, Dave.'

Dave strode past her and threw his jacket across the back of his office chair.

'Sorry,' he said. 'I was just absolutely *sure* I'd be the first one in today.'

She forced a smile.

'There's no trophy or anything, I'm afraid,' she said.

Dave hit the power switch on his PC.

'I'd settle for the short-lived feeling of pride,' he said. 'I hope you've been appreciating it.'

Ishbel dropped her gaze.

'There's coffee,' she said. 'I only just made some.'

He glanced over in the direction of the coffee room, and clapped his hands together, just once.

'You're a star, Bel,' he said. 'Why're you in at this hour, anyway?'

'Why are *you*?' Dave usually trailed in as late as he could manage – and she was surprised to see that now, he was blushing.

'Okay.' He huffed his breath out. 'I may or may not have acquired a new lady friend. She lives here in Musselburgh, so . . . my commute just got shorter.'

Ishbel beamed at him. In the time they'd worked together, Dave had married, divorced, lost a custody battle – and that was just the stuff he told her about.

'Dave, that's brilliant,' she said. 'I'm pleased for you.'

He made a *pshaw* sound and flinched a little, as though dodging her kind words.

'Well,' he said. 'It's early days yet. Look, don't tell everyone, will you? Sorry – I mean, I know you won't. But if Sheila – you know, admin Sheila? If she finds out it'll be all over the place, and we're just testing the waters at the moment. I don't want to scare her away, you know?'

Ishbel reassessed her grin, toning it down to a toothless smile.

'Of course,' she said. 'Mum's the word.'

The word *mum* made her think of Abigail again, and she felt a little sting of anxiety.

'Dave . . .'

He'd begun to move towards the coffee room and now turned, pivoting on one foot, to face her.

'In answer to your question, I'm in early because . . .'

A tight little silence fell. *Just say it.* A second ago she'd wanted so much to tell him about Abigail. She felt a strong urge to just *check* with someone – to make sure she wasn't being irrational, like Aidan seemed to think. But the silence stretched. What if Dave agreed with Aidan? What if he told her she should have been a more attentive mother? What if he told other people that?

'Because,' she said, 'I've got this complaint, and – and I'm struggling a bit with the initial report.'

She watched Dave's face relax. *Okay*, she thought, *I was right not to tell him.*

'Do you think you'd have time,' she went on, 'to have a look at it for me sometime this week? Just to read it. See if you think I'm on the right track.'

Dave threw her an A-okay sign.

'Sure thing, Bel,' he said. 'What are colleagues for?'

Ishbel tried to force herself to focus on the work. She opened up the half-written report, and read over what she'd done so far. She deleted the odd word; rephrased an occasional sentence. She slackened her gaze and allowed the text in front of her to swim. The temptation to open up her emails was almost over-whelming. *No*, she told herself, trying to snap back in. *I have to get this done.*

It was 8.50 a.m. – about the time she'd arrive in the office on a normal day – and she'd made exactly zero progress. The place was filling up: somewhere a few desks over, someone was being asked about their holiday. Behind her, the coffee room was a beehive of voices. Even Dave had begun typing away in earnest. Ishbel took a swig of her coffee, and made a face. It had gone cold.

'Fucking hell.'

She glanced up. The voice belonged to Alison, the woman who worked at the desk facing directly onto her own. Their two PC monitors were back to back, and the women would be able to look one another in the eye, were it not for the partition of cloth-covered chipboard erected between them. At the sound of Alison's profanity, Ishbel found herself looking instead into the eyes of Abigail, aged about nine, beaming down from a photo she'd pinned to that partition.

Alison's blonde, permed head bobbed up above the chipboard.

'Sorry,' she said. 'Sorry for swearing, but – I'm on Twitter, and . . .'

'Twitter, eh?' Dave had stopped typing, and was leaning towards Ishbel. He looked at her and winked. 'Now there's a surprise.'

Ishbel threw him a *You're terrible* look, but something in Alison's voice caught her attention.

'Stop it, Dave,' Alison was saying. 'This is serious. They're saying that there's a shooting. It's happening now.'

A few more heads popped up between the cubicles.

'Where,' someone asked, 'in America?'

Alison raised her voice so everyone could hear.

'No, here. At the college in Edinburgh, it says. It's happening right now.'

Ishbel felt a shudder in her chest, like a car stalling. Around her, other people were logging into their Twitter accounts – she could hear their gasps rising into the air like steam. A small hubbub was growing.

'Which college?' Ishbel spoke but no one seemed to hear. Alison's head had disappeared behind the partition again, but Ishbel could hear her saying 'Oh my God' to herself, quietly, over and over.

'*Ali*son.' Ishbel's sharp tone brought her colleague's face back up over the divide. 'Which college?'

'Three Rivers,' Alison said, and then, 'Oh shit, is that where your wee girl goes?'

Ishbel looked down. For a moment, her vision dropped out, and she could see only spots in front of her eyes. She thought of the way old photographs, the printed kind, could end up with light let in at the wrong time – it looked like that. She blinked, and then through the fog she could see the vague outline of her hands. The diamond in her engagement ring a point of white light.

She heard herself speaking.

'Does it say which campus?'

Alison's face dipped away momentarily, then reappeared.

'Tweed Campus,' she said, her voice like a wince. 'The one over west.'

Ishbel blinked again. Her vision was becoming pixelated. The spots turned into churning patches of grey, with rainbow chimeras glinting in them, like flies' eyes. A loud buzz began to build inside her head, as the sounds of the office around her dimmed.

'Bullshit,' she heard Dave say. 'If it's on Twitter it's probably a hoax. People make shit up on there all the time, drives me nuts. About every six months they all say Bruce Springsteen's dead, and I freak out. It's never true. Bel, you all right? You're looking a bit green.'

Ishbel closed her eyes, but the weird light show didn't quit.

'Her daughter goes there,' she heard Alison say.

Someone grasped the rear of Ishbel's wheely office chair, easing it backwards. Then she felt the soft pressure of a hand on the back of her neck.

'Ishbel.' It was Dave. His voice was very close to her ear. 'I think you're having a bit of a fainting fit, sweets. I want you to just lean forward and put your head down by your knees, okay?'

Her eyes were still closed, but Ishbel nodded. She allowed herself to go limp, and be folded in half by Dave's guiding hand.

'That's a girl,' he said. Then, louder, to someone else, 'She's just gone a bit green around the gills. She'll be fine in a tick.'

Ishbel felt the poly mix of her skirt rub against her forehead. She felt the hair around her hairline making static electricity. *You'll look a sight now*, she thought. She very much wanted to go to sleep. The buzz in her head was almost soothing, and the twisting clouds of rainbowed grey had begun to fade to black.

But Dave was yanking her upright again.

'Okay,' he said. 'Sit up for me for a second. Alison's brought you some hot, sweet tea and I want you to drink it.'

There was a pause.

'That means you have to open your eyes, Ishbel.'

Somehow, she complied. The world was brightly lit and out of focus. She allowed Alison to press a mug into her hands, and then she lifted it and took a sip. It singed her tongue.

Dave was leaning past her and typing on her keyboard with one hand; the other hand was on her back, steadying her as she sat with the mug close to her face, breathing in the steam. The BBC News website appeared on the screen; even through her own private blur, Ishbel recognised the header.

'Reputable source, that's what we need,' Dave was saying. 'None of this Twitter malarkey.'

Ishbel screwed up her eyes, then stretched them wide open, raising her eyebrows as high as she could. *Why am I faint?* she almost asked. Anxiety sat heavy in her ribcage – they'd been talking about something important a minute ago. What was it?

'Oh, holy shit,' Dave said.

Ishbel tensed. *Abigail*, she thought. *Something about Abigail.*

'Breaking news,' Dave read. 'The BBC has received reports that gunshots have been fired at the Tweed Campus of the Three Rivers Further Education College in Edinburgh. Emergency services have been notified, and reports indicate that the unidentified gunman is still at large. As yet, no casualties or injuries have been confirmed. We will be posting live updates on this story as they come in, but in the meantime . . .' Dave trailed off.

Ishbel tilted wildly towards the screen, trying to make the print come into focus. The hot tea leapt out of its mug, and she was vaguely aware of a wet stinging sensation on her right thigh.

'In the meantime *what?*'

Dave didn't look away from the screen. He was trying to scroll down, though there was no more page to scroll to.

'Is that it?' he said, and then, 'Sorry. In the meantime, they've set up a helpline number. But that's it. That's all the information they have. So it can't be bad, right? *Right*, Alison? It can't be that bad, or they'd say more than that. They'd say, like . . . I don't know . . . the area's being evacuated, or something. Right?'

Alison must have come round to their side of the bank of desks, because her voice now came from somewhere behind Ishbel.

'I'm sure you're right,' she was saying. 'I'm sure there's nothing to worry about.'

Ishbel was still peering at the screen. The words *helpline only*, *families*, and *no press* flared in and out of focus.

'Dave,' she said. 'Will you dial the number for me? The helpline number? I can't seem to see straight.'

Without speaking, Dave leaned over the desk again. Though she didn't move her eyes from the screen, she could hear him dialling. He seemed to be doing it very slowly, and she wanted to snap something at him. She was vaguely aware of Alison bending down to sponge up the slopped tea.

'You want me to talk to them?' Dave asked. 'To whoever answers?'

'No.' Ishbel reached out her hand for the receiver, and brought it, shuddering, to her face.

'We are receiving a high volume of calls at this time.' The voice was female, but clearly robotic. 'Please try again later.'

Ishbel stared dumbly, not moving.

'Please try again later,' the robot woman said again, after a short silence. Then she said it again – and again.

'Goddammit!' Ishbel banged the receiver down. Blood pounded in her head. Everything came rushing back: her colleagues' voices, unbearably loud; the overhead strip-lights; the too-bright flare of the PC screen. Dave's cheap aftershave so strong she could taste it. Every single face had flicked round to look at her.

'Redial, please,' she said. She put the receiver to her cheek again, and Dave hit the button.

'We are receiving a high volume of calls—' But Ishbel had already slammed down the phone.

She looked up into Dave's face. He'd gone very white.

'Fuck,' was all he said, but in that word was everything Ishbel needed to hear: *I think it's really true. It looks pretty serious.* Loudest of all: *You should go.*

Ishbel bent double again – this time beyond the hem of her polyester skirt. She scooped her handbag out from the footwell of her desk and clawed around inside it till she found her car keys.

When she stood up, she could see that most of her colleagues were on their feet, too – huddling in threes and fours around computers, glancing over in her direction but then quickly looking away. She turned to Dave.

'Go,' he said, his voice almost a whisper. 'Just go. I'll sort things out here.'

It was enough. Ishbel pushed back the office chair, and ran.

14 May, 9.25 a.m.

Moira's hands were filthy. The shed floor hadn't been swept in years: she was crawling through decades of soot and soil, human dust, parched stalks and dried leaves, the carcasses of spiders. The words *they have to be here somewhere* ran through her head over and over, a kind of demented chant. Beyond the open door, she could see the garden, green and streaked like the inside of a bottle in the still-early light. As she swung her head back and forth – *they have to be here* – the doorway left a bright, pale green smudge on her retina.

A figure stepped into that doorway, and the shed grew darker around her. Before she could look up, she heard a mechanical click: close to her face, familiar and weird.

'Stay still, please.' A man's voice. 'Armed police.'

Moira froze. In her head, that chant: *they have to be here, they have to be . . .*

'I'm going to give you a command now,' the man said. 'But I want you to listen to it all the way through before you move, okay?' He sounded young. Somewhere in his vowels, Moira could hear a slight tremor: fear.

'I want you to stand up for me, very slowly,' he was saying. 'But I need you to keep your hands where I can see them the whole time. Can you do that for me?'

Moira looked at her hands, which were palm down, bracing her weight against the shed floor. It occurred to her that this was the pose she'd made as a young woman – a woman whose tiny son was singing *a horse ride, a horse ride!* for the fortieth time that day. She'd crawled all over that garden, wrecking her back, being Ryan's horse. Now, her hands were getting wrinkled: the dirt from the floor exacerbated their elderliness. Each nail was a skinny black moon.

When she raised her face, she saw the source of the click she'd heard. About twelve inches from her right eye, the long, elegant throat of a rifle hovered. Her heart snapped like elastic.

'I need you to do that for me *now*, please,' the young man said.

Moira squinted past the gun barrel. He was dressed all in black and heavily padded: his chest boxed in Kevlar.

'Okay,' she managed to say. She went through the motions he'd asked for, clicking her limbs into position like a wind-up toy. As she rose to match his height almost exactly, he let the gun hover, so now it pointed at the centre of her chest. She imagined the bullet splintering her breastbone – her torso breaking open like some lush, pink fruit. The thought brought a moment of unexpected calm.

'Good,' the young man said. 'The next thing I'd like you to do is raise your hands so I can see them very clearly, and then turn round in a full circle till you come back to face me.'

Moira flipped her palms up towards him. He'd be able to see every line, picked out in dirt. She turned in a neat circle, picking up her feet like a dressage horse.

'All right.' He sighed the word out, and there was relief in it. 'Now I'd like you to tell me your name, please, madam.'

The *madam* seemed so out of place that Moira actually smiled.

'Moira Summers,' she said.

He lowered the gun barrel, and slung the weight of the big machine onto one arm. The other he raised, and made a sort of beckoning motion.

'Guv!' He barked the words across the garden, sending up a clatter of jackdaws from the nearest, biggest tree. 'We've got the mother!'

Moira allowed herself to be led along the side of the house, and round to the front. The patch of street beyond the boundary wall was full of vehicles: most of them black, and unmarked. There were also people, some helmeted and flak-jacketed: a few on the front lawn, a few in the street with their vans. But the majority of their number, Moira sensed, were now inside her house. She thought of their deep-tread boots on her carpets. She tried to remember how tidy the kitchen was. She'd been in it, last night, for a long time – but she'd been distracted, talking to Ryan. A shiver went through her. She wanted very badly to go back into the shed, and continue her search.

The man who'd been identified as *Guv* by the young, gun-pointing soldier-policeman was now holding on to Moira's elbow. He'd taken off his glove and his fingers were gentle on the sleeve of her cardigan, but there was purpose in the gesture, too. It said *make no sudden moves. Stay calm.* It was a grip that, Moira knew, could tighten much faster than she could ever make to run.

'Mrs Summers,' the man said. 'We have a team of officers searching your house. I need you to tell me if you know of any threat to their safety anywhere inside that house.'

Why? she wanted to ask. *Why are they searching my house?* But instead she began to think about his question: about the loose flap of stair carpet six stairs up; Jackie's vintage cut-throat razor in its old suede pouch in the bathroom cabinet. The breadknife with the blade that sometimes came free of its handle. She knew that was not what he was asking.

'No,' she said.

'I'll be specific. Do you know of any bombs, or any explosive booby traps, inside this house?'

He pointed backwards at the pebbledash, the bay windows, the woody old hydrangea beside the door.

'No,' Moira said.

'Do you know of any guns or other firearms inside this house?'

Moira shuddered. She remembered Ryan's face, hanging in the air across the kitchen table – had that really been just last night, that conversation? She felt like a child caught in the midst of telling a lie.

'Not in the house,' she said, after a pause.

The man tightened his fingers around her arm, just slightly.

'Not in the house,' he echoed. 'But somewhere on this property?'

She squeezed her eyes closed.

'Yes,' she said. 'In the shed. That's what I was looking for. I know what—'

'Can you describe the firearms for me, please?'

Moira kept her eyes closed.

'They're not guns. Not exactly.' Yes, just like a child telling a lie: caught, but keeping the fiction going all the same. 'They're starting guns. My husband is – sorry, *was* – an athletics coach. But they *look* like guns, a bit. Or they do to me.'

She opened her eyes.

'Okay,' the man said. He was speaking more slowly now, as one might speak to someone whose English wasn't that good. 'What *kind* of guns do they look like? He pointed to the young policeman with the rifle. 'Like this, like a rifle? Or like a handgun?'

Moira nodded, though it wasn't a yes-no question.

'Like a handgun,' she said. 'They're very small. There are three of them. Two of them are orange, and I think parts of them are made of plastic. Or they look like plastic. One is mostly black – that one looks most like a gun, I suppose. Like a gun from off the TV. They all have wooden-type handles.'

The man's hand was still there, holding her in one spot. She began to feel glad of it.

'And the last place you saw these firearms was the garden shed, you say?'

She nodded.

'The outbuilding you've just been escorted from?'

'Yes.'

'And you say that you were in the shed because you were looking for these items?'

'I was.'

He nodded.

'But you didn't find them?'

'Not yet.'

'Had you been searching for them long, before we got here?'

Moira's eye was caught by a movement across the street: her elderly neighbour, Frank, opening his front door and stepping out onto the welcome mat in his slippers. She forced herself to focus. *How long was I looking?*

'I don't really know,' she said.

She endeavoured to keep looking at this flak-vested man. On the edge of her vision, Frank was teetering on his front step, watching the comings and goings.

'You're doing well, Moira,' the man said. His tone had softened just a little, and when she blinked, she realised her eyes were wet, her face was wet. Would these men wonder why she was crying? Did they think she looked guilty?

'I just have two more questions for now,' the man was saying. 'The first one is, do you think it's possible that these three firearms have been recently moved out of the shed and taken somewhere else?'

'I don't know what you mean,' Moira said. But she did. She did know what he meant. He knew it, too.

'I'm asking if they could be in the house, for example,' he said. 'Could someone have brought them inside, since you last saw them? Your husband, maybe?'

'My husband is dead. He died two years ago.'

The man blinked, then nodded.

'Okay. Final question for now.' He kept saying that: *for now.* Moira closed her eyes again. *What is this the start of?* she wanted to ask. Nausea had begun to swirl inside her. 'Do you have any reason to think that these guns might now be in the possession of your son, Ryan?'

There it was. Under her feet, the lawn seemed to lurch. In the few seconds of quiet in the wake of his question, Moira weighed up a few options in her head. *No, Ryan wouldn't. No, they belonged to Jackie. Okay, Ryan was interested in them but he'd never. I'm sure they're in that shed. If you look, you'll find them. Let me go back. I'll find them. They must be there somewhere. They must be.*

'I suppose so,' was what she actually said. But then she added, 'Ryan was interested in them, sure. He wanted to know how they worked. But they're starting pistols. I said that, didn't I? They're not guns. They're not dangerous.'

They're not dangerous. The words seemed to come out too loud, to echo off the sides of the vans, off the walls of the houses – she imagined the whole conversation reaching Frank, forty yards away. It wasn't even what she wanted to say. She wanted to say, *Why are you bringing Ryan into this? Why does it matter if he has some old starting pistol in his room, or even in his bag?* But she didn't say it, because she knew why. It was the reason she'd been awake half the night after talking with her son. It was the reason she'd gone out to the shed in the first place.

The man had dipped his head towards his chest, and brought his hand up to the radio mounted there.

'Okay, folks.' The voice he used to speak into the radio was quite different to the one he'd just been using for Moira. 'We're looking for three snub-nosed revolver-style pieces, I'm told they're starter guns. Two have orange frames, one black, all three have wooden or wood-effect grips. The last known place they were stored is the outbuilding in the garden. They could now be somewhere inside the house. They could also have left the property. But if they're here anywhere, then let's find them please, and I mean pronto. Let's get that particular question answered, okay?' There was a pause. His hand was still on her arm. When no answer came, the man added, 'Out,' and brought his head back up to make eye contact with Moira.

'Is there anything else?' he asked. 'Anything else my team need to know about in this house?'

Moira allowed herself to look around again at Frank. He was now at the end of his garden path, chatting over the wall to a white-haired woman. The woman was wearing a raincoat, holding a dog on a red lead. Moira had seen her around – guessed she must live a street or two over.

'No,' she said. 'Nothing else I can think of.'

'Okay.' The man opened his fingers and let go of her arm. 'I need to be elsewhere now,' he said. 'I'm afraid we can't let you back into the house while the search is ongoing, but we do need you to stay nearby. Can I ask you to stay here in the garden for now? Gibbie here will keep you company.'

He nodded in the direction of the young policeman, who was still hefting his terrible rifle on one arm.

'Can I ask . . .' The words came out and Moira wished she could pull them back in again. She both did and did not want to know. But now he was looking at her, waiting.

'Can I ask what you're looking for?' she said. 'Can I ask, is my son – is Ryan okay?'

The two men exchanged looks.

'You've heard that there has been a shooting at Three Rivers College.' It was a statement, not a question.

'Yes,' Moira said. 'On the radio. Is Ryan . . .?'

The man drew himself up a little.

'I'm afraid I don't have information on casualties at this moment,' he said. 'I can't tell you any specifics about any of the students at the scene. I also can't tell you what we're looking for, because at this point we don't really know ourselves. But I can tell you that we're here because we're working to stop what's happening at the college, and to stop anyone else from being harmed. That's why we need your help.'

The young man, Gibbie, had taken a step forward. He was, she could tell, preparing to take charge of her.

'Okay?' the senior officer was saying. 'Is that okay, Moira? Will you help us?'

It was true, then. What she'd suspected – what had begun to settle over her with increasing heaviness as she'd searched in the shed and failed to find what she was looking for – *something happened, and Ryan made it happen.*

'Of course,' she heard herself say.

As the man walked away, she felt Gibbie step forward and slip his own hand into that same groove on her upper arm.

'We'll need to take a proper statement from you shortly,' he said. Then, in a much lower voice, he added, 'I'm sure it'll all be all right.'

Moira looked over at her neighbours, their faces equal parts curious and frightened.

'I don't think it will,' she said.

14 May, 9.25 a.m.

Ishbel couldn't find her car. She'd almost broken her neck on the stairs, almost lost a high-heeled shoe running out across the cobbles of the courtyard. She didn't even know where she was going, but something told her she had to go there fast. A voice had started up in her head – later, when she thought about it, she'd realise that voice had sounded a lot like her own mother, dead nearly twelve years. *Your child is in danger*, it said. *Go faster. Hurry up.*

Now she couldn't find the car. Her body felt like a shaken bottle: full of sloshing, fizzy panic. Surely it hadn't been stolen. Surely someone hadn't done that to her.

Hurry up, the voice said. *You can still save her.*

Ishbel clattered through the car park, between rows of shiny estates and executive 4x4s. Skidding on her heels she disturbed a family of gulls, chattering around an overflowing bin. They took to the air and began circling, throwing down their weird laughter.

Come on, what's wrong with you? the voice said.

The car was hidden behind a Transit van. The van's owner had parked badly, angling his front wheels over the line. The voice that told her to swing open her driver's door and damn his paintwork to hell was very much her own. She climbed in and jammed the car into reverse. As she swung out without looking, her driver's-side corner made contact with the van's flank and there was a shriek of metal on metal that oddly satisfied her. Even in her panic, she was able to think about Aidan's irritated face, about the trouble she'd be in for the ding.

But it's evidence, said the voice. *Later, when you get her home, you can show her. I stopped at nothing. I came for you.*

But the car wasn't moving. Ishbel sat with her foot on the clutch, her mind like stew. She didn't know where to go. To the college? Back to the house? Abigail might not even have made it in on time this morning. Ishbel could drive home, stagger into the kitchen, only to find her daughter sitting at the breakfast bar still in her pyjamas, eating cereal and flicking through Ishbel's *Hello!* magazine.

A thought hit her, obvious as a flung stone. She scrabbled in her handbag for her phone, and thumbed in Abigail's number. It rang out.

'Hey, you've reached Abi H,' the voicemail said. 'I can't pick up right now, so text me.' At the sound of her daughter's voice, Ishbel's vision began to falter again.

Hurry, said the voice.

But she'd barely hung up the call when the phone rang in her hands. It wasn't a number she recognised, but it had an Edinburgh 0131 prefix.

'Baby?'

There was a pause on the line, and then a man's voice.

'I'm sorry – is that Ishbel Hodgekiss?'

Shit. Was this a work call? Was someone actually calling her at *this* moment to talk to her about something other than her daughter?

'Yes. Sorry, yes it is. But I can't—'

'Ishbel, it's Greg Tomlinson here.'

Hang up, the voice said. *Hurry.* But Ishbel's heart kicked.

Greg was one of her old school friends, a doctor. He came over for dinner occasionally and Ishbel and Aidan always argued afterwards. Aidan disagreed with almost all of Greg's views, while Ishbel admired them.

'Greg,' she said, 'I'm sorry, but right now—'

'It's about Abigail,' he said.

Ishbel's body flooded with heat: with a feeling she'd never felt before. Relief – *she's okay! She's – somehow – with Greg!* But also panic – *she's hurt. She's hurt and he knew about it before I did.*

'Oh my God,' Ishbel said. 'Has she called you? Have you seen her? Greg – what's happening? Do you know something?'

'I'm at the hospital,' he said. He paused, but she could make no reply. The two halves of herself were still fighting: *the hospital, good. They'll take care of her*, versus *if she's at the hospital she must be hurt*. The whole time, the other voice, the one that wasn't quite her own, was saying *hurry, hurry*.

But no, Abigail wasn't there – Greg's tone was wrong.

'I thought you'd want to know,' he said. 'We've just had the call to say they're bringing the casualties here. The injured. I mean the students who've been injured.'

The correction came too late. Ishbel heard herself make a weird sound, like she'd been slapped.

'They've called me down off the ward,' he was saying. 'We're down here waiting for the ambulances and it's going to be all hands on deck. We don't know yet what's coming, how many, how bad they'll be. We don't know who.'

Ishbel swallowed hard, once, and then again. The fizzing in her system felt out of control – she thought she might throw up, or burst into tears, or faint again. The thought *Should I even be driving right now?* came to her – distantly, as though shouted from a long way away.

'So,' she heard herself saying, 'you haven't heard from her?'

Another pause.

'No,' he said. 'I just thought. I thought you'd want to know something. I don't know where you are, but if you wanted to, you could come here and see if they bring her in. If she's been hurt in any way, even if it's just cuts and bruises, this is where they'll put her. I shouldn't be telling you this, mind. But if she's hurt – and Christ knows I hope she isn't, Ishbel – coming here would be the fastest way to find out.'

Ishbel said nothing. She was beginning to calculate distances, think about routes. She glanced down at her petrol gauge.

'I think your alternative is waiting for the police to tell you what's what,' Greg was saying. 'And judging by the call we've just had, they're struggling. It's going to be a hell of a day at sea, no matter what the scale of this thing.'

Ishbel shoved the car into first gear.

'The scale,' she said. 'Have they given you any sense of it?'

'No. Like I say, we don't know what's coming. The whole thing's what? Half an hour old? I mean, we're all hoping against hope that all we get is some bumps and flesh wounds. That this gunman was a bad shot, or the police got to him quick. But we don't know. We've got surgeons on stand-by, too. We just don't know.'

Go, the voice was saying. *Go get her.*

'Okay,' Ishbel said. 'I'm coming. But that place is like a maze. When I get there, where do I go to?'

Greg was moving now – she could hear his footsteps, his breath slightly faster.

'Your main problem will be parking,' he said, 'as bloody ever. Just go in the paying section. They'll hand you a bill like you've been at the Ritz, but I'll do what I can about that when this is all over. From there, if you look over at the buildings you'll see a big red sign that says *Emergency Department*. It's a lit sign; you can't miss it. Head there. There's a waiting room. As they bring people in, we'll start a list of the injured and it'll get put up in that waiting room, and we'll update it. There might be a lot of ambulances, a lot of commotion. But if you go there and you stay there, you'll know as soon as anyone will if Abigail comes in. Okay? I'll try and get down at some point to see you, if I can.'

Ishbel was already steering through the car park.

'Greg,' she said. 'Thank you so much.'

'No problem. I hope to Christ she doesn't come in and this has all been a big waste of your time.'

Behind his voice, she realised she could hear a siren.

'Okay,' he was saying, 'this is it, they're playing my song. I'll see you, Ishbel.'

'Good luck.' She was saying it for herself as much as anything, because Greg had already gone.

She threw the phone onto the passenger seat, and gave her head a little shake. The panic was still sloshing in her chest, but she'd calmed it, just slightly. She had a plan.

You were wrong last night, that voice was saying, *but you can make it up to her now. But you have to hurry. You have to go.*

The car peeled out into traffic. She went.

It was difficult for Ishbel to discern the extent to which the A&E waiting room was chaotic. As she walked towards the large, imposing reception desk, she thought, *It might always be like this.* Indeed, a lot of the people milling around, or sitting in the rows of hard plastic chairs, appeared to be walk-ins – people whose condition suggested they'd been nowhere near the scene of a shooting. There were parents with small children in buggies; a woman with a makeshift and blood-spattered bandage tied around one foot; older people in couples, or sitting alone with newspapers. Above the plastic chairs a flat-screen TV was bolted to the wall, showing 24-hour news. Ishbel felt a moth-like pull towards it, but she forced herself to stay on course. The woman behind the desk seemed to brace for impact as she approached, and Ishbel realised she must look quite imposing. She was wearing a dark suit and, she realised, her work face: the 'game face', Abigail called it. *I must look like an inspector,* Ishbel thought to herself – and then, *probably because I am one.*

She reached the desk.

'My name is Ishbel Hodgekiss. I received a call from . . .' Ishbel stopped herself, just, from giving Greg away. His voice drifted through her head: *I shouldn't be telling you this, mind.*

The woman behind the desk blinked at her.

'From a doctor here.' Her voice thickened. Ishbel swallowed hard. 'It's about my daughter. Her name is Abigail. She – attends Three Rivers College.'

The woman studied Ishbel's face. Her eyes narrowed, just slightly.

'You had a call?'

'Yes,' Ishbel said. Her throat felt swollen. *Please be kind to me right now,* she thought. She wondered if Greg had also called Aidan. Somewhere outside, another siren – still far off, but approaching.

'He told me to come here. I was told I could wait. He said . . .' Her voice cracked. *Hold it together*, said the voice. 'He said there'd be a list.'

The woman said nothing for a moment, still studying Ishbel's face. Then she seemed to have a thought that satisfied her, and she waved one hand in the direction of a biro that was sitting on the lip of the desk.

'There's no list,' she said. 'Not yet. There might not be one at all. We don't know yet what information we can release. But if you write your name and your daughter's name down there for me, that'll be a start.'

The woman placed a piece of NHS-headed paper, upside down, in front of Ishbel.

'If she's here, I can update you on her condition as long as you have ID.' The woman was looking at the middle of Ishbel's chest – she realised she was still wearing her proximity card and lanyard from work. 'But you'll need to wait. We're still dealing with people coming in. As you can imagine, this isn't your average morning.'

Ishbel nodded, already scribbling down Abigail's full name – her middle name was Pauline, after Aidan's mother. Tears rose in her eyes, making the words swim, but she pulled them back with a sharp inward breath. *Stop it*. She also wrote down Abigail's date of birth, her own name, and, as an afterthought, her mobile phone number. She let the pen hover for a moment, then handed it back without writing down anything to do with Aidan. He could get his information from *her*, for once. She had the thought, then felt ashamed of it.

'Do me a favour too, will you?' The woman was looking down at the paper, and had lowered her voice. 'Don't tell the other patients why you're here. We've already got a bit of disgruntlement going on, because we're prioritising . . .'

Ishbel was blinking hard, pushing the tears back, and now she could see that this woman was frazzled – and perhaps a little scared – herself.

'I understand,' she cut in. 'You don't need to explain. I won't talk to anyone.'

The woman smiled: a tired, thin-lipped smile, but grateful.

'I don't feel much like talking to anyone, anyway,' Ishbel added, half to herself.

As she returned the biro to the desk, the woman reached over and put one small, dry hand over Ishbel's own.

'If she's here,' the woman said, 'then she's in the best possible place.'

Those tears again. Ishbel closed her eyes against them, and nodded. When she opened them to speak, her voice was a hoarse whisper.

'You'll let me know . . .?'

The woman squeezed her hand, and then let go.

'Soon as I can,' she said.

Ishbel walked over to the nearest seat: next to the woman with the bloodied bandage on her foot. Before she sat down, she found herself casting around for a glimpse of Aidan – surely Greg must have called him, too? She felt a spike of annoyance at him: unlike her, Aidan worked in Edinburgh, and should really have got here first. But no – *stay focused*, she told herself.

The siren was close now. Its persistent, strobing cry touched something primal in Ishbel, like the cry of an anguished baby. She wished there were something she could do to make it stop. She sat down on the hard orange plastic and tried not to make eye contact with anyone. The sound on the TV was damped down, but just audible.

'What're you in for?'

The foot-bandage woman was leaning over, trying to get Ishbel to turn and face her. Politeness took over and she did, wincing.

'It's not me,' she said. 'I'm – I'm just waiting for someone.'

The woman's face made no secret of her disappointment.

'Oh, okay,' she said. Then she waggled her bandaged foot. 'No prizes for guessing what's up with me.'

Ishbel smiled again, but the smile was smaller, tighter.

'Bloody typical,' the woman was saying. 'I get up early, think, I'll get out in the garden today, make the most of this weather. I've got all sorts to do – old shed to dismantle, seedlings to get out, you name it. Anyway, what do I go and do? Only shove the bloody garden fork through my foot in the first five minutes. I ask you.'

Ishbel flinched.

'Yeah, it's not pretty,' the woman said. 'I've had something for the pain, but goodness only knows how long I'll be sitting here. Bleed to death most likely.' She made a kind of snorting sound in her throat. 'Bloody NHS.'

Ishbel froze. The siren had stopped, and now there were sounds of shouting, doors banging, rushing feet, coming from outside the door she'd walked through a moment ago. The woman with the bandaged foot turned her whole body, and leaned out of her seat to ogle.

There were suddenly a lot of people in the waiting room. Paramedics in their green uniforms. Other uniformed people – doctors, nurses? In their midst, a stretcher, bearing a young man with a ventilator mask over his face. His torso, the mask and most of his face were daubed and smeared with red-brown blood. The smell of it hit Ishbel like running into a wall.

'All right.' A male paramedic manoeuvred the stretcher through the space at a clip, the other uniforms gathering alongside, seemingly trying to shield the boy from view.

'This is Jack,' he was saying. 'Bullet entered below the right collarbone, clean exit wound below the shoulder blade, but we've got a perforated right lung, blood loss is . . .'

Jack, Ishbel thought. *Why is that name important?* She scrabbled to remember.

Time seemed to slow down. A movement – a blur of dark clothing – caught Ishbel's eye, and she managed to somehow pull her gaze away from the spluttering, blood-soaked body of the boy. A man in a dark grey coat had stepped, as if out of thin air, into the circle of people clustered around the stretcher. In one fluid, practised movement, he pulled out a mobile phone, pushed it into the throng so it hovered over the beleaguered boy, and took a photograph. Ishbel felt herself jump – physically – as the flash went off, and she realised for sure what he was doing.

One of the paramedics, a woman, spun to face the man.

'Get the *hell* out of here,' she said evenly, and planted the flat of her hand against his chest. Her push was enough to expel him, arms splayed, from the circle, and then the gaggle moved, disappearing the stretcher and the boy through a pair of double doors. Ishbel coughed, and tasted acid.

'Holy fucking Jesus Mary and Joseph.' The woman with the bandaged foot sank back into her seat. 'I guess it really is as bad as they're saying.'

Ishbel followed the woman's nod and found herself looking at the TV – she'd forgotten about it. It showed aerial footage of the college campus, with a red ticker scrolling white text along the bottom. Ishbel's head swam – the text was too fast for her to read more than the odd word, but she caught *fatalities*, *emergency services* and *bloodshed*. She tried to see the college buildings as she knew them, tried to pick them out from the shaky helicopter footage, but she couldn't get her bearings. She realised how long it had been since she'd visited the place, since she'd shown any real interest in Abigail's course. On the screen, the footage cut to grainy, long-lens images of ambulances, standing in a line in the college's car park. Cut to a close-up of two female students hugging, one of them crying uncontrollably. Cut to a close-up of a girl's slip-on shoe, pale green with cut-outs, discarded on tarmac. Stepped out of, maybe, in the rush to get away – or had it dangled and then dropped from the foot of a lifted, broken body? Ishbel swallowed, trying to tamp down her panic. *Where the hell is Aidan?* She tried to tell herself that maybe he was with Abigail, maybe everything was okay ... but she didn't believe it. He'd have phoned. *He would have*, she thought. *He wouldn't leave me sitting here in an abject panic. Right?*

She was aware of someone standing near to her. When she looked up, it was the grey-coated man – his mobile phone still in his hand. He too was looking up at the TV screen.

'You there!' The woman with the bloodied foot had also noticed him. 'What do you think you're about, *photographing* something like that?'

The man turned his head, slowly – up close, there was something almost reptilian about him. He was small for a man, and slight – not much older than thirty, Ishbel would have guessed, though his mousy-coloured hair was beginning to thin.

'What are you,' the woman was saying, 'some sort of pervert?'

The man took a step towards them, and both Ishbel and the bandaged woman flinched. His face bloomed into a small, nasty smile.

'Madam,' he said, 'I'm a journalist. Grant Lockley. You might have heard of me?'

Ishbel hadn't. She wanted very much for him to go away. She wanted to look back up at the TV, or go back to the desk and ask again about the list of names, or do *something*. But she also felt like she had to keep an eye on this man.

'Journalist,' the bandaged woman scoffed. 'The *worst* kind of pervert.'

Grant Lockley looked hurt.

'Not so, madam,' he said. Ishbel shook her head slightly. She felt like she was inside some sort of surreal bad dream. 'Everyone has a job to do. This is mine.'

The woman scoffed. Lockley didn't speak again, but instead lifted the mobile phone and aimed it at the woman. The flash went off, and Ishbel blinked, hard. She could never believe how bright those things were: behind her eyelids, a white streak swam on her retina. When she opened her eyes again, Grant Lockley had gone, and beside her, the woman was opening and closing her mouth like a fish.

'Ishbel.'

Someone else was standing in front of her now, and she looked up. It was Greg. His face was very white. Ishbel looked at his hands, which hung by his sides in two loose cups. He clearly hadn't noticed, but there was something brown and flaking dried onto his cuff: blood. She immediately forgot all about the grey-coated man and his phone.

'Ishbel,' he said again. 'I need you to come with me, please. And I'm going to need you to phone Aidan. I haven't been able to reach him.'

Ishbel stood, and found it hurt to do so, like she'd been left outside for a long time in a hard rain, and rusted over.

'She's hurt, isn't she.' It wasn't a question.

Greg turned to face her, fully, and looked her straight in the eye. Looking back, Ishbel would realise she appreciated that – he didn't flinch, didn't sugar-coat. Years of experience, she supposed.

'Yes,' he said. 'Abigail was shot, Ishbel. I can tell you more, but I need you to come with me now.'

He gestured towards the double doors. A deep, hot fear howled up inside Ishbel, and she allowed it to pick up her feet and carry her out of that room, in the wake of the boy Jack, and the paramedics, and Greg.

To: Helen Birch
From: Alan Gibb
CC: Amy Kato
Subject: Initial statement, Moira Summers
Date: 14/05 16:09

DI Birch,

Please find attached the initial statement taken from Mrs Moira Summers this afternoon. I attended the search at the Summers' property this morning and took charge of Mrs Summers while the search was ongoing. When the request came for her to attend the Royal Infirmary morgue to formally identify her son she asked that I go along with her. Having sought the necessary permission, and taking into account the fact that a FLO had not yet been assigned, I agreed. The body was formally identified as Ryan Andrew Summers and all necessary paperwork completed at 2.35 p.m. today.

I then accompanied Mrs Summers to the station at Fettes Row and took the attached initial statement from her. She is currently still at the station. At this stage she has not been detained. I have now stepped back and have cc-d in Amy Kato who I am told has been assigned the case as FLO.

If you want to ask me anything just give me a call and I can head back to the Command Centre at a time convenient for yourself.

Alan

View attachment:

Initial statement (audio transcript)
Mrs Moira Summers
Date: 14 May
Time of statement: 15:44

I'd been in his room in the morning. It's strange, I don't go in there much, but for some reason this morning I did. It smelled – I suppose all rooms where young men are allowed to do what they like smell that way – like sweat and old food. So the first thing I did was open the window. It was warm: actual warm air came in through the window when I opened it and I remember feeling shocked that spring had arrived, all at once. After I stripped the sheets off the bed, I sat under the window and listened for a while to the jackdaws. They make that strange sound, a sort of a spark – like rolling marbles, when they hit each other. The neighbour's garden has a big tree, and it's full of them.

What did I do in there, let's see . . . Stripped the bed, carried the sheets down to the wash. I suppose you're shocked that I still change my grown son's sheets, but if I didn't, he'd sleep in the same ones for a year. He'd wear them to rags. Then I think I took the dishes out. The usual: coffee mugs with bits of old milk floating on the top. Empty beer bottles, popped bottle lids. A few plates. He eats up there. I don't see him much, especially not since his father died, and that was a good two years ago.

I don't go through his things. I don't rifle. Oh God, a bad choice of words. I mean I respect his privacy. I've been in trouble, before now – throwing things out that weren't meant to go. Receipts, things that looked like litter. This morning I moved some clothes off the floor, just to run the hoover round. The computer screen? It was dark – like they are when they make themselves go to sleep.

I flurried about downstairs. I had the radio on: I always have the radio on. But I was hoovering, and the washer was going, so the first report I didn't hear. The house seemed like it was full of sun, and I was happy. Happy, while all of what happened was happening.

I heard the second report. I heard them say 'Three Rivers College', so I paid attention. Then they said shooting. At first I thought they meant filming, shooting a film. Then I understood, though at some point I went deaf – I just had the sound of blood in my ears. They still didn't know much, but they'd set up the helpline. I couldn't call at first. I'd gone cold all over – I was shivering, and I couldn't feel my hands. Couldn't dial. It took me five minutes and then it was jammed and I had to hold. There was hold music. I still can't believe there was hold music.

What was my thought process? I thought, *My son is dead.* I wished I hadn't washed his sheets, because they would have smelled of him, and if he was dead I would want to smell him again. Then I thought, *No, Ryan isn't dead.* Wouldn't I have felt it, me, his mother? Wouldn't some cosmic force have told me? You read about these things. Then I thought about how big that college is and how many buildings there are. All the places he might have hidden, how he'd know to hide. I thought, *Maybe he was there in the engineering lab and the whole thing happened somewhere else and he sat right through it.* Maybe he didn't even know. I listened to the hold music and those were the things that I thought.

The music stopped and I spoke to a person. A young man. I told him that my son was a student at the college and that he had gone there that morning, and I said his full name, Ryan Andrew Summers. The man said they didn't have any names, they didn't know who was shot and who was not shot. The only thing he told me was that I should not try to call Ryan's phone, because he or someone else might be using it to call 999. And I mustn't go there, to the college. Then he hung up.

I'm hearing now, on the news, that parents did go, they did drive to the college. That they're getting in the way of police. It's odd: listening to that hold music all that time and I never thought, *I have to go there.* I never thought, *Go and get your baby.* What kind of mother . . . I've asked myself this question a thousand times, I mean just today. What kind of mother have I been?

Then the phone rang a few times. I picked it up thinking *Ryan,* but it wasn't Ryan. Each time it was someone who'd heard on the news, wanted to know if he was okay. I cried at them. I wanted them to get off the line, because what if he called? But I couldn't say it. I just cried. I put the TV on.

It was on a loop on the 24-hour news, big red ticker along the bottom like you see in films. They said the suspected gunman was a young man who was a student there. There must be thousands of young male students at Three Rivers, but that was when I had the thought. What if it was *my* young male student, my boy, my Ryan? And once I'd had that thought, I couldn't shake it – it stuck out between all the other thoughts, like a tongue. What if he's dead? *It was him.* Maybe he hid? *It was him.* He'll walk through that door any second, you'll see. *It was him.* It was him, it was him, it was him. Just like that. It filled my head like a loud noise, like someone hammering.

Then I went out to the shed. I knew he'd been fiddling with his father's guns – we even called them that, though they aren't really guns. Or weren't really. I didn't know what he was doing, but they were starting pistols – I didn't think they could ever do harm. And he's a born engineer. Was. Is. I don't know. At six he dismantled this old typewriter we had and showed us how it worked. He loved all the parts, the shapes of them. I liked him working on things. I liked him working on those guns. I can't believe myself.

I don't go out there often so I didn't really know where to look. That shed is a man's place – it was the only real bond they had, Jackie and Ryan, and I didn't get involved with that. It's their place. Was. And after Jackie died I liked Ryan going out there. I wanted him to still have that. But this morning I went out and unlocked it. There's a workbench in there, a few metal cabinets on the walls. Shelves. No sign of those guns. After a while I got on my hands and knees and looked on the floor. I got filthy. I got metal filings stuck in the skin of my hands, and I didn't know where those filings could have come from. And I realised he'd done something. He'd done something to those guns to make them fire, and he'd taken them away, and now there had been a shooting. I got down there on the shed floor and I stayed there for a long time, I don't know how long. Until you found me, whatever time that was. The jackdaws were still playing in the next-door tree, and I could hear the sounds of the house, kind of far off. The TV and the radio still on, and the washer, which came to the end of its cycle after a while and the noise stopped. I looked at the sun moving around the garden. I thought, maybe it wasn't so bad. They hadn't announced that anyone was dead, and I thought, maybe no one's dead. Maybe he was a bad shot. But he wouldn't be a bad shot, would he? He got single-minded that way. He's like his dad. Was like his dad.

I've never thought about death so much in my life as I have today. What does it feel like, to be hit with a bullet? I've tried to think of all the pains I ever felt: all the burns, the time I stepped on the plank with the nail in it. I kept thinking about childbirth, like being beaten up from inside. It never occurred to me that he might be dead as well. I kept thinking I'd need to see him soon, I'd be brought to see him. I'd have to speak to him. And what would I say, to my only son. About the kind of mother I had been.

I could hear the phone ringing in the house. Maybe it's Ryan, I thought, maybe he's calling to say he's okay, he survived. It wasn't him, he threw the guns away. But I couldn't get up. Or I chose not to, I don't know. It kept ringing. Then I thought it was probably some friend or other, asking if I had heard, if he was fine, where was I, what was I going to do. I never thought it might be you, because I never thought he'd be dead, and I never thought I'd be told I'd have to go to the hospital, and I never thought I'd have to walk into that room and see my dead child lying there. I never thought I'd look down at the boy I birthed and see him dead, his face all pulled away. I barely knew him. On that table, I saw him as a grown adult man – I don't think I ever really had before. I understood it, suddenly. The man I raised was an evil man – a man who hurts women. But why? Why would my little boy want to do that? He was never a violent sort of boy. I never would have thought in all my life . . . I thought I could just stay there, quiet as anything, not moving, and listen to the jackdaws.

14 May, 5.50 p.m.

Birch's footsteps echoed through the corridor, her heels making a clop-clop sound like horses' hooves. She was on the first floor, in the Hairdressing department: on either side she glimpsed rows of white sinks and fat black chairs through the training-room doors. All silent now. The light in the corridor was dimming, and no electric lights had yet been switched on. She glanced at her watch: almost six. She'd been here nine hours.

Detective Chief Inspector McLeod was downstairs in the refectory, and he'd drawn all available personnel to him, like moths to a bare bulb. Birch had slipped away from the back row of the briefing after a while: he wasn't saying anything she didn't know, and she'd have to suffer through a private audience with him later, anyway. She needed a few minutes' peace.

And it *was* peaceful up here, though the strong smell of industrial disinfectant hung in the air. Birch stopped walking. Beside her, running along the wall up to about waist height, there was a patch of painted plaster that was lighter than the rest. It was about a metre and a half long. Metal fixings and chewed plastic rawl plugs jutted out of the patch at intervals. There was a rectangle of tape on the floor here, and a number marker-penned onto the waxed surface inside it. This was where the radiator had been. This was where Leanne Lawrie, the ninth victim, had fallen, and been found.

Seven hours earlier, Birch had stood here for the first time, taking an initial tour of the scene with PC David Leake. Leake had been written up as the First Officer Attending – he was PC Park's partner, the one who'd run inside while the shooting was still going on. As he and Birch walked the first floor together, he'd stopped at the radiator – still there at that hour, covered in blood that had run in stripes through its downward grooves, and dried. A further pool of it on the floor below had moved in a slow, tarry stream towards the stairwell, betraying the building's slight tilt.

'Here,' he'd said, pointing to the radiator, 'there was a girl here.' He'd been shaking all over.

'I'm sorry, David,' Birch said. 'I'm sorry to make you do this now. But we need to get as accurate a picture as we can of what you saw. Time is of the essence, and all that.'

'I know. You said.'

He pointed down at a vague line that had been drawn on the floor with some sort of pen – a line that would be firmed up by the tape later on.

'This one had a head injury,' he said. 'When I got to her, I thought she'd been shot in the head. But she had a pulse. I was waiting for the ambulance sirens – I was praying for them. I was off the radio because I didn't want Summers to know I was there. But I was calling it in, in my head – internally, I was screaming it.'

Birch had put a hand on his arm, and felt the quiver through her fingertips. Leake was vibrating, like a struck tuning fork. He knew where they were going next.

They'd walked down the corridor a little way, towards the two zipped body bags, and the SOCOs moving here and there around them.

'These two,' Leake said, 'I came to next. I couldn't find a pulse on either of them, and one of them . . .' He pointed to the furthest away of the two covered mounds. 'She was in really bad shape. Like, very obviously dead shape.'

Birch had shivered slightly herself at this. She'd have the crime scene photos and autopsy reports on her desk soon enough.

'Where did you go next?' she asked. Leake turned and pointed through an open classroom door behind them – another of the hairdressing rooms, with its line of gleaming sinks.

'There was a student in there,' he said. 'The others were all running, getting out of the fire exits. Most of them were gone from this floor by the time I got up here. But there was this girl in there – she made a sound, or something, and I turned round and saw her.'

Birch squinted in through the doorway. The morning's strong, spring light was bouncing up off everything: those glazed sinks, the white Formica desk tops, the shiny waxed floor.

'She was hurt?'

'No,' Leake said. 'She was hiding. Or, not even really hiding. Just sitting there. As if she was unable to move.'

Birch turned her head, calculating the line of sight from the classroom to the two body bags on the floor outside.

'You think she witnessed . . .'

'Yeah,' Leake said. 'I went in, spoke to her. She had her phone in her hand. She didn't want to speak, and didn't want me to make any noise. She was just hissing at me to *sshh*. Eventually she told me her name was Irina. She'd seen these two get shot, seen Summers. She'd watched him walk off. She said she thought he was still nearby, so she didn't want to move.'

Birch had nodded.

'I'll need to talk to her, for sure.'

'I'll happily ID her for you,' Leake said. 'Long black hair, sort of wavy. Skinny girl, Eastern European accent. Lots of gold jewellery, earrings and that.'

Birch had closed her eyes for a moment, allowed a vague mental Polaroid of this witness to form itself. Then she had looked back at Leake.

'What then, David?'

He swallowed hard.

'Then . . .' He pointed down the corridor, through the crowd of SOCOs. 'I walked towards that door. The ladies' loo.'

Leake began to move, slowly, in the direction he'd pointed.

'Summers had walked in blood here, look,' he said, skirting past the two body bags, pointing vaguely down at them. Birch looked, and saw what he meant: big, army-style boots with geometric treads, the prints dried and browning.

'I followed the prints,' Leake was saying, and Birch trailed them with her eyes, to where they seemed to disappear, fainter now, under the toilet door. 'You'll see that they go in, but they don't come out again.'

Birch smiled weakly at the SOCOs as she and Leake weaved between them. A few of them nodded in greeting, or mumbled a 'marm,' as they passed.

'So here I was,' Leake said, as they came to a stop outside the toilet door. 'I'm stood here, thinking, unless he took his shoes off, he's gone in there and he hasn't come out. He's still in that room. But I couldn't – I couldn't go in. I couldn't make myself. I'm sorry . . .'

Birch had placed a hand on Leake's shoulder, and felt for herself as the background shiver became a heave, and then another: huge, quiet sobs had seemed to rise up in the man beside her and then fall out, one after the other.

'David,' she said. 'It's okay. You did right – as an unarmed officer, you did right. You waited for the cavalry.'

Leake shook his head, flicking tears onto Birch's sleeve.

'But he was down,' he said. 'I didn't hear any shots fired in there, so he was down before I even got on this floor. He'd already killed himself. It was safe. And if I'd got in there, I don't know . . . what if those girls were still alive then? What if I could have done something to help them?'

Birch gave his shoulder a small squeeze.

'You didn't know,' she said. 'You didn't *know* that Summers was dead. And as for those four girls . . . I've been given a sense of their injuries. Even if they were still alive, they were beyond any first aid you could have given. They were dead, or they were dying. You did right.'

Leake had looked up at her then, looked into her eyes with so much fury – at her and at himself – that she'd dropped her hand from his shoulder, and taken a step backwards.

'Well, I could have sat with them,' he said. His voice caught in his throat and he twisted out a strange cough. 'I could have been there with them, in their final minutes. But instead I stood out here, doing nothing. I stood here like a fucking coward.'

In her pocket, Birch's phone buzzed, kicking her back into the here and now. She'd sleepwalked as far as the toilet door, which was sealed off with signs and tape: there was further forensic work to be done in there. Birch shuddered. It was a small bathroom, with only two cubicles – yet Summers had cornered four girls in there. She hoped they'd been in there anyway, maybe fixing their hair before going to class, chatting, sharing lipstick. She hoped they hadn't run in there to hide, and been punished for their mistake. A bathroom wasn't a stupid thought: in the US, kids were told to run into toilet stalls and stand on the toilet bowl in the event of a shooting. Birch remembered this from a viral Facebook post a while back: a cute little three-year-old girl who'd been trained to do this at kindergarten in the wake of Sandy Hook. School shooters were always male, and social programming runs deep – even on a rampage like this, they'd be likely to hesitate before entering a ladies' bathroom. *But,* Birch thought, *he wanted to kill girls. Women,* she corrected herself. All the dead were female, and only one of those in critical condition at the Royal Infirmary was male. Birch turned her back on the toilet door.

'This is about girls,' she said, quietly but aloud, into the long, empty throat of the corridor. 'He had some issue with women. I'd bet all the money I have.' She flipped her phone out of her pocket: a text from McLeod. She was being summoned.

As she walked back down the length of the first floor – past the tape marks and the pale swatches of floor where the bloody bootprints had been scrubbed at – she re-read the email with Moira Summers' statement in it. She'd listen to the audio itself later, listen for the cracks and pauses and quirks that might give something away. But in the transcript there was no mention of women, relationships Summers might have had. No break-up. But then, that line: *I don't see him much, especially not since his father died.* How well did his mother really know him? It sounded like Mrs Summers had been asking that herself.

The light in the corridor was fading rapidly, and up ahead Birch thought she saw a shadow move, briefly, across one wall. She stopped. In spite of herself, she shivered. *They always demolish the buildings where shootings take place,* she thought. *Too many ghosts.*

In the stillness, she listened for a shuffle or a footstep, but nothing came. Yet, yes – there it was again. Movement: a distortion of the dim, grey light. One of the SOCOs, still here? Or a cleaner, maybe?

'Is someone up there?'

Ahead of her, silence yawned. But just as she was about to shake herself and continue walking, a figure stepped out of one of the classroom doors, and into the corridor in front of her.

Birch felt her heart accelerate. Her hand went to her hip: an old, habitual movement from many years of carrying a baton, though of course she didn't have one now. The figure in front of her was indistinct, but she could see the person was slight. A woman, or a very slim man. A student? Could a student have hidden for this long, and gone undetected by the SOCO teams? *Surely not*, she thought.

'Who is that?' Her voice had a tremor in it.

Above her, the corridor's panel lighting began to clunk on, and the sudden change made her blink. When she focused, she could see who it was up ahead of her, maybe thirty feet away, leaning on the bank of light switches.

'Hello, DS Birch.'

Birch let out a long breath through her nose.

'Grant Lockley,' she said. 'I suppose it was only a matter of time before *you* turned up.'

Lockley took his hand off the switch and pressed it to his chest, a wounded gesture.

'I don't know *what* you mean,' he said.

'Yes, you do.' Birch was doing rapid mental arithmetic: *How did he get in here? Has he contaminated the crime scene?* 'You're as predictable as worms after rain.'

'I take offence to that, Detective Sergeant,' he said, but he was smiling.

'You claim to know everything, Lockley.' Birch began walking up the corridor towards him. 'In particular, you know everything about *me*. So I know that you know I got my pips recently. I'm Detective Inspector now, this is my investigation, and I'd like to know who the hell let you get into the middle of it.'

Lockley's smile grew. It was a smile she'd come to know well – too well for her liking – though mercifully she hadn't seen it in person for some years. Lockley had had his teeth in other people lately. He looked like a shark, Birch thought, with his sawn-off grin and his eyes just a little too far apart. There was no better career for him, really.

'Just goes to show, doesn't it?' he said. 'This college is a nightmare, security-wise. Even crawling with police personnel, it's vulnerable. No one *let me in*, Detective Inspector. I found an unmanned door and simply let myself through.'

Birch stopped walking. She was maybe four feet from him now, close enough to see the product in his hair. He looked the same as he always had, really – a little crinklier around the eyes, perhaps. But otherwise, the same. Standing this near to him made the hairs stand up on Birch's arms. The encounter felt as risky, as intimately dispiriting, as running into an ex.

'Don't you think it's a serious oversight?' Lockley was saying. 'Since Dunblane, schools are all sealed up like Fort Knox. Yet there are students here who are still children – fifteen, sixteen years old – and no high security for *them*, eh? Anyone could have walked in here, easy as I did. People are going to question that. They'll want to see heads roll . . . and campus security's just the start of it.'

In her hand, Birch's phone buzzed again. McLeod, no doubt – he didn't like to be kept waiting.

'I bet it is,' she said. 'I bet you've got six months of hit-pieces lined up, haven't you, Lockley? This shooting's a real turn-up for the books in terms of your career.'

Lockley did, this time, look genuinely wounded.

'I'm a public servant like you, Detective Inspector.' He pronounced her title pointedly, spittily. 'Free speech is a basic human right. People are desperate for the truth, and they want it without spin. I give them that. Can you say the same?'

Birch rolled her eyes. She knew what was coming next – she could, had she wanted to, have mouthed the words in perfect sync as Lockley said them.

'I'm just doing my job.' That hands-up, *what can I do?* gesture. She remembered him feeding the same line to her mother one night, when he'd woken her going through the family's bins, and scared her half to death. He'd ended up cornered by the back garden's high wall, and he'd thrown up his hands in that exact same way, as though Birch's grief-stricken mother might have thought to attack him. 'I'm just doing my job, Mrs Birch. We all want the same thing, here – we all want to find Charlie.'

Now, she found herself scowling.

'As much as I'd love to stand here and discuss your virtues all evening,' she said, 'I have about five thousand more pressing things to do right now. So how about you let me escort you out of my crime scene? If you leave now, I'll overlook any potential criminal intent on your part.'

Lockley cast his gaze around the corridor, ignoring her.

'Of course,' he said, 'the main thing the public will want to know is *why*. Why did Ryan Summers do this? What makes a seemingly ordinary young man go out and kill a bunch of his classmates? And not just on impulse, either – in a cold, premeditated attack.'

'We don't know what this was yet,' Birch said. *Shit*, she thought. *Surely this investigation can't already have a leak?*

Lockley raised an eyebrow.

'This is Scotland. People don't just have guns lying around the house. This kid went out and got himself one – and through highly illegal channels, I'll wager.'

She relaxed a little. Perhaps all Lockley had at this point was speculation; not that he ever needed much else.

'Yes,' he was saying, 'people will want to know why. And the answer will lie with the parents. It basically always does. Little Ryan wasn't loved enough as a kid, maybe. Little Ryan was allowed to listen to violent rap music. Little Ryan's dad died and he never got over it . . .'

Lockley tilted his head like a bird's.

'Am I getting warm, DI Birch?'

Birch forced her mouth into a hard line. She could not – *could not* – let her past encounters with this man interfere with her work.

Not with a case this delicate. The investigation felt like a live grenade she was cradling in her hands; if she let him, she knew only too well that Lockley would rip the pin out and run.

'We're done talking, Lockley,' she said.

He shrugged. 'For now, maybe. But if you think I'll leave this investigation alone, rest assured, I won't. I know you lot are mainly interested in a quiet life. You'll want to close up this case for good and hope people forget about Ryan Summers, but I won't let that happen. I'll find out why he did this. If it turns out his mother knew it was coming, I'll find out. If it turned out he had accomplices, I'll find that out too. It's my job to do that – just like your job is to put the bad guys away. I think our motivations for getting out of bed in the morning are roughly the same, really, aren't they? I think I know you well enough to say that, what with our ... personal history, and all.'

For a moment, Birch's hearing gave out, and her vision stuttered red, black, red.

'My *personal history*,' she said, through her teeth, 'does not come to work with me ... and I don't want it mentioned. You understand?'

Lockley looked down at the sleeve of his dark grey coat. It was corduroy, Birch noticed, and cheap. He pretended to see a speck of something, and brushed it away.

'What I understand,' he said, 'is that your brother was exactly Ryan Summers' age when everything went down. And your mother died just recently, am I right?'

Birch drew herself up a little taller.

'I won't discuss my mother with you, Grant.'

He was still smiling. He seemed always to be smiling, as though that smile were his work uniform.

'It must be hard for you,' he said, as if she hadn't spoken, 'thinking about Charlie all the time when you're trying to focus on your work. And don't tell me you're not. It's a little puzzling to hear you say you don't bring your personal life to work with you when you also told the *Scotsman* newspaper – many moons ago, I admit – that your brother was the very reason you *became* a police officer.'

Birch cursed inwardly. She hadn't always been this wary of journalists, and had learned the hard way about making idle chit-chat with them.

'My brother's case has been cold for over a decade. You looked over every last scrap of the public record at the time, so you know there's nothing there you could possibly write about – and if there were, I'd know about it long before you.'

Birch took a long step towards him, into the shoving crowd of his aftershave, and lowered her voice.

'I won't let you hurt me again,' she said.

Lockley opened his mouth to speak, but as he did, the fire door at the end of the corridor swung open.

'Birch?' McLeod was framed in the doorway that led to the stairs. Lockley turned, and Birch watched the two men rearrange their faces as they recognised one another.

'What the fuck?' McLeod began stomping down the corridor towards them. 'What the *fuck* is this degenerate doing in my crime scene?'

Birch grimaced. Words would no doubt be had, later, about this.

'He's leaving,' she said. She looked hard at Lockley. 'Right this minute, sir.'

Shooting

At approximately 8.15 a.m. on the morning of the shooting, Ryan Summers was witnessed alighting from a bus at the main road entrance to the Tweed Campus. From there he walked to the south-west corner of the campus and entered the college buildings. Summers gained entry not via the main reception, but through a secondary entrance at the Jackie Stewart building, the college's purpose-built engineering block where Summers spent much of his time as a student [6][7][10]. Summers was wearing dark-coloured clothing, including a long black hooded sweatshirt, under which was concealed a makeshift holster containing three identically modified blank-firing revolvers [10][12]. Summers was witnessed by several fellow students as he made his way through the Jackie Stewart building and entered a men's bathroom. It is believed that he used the bathroom to check and load his weapons, and to put in earplugs [10][32].

At approximately 8.30 a.m., Summers entered the Tweed Campus refectory and approached 19-year-old Abigail Hodgekiss, who was seated at a table with her boyfriend Jack Egan, 21, and five other students. Hodgekiss was in her first year of a HND qualification in Acting and Performance at Three Rivers College. After a brief exchange, Summers produced one of the three modified Bruni Olympic .380 BBM revolvers and fatally shot Hodgekiss at close range [10][12]. He then fired upon Jack Egan, who sustained a gunshot wound to the shoulder and fell to the ground. Egan was later treated in hospital and survived [13].

Witnesses report that as chaos erupted in the refectory, Summers turned his revolver towards 20-year-old Mary-Ann McEwan and

19-year-old Dawn Black and shouted, 'Put your hands up!' [10]. McEwan and Black had been sitting at the same refectory table and were attempting to perform emergency first aid on Abigail Hodgekiss [15]. McEwan was yelling at Summers when Summers fatally shot Dawn Black, and then McEwan [10][14]. As Summers bent over to look at Hodgekiss, he was tackled by 17-year-old Liz Gill, who had recently enrolled as a BTEC student in Sports Coaching [15][16][17]. Gill attempted to disarm Summers, but during the scuffle Summers fatally shot her in the chest at point-blank range [15].

Summers then fatally shot 27-year-old refectory counter assistant Kerry McNaughton, a student on the college's SVQ Level 1 Professional Cookery course [10][15]. McNaughton had been pulling other students to safety, encouraging them to take cover behind the refectory counter and then exit the building via the kitchen entrance [15][16]. Among the students who escaped this way was 23-year-old Ella Ostrowska, who placed the first 999 call from the scene [10][13][15].

After killing McNaughton, Summers exited the refectory and walked in the direction of the building's central stairwell, where he discarded the revolver he had used to shoot his first six victims [12]. Adult literacy tutor Isobel MacNab witnessed Summers entering the stairwell with the weapon in his hand as she unlocked a nearby computer lab for fleeing students to take refuge in [10][23]. From the computer lab MacNab placed a 999 call and some of the students with her sent tweets and Facebook messages describing what was happening [18][19][22].

As he moved up the stairwell, Summers encountered 29-year-old Victoria Cho, an international student on the college's HNC in Retail Management. Witnesses said that Cho approached Summers and spoke to him, not realising that he was the gunman [10]. Summers shot her twice with the second revolver, and she later died in hospital [20].

Summers exited the central stairwell on the building's first floor, where dozens of students were milling about [10]. Because the time was only approximately 8.40 a.m., the majority of the campus classrooms had not yet been unlocked for 9 a.m. classes [10][23]. Summers approached a group of female students and began firing apparently at random, killing 22-year-old Mhairi Crosbie and Sarah Reynolds, also 22 [10]. 21-year-old Leanne Lawrie was jostled in the ensuing panic, causing her to fall, hit her head against a radiator, and sustain a serious head injury [20][21]. She later died in hospital [10][20]. Witnesses reported hearing a clicking sound from the second <u>revolver</u> after these shots were fired, suggesting that Summers attempted to continue discharging the gun after the chamber was emptied [10][12][25].

At approximately 8.45 a.m., Summers entered a women's bathroom near the central stairwell on the first floor of the building [10]. Janitor Jim Robertson reported hearing cries for help from the bathroom as he ran along a first-floor corridor unlocking classrooms for students to hide in [23][24]. 25-year-old Evie Kesson, 22-year-old Catriona Brown, 22-year-old Gemma McGregor and 19-year-old Chantal Walker were all shot and killed, execution-style [32], in the first-floor bathroom [2][10]. Moments later, Summers shot himself in the right side of the head at point-blank range with his last round of ammunition [3][10][12][25].

Two days later

MOIRA ANNE SUMMERS

DATE: Thursday, 16 May
TIME: 14:06
PART 2 OF RECORDED INTERVIEW
DURATION: 54 minutes
LOCATION: Interview Room 4, office #20188
PRESENT: Moira Anne Summers (interviewee), Anjan Chaudhry (legal counsel) Det Inspector Helen Birch C#4138E, Det Chief Inspector James McLeod C#1666E, Police Family Liaison Officer Amy Kato C#901E
PAGES: 8

McLeod: This interview is being recorded; the time is 14:06 hours. I am DCI McLeod, resuming our interview with Moira Anne Summers. Also present are DI Birch and Amy Kato, Mrs Summers' FLO. Mrs Summers' legal counsel is Mr Anjan Chaudhry, and Mrs Summers, in the first part of this interview you stated that you would like to be called Moira throughout. Can you confirm that this is still the case?

Summers: Yes, that's right.

McLeod: And Mr Chaudhry, I am led to believe that you wish to make a statement for the record before we proceed with the interview?

Chaudhry: Yes.

McLeod: You may do so.

Chaudhry: Thank you. I would just like to put it on record that Mrs Summers has been under considerable emotional strain over the past two days. Not only is she coming to terms with the death of her son, but she has also been bombarded with attention from the press and from members of the public, most of which has been negative. I know, DCI McLeod, that at present you and members of your team here are investigating several anonymous death threats and threats of bodily harm that have been made against Mrs Summers. I know that local police are also monitoring the behaviour of those members of the press who are currently camped outside Mrs Summers' house. As I am sure you can appreciate, this set of circumstances is extremely difficult and highly unpredictable. Therefore I'd like to ask that all efforts are made over the course of this interview, and in any subsequent interviews, to take into account the circumstances under which Mrs Summers comes to speak with you. I'd also like to take this opportunity to recognise, and to praise, the work done these past two days by Ms Kato. Mrs Summers has led me to believe that your presence has been invaluable, and a great comfort.

McLeod: Let the record show that this last remark was made directly to Officer Kato.

Summers: Yes, thank you Amy. Amy really has been wonderful.

McLeod: Thank you, Mr Chaudhry, for your statement. I assure you that we are fully aware of the wider circumstances surrounding Mrs Summers' presence here today.

Summers: Thank you, Anjan.

McLeod: Unless there are any further pre-emptive statements, I would like to proceed with questioning. Let the record show that Mr Chaudhry nodded his head indicating that the interview may proceed. Are you happy for us to proceed, Mrs Summers?

Summers: Moira. Yes.

McLeod: Moira, my apologies. Okay then. We've already spoken about your movements on the morning of the shooting. Today I'd like to ask you some questions that are focused on your son, Ryan. We'd like to get a better picture of the last few days and weeks of his life.

Summers: Okay. Okay. I will do my best.

'I don't know how you work with him.'

The lawyer was standing in a stripe of afternoon light, a floodlight aimed at the corridor's waxed floor. His shoes gleamed. Beside him, the bulb of the water cooler gargled air.

'Hello, Anjan.'

Birch approached him with caution: she felt rumpled and scruffy next to this man. At sternum height, a gold tie-pin winked, its small ruby matching his wine-red tie, cufflinks, even his socks.

'You look tired, DI Birch,' he said. 'Congrats on the promotion, by the way.'

She reached down for a plastic cup. They were the cheap, ribbed kind: the kind that crackle and split under the slightest pressure.

'That feels like years ago,' she said. 'So much for thinking I'd ease in gently. I've had, what, about six hours' sleep since the shooting? And an hour of that was in my car this morning. You'll have to forgive my appearance.'

The water cooler chugged.

'Well, you're the chosen one.' His tone was not warm. 'He says jump, and you say—'

'And I say, "Yes, guv." It's my job, Anjan. He's my boss.'

'He's a pig.'

'Come on, don't make me do this. And keep your voice down.'

Birch dipped two fingertips into her cup of cold water. She lifted them to her right eyelid, closed her eyes and daubed the water across the thin skin. She repeated the gesture for her left eye, then looked up at the lawyer, water beginning to run down her face like tears.

'Feel better?' he asked. He was smiling now.

'Not really.' With her free hand, she patted herself down for a tissue, and wiped her face. 'I'd feel better if I knew what it is your client isn't telling us.'

'You mean Moira?'

Birch closed her eyes for a moment. In spite of the water, they felt sticky, hard to keep open.

'Who else would I mean, Anjan? I mean, I feel for her, but – she's just being a little too co-operative. There's something she's hoping we won't find out about . . . and I suspect that you know what it is.'

The lawyer arranged his face into a neat mask of neutrality.

'I can't say that I know what you're referring to.'

Birch rolled her eyes.

'Of course. Oh well. I suppose we'll just have to keep on keeping on.'

Anjan flashed her a smile.

'I suppose you will.'

There was a pause. Around them, the station ticked and hummed. Birch frowned, and felt the frown deepen until she had to speak.

'I just – I just want to know why. Ryan Summers, I mean. Why do that? Why the *hell* would anyone do that? Did he not think about what he'd leave behind? I mean, look at his mother. Two full days she's been in here getting questions fired at her. She's got death threats, she's got rape threats, she's got paparazzi in her garden hedge, she's got nutters on the doorstep. Didn't he realise that would happen to her? Didn't he give a shit? She's his mother. And I'm not even letting myself think about the girls. The victims. What about *their* mothers? What about the journos in *their* hedges, nutters on *their* doorsteps? He unleashed all of that, and that's just the fall-out we know about. Why – why do that? Or perhaps the more pressing question is – what can any of us do in the face of an act like that?'

When she finished speaking, a thick quiet seemed to ebb into the corridor like smoke. There was no one else around, just Birch and the lawyer – not just any lawyer, but the best lawyer, Anjan Chaudhry – the guy they used to call The Brain at her old station. She'd always liked him. He was tough, but he wasn't an arsehole. He was loaded, but he hadn't gone into the law to get rich. He cared about what happened to people. He rarely defended anyone who was truly guilty. One of life's good guys, Anjan, she thought. And, as if to prove it, he took one step towards her, and put his free hand onto her shoulder.

'You're doing okay, Helen,' he said. He jiggled his elbow a little, shaking her, to make her look him in the eye. 'I mean it.'

She looked at him for a second, then past him, into that stripe of light. Dust specks swirled, pulled in the small slipstream of their movements.

'What do we do, though?' She looked down at the tie-pin, its ruby like a point of blood, shining. 'When the crime is so huge, but we already know who did it? We know *how* he did it. I guess we'll never really know *why* he did it. So what do we do? What is it for, all this? The questioning. The not sleeping. The bitching about my boss. What is it for?'

Anjan was looking at her face, but his eyes became unfocused: he'd gone inside himself somewhere for a moment, to think. He shook her again, less urgently, and his voice was quiet and certain.

'I believe,' he said, 'that you – that the police – give people hope. That's not true in many countries – it's not true where I come from. But it's true here. Everyone's scared. More scared than you, Helen, because remember, you have information that they'll never be given. Everyone's wondering why this happened, what makes a person turn into a monster. They're scared because they look at a kid like Ryan Summers and think, what if, actually, he was normal? What if what happened inside him happens inside me, and *I* become capable of something like that? But through that fear, they also see that you're doing something – you, the police. Someone's *doing* something. Something's being *done*. That helps. That isn't a small thing.'

Birch nodded, slowly, then shook her head as if trying to dislodge something. She nudged his hand away, straightened up.

'You're right, Anjan. Thank you, you're right. I'm just tired. I need to pull myself together.'

She downed the water – tinged blue-green by its plastic cup – a little lukewarm now.

'No problem.' Anjan stooped to fix the line of his jacket. 'Oh, incidentally: my office has been receiving some phone calls from a Mr Grant Lockley. I believe you two know each other?'

Birch felt her shoulders crumple inwards.

'Oh for goodness' sake. Yes. We've had some previous, Grant and I. Some . . . less than pleasant personal dealings, from before I joined the force. It's a long time ago. What's he after?'

Anjan extended an elegant hand, studied the nails.

'I couldn't possibly tell you,' he said. 'For the simple reason that I haven't returned any of his calls – and nor do I intend to.'

'Good,' Birch said. 'I'm glad to hear it. It's not you he wants, anyway – he's just trying to get to Moira.'

Anjan put his hand back in his pocket, and looked up at her.

'I gathered that, Helen,' he said. The smile was returning to his face. 'I've been in this game a little while now, you know.'

Birch summoned a weak smile. Her empty cup rang against the side of the metal bin.

'See you in there, Mr Chaudhry.'

McLeod: Moira, you said in your first statement – I am referring to the statement you gave on the day of the shooting – that you liked the fact that Ryan had shown an interest in restoring your husband's old starting pistols.

Summers: Yes.

McLeod: Can you say why that is?

Summers: Well, I know it sounds terrible now, but I was just relieved. That he was telling me about things again. That he was asking me things.

McLeod: I'm sorry – when you say 'he was telling me about things *again*', what exactly do you mean?

Summers: Oh, sorry. I mean again, since his father died.

McLeod: You're referring to your husband, Jackie.

Summers: Yes. He died a little over two years ago. He'd been ill for some time.

McLeod: And Ryan didn't react well to his father's death?

Chaudhry: DCI McLeod, I wonder if you can bring this questioning back to the matter at hand? It seems mildly insulting to suggest that a son ever *would* react well to the death of his father.

McLeod: I apologise, Moira, if that was the impression my question gave.

Summers: That's all right, I knew what you meant. And you're right. Ryan reacted very badly to Jackie's death. He became very withdrawn around me – especially around me. After a while he went back to his job, and then his employers said they'd pay for his college course and he went off to college. But when he was at home he was very . . . subdued, I think, is the word.

McLeod: Can you give some examples of what you mean, Moira?

Summers: Just small things, I suppose. But things that felt big to me. Like, he didn't like to eat with me, he liked to eat in his room. I let that go on for too long after Jackie died, I suppose. And when he did come down to sit with me he'd just look at his phone all the time. It got so he barely spoke to me.

McLeod: But things improved, in your opinion, when Ryan started to show an interest in the starting pistols?

Summers: Yes. He was down out of his room more often. He'd be out in that shed a lot more often, and sometimes when he came in for a cup of tea he'd stand in the kitchen and drink it with me. And we ate together a little more. I thought it was progress I was seeing.

McLeod: And this progress – it seemed to continue right up until the day of the shooting?

Summers: Yes.

McLeod: So you didn't see any further changes in Ryan's behaviour in just, say, the past couple of weeks? Or the past few days?

McLeod: Moira, I'd really like you to answer that question.

Chaudhry: Take your time, Moira.

Summers: No. No changes in behaviour that I can put my finger on.

McLeod: What about conversations the two of you had just recently. Did Ryan say anything to you that made you anxious or worried in any way?

McLeod: Moira, I know this is upsetting, but I do need you to answer that question.

Chaudry: DCI McLeod . . .

Kato: DCI McLeod, I think Moira could do with a wee break quite soon. Don't get upset Moira, you're doing great here.

Birch: You're being very helpful, Mrs Summers. We greatly appreciate your co-operation.

Summers: I can't believe myself, honestly.

McLeod: What can't you believe, Moira?

Summers: That I didn't see it coming.

McLeod: Which you didn't? You genuinely didn't have any concerns prior to the shooting?

Chaudhry: I think she's just answered that question.

Summers: No, I didn't. I thought this was just what boys Ryan's age were like. I thought he was like any other boy. I used to talk to my friends about their sons, like you do. You know, asking how they were. And they'd tell me, they'd reassure me, their sons were just the same. Always in their rooms, on their computers. Always with their mobile phone out at the dinner table.

McLeod: So you must have had some concerns, because you asked friends for reassurance.

Chaudhry: Moira, that's not something you have to answer if you don't want to. Once again, that wasn't a question, DCI McLeod.

Summers: No, it's all right, Anjan. Thank you. I suppose I asked my friends for advice about how sullen Ryan could be because sometimes I did get frustrated about his behaviour and I told a few of them how I felt about that. Then we'd end up talking about how much time our sons spent in their rooms playing these video games, or whatever. But that was it really. You know the kinds of conversations mothers have. Or maybe you don't, I don't know.

McLeod: And you never had any conversation with Ryan about guns, with the exception of the starting pistols? He never spoke about guns with you?

Summers: Never.

McLeod: And you never spoke about guns with anyone else?

Summers: No. It's not something you really talk about, is it?

McLeod: Not even the starting pistols? You didn't tell anyone else that Ryan was interested in them?

Summers: No, I didn't. I wish I had now. They might have warned me that that wasn't right.

McLeod: But you never yourself felt that it wasn't right, that Ryan was doing something with these starting pistols?

Chaudhry: My client has already answered that.

McLeod: Very well. Moira, did you have any idea why Ryan was so interested in the starting pistols? Did you never wonder what he intended to do with them?

Summers: He said he wanted to see how they worked. We had one conversation about it, Ryan and me. Ryan asked me about the old guns in the shed. Like I say, we called them 'guns'; that's how we referred to them. Before that point I actually didn't know they existed, I had no idea Jackie had kept them and I hadn't been out to that shed since before he died. I never realised they were illegal – I didn't know starting pistols could be. I did want reassurance from Ryan that they weren't dangerous, and I said he could only work on them as long as he never took them out of the shed. I was worried that someone might see him carrying one and mistake it for a real gun. So Ryan asked could he take them apart to look at the parts, and I said yes. Ryan told me that if he took them apart, he'd probably never be able to put them together again properly. And I believed that. I felt okay about it because he'd said that, and I never really gave it much thought after that. I'm so ashamed of myself. I'm sorry, Detective Chief Inspector. I really am sorry.

16 May, 4.45 p.m.

Birch was the only woman in the staff canteen. No one else had come to sit at her table. The canteen was badly lit, bland and weird, an old-fashioned space with ceiling tiles and a kitchen hatch. Efforts to modernise it seemed only half done: new lino, dated already; colourful moulded chairs that looked like Play-Doh; felt-backed pinboards tacked with posters for PolFed and UNISON meetings. Birch felt like she was back in school again – alone at the lunch table with her head stuck in a book, like she was surrounded by some force field that other people could all see. *Especially boys*, she thought: they'd always given her an extra-wide berth.

Except instead of a book, her head was stuck in the mounting pile of case notes for Three Rivers, and her colleagues were avoiding her because they didn't want to be given something to do. That was what she hoped, anyway. No one had slept much – everyone looked grey-faced and stretched. There was nobody here who'd ever worked a case like this, and all the boring police-work of a regular day didn't just go away in the event of a mass shooting. Birch was the one who was adding extra work to just about everyone's desk. If no one would meet her eye, it was totally understandable – right?

Birch forced herself to look back down at her notes. Now she had FLOs in place, she'd been able to organise a gathering for the families of the victims – or as many as they could bring in by tonight. One of the victims was an international student, her parents thousands of miles away in Korea. Sorting out the release and transport of her remains was going to be a real headache, later on down the line – involving paperwork and consulates and overseas funeral directors, none of which Birch wanted to think about right now. She hoped that girl's parents were being adequately supported. She could only imagine how vast that distance must feel.

Look, she forced herself to think, *at your bloody notes.*

It was unorthodox, this meeting she was organising, but this was a case – and a crime – like no other, and the gathering would help her tick a lot of boxes. First, she had a lot of information that needed to be imparted to the families: as soon as they'd been allocated FLOs, they'd started asking questions, and Birch's bewildered team were struggling to keep up. They were mostly hard questions – parents wanting to know when their child's remains would be released to them; siblings asking if they could meet with FLOs alone because their parents were struggling too much with their grief. Everyone was in need of a level of victim support that Birch had never before orchestrated. As well as the FLOs, she'd invited as many Victim Support Scotland workers as she could rope in.

Secondly, McLeod was worried. When school and college shootings happened in America, families of victims routinely tried to sue the police. The emergency response to Three Rivers had been not-great – as one of the first officers on the scene, Birch would readily attest to that. McLeod wanted to get as many of the families in one place as he possibly could, essentially to try and butter them up. 'Damage control,' he'd said to Birch. She'd made a face at him as soon as he turned his back, but had to admit: it wasn't the worst idea he'd ever had.

Thirdly, Birch hoped that the families might get some comfort from coming together in the same room. It would be a meagre comfort, she imagined, but she also knew from experience the quietly restorative power of community. Her mother had only begun to recover, after Charlie, when she began talking to people – and trusting them – again.

Lastly, and secretly, Birch hoped that she might get the chance to warn the families away from Grant Lockley and his ilk. She knew the tabloids would soon start doorstepping them, offering dizzying sums of money for tell-all stories. It would be better for everyone involved if the personal stories of Three Rivers families were kept out of the papers: her own bitter personal experience with Grant Lockley had convinced her of that much.

Birch opened her laptop. Her head felt fizzy, like she'd been picked up and shaken. She couldn't settle to anything. As the screen lit up she clicked open the folder she'd made in order to keep track of the death threats being sent to Moira Summers. There were a lot: she'd told Amy not to let on to Moira quite how many. Analysis had started to come back on them, and most, it seemed, were one-offs – sent online, some within half an hour of the press conference at which a police spokesperson had confirmed that Ryan Summers was indeed the Three Rivers gunman. But a few people were proving more persistent, and there were a couple of individuals, still unidentified, who analysis felt were credible. There were people out there who might really want to kill Moira Summers.

It wasn't a stretch to see why. In her first couple of years on the force, Birch had routinely chided herself for privately understanding why a perp might have wanted to commit the crimes that they did. Jealousy, grief, desperation: more than once, she'd thought, *Yeah, I'd have done the same in your shoes*, and then punished herself for even entertaining the thought. These days, she gave herself more of a break. After all, if Moira Summers really *had* known what her son was planning – really *had* stayed silent and let him do it – then some measure of justice would have to be meted out. Birch could understand the men and women who were volunteering themselves as vigilantes, willing to do just that. She planned to stop them by any means necessary, but she understood them nevertheless. Birch had sat in the interview room with Moira: had held her gaze as the woman dissolved into tears over and over again. *Surely*, she thought – *surely, that distraught and ashen woman cannot have been the silent accessory to thirteen murders?* No: she shook the thought away. The idea was too unpleasant to hold on to for long.

Birch clicked into her emails and opened the most recent one from Marcello, a criminal intelligence analyst she had a soft spot for. Marcello was Italian, and the least subtle person Birch had ever met: he spoke loudly and laughed often, with his whole body. It was an excellent cover for someone who worked in intelligence, she thought. Each time his name popped up in her inbox, she smiled. He had a gap between his front teeth, and the most startling blue eyes. If she thought she'd be able to find the time, she might have tried to get the courage up to ask him out for a drink. But it wouldn't end well. Birch's relationships never did: not since she married this job, what – twelve years ago? She sighed. *Come on*, she thought. *You have to do this work. Concentrate.*

Marcello's expert eye had picked up on a thread in the general noise of death and rape threats – Birch grimaced at the number of those there were, too – that he thought she should pay particular attention to.

I'm calling this man, and I'm certain it is a man, correspondent C, he wrote. *In the attached spreadsheet, I've highlighted the various threats I believe have been sent by him.*

Birch clicked open a preview of the document, let it hover alongside the text of Marcello's email. A few lines of cells in the white spreadsheet were coloured in green.

There aren't many, he wrote, *not as many as some of our other correspondents. But I believe his threats are the most credible, and by far the most worrisome. Correspondent C is careful with his wording, and he repeats the same sort of phrases and imagery. It's my belief that he has clear ideas about how he would like to hurt his target.*

There was more text, but Birch was still struggling to focus. In the bottom right-hand corner of the screen, the laptop display informed her it was 17:21. *Maybe* . . . she thought, and reached for her mobile. Marcello answered after two rings.

'Detective Inspector Birch!'

Birch flinched, and moved the phone away from her ear just slightly.

'Marcello,' she said, 'I'm so pleased you're still there.'

'Waiting for your call, my darling,' he said, and then his trademark laugh. 'And if you think I'm getting to go home by five these days, you're dreaming.'

'Sorry,' Birch said, 'that's largely my fault, isn't it?'

He laughed again.

'Let us say it's Ryan Summers' fault.'

Birch pushed aside the desire to make small talk. *You have to do this work*, she told herself again. Plus, she wasn't sure she had the energy for anything other than what was right in front of her.

'Listen,' she said, 'I'm reading your notes about Correspondent C. I share your concerns.'

Fibs, she thought. *What you mean is, I don't know what I'm doing, Marcello, and I need you to tell me what's up.*

'Yes, he's credible for sure. A very interesting man, I think.'

Birch rolled her eyes. She'd always been amazed at the knack that certain cadres of police personnel had for totally distancing themselves from the human realities of a case: perps and victims were all just numbers to be crunched, patterns and quirks to geek out over.

'What can you tell me about him?'

She felt something quicken on the line between them. Marcello was preparing to give her a theory.

'Well,' he said, 'I have a hunch, one that I cannot prove yet. What I know, almost for certain, is that Correspondent C is a man. He's an older man – a lot of the one-off threats came from individuals under twenty-five, as I mentioned. But the length, vocabulary and general style of these messages suggest an educated, professional person.'

Birch was nodding again: nodding at a person who couldn't see her. It was a bad habit she'd long been aware of, but had yet to do anything about.

'Okay,' she said. 'What else?'

Marcello was making a clicking sound between his teeth. In the background, she could hear him typing.

'Ah,' he said. 'Here we are. Okay, so he's gone to some lengths to hide his identity, and to make it look like these threats came from different people.'

'Like what?'

There was a pause.

'You *got* my email?' Marcello was laughing at her.

'Yes,' she said. 'But lack of sleep is messing with my reading comprehension right now.'

'All right,' he said. 'Well, he tries on linguistic disguises . . . attempting to write in a way that he thinks is distinct each time. It's not very sophisticated, but he's trying. And he's used different computers, with different IP addresses, but it looks like they're all in Edinburgh. These are the things that make Correspondent C worrisome. He's persistent – not content with just sending one threat. And he lives locally. He will have local knowledge. He could easily find his target.'

'So you're about to ask me if you can go to the ISP and get more specific information,' Birch said.

'Yes,' he said. 'We'll need a warrant for that. And I don't think he'll have been stupid enough to send anything from his home address. But I suspect at least one of the computers being used is at his workplace . . . simply because that's a strangely common thing these people do.'

Birch scribbled a note on top of her file. 'Okay, I'll get onto it. Now . . . what's your hunch?'

'Aha. You are keen to . . . "cut to the chase", as they say in the movies.'

Birch rolled her eyes again.

'So,' Marcello was saying, 'I can't prove it yet, but as you know, DI Birch, I am always right . . .'

'Of course.'

'. . . so I will be extremely surprised if it doesn't turn out that this man is personally connected – closely connected, I think – to one of the shooting victims.'

Birch sat up straight.

'You mean . . . a family member?'

'Could be,' Marcello said. 'He could be a friend, or a teacher, but . . . yes, I think this is a close relative of someone who died. An uncle, maybe. Maybe even a father. There are just little things in the wording. Little quirks. You know?'

Birch nodded.

'Marcello,' she said, in her best *give it to me straight* tone, 'just how confident are you about this?'

'Confident.' Again, that loud laugh. 'Confidence, my darling, is my middle name.'

Birch hung up and looked around her. The canteen had emptied out. At the far end, a couple of guys whose names she didn't know were sipping terrible coffee from corrugated paper cups. About three tables away, a uniformed female officer was typing something on her phone, her thumbs going so quickly they were almost a blur.

She made a *pfft* sound, the shoved-out breath lifting her fringe off her face.

'Focus, woman,' she hissed to herself, apparently loudly enough for the uniform to flick her face up and look over.

Sorry, she mouthed. The woman shrugged.

Birch's cup of tea had gone lukewarm at her elbow. An oily film had begun to form on its surface. She stared down at it, watching the quivering reflection of the ceiling tiles, and chewing over what Marcello had told her. Maybe this evening's hastily arranged meeting would serve another purpose: she could watch the male family members for signs of criminal intent.

Someone's uncle, she thought. *Someone's father.* Would a bereaved father really turn his thoughts to revenge before his child's body was even shelved in the morgue? Birch thought about men, what she'd seen of them as perps, as victims. *Yes*, she thought. *Some fathers are like that. I could believe it.*

Birch's phone rang: Marcello's department landline.

'DI Birch?' she answered, as though asking herself a question.

'Marm.'

She sighed. The voice was not Marcello's.

'Jim?' she tried.

'John,' said the voice on the other end. 'But close enough.'

'Sorry.'

'It's okay. I'll answer to anything, as long as it's not rude.'

'It's because I usually deal with Marcello,' Birch said.

'I know,' John replied. 'He just left. You'll have to deal with me this time, I'm afraid.'

'If this is about Correspondent C, I just—'

'Yeah, I know,' John said. 'But no, it's something else. I've been looking at those forum posts for you.'

Birch blinked.

'Forum posts?'

'Oh. Yeah – I sent you an email?'

Birch pressed one palm to her forehead.

'Sorry, John. I'm . . . struggling to prioritise over here.'

'That's all right. I'll start from the beginning. We got a tip-off – I'd assumed it had been passed up through you, but if not, no worries – about some posts on an online forum. Posts written over a period of several weeks earlier this year, which seemed to make reference to a Three Rivers-style event. We had reason to believe they might have been written by Ryan Summers.'

Birch scrabbled for a pen, and some white space to write on.

'Okay,' she said. 'You have my full attention now.'

'Don't get too excited,' John said. 'I was mainly phoning to say that we've looked over them, but come to the conclusion that it's going to be tricky to prove for certain that they were written by Summers. There are a lot of nutters on these forums, and they say all sorts of outlandish things – usually, they're fantasists who can't function in the world beyond their keyboards.'

'This is an MRA forum?'

John paused.

'You *did* read my email.'

'No.' Birch felt her mouth harden into a line. 'Lucky guess, based on the all-female body count. God, but I hate it when I'm right.'

'So our problem,' John said, 'is that usually, these anti-feminist and Men's Rights types frequent lots of different fora, all over the internet. They tend to always use the same screen name, or a variation of the same, so they can keep tabs on each other. They have lots of little in-jokes and hashtags and creepy little codes that they speak in. But . . . this one profile, the one that made these posts? I can't find him elsewhere in the wider MRA community. His screen name only appears in one other place, and then only once, making a fairly benign comment about something.'

'What other place?'

She listened to nothing: the sound of John checking his notes.

'Truth Unifies,' he said. 'It's a conspiracy theorist website. No real MRA connection, though there is some crossover between MRA and conspiracy theorist circles. But the screen name could well be a coincidence. Could be someone totally different.'

'What's the screen name?'

'theobviouschild,' John said. 'It's a weird one.'

'Isn't that a Paul Simon song?'

'I dunno, marm, is it?'

'Yeah . . .' Birch hummed a little of the tune, almost to herself, and then blushed. The uniform a few tables away seemed to be focused on not looking at her. 'Ring a bell? It's on the *Rhythm of the Saints* LP.'

John laughed.

'I'll take your word for it.'

'That album came out when I was . . . twelve or so?' Birch allowed herself a fleeting memory of the early nineties, sitting in the back of her dad's car, listening to the song's battering drum solo playing on cassette, a hot wind coming in through the hand-wound windows. 'You must be too young to remember. It's certainly a weird reference for a twenty-year-old to make, if it *is* Ryan Summers we're looking at.'

'Sure,' John said. 'So it may well not be him at all. But the things this guy's threatening to do certainly match up with the events at Three Rivers . . . so if it's not him, it's spooky.'

Birch scribbled.

'Okay,' she said. 'Keep at it for me, would you, John? It's awful, but I think that if we could point to MRA-type tendencies in Summers for sure – if we could pinpoint something that might reasonably be called *motive* – that might bring a degree of closure for people.'

John 'mm-hm'd into the receiver.

'I can't promise anything,' he said, 'but we'll do what we can. Look at my email, when you get a minute; there's some more detailed analysis there. But for now, the only certain thing we can say about this obviouschild guy is ... well, he's got some really weird ideas about women.'

I knew it, Birch thought, as she swiped to end the call. *I hate it when I'm right.*

The room she'd booked for that evening's gathering – *the gathering*, she'd called it in her head, a daft-feeling term that she now couldn't shake – was woefully inadequate. In one bank of ceiling lights a fluorescent bulb flickered on-off, on-off, whispering *link, link, link* to itself. Birch had ordered teas and coffees for eighty – families, police personnel, Victim Support and college staff were all invited – and now a line of giant stainless-steel urns hissed and laboured on a side table, rattling the teaspoons in their saucers as they boiled, cooled, boiled again. The room had been set up with a wide circle of chairs, padded ones, at Birch's request, scrounged from offices and waiting areas, so few of them matched. The room looked like something out of a horror movie, or like the set-up for an AA meeting straight out of the seventies. In a half-hour or so, people would start arriving. Birch paced inside the ring of chairs, as though trapped by its grim fairy circle. Any minute now, McLeod would make his entrance, and she'd have to bow and scrape.

The FLOs had already begun to file in – *good*, she thought. She wanted to pass on Marcello's findings to them before the families arrived. Rehan Ibrahiim was first: this was his FLO debut and he was keen to show his commitment. Some of the more experienced FLOs arrived shortly after Rehan in a gaggle – a clique, even, Birch guessed. Among them was Rema Mohamed, an officer whose rep in the city was legendary. Standing at five feet tall, Rema was tiny but mighty. She'd been a vocal campaigner for the hijab to become an official part of the Police Scotland uniform, then when it did, she'd spoken to the press about the fact that the uniform rule was only the tip of the iceberg: there needed to be a concerted effort to recruit more Muslim women into the force. Birch admired Rema, and disliked the fact that her male colleagues had a tendency to speak of her as a fly in the workplace ointment. Some even referred to her as 'the headscarf wifey' – Al, the Gayfield custody sergeant, included. *They're just scared,* Birch thought, watching Rema cross the room towards her. *She'll be their chief superintendent in no time, and they know it.*

'Evening, marm,' Rema said, stepping into the circle of chairs. She handed Birch a cardboard cup – tea, thank goodness, though the little tag on the teabag's string had fallen in and been submerged. 'You look like you need this.'

'Thanks, Rema,' Birch said. 'Hydration is key, or so I'm told.'

Birch had assigned Rema to the family of Liz Gill, the student who'd grabbed Ryan Summers in a bid to disarm him, and been shot at point-blank range for her trouble. Birch hadn't even seen the crime scene photos when she made that decision. The Gill family were going to need a special kind of support, having clearly lost a very special daughter to truly horrifying injuries. Liz had been a twin, too.

'How are they doing?' Birch didn't need to specify who she meant.

'Devastated,' Rema said. 'The worst I've ever seen, though I guess that makes sense.'

'The sister?'

Rema shook her head, her eyes closed for a moment. Birch noticed the glitter of silvery powder on her eyelids.

'Wee scrap,' Rema said. 'She's just zombiefied. And yet you can see her trying to take care of her parents, trying to be the strong one. It's the worst thing.'

Birch nodded, blowing on her tea.

'Such a drama with the press, too,' Rema went on. 'Everyone wants a piece of them. I daresay all the families are finding the same . . . but because of what Liz did? Everyone wants the exclusive with the *heroine's* family. My phone's ringing all hours of the day and night. They've been doorstepped more times than I can count. We had one journo turn up at the front door pretending to be a vicar. *A vicar,* with the costume-shop dog-collar and everything. A woman, too – for some reason I imagine they'll know better, but no.'

In spite of herself, Birch smiled. Rema's patter was effortlessly engaging, no matter the subject.

'Honestly,' Rema said, throwing up a hand. 'If you didn't laugh at these people, you'd cry.'

Birch thought for a moment.

'You've formally logged the fake vicar episode, though, right? We could talk about threatening behaviour.'

Rema raised an eyebrow.

'No need. It was me who answered the door to her. Trust me when I tell you she'll not be pulling a stunt like that again for a good while.'

Birch laughed, too, and then stopped herself.

'Sorry,' she said. 'I know you just said *if you didn't laugh you'd cry*, but . . .'

'Feels wrong, doesn't it?' Rema said. 'I know. Being in the midst of it, in the family home, and seeing them so besieged on top of it all . . . it makes you wonder if there's humanity left in this world.' She paused for a moment, her eyes upturned. 'But in a way – and I'd never say this to them, of course, or not in so many words – I think they've got the edge, the Gills. On the other families, I mean. It's the smallest silver lining round this cloud of grief that is just *massive*, but . . . they're proud of her. That she died that way, trying to save her friends. The kid was a superhero. I couldn't have done what she did.'

Birch felt a lump forming in her throat – took a gulp of too-hot tea to try and dissolve it. *Yes you could, Rema,* she thought, but she didn't say it.

'And imagine,' Rema went on, 'if she'd succeeded. Imagine if she'd rugby-tackled that little shit to the ground, and actually disarmed him. She must have been *so close* to doing that. She must have known it was possible, right? Or she wouldn't have tried it.'

Birch tried to remember what Liz Gill's father looked like – what his profile was. *Dear God,* she thought, though she was praying to Marcello, really, *please don't let it be him.*

'Ah,' Rema said, gesturing towards the door, 'time for me to make myself scarce.'

As Birch looked up, Rema melted out of her eyeline. McLeod had arrived, with the last few FLOs and a good number of other police personnel, uniformed and not, straggling in his wake.

'Showtime at the Apollo,' Birch muttered, and stepped out of the circle.

16 May, 6.57 p.m.

Ishbel stood on the pavement on Fettes Avenue, looking up at the police buildings behind their railings. Around her, cars drew up and pulled in to the on-street parking, their passengers skip-walking across the road between after-school traffic from nearby Broughton High School – the same school Abigail came to for football. *Or used to*, Ishbel thought, her throat thickening. Some of the people who filed into the police station wore lanyards round their necks, or carried briefcases. Ishbel could identify other Three Rivers family members easily: they were either crying, or looked like they were trying not to. Even the men looked numbed, lost.

Ishbel wasn't sure how she'd got there herself. She had no memory of the short drive over, though she knew she had done it: right now she was leaning against the back corner of the car to cover up the shaking in her legs. This was the first time she'd changed her clothes in two days, and she'd taken them from the drawer and put them on without really looking at them. Now, in the car window she could see her own gauzy reflection: a work blouse that needed an iron, a clashing floral cardigan Pauline had given her. Her short hair stuck out at angles. Her eyes were so swollen with crying that she started a little – her crow's feet had smoothed with the swelling, and she looked like she'd been punched. Reflected behind her was the sky, beginning to turn pink, wisps of high cloud purpling on it like peripheral bruises.

Aidan was walking up the pavement towards her. She was supposed to be keeping an eye out for his car, but had missed him, looking at herself. As he neared, she could tell from his face that he'd been crying, too – the whites of his eyes were bloodshot, and his cheeks were red. She hadn't seen him cry thus far: he'd been disturbingly, angrily stoic throughout the process of being told that Abigail was dead, throughout the awful identification and paperwork in the morgue, throughout the meeting with Rehan – the young officer assigned as their police family liaison. On the day of Abigail's death, they'd stayed in the hospital for a long time: by the time they left, dark was falling outside, and Ishbel had shied away from the car park with its long blue shadows and taxi-engine noise. It had seemed like such a halfway house, that brightly lit place with its disinfectant smell and squeaking floors, that she felt if she could just stay there till morning, she might find that none of it had really happened. The hospital felt like a dreamscape, and she wanted to wake up.

She'd made the mistake of saying this to Greg and Aidan, standing at the threshold of the exit door engulfed in sobs, not able to walk out. Greg had told her to wait, and disappeared, and in the quiet after he clicked away, Ishbel listened to her own wet, ragged breaths.

'Aidan,' she'd said, baffled by her husband's upright silence. 'Abigail is dead. She's dead.'

He hadn't replied, just looked at her as one might look at a whimpering animal – with pity, and slightly askance.

'Don't you understand?' She'd heard her own voice raised, become aware of faces turning to look at her. 'What's *wrong* with you, Aidan? *Say something.*'

When he turned his gaze on her properly, she'd flinched.

'I understand.' She'd seen then the form his grief was taking: he was furious. There was a glitter in his eyes, but it wasn't tears. For the first time in the twenty-five years she'd known him, Ishbel had felt afraid.

Greg had returned with a plain white box, which he pressed into Ishbel's palm. Looking down at it, she could see the top of a prescription slip sticking out of the carton: these were sedatives. To her surprise, when she looked up again, Greg was hugging Aidan: one of those powerful bear hugs men reserve for rare times of true need. When they broke their embrace, Greg's eyes were wet, but Aidan's still weren't. Ishbel wanted to be held, too – by either of them, or by anyone – but Greg only placed his arm lightly around her shoulders, and pointed down at the little white box in her hands.

'If you need one,' he'd said, 'take one. I know nothing can help, really, but . . . you know.'

Ishbel had made it across the car park, then dry-swallowed two of the pills before she'd fastened her seatbelt. She'd woken hours later on the sofa in the house – Aidan had driven her home. He must have carried her in and left her there, fully clothed, in the dark.

'You've been crying,' she said to him now, as he reached her. She was smiling, and she knew that was wrong, but it was a relief to see him show what felt like normal emotion.

'A little,' he said. 'In the car.'

Ishbel had been asleep for most of the past two days, thanks to Greg's pills – only really awake for the brief meeting with Rehan – but she'd somehow felt Aidan moving around in the house, and leaving, and coming back, and leaving.

'Where have you been?' she asked.

He paused, and blew air out of his nose, as though suppressing some initial response.

'I had to duck into work,' he said.

Ishbel frowned.

'Just for a half-hour,' he said. 'They were worried.'

He looked away from her, glancing up and down the street to check for traffic. Ishbel felt that same, strong urge to be held by him – the one she'd got in the hospital doorway – a thing she hadn't felt for years until now.

'Aidan . . .'

She reached out to take his hand. He had big hands, with fine blond hairs on their backs – *hands like spades*, Pauline had said once – and Ishbel used to love watching them doing whatever they did, whether that was washing up or writing shopping lists or changing Abigail's nappies. If he'd been crying, she thought, perhaps that meant he'd be softer now – softer perhaps than he had been for months, since the Telford case, when Ishbel had stopped paying attention. But he flinched away from her.

'Come on, now,' he said, not unkindly, but his voice was even. 'We're late as it is.'

Aidan needn't have worried about them being late. They were led through the corridors of the police station's ground floor by a young officer in uniform, but when they walked into the room that she directed them to, there were no signs of the meeting having officially begun. As Aidan held the door for her and she edged inside, Ishbel balked: there were far more people here than she had expected. In the centre of the room, a circle of chairs had been laid out, and inside it, those who were obviously family members of victims had begun to sit down in small groups, talking quietly, some of them crying already. Among them, people in suits with police lanyards were dotted about: the various FLOs, Ishbel assumed. But standing elsewhere – in knots of four or five outside the circle, or leaning up against the walls – there were uniformed police, Three Rivers staff whose lanyards were red instead of blue, and some of the briefcase-carriers Ishbel had seen outside, whoever they were. Ishbel wasn't quite sure what she'd expected, but it wasn't this. She felt her body sag, and Aidan closed one hand around her arm to steady her. After two days of waiting for contact, his touch shocked her.

Rehan picked his way across the circle, and took Ishbel's hand in his own. His handshake was damp, and not very firm, but he said, 'Ishbel, you made it,' and waited until she looked him in the eye. Then he broke free of her and did the same to Aidan. When he turned, Ishbel stumbled after him into the circle, and sank into a seat.

'There's tea and coffee,' Rehan said. 'Would either of you . . .?'

Ishbel shook her head, but Aidan, who had not yet sat down, said, 'I'll get it.' She watched him stride towards the hot-water urns.

She tried not to make eye contact with anyone. She didn't want to have to talk about Abigail, or even reveal who she was. She didn't want to admit that she was the same as these people: here because her only child had died. But, as she glanced round the circle, she felt a flicker of comfort, seeing the other women were also dishevelled and shrunk. No one else seemed to want to make eye contact, either – the families were mostly talking amongst themselves, with their respective FLOs. In some of the little groups there were siblings – young people holding fast to their parents' hands with whitened knuckles. One woman sitting near Ishbel – undoubtedly a mother, too – was staring dead ahead at a bare patch of wall, while a man who may have been her husband talked to their FLO through the straight, invisible beam of her gaze.

Beyond the circle, Ishbel was able to pick out DI Birch, the female supervising officer who'd visited them, very briefly, to introduce Rehan. She was taller than most of her female colleagues, and Ishbel found herself leaning a little to see if the DI was wearing heels. Her hair was a mousy reddish-brown, all of it pulled into a ponytail except for a long fringe that looked in need of a cut. She looked tired. Ishbel was just hazarding a guess at her age – forty? Not much older than that, anyway – when she remembered, for the five thousandth time, who she was. Why she was here. *You're not at work*, she reminded herself. *You don't have to appraise everyone.* But in the absence of Aidan, and with Rehan looking down at his smartphone, there wasn't much else to do but think about Abigail, and no, that was unacceptable.

A plain black suit and pale shirt seemed to be standard issue for more senior officers, though DI Birch was speaking to a man in an ensemble that was just a touch flamboyant. His suit was a deep blue, with a wide pinstripe and shoulders that were clearly tailored to fit. This was a person of high rank, she could tell: the other officers looked at him differently, and when they passed, made a wide circle around him. At DI Birch's side there was a young Asian officer, wearing a new-looking lanyard under a long sheet of dark hair – she wasn't quite the DI's height, in spite of her towering high heels. The young woman's face was a mask of worry, and from under that mask she occasionally glanced up at the pinstriped, high-ranking man.

Rehan had dimmed his phone screen, and pushed the small machine into his pocket.

'Who's that?' Ishbel asked him. He followed her gaze.

'With DI Birch? That's Detective Chief Inspector McLeod. He's here to . . . oversee proceedings.'

Ishbel frowned.

'No,' she said, 'the young woman.'

She watched Rehan's mouth slacken.

'Ah,' he said. Then, after a pause, 'That's Amy. She's a family liaison officer, like me.'

Ishbel cast her eyes around the circle.

'Her . . . family. They're not here?'

Rehan tensed up, and glanced behind him, to where Aidan was stirring a cup of tea with a little wooden stick.

'What?' Ishbel said.

Rehan turned back to her, and when he spoke again, his voice was low.

'Amy has been assigned to Moira Summers.' When Ishbel frowned, he added, 'Moira Summers is the mother of Ryan Summers, who . . . the gunman.'

Ishbel felt a jolt of something run through her. Panic, maybe.

'I know,' she said. 'But – Rehan, does that mean she'll be here, tonight? The – Moira? The mother?'

Rehan placed a hand on Ishbel's arm. Again, she felt the electric shock of human contact.

'It's okay, Ishbel,' he said. 'No one here would think that was appropriate.'

Ishbel's brow furrowed deeper. *Why not?* she wanted to say, but she knew why not.

Her head was swimming: either the sedatives were still in her system, or she was suffering some sort of withdrawal symptom. The room felt hot, too full of limbs and eyes. She got the feeling that Aidan was deliberately keeping away from her, watching her from a distance for signs of madness. Every thirty seconds or so – a pattern that had kept up for two days now, as long as she was awake – she remembered that Abigail was dead. The remembering throbbed inside her, as though she'd swallowed some cold and terrible engine.

DI Birch had pulled herself from the suck of her DCI's attention, and now stepped into the circle of chairs.

'Good evening, everyone,' she said. Her voice was quiet, low for a woman's voice, and she spoke slowly. 'I think most of you know me. I'm Detective Inspector Helen Birch, and I'm doing a lot of work on . . . this investigation. I want to thank you all for coming to this meeting tonight. I can only imagine how hard it must have been for many of you to leave your families and support networks to come in and see us. We really are very grateful.'

Ishbel's attention drifted. She thought of her own 'support network', as DI Birch called it. These past few years, it had grown thin. She had Aidan, of course, and Greg, though she saw him rarely, and Pauline was a regular presence in the house. She got on well enough with her mother-in-law, but she was still her mother-in-law. Ishbel's own parents were dead – her mother *long* dead now, it felt like. When it came to friends, she had a great rapport with her colleagues: on the rare occasion she went to the pub these days, it was always with them. The job they all did was esoteric, misunderstood, sometimes even hated – it was hard to explain to anyone else. They hung out together and bitched and commiserated, offered advice – but, Ishbel realised, really only ever talked shop. They'd send Christmas cards to each other with 'and family' tacked on; occasionally, someone would ask about someone else's kids. They were great people, and she loved them, but there was no one among them she felt could join her 'support network' at a time like this – not even Dave, her secret favourite of the bunch.

I have one best friend, Ishbel realised, *only one*. She and Caroline had been joined at the hip at uni: St Andrews, where they'd both studied sociology and bunked out of lectures, scoffing at the posh toff students who went to the society balls and wore the ridiculous optional scholarly robes. Later, Caroline had dated a friend of Aidan's for a while, a guy called Sandy who looked like a male model, and she and Ishbel had chattered excitedly about the prospect of a double wedding. But Caroline was restless in Edinburgh: the city was too small, too parochial to hold her big ambitions. She trained as a psychotherapist, and had moved to America – Abigail was small at the time – nearly twenty years ago, Ishbel was shocked to realise. Now, Caroline lived in New York, and had a fancy private clinic in a brownstone on a tree-lined street. She hadn't been back to the UK in a decade. Ishbel hadn't visited her in five years. They mostly communicated via email, and the emails had become more and more scarce.

Ishbel shivered. Caroline probably didn't even know about Abigail, not yet. But the idea of phoning her, the idea of having to say the words to someone, Ishbel could barely even give the thought space in her head.

My support network, she thought. *My support network is standing over by the coffee urn, not taking part.*

But as if he'd heard her thought, Aidan picked that moment to slip back into the circle, and down into the seat between her and Rehan. The tea in his hand was already half gone. Ishbel put her hand onto his knee, expecting him to nudge it away again. When he didn't, tears rose in her eyes. Was he not lost to her, after all? She couldn't tell. If he was, she suspected it had happened long before the shooting, in some quiet moment when she wasn't paying proper attention.

DI Birch had been speaking all this time: something about talking to the media that Ishbel had only half heard. Now one of the men inside the circle spoke up, interrupting her.

'Of course *you* don't want us to talk to the media,' he said. Ishbel recognised the voice of someone who was trying to sound brave, trying to keep his voice from cracking. 'You want a nice clean cover-up!'

Hurt registered on DI Birch's face: just a flicker, before she swept it away.

'Sir,' she began, but she was cut off by DCI McLeod stepping into the circle, moving himself in front of her as if to shield her from physical attack.

'Mr Kesson.' Ishbel flinched at the name. She knew who these people were, of course she did – but it rattled her, hearing the surname of one of the other girls killed, a name she'd heard read out on the news on the hospital TV, alongside Abigail's own. 'I'm Detective Chief Inspector McLeod, and this is my investigation.'

To her surprise, Ishbel saw Amy, the young officer across the room, raise one eyebrow and make a face in DI Birch's direction. The DI's expression remained impassive.

'No one,' DCI McLeod was saying, 'wants to create a cover-up, I assure you. In fact, it's likely there will be a government inquiry in due course. Transparency is one of our greatest priorities here.'

Ishbel studied the man's body language: his large frame blocking the space between Mr Kesson and DI Birch, a gesture that could have been protective, or could have been dominant, she couldn't tell.

'We just want to make sure,' McLeod went on, 'that no one gets exploited, or feels wronged. To the tabloid press, your vulnerability at this difficult time makes you easy targets.' He cast a sweeping glance around the circle. '*We*, on the other hand, want to try to understand, and support you. So however tempting it may be to call up a journalist, we'd encourage you to call *us* if you need to talk through something.'

Behind him, DI Birch was nodding. DCI McLeod watched Mr Kesson until he seemed satisfied that the other man wouldn't speak again. Then he turned to Birch, and made an *over to you* gesture that was nearly a bow.

'Apologies, DI Birch,' he said. 'Carry on.'

He dyes his hair, Ishbel thought, as he turned his back to walk out of the circle. *No one's hair is really platinum.* Then her thirty seconds were up, and once again, she remembered why she was there. Something at the centre of her bucked and yawned.

'Okay,' DI Birch said, trying to right herself again after the interruption. 'Thank you for your patience, everyone. I won't speak for much longer. In a few moments, I'll pass you over to the fine people from Victim Support Scotland, who are also here with us tonight.'

The rest of the meeting seemed to blur into one long continuation of people standing up to speak, and Ishbel not quite managing to listen properly. Though she'd slept on and off for most of the day, she began to feel herself longing for the oblivion of silent, dreamless darkness once again. The knowledge of her daughter's death was like a long, cold shadow, and just being awake under it was a physical strain like nothing else she had experienced. At one point, she realised her hand was still on Aidan's knee. When she lifted it, the palm was slick with sweat and had left a damp print on his trouser-leg. As the meeting drew on, she was aware of him shifting, clearing his throat – he was struggling to focus, too.

She was surprised, then, when he hung back at the end of proceedings – not standing when Ishbel did, but staying in his seat, speaking quietly to Rehan. Ishbel swayed on her feet. She felt a spark of annoyance at the fact that Aidan had gone off somewhere that afternoon, and come in his own car; she'd have to drive home again on her own, with him following. But the anger went out as soon as it had flared. She half closed her eyes, longing for the spare-room bed, and the white box of sedatives – the precious gift from Greg.

Mr Kesson had edged across the circle. A few of the other men had gathered beside him: a show of solidarity over his tackling of DI Birch. *How are men*, Ishbel thought, *so very capable of doing that? Of keeping calm and carrying on?* But she knew the answer – she'd lived with Aidan's own personal brand of masculinity for long enough. They did it because they had no choice. Strength was what was expected of them.

Now Aidan stood and went over to Mr Kesson, too. Not wanting to be sitting alone – vulnerable to strangers who might want to speak to her – Ishbel trailed in his wake.

'Mr Kesson.' Aidan held out his big hands, and took Mr Kesson's smaller one between them to shake it. 'Aidan Hodgekiss.'

'Barry,' Mr Kesson said. 'I'm sorry for your loss.'

'Likewise,' Aidan said, and Ishbel saw him squeeze the man's hand before letting go. He looked round at the other men gathered there, some of their wives hovering, as Ishbel was, like ghosts on the huddle's edge. 'And to all of you,' he said.

'What a terrible business this is,' Barry Kesson said. 'What a terrible, senseless thing.'

Ishbel's eyes prickled.

'We were just talking,' the man went on, 'about starting up some sort of . . . foundation, or charity of some kind. In the names of the – well, all our loved ones. Something good to put into the world. A sort of . . . attempt to set things right.'

Ishbel was looking at the back of Aidan's neck. She watched his head cock slightly to the side – a sign that something had vexed him.

'Set things right,' he echoed.

'Yes,' Barry Kesson replied. The men around him made rumbles of agreement. 'Well, you know.'

'I like the idea of a foundation,' Aidan said, after a pause. Under other circumstances, Ishbel would have been surprised – Aidan didn't much go in for charitable giving. 'And I'd be happy to hear more about it. But I don't think anything that's done by us can "set things right". I think those efforts have to come from elsewhere.'

Barry Kesson narrowed his eyes. He was an older man, Ishbel noticed: she suspected his daughter Evie, about Abigail's age, might have been what Pauline would call *a wee surprise*. The thought made her want to cry all the more. *Her daddy's wee surprise*, lying in a steel drawer in a freezing morgue.

'I'm not sure what you mean,' Mr Kesson said. 'From the police?'

Aidan shrugged.

'They'd need to be involved,' he said, 'yes. But what I'm talking about is the family of Ryan Summers being brought to justice.'

Ishbel's eyes widened. Around them, the room fell silent. Aidan was the first person all night to speak the name of the man who'd taken their daughters and sisters from them. Beyond the pale hill of her husband's shoulder, Ishbel saw the face of Amy, the young Summers FLO, go pale.

Barry Kesson took a step towards Aidan.

'Now,' he said, 'I don't think this is the place for that sort of talk, when—'

But Aidan shrugged again.

'It's terrible, I know,' he said, cutting off the older, smaller man. 'I don't want his name in my mouth any more than you want to hear it. But the fact is, none of us would be here if not for that boy. If not for the fact that no one was warned about him.'

Amy was speaking rapidly to DI Birch, leaning close to her, as though talking into the lapel of the DI's black suit jacket. The DI's attention had sharpened. DCI McLeod seemed to have vanished.

'I'd like to know,' Aidan said, raising his voice slightly so the police personnel in the room would know they were being addressed, 'when someone is going to bring in Ryan Summers' mother on charges of accessory to murder. I don't believe for one second that you can live in the same house as someone and not *know* that they're planning to kill thirteen innocent people.'

Barry Kesson looked abject, discomfort shining out of him like a sickly green light. Ishbel cast around for Rehan, and saw he was at her elbow, standing in her blind spot. When they made eye contact, she found he was looking at her in the same way as she was looking for him: *Do something*, his eyes said. But around them, some of the men in the huddle were muttering in agreement.

'Accessory to murder,' one of the men echoed, 'on thirteen counts.' He looked back over his shoulder at no one in particular. 'I'm sure someone in this room could tell us what sort of sentence that carries.'

Aidan was nodding vigorously. Ishbel cleared her throat in a feeble attempt to get his attention, but the sound came out so hoarse that even she barely heard it.

'Do you think the police will act on this?' Aidan was addressing the general company. Ishbel felt a tiny flashback, remembering his face at the hospital exit door: that cold anger. That anger had an audience now – the whole room was tuned into it, though some people were taking care not to look at him. 'Does it look like they're going to?'

Ishbel reached out from behind her husband and wrapped a hand around his upper arm. She felt exhausted.

'Aidan,' she said. 'Aidan.'

The two syllables of his name were all she could manage.

Aidan turned, and that seemed to break the spell the room was under: around her, she felt a general letting-out of held breaths. Released from Aidan's gaze, Barry Kesson turned away. Rehan stepped in next to Ishbel, and took hold of her husband's other arm.

'Aidan, mate,' he said. Ishbel blinked at this familiarity, but Aidan seemed not to notice. 'If you want to talk about what the police are doing, you'd best talk to a police officer, no?' He smiled a nervous, stuck-on smile. 'It just so happens that I am one of those. Let's talk about this – at home, perhaps.'

For a moment, Ishbel, DI Birch, Amy and the gaggle of men watched to see what her husband would do. Silence yawned. But then Aidan's face seemed to relax, just a little.

'Sorry, Reh,' he said. Ishbel blinked again – she hadn't been invited to use this pet name, and she hadn't heard a man call her husband 'mate' in a very long time. 'That was heavy talk.'

Rehan glanced at the men still gathered around them, and Aidan turned back.

'I'm sorry,' he said. The men made supportive noises, some of them nodding or shrugging their collective *It's okay.* Only Barry Kesson, who'd moved back to stand with his family, made no response. Rehan led Aidan away, and Ishbel, now so tired that her vision was fraying at the edges, trailed after them, helpless as a loose thread on a coat.

IS THE TRUTH ABOUT THREE RIVERS COLLEGE BEING COVERED UP WHILE TAXPAYERS FOOT THE BILL?

By GRANT LOCKLEY
PUBLISHED: 16:15 16 May | UPDATED: 17:03 16 May

It's been two days since the brutal shooting of thirteen young women at Three Rivers College, Edinburgh, and details about what supposedly happened that day are, at last, being released.

According to official statements released by Police Scotland, the deranged gunman – 20-year-old Ryan Summers – used three Bruni Olympic .380 BBM revolvers to brutally slaughter his thirteen victims. He then shot himself at the scene, which seems to be standard practice for the cowardly individuals who commit such acts. For those of you who are unfamiliar with gun-talk, a Bruni Olympic revolver is a blank-firing starting pistol that was deemed illegal to use or possess in 2010.

Police Scotland claim that Ryan Summers used the skills he'd learned in his engineering lessons to modify the starting pistols, allowing them to fire deadly live ammunition. Can I be the only one raising an eyebrow at this? What exactly is it that they're teaching the young people at Three Rivers College?

<u>We've put together our own detailed ballistics report: read more here</u>

Police Scotland also say that the guns – which should have been turned in during the 2010 firearms amnesty – belonged to Summers' father Jackie, who died two years ago from infective endocarditis, a type of heart disease.

To this columnist, that all seems a little tidy. The illegally owned guns belonged to Dad, who's conveniently no longer with us? It all sounds a little like the police want to save themselves the bother of dealing with a firearms possession charge.

Then again, it's possible that the gunman's mother, Moira Summers, may still be charged in connection with the shooting. Mrs Summers has been in police custody since the terrible tragedy occurred, which seems right and proper to me, but she has not yet been officially arrested or charged with any offence – which very much does not. In a statement, Police Scotland said that Mrs Summers is 'currently helping the police with our enquiries', and refused to comment on whether or not she is considered a suspect.

I'd love to hear your thoughts in the comments section. My guess is that the majority of right-thinking people believe that this woman ought to be locked up as an accomplice to mass murder. Can you live in the same house as someone who's modifying handguns and plotting to kill at random, and not know that they are up to something? It's even less plausible when you consider the close relationship between mother and son. If I were interrogating Mrs Summers, I'd be asking her to do a polygraph test, and asking her about maternal intuition. I refuse to believe she knew nothing.

Three Rivers: for a blow-by-blow account of the fateful day, click here

The public clearly have their own views. In the early hours of Wednesday morning it was reported that the Summers family home – a comfortable double-fronted, detached property in Edinburgh's affluent New Town – had been vandalised by outraged locals. Uniformed police are now guarding the Summers' home around the clock.

Yes, you read that right. Round-the-clock security has been provided for the home of a murderer: a house that, at present, stands totally empty. Apparently that's all part of the service offered by our boys and girls in blue, with the taxpayer footing the bill.

Take our poll: does the mother of a murderer deserve protection from the police? Have your say here

The murderer's father, Jackie Summers, a high school PE teacher and part-time athletics coach, died just over two years ago. It's believed that his infective endocarditis was linked to a bout of rheumatic fever he suffered as a young man.

Ryan Summers' mother, Moira, quit her nursing job shortly after her husband's death. According to her stunned neighbours, her recent behaviour was stand-offish, as though she might be hiding a secret.

I spoke to Frank Cole, 84, a neighbour who lives just a few yards from the Summers family home.

'After Jackie died, she [Moira] kept to herself a bit more,' he said. 'We used to chat quite a lot if I saw her in the street but I haven't seen very much of her this past year. I think Jackie's death was quite a shock for the family. I saw a lot less of the son [Ryan] after that, as well.'

Mrs Summers' attorney was approached for comment, but made no response. Make of that what you will.

In pictures: our tribute to the Three Rivers College shooting victims

Elsewhere, Police Scotland seem to be struggling to respond to what is surely the most devastating crime the unified police force has dealt with to date. Criticisms of police actions on the day of the shooting have already begun to surface, with many asking why it took so long for first responders to secure the Tweed Campus site.

This columnist was able to access the scene of the shooting late on Tuesday. I can report that security around the sprawling campus site did seem lax – should I, for example, have been able to walk through an unguarded door and access the college buildings without reporting my presence? I can also tell you that some police officers at the scene seemed pretty confused, even disorganised, and they didn't take kindly to yours truly turning up to try and get at the truth.

Meanwhile, members of the local community continue to express their shock and grief in the wake of this tragedy. The names of the thirteen victims were released late on Tuesday night, triggering an outpouring of sympathy and support from across the globe. A candlelit vigil has been set up at the gates of the Tweed Campus, and <u>an online crowdfunding campaign</u>, set up to gather donations for the victims' families, has already raised almost £250,000.

See more from Grant Lockley

Share or comment on this article

TOP COMMENTS

rEdWhiteblue1 The mother is in police custody? Good. She should stay behind bars forever for bringing this monster into the world. God bless the families of these precious girls, you are in our hearts.

 ^ 2364 people liked this

Kingdom77 when you say the house was vandalised i hope you mean burned to the ground . . . those girls can never go home so why should SHE!!!!!!!!!!

 ^ 2041 people liked this

USAimee I hope the police are squeezing Moira Summers in interrogation. I have three sons and there is no way I wouldn't know if they were planning something like this.
This sure was PLANNED! Even if he didn't tell her about it then mother's intuition must have kicked in. If it turns out she knew about this and told no one then she can ROT IN JAIL and then BURN IN HELL.

 ^ 1997 people liked this

magdadgam beautiful girls who were killed by this psyco (sp???): u were loved, may god bless u, u r in all our prayers. 13 new angels got their wings that day xxxxx

 ^ 1679 people liked this

One week later

21 May, 10.00 a.m.

The driveway had filled with flowers. It had started the night of the shooting, when the first few victims' names had been officially released to the press, Abigail's among them. At first, it was just a couple of bouquets: Rehan had needed to move them in order to squeeze his car in behind Ishbel's. When he'd mentioned them, Ishbel assumed that the bouquets had been left by the neighbours on either side – neither household could ever bear to be outdone by the other. But two days later – the evening that Ishbel had forced herself to get up, get dressed and drive to Fettes Avenue for the meeting with the other victims' families – she'd unwittingly driven over a soft buffer of flowers as she backed out of the driveway. Now, Rehan had been forced to find a parking space down the street. The pile of flowers formed a small hedge running the full length of the property, and the bouquets had encroached so far up the driveway that some were leaning against the Qashqai's back wheels.

'There must be hundreds now,' Rehan said, taking off his coat in the hall. 'People really do care.'

Ishbel turned away. She was still in her dressing gown, though it was mid-morning. She'd been in her dressing gown most of the week, in fact. She was aware that Rehan must be noticing her hair, pulled into greasy spires after days of going unwashed; must be noticing her red face, puffed and bruised as a boxer's from crying. Rehan seemed very young to her – too young, surely, to be doing a job like this. His dark hair was cropped very short and he wore those large-framed glasses that seemed to be so fashionable. In a line-up, Ishbel would have pegged him as an art student, not someone whose job it was to help people through the darkest hours of their lives. Not that he seemed to be helping a great deal.

Through the fog of her grief, she resented his almost-constant presence in their house; it seemed that whenever she woke up, fuzzy from the pills Greg had given her, he was there. And she resented the esteem in which her husband seemed to hold him.

She drifted into the living room, to squint out of the big window as best she could. Journalists were regular visitors to the street, now – and to the house. They tried their luck, flitting in and out of the garden like bats, seeing how close they could get. Some were brass-necked, marching right up to the door and ringing the doorbell. Others phoned the landline repeatedly, sometimes stood at the bottom of the garden in plain sight, their phones clamped to their ears, hopeful as dogs. Cars lurked at the end of the driveway. The bins were rifled, the recycling. The front lawn was muddled by boot-prints, and at the garden hedge the gaggle ebbed and flowed, stashing their cigarette butts in the privet. One night – she wasn't sure when, how long ago – Ishbel had woken in the spare-room bed to hear Aidan's creaky tread on the loft-ladder; the sound of him rooting about in the loft above her head. A stray thought had come to her: *what if he's making a noose?* She imagined him swinging out into space, his feet and legs crashing through the ceiling to rain plaster shards all over her. The thought came to her because she'd considered it herself: under the heavy cloud of the sedatives she'd half dreamed of running a bath, putting her face under the sudsy surface of the water, and just never coming back up.

As it turned out, Aidan had been in the loft searching for the old net curtains – a vain attempt to keep the press from aiming their lenses into the windows. Beyond the grubby lace, the garden was shrouded in a thick fog, as though the very weather itself had been brought low by the shooting. At the foot of the short drive-way the gaggle of journalists dithered, like spectres.

'I could bring you a few in, if you like.' Behind her, in the living-room doorway, Aidan was speaking. 'While I'm out there.'

Ishbel didn't look round. She was watching Rehan, who'd gone back outside. He was setting up an old black music stand of Abigail's on the lawn, a few feet out from the front door. She was remembering that night – last night? A few nights ago? She honestly didn't know – that she'd heard Aidan scraping about in the loft space. She'd been naive, she thought: Aidan was far too pragmatic for suicide. Too angry. His eyes cold at the hospital; again as he sized up Barry Kesson.

'Bring me a few in . . . of what?'

She heard him sigh.

'The flowers, Bel. The bouquets. Reh says some of them have cards on.' This pet name Aidan seemed to have permanently adopted: pronounced *Ray*. Ishbel didn't know how he could stand to be so familiar. 'I thought you might like to read what people are saying. About Baby.'

Outside, Rehan walked backwards a few steps, studying the music stand.

'What could they possibly have to say? They didn't know her.'

He didn't make any noise, but Ishbel could tell that Aidan had advanced towards her. When he spoke again, his voice was closer.

'I'm just trying to be . . .' He paused. 'Constructive, here.'

One of the journalists had called out to Rehan. He was walking down the garden towards them. Ishbel watched as his shoes began to glitter with the moisture from the wet grass.

'You know I don't agree with this,' she said. 'With what you two are doing.'

Aidan took another step towards her – now, she could hear his breath.

'Bel,' he said. 'Reh thinks it's a good idea. Get the press on side. He says that giving a press conference will give them something to write up – get at least some of them to go away. We want that, don't we? Some privacy?'

Ishbel turned her head a little. He was standing almost directly behind her, watery in the corner of her vision.

'Going out there and parading in front of them isn't privacy,' she said.

There was a silence, which seemed to stretch and vibrate, and then the crackle of paper.

'I thought you might like to read this,' Aidan said. 'The statement I've written. Tell me if there's anything you want to add.'

Ishbel turned her head slightly further, far enough to glimpse the typed A4 sheet that Aidan had unfolded and held out towards her.

'No,' she said, turning back to the window, and away from him. 'I don't want to add anything. I don't want you to *do* this, Aidan. I don't want you to say anything at all.'

She heard him sigh again.

'Why are you making this so hard? I don't want to have to go against your wishes.'

Rehan had almost reached the reporters – though he had to stop to pick up and rearrange some of the flower bouquets. That morning when he'd arrived, he'd tunnelled a small path through them, and some had fallen back into it, or new ones had been placed over the top.

'Then don't,' Ishbel said. 'For once, you could do as I ask.'

Aidan made a clucking sound in his teeth.

'Bel,' he said, 'you're grieving. You're barely awake. You're not yourself. I really don't think you know what's best right now.'

She whipped her head round and looked at him properly. In one hand, he was still holding the typed statement. In the other, bizarrely, an empty picture frame.

'And you do? You're just totally clear-eyed right now, are you?' She dropped her gaze, and her voice became quieter. 'I don't know, maybe you are. Maybe that's because you're *not* grieving.'

She heard her own words hanging in the air between them, and regretted them.

'Or not in any obvious way,' she added.

'Someone,' Aidan said, the word coming out slowly, from bared teeth, 'has to do the things that need to be done. Someone around here has to be responsible right now. We can't *both* just float around the house rending our garments.'

Ishbel turned back to the window. *Don't let him see you bleed*, she thought, swallowing down tears. Outside, Rehan was waving the first of the journalists through the little path he'd made in the bank of flowers. He was pointing towards the music stand, which looked like some absurd sculpture in the middle of their small lawn.

'It's getting to the point,' Aidan was saying, 'where we need to start organising our daughter's funeral. I need you to pull it together for that.'

Ishbel began to shake her head, and then found she could not stop. The word *funeral* rattled about in her head, and she wanted to shake it loose – to shake loose the very suggestion.

She was still shaking her head when Aidan finally added, 'I gave Reh the photo of Baby off the top of the piano.'

She stopped, abruptly. The photo frame in his hand: she could place it now.

'Why?'

Aidan sighed again. It seemed to her that over the past few days he'd become adept at sighing – sighing his impatience as they waited at the hospital to be told of Abigail's condition; sighing his stoic acceptance in the morgue as they formally identified their daughter. He'd sighed a thousand times at Ishbel's more untidy responses to the events of these few days. She'd listened to the sigh of his snore, drifting down the landing to the spare room where she lay, wondering how on earth he – or anyone else on this godforsaken earth, for that matter – could sleep, when such events were allowed to unfold.

'For the press,' he said. 'I want them to stop running that dreadful picture of her they pulled off Facebook. It's years old. She looks like a child.' He waved the empty frame. 'This is a much better photo. *She*'d have preferred it.'

Ishbel closed her eyes. She'd looked at that photo many times: a studio portrait they'd booked for Abigail as part of her eighteenth birthday present. For the occasion, Abigail had worn her favourite top: coral-coloured, with a boat neck, made from a poly-cotton blend so soft that Ishbel was always surprised by the feel of it among the laundry. Ishbel felt a sudden ache for that top, folded quietly into its dark drawer in Abigail's upstairs room. Outside, Rehan had amassed a small crowd of journalists: some with tablets and smartphones, audio recorders; some with TV cameras hoisted onto their shoulders.

'You should go,' Ishbel said. 'Your public's waiting.'

But Aidan had already left the room. As she spoke, he stepped out of the front door, walking into her line of sight, and a flashbulb lightning storm.

Ishbel remembered the day they'd moved into the house. It was 1991, about the worst possible year they could have picked to enter the housing market. They'd been searching for months, and had fallen into a terrible pattern: on finishing work, they'd meet up at the latest house or flat for a viewing. Inevitably, one of them would love it, and the other hate it. They'd trudge to the nearest bus stop in silence, ride back to their fifth-floor rented flat in silence, and climb the hundreds of cold tenement stairs in silence. Then they'd argue into the evening – over the property they'd just seen, over money, or over the question of children. This was, of course, before Abigail, but Ishbel was convinced they ought to try and buy a place where they'd have room for a child. Aidan argued that they couldn't afford anywhere that big, that they should buy small and scale up once the recession passed. Ishbel would ask him how he knew that it would. Aidan would laugh in the face of her naivety, and then Ishbel would accuse him of not really wanting children at all, and just being too cowardly to admit it. The evening would usually end with at least one slammed door.

Then Aidan's father had died, suddenly, of what Aidan called 'a good, clean, Scotsman's heart attack'. Aidan's mother, Pauline, hadn't wanted to stay in the big house in Primrose Bank alone: 'I'm positively rattling around in it, hen,' was how she'd put it. She'd given the house to them as an exchange. 'Give me some braw wee grandkids,' she'd said, 'and we'll speak no more about it.'

Remembering her promise to her mother-in-law made her cry new, quiet tears now – though she wasn't sure what they meant. It physically hurt to do so, but she tried to breathe slowly and examine the various feelings that were sloshing through her, unbidden. There was that long shadow of grief, which pulsed with the words *she's dead, she's dead, she's dead* – it felt like a cold fist opening and closing around Ishbel's heart. There was anger, certainly – a scattergun kind of anger with nothing, really, to aim at. There was weariness that verged on boredom: an almost overpowering desire to just no longer be awake, to turn off all thoughts, cut off the air supply. But bigger than all of these things, she realised, with a loud, unbidden sob, was *guilt*. Guilt at having lost her child, her only child, at having failed to protect her, to do the one thing a mother is supposed to do. Guilt at having reneged on the deal with Pauline. Guilt at the fact that, five minutes ago, she had implied that her grief was somehow more legitimate than Aidan's, more pure – and guilt that yes, she believed it, though some part of her knew it wasn't how such things worked.

She watched her husband turn from the circled pack of journalists and walk back up towards the house – that very same house – and wondered if there was a limit to how much one person could cry. If such a limit existed, she thought, she must surely be edging near it.

Aidan walked into the room, and Ishbel felt a twinge of anxiety.

'Did you shut the front door?' she asked. Her voice sounded more combative than she'd intended. 'I didn't hear it.'

Aidan threw a glance behind him, and then turned back.

'No,' he said, and in his voice was that same irritation she was starting to get used to. 'Reh's right behind me.'

He gestured vaguely backwards, toward the sound of footsteps in the front hall. Ishbel looked back out of the window.

'He isn't,' she said. A knot of fear formed in her throat. 'He's still out on the lawn, look . . .'

Aidan didn't often look panicked. He prided himself on his composure – had continued to do so, even after the shooting. But now, he looked panicked.

'Then, who—?'

They both turned to face the doorway. Standing there: a thin man in a dark grey coat.

Police, Ishbel heard herself thinking. *He must be a policeman – who else would think it acceptable to walk right into the house?* Something bothered at her, an itch near the back of her skull: she recognised this man from somewhere.

'Mr and Mrs Hodgekiss?' The man looked pleased with himself, like he was trying not to smile. 'My name is Grant Lockley. I'd like to ask you some questions, if I may.'

'I'm sorry,' Aidan said. Ishbel could feel him weighing up the situation, running through possible scenarios in his mind. She could hear it in his voice. 'I don't know who you are. Can we see some identification?'

The man only loosened his smile, made it wider.

'I'd like to ask if you have any theories,' he said, 'about why Ryan Summers might have committed this terrible atrocity. I know Abigail was the first of the victims to be killed. Do you have any idea why that might be?'

'Listen,' Aidan said, 'I don't *like* this line of questioning. I won't answer that question, or any other for that matter, until you tell us who you are.'

Ishbel knew her husband had spoken, but she didn't really hear him. She could feel her face and hands prickling, and little sparks began to appear in her vision. No one had told her that Abigail was the first.

Ishbel watched as Aidan's posture shifted, just slightly – he was. trying to intimidate the smaller man, bracing himself as though this interloper might run at him. She could swear she saw, on the back of his neck, the fine, blond wisps of his hair lift, like the hackles on a dog. She opened her mouth. She wanted to speak, though she had no idea what she might say. Instead, she found she could only gulp at the air, her mouth slack. Aidan seemed unmoved by this information: it wasn't new to him. Rehan must have told him, sometime over the past few days, while she was asleep. She ought to be angry about this, she knew. But her brain was chanting, *Why would she be first? Why would he shoot her first?*

'My name is Grant Lockley,' the man said again. 'I'm trying to get to the bottom of why Ryan Summers did what he did. There are a lot of people out there who want to know.'

Fear vibrated inside Ishbel like a struck piano wire: this was the man she'd seen at the hospital, the man who took the photograph of the boy on the gurney. She kicked herself: until now, she'd forgotten all about him. And now he was staging an ambush.

'You're a journalist, aren't you?' Aidan said.

The man placed one hand on his chest.

'I'm the person who's going to get to the bottom of all of this for you, Mr Hodgekiss – sort this out. I see that as my job, in this whole sorry mess.'

Maybe it was coincidence, Ishbel heard herself think. *Maybe she was just in the way.*

Aidan balled his fists.

'Reh!' he bellowed. Ishbel glanced out of the living-room window to where Rehan was still standing in the gaggle of journalists, answering questions. She saw his head flick upwards.

'Reh!' Aidan shouted again.

When Ishbel looked round, Grant Lockley seemed to have fixed his gaze on her. Once again, she became very aware of her dishevelled appearance: her grubby neck and dirty fingernails; the white, unshaved legs sticking out from the bottom of her dressing gown.

'Mrs Hodgekiss,' he said, his voice quieter now. 'Don't you want justice for your daughter? Don't you want to find out why she was so senselessly killed?'

The wire inside Ishbel snapped. She elbowed Aidan out of the way and flew at the little man in the doorway.

'Get *out* of my *house!*' Her voice sounded like broken metal, high-pitched and scraping. 'You don't care about my daughter – you only care about what you can get! You people are all *vultures*—'

She felt Aidan's hand close around her arm, and Reh tumbled into view behind Lockley.

'Oh, I care all right,' Lockley said. His face had darkened: the smile was gone. 'I care about finding out the truth – about making sure that people have the facts. And let me tell you, Mrs Hodgekiss ... I'm hearing some *truths* about your daughter that might just shock you.'

Behind Lockley, Rehan was speaking rapidly into his mobile phone. Ishbel caught the words *immediate back-up*, and the journalist did, too. He wheeled round.

'All right, I'm going!' He held his hands up over his head, as though Reh might shoot him. 'You should tell the cavalry to stand down, unless you want a story about yet more wasted police funds.'

Lockley raised his voice, so whoever Rehan was talking to on the phone could also hear him.

'You can't get me for anything,' he said. 'Breaking and entering won't stick – Aidan here practically held the door open for me! And now I'm going.'

'*Good*,' Aidan said. His grip on Ishbel's arm was painful, she realised, but she was also glad of it. Her heart spat and popped in the furnace of her chest. *Maybe it was indiscriminate. She was just the person closest to him.*

Lockley shimmied past Rehan, and turned his back on the three of them. He stopped, and looked back over his shoulder, right at Ishbel. The spike of fear he'd shown in the face of Rehan's call for assistance was gone as soon as it had come.

'You'll hear from me again,' he said, and was gone.

Ishbel's pulse was battering away, like a loose door in a high wind. For the first time in a week, she felt fully awake, and the pain of Abigail's absence felt so acute that she could barely stand. Rehan was still speaking into his mobile phone – more gently now, explaining what had happened. Aidan was still a pace or two in front of her: he'd turned slightly to watch Lockley flee out of the front door and down the garden into the security of the paparazzi gaggle. Ishbel could see a vein standing out on the side of her husband's neck, the blood flashing through it in time with her own racing pulse.

'The nerve,' he hissed. Rehan looked up.

'I'm sorry, Aidan,' he said. 'Both of you, I'm sorry – you shouldn't have had to deal with that intrusion.'

But Aidan was looking past Rehan, at the door that Lockley had slammed behind him.

'If anyone's going to *sort this out*,' Aidan said, mimicking the journalist's sibilant tone, 'it'll be me.'

He turned, and without looking at her, walked past her into the kitchen. Her legs began to give out, and she sank onto the faded sofa. Outside in the garden, she could hear the paparazzi's distant laughter, and Rehan's quiet phone voice in the hall. But mostly, the room was full of Aidan's rage: she fancied she could hear it buzz, like static – an extra layer of noise on the edge of everything.

MURDERER'S MOTHER RELEASED FROM CUSTODY – THEY SAY SHE'S INNOCENT, BUT THERE'S BLOOD ON HER HANDS

By GRANT LOCKLEY
PUBLISHED: 10:55 21 May

Good news today for Moira Summers, mother of the depraved Three Rivers College murderer Ryan Summers. She's getting to go home.

Mrs Summers is due to leave the former Lothian and Borders Police Headquarters on Fettes Avenue this morning. From there she will be transported – with a police escort, would you believe – to the Summers family home in Edinburgh's New Town.

Mrs Summers has been 'assisting police with their enquiries' – that's what they're calling it, anyway – for almost a week. I know I'm not the only one who's been shocked at the fact that no charges have been brought against her. It is believed that for some of that time she has been in protective custody following a string of anonymous death and rape threats made towards her.

As a result, the Summers house is currently being guarded by uniformed police officers round the clock, thanks to the contributions of the British taxpayer. I don't think it's overly cruel of me to believe that Mrs Summers really does deserve whatever angry words the public might wish to fling at her. I also believe that it is ludicrous for our hard-earned taxes to be spent on protecting her from what are, most likely, empty threats made by people who just want to get that totally understandable anger off their chest. I mean, who among us would not have some choice words for this woman, were we to run into her in the street?

Related reading: is the truth about Three Rivers College being covered up while the taxpayer foots the bill?

One week on from the horrific shooting, and we are still no closer to knowing why Moira Summers' only son, 20-year-old Ryan, went on a killing rampage that left thirteen of his female classmates dead and many others injured.

Many have speculated – myself included – that Mrs Summers must have had some idea that her son was planning to commit the terrible crime. It's certainly interesting that, very soon after news of the shooting broke, Mrs Summers hired the services of top defence lawyer Anjan Chaudhry, allegedly one of the best criminal lawyers in the business. This columnist asks: does that seem like the action of an innocent woman?

If Mrs Summers did indeed have some idea that her psychotic son was planning to gun down his classmates in cold blood, then she must be held accountable – and, in my view, treated as an accomplice to murder.

Take our poll: do you think Moira Summers suspected her son in the run-up to the Three Rivers shooting? Have your say here

In related news, a statement was made to the press earlier today by Aidan Hodgekiss, the father of one of Ryan Summers' innocent victims. Abigail Hodgekiss, who was 19 and a drama student at Three Rivers College, was the first person to die by Summers' hand. Mr Hodgekiss is the first of the victims' loved ones to speak publicly since the shooting took place.

In his statement, Mr Hodgekiss said that he and his wife 'cannot find the words to express our grief in the wake of this terrible tragedy'. He added, 'Because of the unspeakable anger and hatred of one man – Ryan Summers – we will forever be denied our chance to meet the woman she [Abigail] would have grown into.'

Victim's dad Aidan Hodgekiss's emotional public statement: read it in full here

Mr Hodgekiss's wife Ishbel, who works as a social care regulator, did not appear in front of the cameras today. Her husband – a dentist

– spoke on behalf of the whole family when he thanked the general public for 'the great outpouring of sympathy that has been extended by the people of this country, and the world'.

Mrs Hodgekiss is perhaps shunning the limelight because this tragedy has taken a toll on her mental and physical health. This columnist had the opportunity to speak briefly with her today, and she seems to be almost delirious with grief over the death of the couple's only daughter.

Mrs Hodgekiss's demeanour begs the question: to what extent can a loved one get over a tragedy of this magnitude? Will Ishbel Hodgekiss ever be able to return to her high-powered career in a field where nuance is everything? Or has Ryan Summers taken that away from her, too?

See more from Grant Lockley

Share or comment on this article

TOP COMMENTS

isjusticejustICE Having watched the Aidan Hodgekiss statement on Youtube . . . surely I can't be the only one who thinks . . . he doesn't seem very upset? If his wife has lost her marbles that's much more understandable.
^ *16 people liked this*

StillYes45 Surely Police Scotland will investigate Moira S further? Cannot believe her story. Says she didn't know about the guns, didn't know about the plan, didn't know anything was going on with her son? I smell a rat.
^ *29 people liked this*

SAPPERGEO Three Rivers was a set up!!! False flag event, Ryan Summers is still alive. Wake up at truthunifies.com
^ *31 people liked this*

21 May, 5.35 p.m.

~~To whom it may concern,~~
~~Dear world,~~
~~Dear everyone,~~
~~Dear reader,~~
~~Dear Reader,~~
Reader,

I don't ~~think I~~ need to introduce myself. You already know my name. Or if you don't, then you know my son's name. My son is the ~~boy~~ man who, just a few short days ago ~~— though already that passed time feels like years —~~ walked into ~~the canteen at~~ the Tweed Campus of Three Rivers College, and opened fire on his ~~friends and~~ classmates. He killed thirteen ~~young~~ women. His name ~~is~~ was Ryan Summers, and I am his mother.

Why am I writing to you? That's a good question. ~~Someone told me that 'the open letter' was the latest way to say what you feel.~~ Over the past few days, I've been told many times that I should ~~repent~~ apologise for ever creating the ~~boy~~ man who ~~is~~ was my son. I can't do that. ~~For twenty years, Ryan was my only child and he always brought great joy to~~ But what I can do is apologise for ~~what he did his selfish acts~~ the horrendous acts he has committed. I want to say sorry to the families of the ~~girls~~ young women who were killed. I know that these young women were each, in their own way, brilliant and gifted, just starting out with their studies, just starting out with their lives. ~~My son~~ Ryan took away so much when he killed them, and for that I ~~apologise~~ say: I'm sorry. I also want to say sorry to the ~~other~~ students and staff who were on the campus that day. I'm sorry for what you ~~saw witnessed~~ had to witness. And I want to say sorry to anyone else who is hurting as a result of ~~in the aftermath of~~ this tragedy. ~~So many of you have told me~~ I know that so many of you are hurting.

I want to tell you that I am hurting too. I spent almost a week inside a police station, after the shooting. I have offered up the last twenty years of my life as evidence to be picked over. I have answered the same questions dozens of times. I have been asked again and again why ~~Ryan~~ my son Ryan did what he did. I have said again and again that I don't know. ~~Like all of you, I wish I knew.~~

I am now at home, in the home where I raised my son, alone but for the armed policemen standing outside my front and back doors. I have lost count of the number of death threats and rape threats that have been made towards me. Even if I felt brave enough to ignore those threats, I cannot go outside without facing the dozens of representatives from the world's press who are watching my movements day and night, blocking my road, and inconveniencing my neighbours. I will have no visitors, as no one will want to be associated with me. I can't talk to anyone except for the police. I probably won't even publish this letter.

Moira mashed the paper into a ball, closing her fist around it. She'd been planning the letter all day. It started in her head, in the interviews, while Anjan or the police were talking. Then she'd fleshed it out as she sat in the back of the unmarked car – dark glasses on behind the tinted windows – being driven towards this house with its spitting ring of paparazzi, news helicopters taking turns at fly-pasts over the street. Amy had advised her to pull her coat over her head, and then Amy and a uniform had guided her up the path and into the hallway, their six feet lit in a dizzying snowstorm of flash.

The tea that Amy had made her was still by her elbow, stone cold, a sheen forming round the rim.

'The panic button's for emergencies,' Amy had said, placing the tea in front of her. 'You shouldn't need it. It's really unlikely that anyone will try anything, not with two uniformed police standing right outside. Two scene guards will be there the whole time. They'll change over about twice a day, but there'll always be someone there. And you have my number, and the station number. Don't even think twice about it if you want to talk to me – just pick up the phone. You're my biggest priority right now, okay? Okay, Moira?'

She'd nodded, trying for a smile.

'Oh,' Amy had added. 'I wouldn't recommend going on the internet right now.'

Moira looked around. She'd been sitting at the table for what felt like a long time. Initially, after Amy left, she did nothing – just sat, listening to the shuffle and mutter of the men outside. The house had never felt this empty: no TV on, no radio, no washing machine. And there were no shuffling footsteps above her head, no clatterings: she'd never hear the sound of her teenage son, just existing somewhere in this house, ever again. She thought of the muffled gunshots from his video games – the way they had become just another part of the house's background noise – and shuddered. She remembered times soon after Jackie had died when everything was so wholly desolate that she'd found them comforting, those sounds: the distant, constant rattle of Ryan's simulated gunfire. She'd spent many an evening sitting on her sofa in this very room, feeling reassured by the fact that because of those sounds, she knew her boy was nearby – with her, almost. Her one precious boy: he was safe inside the four walls of the house. 'You're the man of the house, now,' she'd said to him in a thin, wet voice, the day they came back from his father's funeral. They'd stood in the hallway and she'd looked up into his face – he was so tall, it still surprised her sometimes – and tried to pick up his gaze. But Ryan kept his neck bent, his head like a rain-heavy flower, and his eyes on the ground as she pushed out the words through spit-bubbles and hot tears. She remembered feeling angry with him then: his sullen blinking back of any emotion. 'Okay, Mum,' he'd said at last, and she'd turned away, released him to slink off up the stairs and be alone. *I should have hugged him,* she thought now. The memory wedged in her ribs, like a hot blade pushed deep. She felt angry again, but the anger was turned inwards, towards her own sluggish heart. *Maybe I didn't hug him enough. If I'd only hugged him that day, or touched his arm* . . . She flinched and shivered, and the memory dispersed a little, like fog. A small blessing.

Something within her itched to press the panic button Amy had left for her, just to see what happened. She couldn't quite believe that there were people out there who might want to kill her . . . but then, she could also believe it just fine. She tried to imagine what she'd have felt if the roles were reversed – if someone else had walked into Three Rivers College that day, and killed Ryan. Would she have wanted to hurt the woman who put that person on the earth? The idea was slippery, as though coated in some sort of dark oil: she couldn't quite keep hold of it. *Could I hurt someone?* she wondered. *Really hurt them?* She shivered so hard that the chair she was sitting on creaked. *It doesn't matter. What matters is people want to hurt you. People who don't even know you.* She'd reached for the notepad then.

But no. Of course she couldn't write an open letter to the world – though plenty of places, she knew, would be interested in publishing it. No matter how careful her wording, someone out there would read it wrong: dissect it, and find something she hadn't intended in between the words. Something to show she was a bad mother; that she'd birthed some sort of monster – *look, this woman knew her son was evil, and she did nothing!* The world had already made up its collective mind.

The police had taken the brick away before she arrived – she'd assumed it was a brick, but it could have been some other missile. They'd hammered chipboard hoarding over the window, so the room was oddly dark. She knew about the brick from watching TV news in the police station anteroom: a lull between interviews, Anjan and Amy not with her, but somewhere nearby. There was no sound on, so she'd blinked in shock as the camera panned to the front of her house: reporters milling around outside, and the hoarding already in place. The words DEATH IS TOO GOOD had been sprayed in dribbling red paint on the wood, the vandal apparently interrupted before they could finish the thought. Because she'd come in with her coat over her head, Moira had no idea if the words were still there.

The glass that had detonated into the room was still there, though, in the carpet. When they came in, Amy had begun picking it up with her bare hands – not stopping until Moira had shooed her away.

'I'll just get these big bits, then,' Amy had said, dumping the shards in the kitchen bin. The carpet was still sugared with lethal glass dust. *I ought to hoover*, Moira thought, but she didn't move.

The letter was clamped inside her fist, the paper now slightly damp.

'What did I do wrong?' someone said. The voice was her own, only tired, and with an angry edge of something in it. 'What did I do, Ryan? What did I do to make you *do* that?'

The silence in the house seemed louder now that she'd spoken into it. *You know what you did*, it seemed to say. She wished Jackie were here: she'd feel safer. It was a feeling she'd had a few times since he'd died, but never so acutely as right now.

'Get a hold of yourself, Moira.' That was better. That sounded more like her.

'Do something,' she said. 'Come on. Stand up.'

As though her body had been waiting for a verbal command, she stood.

'Good girl,' she said. 'Now, let's go into the kitchen and put this infernal thing in the bin.'

She pushed open the glass door. The kitchen was darkish, too – someone had pulled down the wooden slatted blind, and swivelled it fully closed. Amy, perhaps. The triangles of glass glittered dimly as Moira toed open the pedal bin. The sweet smell of rotting food rose up: of course, the house had been empty.

'How do I put the bins out?' she said. A muffled voice on the other side of the kitchen's back door responded, making her pull the air in through her teeth in a frightened whistle.

'Mrs Summers?'

'Yes? Who's there?'

'PC Phillips.' It was a male voice. She remembered: the policemen. 'Is there something I can help you with?'

Moira frowned.

'No, no. I was just ... having a little conversation with myself. I'm sorry.'

She waited for an answer, but if any answer came, she couldn't hear it.

The letter was still in her hand, unballing itself slowly, like the bud of a peony. She found a corner and pulled, until she could see the whole page.

'You stupid girl.' She was whispering now. She ripped the letter in half, then in half again, and began shredding it, dropping the tiny strips of inky foolscap into the bin. She shuffled her foot away and the metal lid dropped with a clang.

'There,' she said. 'You did that. Let's do something else.'

As she turned, her attention was caught by the three green bottles lined up on the worktop: striking, now she noticed them, against the white tiles.

'No, Moira,' she said.

Should I be worried? she thought, wandering back into the dining room to look at the shattered glass. *I'm talking to myself.* As she walked towards the wrecked window, her footsteps began to crunch. The glass was everywhere. In the thin light the carpet looked grey, and the lethal flecks were dusted all over, like ash. She realised that vacuuming this would cripple her hoover – she needed a stiff brush, and maybe tweezers, first.

'Oh God.' She put out one hand and leaned against the empty window-frame, fingers brushing the splintery wood beyond.

The house was a shallow U-shape: a double-fronted, detached job that Jackie had done up years ago. The long kitchen ran along the back, with the dining room on one side, the good living room on the other. The dining room was where the family did everything: ate dinner, watched TV. She thought of all the Christmas trees she'd put up in this big bay window – all the times she'd watched as Ryan hung up tinsel and paper angels he'd made in school. *No, don't think about that. How can I stop myself from thinking about that?* She stumbled back to the kitchen, the smell of the bin, and the clean white tiles. She picked up the first of the three bottles by its neck: a brick-shaped three-quar-ter-litre of gin. Somehow, a glass tumbler appeared on the counter, but her hand shook as she tipped the bottle, and the liquid didn't come.

'Come on, woman,' she said, teeth clenched hard.

Gin sloshed into the glass: one finger, then two. When she picked it up, the tumbler's sides were wet. The tonic in the fridge was flat, but her shaking hands coped better with the plastic bottle, its grippy shape. She wondered about cutting a slice of lime, but didn't trust those hands with a sharp knife.

'Cheers,' she said, and took a long slug off the top of the glass.

The buzz was almost immediate: she remembered too late that she'd eaten barely anything for a week – not since that day, the day of crawling around in the shed, when she'd figured out about Ryan.

'Sit down,' she hissed, aware of the policeman on the back doorstep, 'before you do yourself a mischief.'

The dining room was too grim: she couldn't handle it. She'd have to go upstairs. As she left the room, she passed the kitchen noticeboard and saw, before she could stop herself looking, the photograph of Ryan she'd pinned there only a couple of weeks ago. It was a photo of him aged ten or so, in the back garden of this house. One jutting hip of the shed was visible behind him. It must have been a sunny day: he was standing inside the ring of a fallen hula-hoop, its white plastic slightly blurred, reflecting the sky's brightness. He looked like he was standing inside some kind of fairy ring, some force field of protection. He was smiling. No, he was laughing – at himself, his own inability to do the silly thing she'd asked of him. She remembered the moment: trying to catch in a photograph the few seconds where he'd managed to keep the hoop aloft around his waist. She'd been mad for hula-hooping as a child, and told him this was the way his mummy used to have fun. She used to love it when she could make him laugh. It hadn't happened much lately.

She was halfway up the stairs before she really knew where she was going: in a blur of tears, she'd crunched back out through the dining room and into the hallway. Behind the frosted glass front door, the neon pillar of a policeman. She climbed the stairs, gripping the banister with one unsteady hand, the other still clutching the slippery tumbler.

At the top of the stairs, she took a long mouthful of the stinging gin. It had started to feel warm.

'Ryan?'

It was habit. It was what she always did.

'Are you decent, sweetheart?' Her throat made an odd, chuckling sound. She stood outside her son's bedroom door and laughed at her own ridiculousness.

'All right,' she said. 'Time's up, I'm coming in.'

But her little charade on the landing – even coupled with the gin – hadn't prepared her for her dead son's bedroom. The scene-of-crime officers – Amy had laughed and abbreviated them to 'SOCO, like so-and-so' – had torn the room apart. The divan bed had been tipped onto its narrow end, and now obscured the window like a monolith, its mattress stacked against it. The fabric sides had been ripped back so the divan's cavity could be searched. All the furniture was pulled out into the middle of the room: her face stung with embarrassment at the dust and detritus they'd revealed. The washing basket and drawers from the dresser had been upended, on top of a pile of clean cotton shirts she'd ironed only days before. The computer desk was the only thing that looked wrong in this disaster zone. It had been swept completely clean: every item Ryan had piled on it had been taken away somewhere. The big PC monitor had been there so long that, now it had been removed, the square of wallpaper it had stood against was darker than the rest of the room. She could see the strange residue left all over by the fingerprinting kits. She pressed the light switch, but for some reason, the bulb in the ceiling light had been taken.

Moira skirted into the room.

'Look at this mess,' she said, her voice guttering like a candle flame. 'Makes you look practically tidy, Ryan.'

She sank fast into the leather computer chair, slopping a little constellation of gin across the carpet. Her face was damp. The chair was covered in fingerprint powder – and now, she guessed, so was her skirt. The wallpaper began to swim.

With her free hand, she reached up and slapped herself in the face. The slap landed with a pleasantly wet sound, but she barely felt it. She tried again. This time, a sting. The third time, a little blistering of stars across her vision.

'Jesus,' she said, through her teeth. 'Pull yourself together.'

She sat in the computer chair for a long time. She could feel herself sliding down into more of a crouch – slowly, a millimetre at a time. She realised she was enjoying the sensation. In the quiet, she could hear the paparazzi talking outside: there was no hoarding on this window to dampen the sound. She was surprised – and oddly disappointed – that the few voices she could pick out from the throng were not talking about her, or Ryan, or the shooting. Instead, they seemed to be using that macho code that signalled they were speaking of a forthcoming major sporting event. She tried to follow, but she couldn't even guess the sport, let alone the occasion. She wondered why on earth they were here, who on earth could think it was a good idea to be paying them. She didn't think about how long they might stay.

The watery sun fell behind the roof of the house across the street, and the light in the room changed. Vehicles began to pull up at the cordon, a few houses down: Moira could hear their distant chug, the whoosh and slam of their sliding side-doors. These were the TV news trucks, coming with kit and correspondents to broadcast live for the evening audience. Amy had warned her they'd come, and as she'd said it, Moira found herself wishing the front garden was tidier, the downpipes more recently painted. She could hear these new arrivals shouting commands, clinking tripods and the poles of booms. The glass was empty, its sides sticky in her hand. If they were going to broadcast, she thought, then she might as well watch.

She abandoned Ryan's wrecked bedroom, and walked back out onto the dim, windowless landing. She paused for a moment, peering down the stairs into the hallway. From here, she could make out a wedge of front door, that yellow smudge of the policeman's neon coat hanging in the panel of frosted glass. She closed her eyes, listening for the scrape of a key. As if any minute now, her son would come slamming into the hall, dump his bag and shoes, and – if she was lucky – shout a gruff *hello* on his way up the stairs. *I'm asleep*, she thought, *and this is just one of those dreams you have, the kind that shakes you enough that you tell it to your friends.* A wave of tiredness settled over her, but something in her brain kicked in to flick her eyelids open again as she swayed.

'Ryan,' she whispered, 'sweetheart.' But behind her, the trashed room was still trashed.

Moira stumbled along the landing to her own bedroom, and found that it had also been searched. More of an effort had been made here to restore things to their natural order, but the room still looked like a high wind had blown through. The chest of drawers had been rifled, its contents unfolded and stuffed back in. The fabric covering on this divan had been slashed, too, though the bed had been returned to where it lived, and the sheets thrown roughly back over it. The TV was still in its corner, surrounded by the prised-open boxes of DVDs, discs scattered on the black ash top of the unit. Moira found the kicked remote on the floor, and switched the TV on.

It took around thirty seconds for the studio newsreader to say her son's name.

'The gunman, Ryan Summers,' he began, and she scrabbled for the mute button, 'was pronounced dead at the scene.' Too late. They cut to a picture of Ryan's face. His last school photo, a few years old now: Ryan in his navy school sweater, the stiff white collar of his shirt sitting wonky in its pilled V-neck. He was smiling, but he didn't look happy – a handful of years back he'd decided he hated having his photograph taken – and they'd cropped out the sky-blue backdrop so the details of her dead son's face filled up the screen. The school must have supplied the picture to the police. Ryan looked uncomfortable, she thought, impatient with sitting there. She remembered the fuss they used to have, getting him ready for the school picture. Back when Ryan was little Moira had a friend named Tanya, a trainee hairdresser. She wasn't very good, but she drove around the city doing cheap haircuts for the kids of friends. Ryan felt an irrational hatred towards Tanya, Moira remembered: he associated her with the hated day of the school photo. She'd turn up in her elderly red Ford Escort and Ryan would spend the next forty minutes being

as rude to her as he thought he could get away with under his
mother's gaze. Moira shivered. These past couple of years she'd
lost touch with Tanya – she'd finally got a chair in a salon in town.
What if the press find her? Moira found herself thinking. Tanya
could tell some stories about Ryan: that he was sullen, underhand,
manipulative.

'That's not who he *was*,' she said aloud, to the newsreader
whose mute lips were moving rapidly. 'I know him better than
anyone.' But she realised that meant nothing now. She wasn't even
sure if it was true. She had let this happen, after all. She didn't
want to think about it.

Ryan's photo came up on the screen again, and Moira studied it through a film of fresh tears. The expression would be
read by those who didn't know him as creepy: they'd think they
could see something obviously wrong in his eyes. Moira reached
out and touched the screen, her fingertips prickled by static. But
Ryan was gone. They switched to aerial footage of the college
car park filled with kids and white police vehicles with blue-
flashing roofs.

She sat down on the corner of the bed. The curtains had been
pulled wonkily shut, and in the gloom the muted TV glowed so
brightly her eyes smarted. Photographs of young women began to
appear on the screen, in a kind of slideshow: a girl smudged with
mud, grinning on a hockey field; a girl in a satin prom dress, wearing a beaded tiara. Moira counted them. They were all beaming,
and unbearably beautiful – these were photographs their families
had been allowed to choose. *Their families.* What were *their* lives
like, right now? Did *they* have police scene guards, crowds of journalists outside their houses? What must they think of her? Moira
simultaneously wished she knew, and hoped she would never find
out.

The final photograph lingered on the screen longer than the
others, and Moira knew without turning the sound back on that
they were talking about Abigail Hodgekiss. Her photo was a fancy
studio portrait, probably done for her eighteenth, Moira guessed,
or perhaps for high school prom. She was wearing coral-coloured

lipstick that made her teeth look very white. A fat, yellow locket hung around her neck. She wasn't the perfect-looking girl that Moira realised she'd been imagining. She had freckles. She didn't look like the sort of woman men killed for.

Moira felt a flash of anger – blood draining out of her head towards her heart, making her feel faint. She closed her eyes, and saw patterns. What had she done, this Abigail, to Ryan? Ryan, the little dark-haired boy, laughing in the back garden, in the bright ring of the hula-hoop. Surely this girl had hurt him. She'd done something to him that was so bad, he'd become angrier than he'd ever been. There had to be – *had* to be – a reason.

Moira leaned over, put her face next to the screen. Up close, she could see the million tiny coloured dots that made up Abigail's eyes.

'What did you do?' she hissed, but the fight was ebbing out of her as fast as it had come. When she leaned back, she realised Abigail was small – fine-boned, thin-limbed. Awkward-looking. This girl was weak. Had been. Moira knew she hadn't done a single thing.

The shot cut back to the slick, grey CGI studio. Ryan's photo hung in the air to the left of the newsreader's head. The news-reader's mouth opened and closed, but Moira was looking at her son. When she'd got that photo, she'd put it in a fancy wooden frame; she knew it was still there, sitting on the bookshelf in the good living room. She should go downstairs and move it. Throw it out, or maybe hide it somewhere for now. In a minute. She'd do it in a minute. She couldn't move her eyes from the warm pull of the TV.

The phone rang, making her jump. She felt the wave of an old habit run through her, and before she could stop herself, she called out, 'Phone!' The extension sat on a small table on the land-ing outside Ryan's bedroom door. She'd yell every time it rang, in the hope that one day, he might walk out and answer it. He never did. *Now*, she thought, *he never will*.

She huffed off the bed and stumbled back out of the room, onto the landing. When she got to the little cordless phone, sitting upright in its cradle, she saw its low battery light was blinking. The SOCOs must have unplugged it, or done something to it. Taken it apart, maybe, in the search – though why they might do that she had no idea. She picked up, expecting to hear Amy's voice on the line.

'Hello?' she said.

There was a pause, as though the person who'd called hadn't actually expected to hear a voice.

'Good evening.' A man's voice, with a very mild Scottish accent. 'Am I speaking to Mrs Moira Summers?'

'Yes,' Moira said, and then kicked herself. *This could be anyone.* But the voice on the other end switched from neutrally polite to positively beaming.

'Oh, I'm so pleased I was able to reach you,' the man said. 'I apologise for disturbing you at home, and at this very difficult time.'

Moira said nothing. Who *was* this?

'My name is Grant Lockley,' the man said. Then he paused again, as though expecting a reaction.

'I'm sorry,' Moira said. 'That name doesn't mean anything to me.'

'Oh, that's not a problem,' the man said. Indeed, he still sounded pleased. 'I thought perhaps your family liaison officer might have mentioned me.'

'No,' Moira said, 'Amy didn't say anything.'

'Amy,' the man said. He drew the word out a little, as though saying it while also writing it down. 'Right. Well, as I say, not a problem.'

'Can I ask . . .' Moira reached out her free hand and pressed it against the wall. Her head was swimming with fatigue, and the sour buzz of the gin. Standing up for this length of time was taking its toll.

'Oh yes, yes,' the man said. 'I do apologise. I was phoning you to – well, I was hoping I might be able to ask you a few questions.'

Moira frowned.

'Are you with the police?'

The man went on talking as though she hadn't spoken.

'Firstly, Moira – do you have any theories as to why your son might have done what he did? Is there any reason you can think of that might make sense? I know that's the one thing everyone wants to know, and if anyone can help us understand, it's you.'

Moira's hand skidded down the wall a little, and she staggered to right herself.

'What *is* this?' she said.

'Did you,' the man was saying, 'have any conversations with Ryan, prior to the shooting, that maybe, with hindsight, seem suspicious?'

Moira's stomach churned.

'You're a journalist.'

On the other end of the phone, the man's demeanour transformed.

'What did you know, Moira?' His voice was spiky, louder now. 'Why didn't you do something to stop him? Why didn't you tell the police?'

She let out a small, choked cry. The phone fell from her hand, and hit the landing carpet with a soft thud. From the receiver, she could still hear the tinny drift of Grant Lockley's voice.

'The public want to know why Ryan did it, Moira. What are you hiding?'

In a moment of sudden, piercing clarity, Moira reached down and yanked the phone's cable out of the wall.

Back in the bedroom, it was as though no time had passed. The shooting was still being talked about on the news: the correspondent standing in someone's garden, the daylight behind him fading. *Live from the home of Aidan and Ishbel Hodgekiss*, the superbar informed her. The TV was still on mute, but Moira could see that there was some kind of continuity delay, the correspondent's face impassive and white under his crew's erected lights. Moira sank onto the bed, her hands shaking. She thought about the talk they'd had – just her and Ryan, in the kitchen, the night before the shooting. She hadn't mentioned that talk to the police in any of the many interviews they'd put her through. She'd tried to avoid even thinking about it.

'What did you know, Moira?' She heard herself repeat Grant Lockley's words, aloud.

She leaned back against the haphazard pillows, and closed her eyes. Her mind raced for an answer, but there wasn't one. There was only Ryan's school portrait face, hanging in the dark: the streak of his white shirt collar, and the black hole of his scowl.

21 May, 6.25 p.m.

Birch got back from her final briefing of the day in time to catch the end of the six o'clock Three Rivers news coverage. She'd finished up the meeting by grovelling to her team about how late she'd kept them. One week on from the shooting, and the workload wasn't slowing – in fact, the workload was a literal pile of paper she'd had to slide her forearms under like a forklift and wedge beneath her chin. The team had largely given up on email: everyone's inboxes were too clogged to make sense of, and things were being missed. Therefore, a new system: priority intelligence and updates were printed. Sensitive information was marked in red. The result was Birch staggering back to her office with a metric ton of paperwork, red ink on the cover of every cardboard file. *So much for our paperless workplace targets*, she thought. The stack of briefing documents landed on her desk with a thud, like a body hitting the ground. It immediately tilted and slid, its top layer spilling. Birch kicked the door shut behind her, and swore.

Now, on her tablet screen, the six o'clock news. She wished they'd stop running that same photo of Ryan Summers. It had been badly cropped – on one side, part of his ear was sliced off – and because of the crop his face seemed too close, filling too much of the screen. Sullen, Birch thought he looked. Not evil, just mildly pissed off and bored. He looked like the sort of kid who couldn't bear to be bored. Or did she just think that because she'd read his profile?

She looked at it now, sitting at her feet, where it had skidded to the floor. It had been updated by Marcello and John, by Amy, and by various other members of the team who'd added notes and memos since she'd last looked at it. The front of the flimsy card file was stamped and re-stamped with the red ink denoting *sensitive*.

'In other news,' the voice inside her tablet said, and Birch flicked the screen off. She laid the tablet gingerly on the desk, watching the precarious stack of briefing files as she did so. It was an absolute pit in here. She'd never had her own office before – at Gayfield Square she'd worked in the open-plan bullpen with everyone else. Sure, her desk had never been the tidiest in the place, but she hadn't realised until now the extent to which her former colleagues' watchful eyes had kept her from sliding into the inevitable chaos that now surrounded her. Birch was glad that one-to-one style meetings had largely been abandoned with this investigation: it was much more efficient to get as many people into a room at once and put as much new information in front of them as you possibly could. Her only truly private interactions at the moment were with McLeod, and he preferred to have those in the comfort of his own office. It was, needless to say, much larger than hers, and also immaculate.

Birch stood looking at the slithered files at her feet; at the collapsed pile on the desk; at her overflowing in-tray, and at the lever-arches piled up on her swivel chair. Under the desk, the bin spewed brown-stained canteen paper cups.

'Fuck,' she said aloud, as she pushed her forearms under the remaining stack of paper once more, and huffed it backwards so it crashed against her ribcage, and she was able to lift it. She let herself half fold, half fall into a cross-legged position on the floor. Then she laid the stack down in front of her, and repositioned the already-spilled layer back on the top. The result resembled a ragged Jenga tower: one thousand paper-cuts waiting to happen. The pile was nearly as tall as Birch now that she was sitting with it – she stared it down like a chess opponent, like it might play some dirty move on her.

'Fuck,' she said again, this time with less fight.

This is your investigation, she thought. *This. Looking at you.* For a moment, she experienced what felt like the spins, as if she'd been out drinking all day. The sensation came over her whenever she thought too much about the big picture – whenever she or one of her officers got too near to the question, 'What the hell are we doing?' Because there *was* no way to 'solve' a crime like this: there was no logical end-point, no closure to be found. When Ryan Summers discharged his last round, he'd frozen time: he'd forever be the bad guy that no one could bring in. The girls he'd killed would forever be tragic victims: rain-spattered photographs pinned to bouquets at some vigil somewhere. Liz Gill would forever be the fallen martyr, Kerry McNaughton forever the brave girl who helped her classmates and died for her trouble. Abigail Hodgekiss: forever the first to die. Chantal Walker: forever the last.

Nothing, Birch thought. *That's what the hell we're doing. Nothing whatsoever of use.* Any 'end' this investigation had would be purely bureaucratic: it would end when every last bit of paper had been filed away. When every last fact had been accounted for, when she and her colleagues knew literally all that they could know, then it would be done. There was no justice in that, she knew that only too well from Charlie's case: her brother, the invisible man. When you can't find the missing person, all you can do is file the report. When you can't bring the shooter to justice, all you can do is obsess over his every move until you've got a timeline that's to-the-minute precise. And McLeod was probably right: then there'd be an inquiry, the IPCC, coroners upon coroners, lawyers upon lawyers, the press – it could go on for years. *But it still won't help*, she thought. There was nothing in this stack of paper that could bring anyone back from the dead, no matter how it was picked through. No matter how efficiently filed.

She closed her eyes. In the blackness, the image of the briefing stack still floated, taunting her. It was knocking seven. She could be here all night. McLeod had gone home nearly three hours ago.

'Come on now, Helen,' she said, aloud. Her first attempt to re-open her eyes seemed to fail, so she pushed out a short, hard breath and said, 'O*kay.*'

When her gaze focused, Ryan Summers' profile was still on top of the pile. She lifted it carefully: the file wasn't entirely bound, and it had some heft. She laid it in her lap and flicked the cover.

Paperclipped to the inside, that same photograph: Summers in his school tie, looking bored.

In the margin, Marcello and John had stuck their Post-its – standard dusky yellow for John, and lime green for Marcello – showing her where the newly added information was. She found the first green one and stuck her finger into the sheaf, flipping straight to Marcello's intelligence.

Newly gathered eyewitness statements, the Post-it read. The handwriting was flamboyant and looped, but small. *Section one: believed credible. Section two: credibility unclear. Section three: confirmed false.* Scribbled at the top of the first printed page, in that same swooping hand: *statements marked with an asterisk were gathered via the Crimestoppers helpline.*

Birch looked at section one. It was by far the slimmest of the three – in fact, there were only two parts. She sighed: only two credible witnesses. She skimmed through Marcello's introductory flourishes to get to the good bit of the first – it was dated 'early April', as the witness could not remember the date.

- *Eyewitness describes seeing a twenty-something male subject, approximately 6'2", dark hair, and wearing a light grey hoodie.*
- *Subject witnessed walking from Niddrie Mains Road onto waste ground [eyewitness referred to, quoting, 'the scrub by the railway tracks'] between Craigmillar and Niddrie.*
- *Eyewitness describes seeing the subject setting up targets (likely cans or bottles) and discharging two small firearms.*
- *Eyewitness claims he was not alarmed at the time: this area is a popular site for [quoting] 'kids with air rifles and stuff'.*

Birch scribbled a note in the margin and looked at it, wondering if she'd be able to read her own handwriting later. Then she read on, to the second eyewitness statement, which was only a few sentences. This one was dated 21 April.

- *Eyewitness was cycling east on the Innocent Cycle Path in the area between Duddingston Golf Course and Niddrie Mains Terrace.*

- *Eyewitness describes hearing distant popping sounds, like cars backfiring.*
- *Eyewitness describes seeing a tall man in light clothing moving around in undergrowth off the cycle path.*

Section two was uninspiring – Birch knew that the words *credibility unclear* really meant, *this might have been a Ryan Summers sighting, but we can't tell and will probably never know.* There was a well-known perp who'd come forward to say he'd sold modified ammunition to a tall young man with dark hair. Birch's heart leapt, though she suspected – as Marcello obviously did, too – that this might be a fabrication. The gent in question was fairly desperate to get put back in jail, where he'd have three meals a day and access to all his old brethren. *Recidivism*, it was called – guys that were referred to as 'HOs', habitual offenders. More out of forlorn hope than anything, Birch underlined the old perp's statement, and drew an arrow in the margin suggesting it be moved from section two to section one. *FOLLOW UP*, she wrote, next to the arrow. She'd give anything to find out where Summers got his ammunition from – it was a hole in that timeline she was building, and it was bothering her.

Section three was several pages long, and it was where the nutters and time-wasters lived. There were people who claimed they'd seen Summers walking around, alive, in the days since the shooting. There were calls to say he was innocent, he was framed – *I know who did it,* or *I know it wasn't him because it was me, I'm the real Three Rivers gunman.* There were plenty of calls from people with feverish theories about Moira Summers' involvement in her son's activities: fabricated witness statements putting Moira at the scene; casting Moira in the role of criminal mastermind, and Ryan as her helpless dupe. Birch could see from some of the wording that Marcello had quite enjoyed summarising the various weird and wonderful statements taken from walk-ins or from the Crimestoppers line. *The eyewitness was really quite insistent,* he'd written in one summary, *that the young man in her dream was indeed Ryan Summers.* Birch tried to raise a smile, but she struggled with this sort of stuff. Not only because it was a waste of police time – how long had it taken to transcribe all those Crimestoppers calls? – but also because it felt intensely *personal*. After Charlie's initial disappearance, Birch and her mother had worked with the Missing Persons Helpline; they'd made posters and a website; Birch had driven to Glasgow, Dundee and Aberdeen to staple the posters to flagpoles and hand out flyers. She'd emailed the posters to friends in London to print out and put up anywhere they thought might help. At first, the calls they got were mainly from old friends of Charlie's who hadn't realised he was missing, and who were concerned. Reaching out. But then Lockley had got involved, and suddenly Charlie was in the papers. People started calling. Emailing. So many people that Birch began driving round and taking the posters down again. People called saying they knew where Charlie was, demanding a financial reward. People called to say Charlie was dead. The worst were the people who called and emailed pretending to *be* Charlie. Birch's mother had been taken in a couple of times – trusting that surely, no one would do that out of malice. But they did. They had. As far as Birch knew, none of the correspondence that came through post-Lockley was genuine.

She was too annoyed to read the whole list, so she flipped through to the next Post-it: a yellow one, which read *statements from known associates – newly added*. Birch was familiar with this section of the file: it contained summaries of Moira Summers' remarks about her son, taken from her various interviews over the past week. The slightly rambling audio transcript she'd given to Gibbie on the day of the shooting had been reduced to little more than bullet points: *I cleaned Ryan's room. I did not find anything suspicious there. I heard the first radio report about the shooting.* Now, statements had been added from a handful of Three Rivers College staff, and she skimmed through them.

In practical elements, extremely adept, one read – Ryan's mechanical engineering tutor. *Ryan had an exceptionally keen understanding of how things worked and his practical assessments were always marked very high. I knew he was a bit of an inventor and he mentioned to me that he had a kind of workshop at home, where he made things.*

Outside of the practical, Ryan struggled a little. His academic work put him in the lower half of the class. He hated essay writing. I have long suspected Ryan was dyslexic. Myself and another colleague both referred him for a dyslexia test but he did not attend.

Birch turned the page. Next, a statement from one Mr Welsh: the introductory line told her he worked as a support tutor, and oversaw the Three Rivers Student Union.

Ryan was the TRSU rep for his engineering class. He attended union meetings reasonably regularly. He'd been a member of the TRSU for about six months. Ryan was a quiet presence, and would usually only join in discussions when prompted. But he was a functioning member of the group and I had no concerns about him. He never spoke to me about anything relating to violence of any kind and he never appeared to be unpleasant or antisocial towards his peers. I might have described him as a little withdrawn. Ryan did not enjoy reading and writing, taking minutes at meetings, for example, but he liked practical tasks. Ryan was a student I had been hoping to get to know better. It was my hope that I could bring him out of his shell.

Birch yawned. There was so little here, so little to be done. She knew that a large sub-section of the general public was desperate for some concrete *reason* why Ryan Summers had done the things that he did, some extreme characteristic or habit or historical detail. Something they could point to and say, 'See, that's why – he wasn't like the rest of us, he was an outlier.' And Birch knew full well that that wasn't how things worked, but she realised that some small part of her was looking for it, too. If Ryan Summers really was just a bit of a shy kid who liked tinkering with things and happened to be very skilled at it – well, how many kids out there could that potentially be true of? If there was no definite *why*, that meant that the Three Rivers shooting simply came about because one seemingly ordinary young man found himself at the intersection of a very specific set of circumstances. That idea, that *under the right circumstances, anyone is capable of this* was terrifying. As much as she hated it, Birch understood why Lockley's readers were so desperate for him to uncover something.

Maybe that something was here: Birch thumbed the pages until she came to John's next yellow Post-it, which read, simply *theobviouschild*. Here was a copy/paste of all of this user's posts from a partly buried sub-section of a fairly well-known MRA forum. *For full threads*, John had written at the top, *with datestamps and replies from other users, see email*. Birch sent up a silent prayer at John's good sense in not printing out the entire shooting match. Marcello had shown no such restraint with the obviously fake witness statements.

theobviouschild: *You lot always on here whining about feminists. You are always saying there needs to be a reckoning. So who's going to do something then? Anyone here man enough to actually follow through on yr posturing?*

John had typed in: *[JS note: theobviouschild was not the original poster (OP) but replying to a post by username Cuck_Norris. theobviouschild's reply was the sixth in the thread.]* Birch read on.

theobviouschild: *Even Elliot Rodger killed more men than women. He called it a retribution but he failed. Someone needs to actually do something.*

[JS note: at this point theobviouschild goes quiet for several days, but these two comments attract replies from 17 different users, mostly goading him and asking what he plans to do himself.]

theobviouschild: *I'm going to actually do it, is what I'm going to do. I am a college student. I am surrounded by women my age every day and I am invisible to them. I have been invisible since I was a kid. I am going to step out of the shadows and make them all remember me.*

theobviouschild: *I have access to three guns and I am going to use them. I am going to shoot as many of them as can't run away. I'm going to count my rounds and when there is only one left I will put it in my head. Otherwise every round has a female name on it.*

[JS note: with the above reply the thread became extremely busy. theobviouschild's plan prompted a flurry of over one hundred replies, with some users goading him to do it, many doubting that he would, and some trying to talk him down.]

theobviouschild: *Those of you saying I can't can fuck off. I am an excellent shot and I've been training and practising for this event. I made these guns and I know them well and I know what they can do. I* *know everything about the building and I will work out a route through for maximum opportunity to shoot without being stopped. I won't be stopped. Just wait.*

Birch let her eyes drift down through the comments. There seemed to be a general pattern of call and response: theobvious-child stating his intentions – which, though horrifying, were maddeningly vague – and other users doubting his ability to follow through. According to John, the thread had gone back and forth in this way for several weeks, with theobviouschild posting only intermittently, and with each of his posts being left to accrue hundreds of replies in his absence.

Birch read and re-read the posts until her vision swam. Sticking her index finger in the file to mark her place, she flicked back to the paperclipped photo in the front of the file. She looked at the boy – and to her, he looked very much a boy, rather than a man – in the school jumper, wearing his petulant face. Though she knew that many people would be keen to, she couldn't quite match that face to the frightening words that theobviouschild had posted; couldn't quite convince herself that they were one and the same.

'What were you thinking, Ryan?' she said, aloud, to the boy in the photo. 'I know it was in some way about women, but . . . seriously, what were you thinking?'

Birch listened for a while to the quiet that answered her. Then she gave herself a small shake. *No*, she thought. *You don't know it was about women. None of us knows anything yet.* She didn't want to get like McLeod, who'd said to her earlier, 'I blame these violent video games,' and she'd had to stifle a smile, because he sounded like someone's gran. And she certainly didn't want to get like Lockley. She remembered him in the college corridor the evening that he'd broken in, reeling off his theories.

'Little Ryan wasn't loved enough as a kid, maybe. Little Ryan was allowed to listen to violent rap music. Little Ryan's dad died and he never got over it . . .'

The memory of his voice bothered at her, like a fly at a window. *No.* She didn't know why he'd done it – no one did, yet. She looked down at the photo again.

'We'll probably never know, will we?' she said, to Summers and his scowl. A thought occurred to her. 'Maybe *you* didn't even know.'

This was nuts. *Come on, Helen.* She tossed her head back and flipped the file open again, to where she'd left her finger marking theobviouschild's page. At the bottom, John's briefing notes:

JS notes: Hard evidence wise, there is still very little we can use to decisively pin it to Summers. But of course there are striking similarities. theobviouschild mentions three guns. He mentions counting rounds, which suggests a shortage of ammunition and a need to make each round count (as Ryan Summers did). He refers to rounds rather than bullets – this specificity could be connected to the use of modified pieces and ammunition. He refers to having 'made' the guns. And of course he claims to be a college student.

We're in the process of finding out where theobviouschild is recorded as having posted from, but a lot of users on sites like these use a proxy server, which masks their IP address. We're also analysing theobviouschild's writing style, turn of phrase and keywords to see if we can find him elsewhere on the internet under another alias. More soon.

Below this paragraph, John had handwritten on the print-out: *As yet unconfirmed! Should NOT be released to press!* The word 'NOT' was underlined three times.

Birch carefully rifled the folder, to try and keep its stacked paper square. She appreciated John's note. Much of that evening's briefing had been devoted to discussing the apparently mounting problem of press intrusion and what to do about it. Although Birch had radar for Lockley in particular, he was only one of many. Three Rivers was selling papers, generating clicks. Birch's FLOs were reporting, almost to a man, that their assigned family's houses were besieged. Birch had watched the footage of Moira Summers being hustled into her New Town semi earlier that day: some channels had sent *helicopters*, for goodness' sake. Her initial hope that the first week would be the worst, and then interest would die down, was starting to feel like a false one.

The last part of the briefing had been rather strained.

'Okay, folks.' Birch's throat had begun to get sore: there were a lot of people in the room and she'd had to really project. 'We need to talk about disclosure, and who's talking to who beyond these four walls.'

No one had wanted to meet her eye.

'Listen,' she said, feeling the mood of the room change. 'I'm not about to suggest we have a mole, or anything of that ilk. In fact, transparency is vital, and we've already talked about the importance of record-keeping in this investigation.'

A few nods from around the room, and a kind of soft, collective groan. Birch knew that as a result of her record-keeping directives, everyone's desk had a sliding volcano of paperwork on it.

'I actually want to talk about clarity,' she went on. 'We've just talked at length about the press, and how difficult we're all finding them . . . right? You're all being exceptionally patient and putting up with a hell of a lot.'

She took a deep breath. Scanning the room, she caught Rema's eye, Amy's eye, and then Marcello's – which made her flinch her gaze away.

'We just need to make sure that when we speak to members of the press, whether on the record or not, we are totally *crystal clear* about what we say.'

She'd rummaged on the table in front of her, and dug out a half-folded newspaper. She held it up and pointed to a story below the crease.

'Here, for example, someone spoke to . . .' Birch paused to glance at the byline. 'Cameron Inglis, apparently . . . Someone he's identifying as a police spokesperson told him that there were fourteen victims at Three Rivers.'

The room had shifted again: a shuffling of feet.

'Now, there isn't going to be a witch hunt.' Birch's voice crackled in and out like an old radio. She really needed to stop talking soon. 'We just have to make sure that we're all saying the same thing. Now, personally? Yes, I believe there were fourteen victims at Three Rivers. Fourteen people died. Ryan Summers was as much a victim of his own actions as any of the others. *However,* the official line is, we do not use the word "victim" to describe Summers – okay? If they ask how many casualties, we say thirteen students, and Ryan Summers. If they ask how many victims, we say thirteen, and Ryan Summers. We do not simply say *fourteen*. I think it's important that we're seen making the distinction ... from a PR point of view.'

She'd felt her own skin creep, then – most of that speech was an echo of one McLeod had given her, earlier that day, in his office.

Now, Birch tried to stretch. One leg had begun to fade into pins and needles. The Summers profile had several more green and yellow Post-its that she hadn't yet looked at. She could see that the next file on the top of the stack was marked *Moira Summers: death threats analysis* in Marcello's elegant handwriting. At least fifteen bright green Post-its stuck out of that file, too, each one at neat right angles to the sheaf. She glanced at the clock: 7.15 p.m. She put the Ryan Summers file down, and rubbed her eyes with two closed fists, the way that sleepy children do. Then with both arms and the leg that wasn't yet numb, she levered herself up out of her sitting position, and stretched. She opened the office door. This, she'd realised, with a sinking heart, was going to require coffee.

Emergency response

The first 999 call from the scene was placed at around 8.40 a.m. [10] by 23-year-old Access to Nursing student Ella Ostrowska, one of the students pushed into the kitchen and to safety by Kerry McNaughton [16]. Ostrowska told the emergency operator, 'A boy just shot a girl at my college' [10][27]. In the background of the 999 call recording, two gunshots can be heard: it is believed that these are the shots that killed Liz Gill and then Kerry McNaughton [10][15][27][32].

The second 999 call from the scene was placed at 8.44 a.m. [10] by adult literacy tutor Isobel MacNab, who said she had seen 'a student with a gun' and heard noises that she thought were gunshots [24][27]. As Summers began to move about on the building's first floor, numerous other 999 calls were placed as students and staff began to realise what was happening [27]. By this time, several students had also made posts about the incident on Twitter and Facebook [18][19][22].

It is believed that the final shot was fired at or just before 9 a.m. [10]. The first police response unit arrived at the campus at 8.56 a.m., with the first ambulance arriving on the scene at 9.08 a.m. [26]. The police were criticised by some students [13], local families and news outlets [3] [26][28] for failing to respond efficiently to the incident. Although emergency response teams arrived on the scene within thirty minutes of the first shot being fired, it took over forty-five minutes for an armed response team to make its way to the campus [3][26][32].

Police reported that Summers was found wearing black jeans with a homemade belt that provided a concealed holster for his three guns [12][25]. In his jeans pocket investigators also found a spring-loaded stainless-steel <u>butterfly knife</u>, which was not used at the scene [25][28]. Summers fired only eighteen rounds of ammunition in total, and only two of his victims were hit multiple times [21]. Twelve of Summers' victims died from gunshot wounds; one, Leanne Lawrie, died from a head injury [20][21]. A police statement released the day after the incident noted it was 'extremely unlucky' that so many fatalities had resulted from such a small number of shots fired [12].

Two weeks later

Rehan,

Thought I'd do the decent thing and reach out to you first rather than trying to contact the Hodgekisses directly. Attached is the draft text of a story I'm running tomorrow to coincide with Abigail's funeral. I wondered if you could pass it on to them and ask if they would like to give a quote (either of them, but perhaps Ishbel would be particularly interested).

Best,
Grant

View attachment:

[Suggested headline – GL]:
Three Rivers victim Abigail Hodgekiss is laid to rest today as family skeletons come out of the closet
[insert byline, publication date/time –
not to be released until 28 May]

Today family and friends of Abigail Hodgekiss, the beautiful 19-year-old drama student who was first to be mown down in the terrible shooting at Three Rivers College, will gather for her funeral.

Abigail was fatally shot when her psychotic classmate Ryan Andrew Summers charged into the canteen area at the Tweed Campus of Three Rivers College, Edinburgh, on 14 May, armed with three handguns he'd modified himself. He opened fire as students waited for their 9 a.m. classes.

Abigail's remains will be cremated following a small service for close family and friends, to take place at an undisclosed location in the city later today. Her family have said that her ashes will be scattered in 'a place close to Abigail's heart' at a later date.

**Readers' tributes to Abigail Hodgekiss and the victims
of the Three Rivers shooting: read more here**
[insert link – GL]

Though this is undoubtedly a sad day, members of the public are still searching for answers. Many want to know why these young women were so brutally murdered, and what the police – whose investigation seems to have gone quiet – plan to do to restore a general feeling of confidence and safety in the wake of this deplorable crime. We're now two weeks on from this terrible crime that really did shake our entire community to its core. It's about time we were given some answers.

One reason for Abigail's death could perhaps be traced back to Abigail herself, in light of shocking new evidence that the 19-year-old was involved with using and distributing Class B drugs.

In an exclusive interview for this publication, Abigail's boyfriend Jack Egan – himself wounded during the Three Rivers shooting – revealed that the pair had been peddling cannabis and pills to fellow students at the college.

'I'd been doing it on and off since high school,' says Jack. 'Then I met Abi on the first day of college and we started dating. I asked her if she wanted to come in with me and help grow the business.'

**Three Rivers gunshot victim Jack Egan tells all:
read the exclusive interview in full here!**
[insert link – GL]

'Abi wasn't keen at first,' he goes on to say. 'But she could see I was making a bit of money from it. And it turned out we were a good team, a good business team. She'd have done anything for me and I could depend on her.'

In the heartfelt interview, Jack also says he misses Abigail every day. 'She was so innocent and sweet,' he says. 'A real sweetheart. I could tell that she liked me from the first day we met, and I was drawn to her. Some people didn't like us being together, but we were in love, we just fell head over heels for each other. I wake up every day thinking it's all been a bad dream, and then I remember she's dead, my Abi. I miss her so much.'

When asked why he thought Ryan Summers committed this terrible act, Jack speculates, 'He might have been jealous of the two of us, of what we had. That's why he shot both of us. I think he wanted to kill me too, but he failed. He was jealous of people being happy and successful, like me and Abi were. He was always this weird creepy guy that no one talked to.' Was Summers involved in drugs, too? Could his rampage – as many of our followers have speculated – been drug-fuelled? Jack says no. 'He hated it. It was just another thing that pointed to the fact that he didn't belong. Abi and I used to joke that it might do him good, but I can't imagine anyone less likely to get high. I think he was too much of a control freak.'

[GL – space for Hodgekiss family reaction quote and words about it]
**In pictures: thousands of well-wishers leave tributes
outside the homes of Three Rivers shooting victims**
[insert link – GL]

Why would a bright, pretty 19-year-old like Abigail Hodgekiss – a girl with her whole life ahead of her – get into drugs? Jack Egan revealed his theory in the second part of his exclusive tell-all interview, which will be available to read in full in Saturday's paper.

'Abi found out that her dad was having an affair a few years back,' Jack said. 'She'd promised him she'd keep it a secret, but she told me it was eating her up inside.'

These revelations are bound to rock the Hodgekiss family. Questions have already been raised about the state of Ishbel Hodgekiss's mental and physical health, as she has now been photographed several times looking pale and thin and behaving erratically.

Become an online supporter and read Part Two of Jack Egan's explosive tell-all interview before it hits newsstands!
[insert link – GL]

[GL – space for Hodgekiss family reaction quote and words about it OR: The Hodgekiss family were approached for comment but have yet to respond.]

27 May, 9.33 p.m.

When it got to nine o'clock, Birch had just walked out. She'd become so tired that she couldn't walk in a straight line, couldn't do two things at once, couldn't stop yawning. Her desk was disappearing under a pile of paper, but she'd got to the point where all she could do was sift – as if she believed that by arranging and then rearranging everything she might find some magical combination in which all these folders and papers and crime scene photos made logical sense. But nothing made logical sense any more. She was hungry all the time. Her head felt like it was full of cotton wool.

She couldn't remember much about the drive home, but she came to after parking the car in its usual space, and opening the driver's-side door. China Express's smell of starch and hot grease poured into the car like warm water. She forgot all about the box of SOCO paperwork she'd stuffed into the back seat on her way out, having had the vague idea that, in her sleep-deprived state, she might somehow get more work done at home. Instead, Birch grabbed her handbag off the passenger seat, locked up the Mondeo, and followed her nose into the tiny vestibule of the China Express. She ordered tofu and cashews in black bean sauce, with veggie spring rolls and egg fried rice. The elderly woman behind the counter looked at her with sympathy, and Birch realised she'd been avoiding mirrors.

'Long day, hen?'

Under her hairnet, the woman's elaborate silk-white hair quivered in its bun.

'A long fortnight,' Birch replied. Her mouth was watering so much that she wondered if the woman thought she was rabid.

'Some good food will fix you,' the woman was saying. 'You came to the right place.'

Birch sat down on one of the two plastic chairs that had been squeezed into the little space. On the other, someone had left a discarded newspaper, half folded, the red top and 200-point headline face up. MURDER MUM MOIRA WALKS FREE, it read. Birch rolled her eyes and flipped the paper over. On the other side, that photo of Ryan Summers' face. If someone had asked her before the shooting to imagine a stereotypical teenage boy, Summers' was almost exactly the face she'd have pictured.

Somewhere in the depths of her handbag, her phone rang. *Rehan*, the display told her. And, in brackets, *Hodgekiss FLO*.

'Birch,' she said into the phone, too tired for any further greeting.

There was a pause, for just a fraction of a second, on the other end.

'Good evening, er, marm,' Rehan said. 'I hope I'm not disturbing you? It's Rehan. Ibrahiim.'

In the kitchens beyond the vestibule, there was a clatter and a shout. *I'm right in the middle of dinner*, Birch thought.

'Not at all,' she said, 'I'm just on my way home. Can I remind you that you should call me Helen?'

Down the phone, she felt him relax, just a little.

'Sorry – Helen.' His voice was stagey, like he was trying on the informality for size.

Birch felt like her stomach had detached itself and was roaming around inside her, beginning to eat other internal organs. She stretched up like a meerkat and peered over the counter.

'I was phoning,' Rehan was saying, 'to update you on something over here in Trinity.'

'Trinity?'

'The Hodgekiss house. Aidan and Ishbel? Parents of Abigail?'

'Oh.' Birch felt a sting of anger. She knew the Hodgekisses' names, and whose parents they were. She was just tired. 'Yes, I know. When you said Trinity I thought you meant the station there. The police station. Except there isn't one. And now I'm waffling. Do go on.'

There was another pause on the line. *Great,* she thought. *He believes I'm a lunatic.*

'Something's happened,' he said, slowly. 'I thought I ought to let you know.'

What, let me know what? There was a thread of worry in his voice, she could hear it now, and it was catching. All thoughts of her takeaway evaporated.

'So,' he was saying. 'You already know that tomorrow is Abigail's cremation. But . . . something's going to happen tomorrow morning that I think is going to cause a real problem.'

Birch's mind was racing. *Spit it out,* she thought.

'*What*'s going to happen?' It was snappy, but he was going too slowly.

'Grant Lockley,' he said. 'He's running a piece about Abigail – and about Aidan. It's pretty bad.'

Birch closed her eyes, but under the China Express's strip-lighting, she could see the inside of her eyelids, swimmy and red. *Lockley.* Popping up once again to bother at her emotions. She was trying not to *have* emotions right now. She didn't want to be thinking about her brother all the time. *My baby brother:* the thought occurred in a bitter-sounding version of her own voice.

'Jesus,' she said. 'How bad are we talking?'

'He makes two pretty big claims,' Rehan replied. 'First, that Abigail was mixed up with drugs, and second, that Aidan has, at some point, had an affair. And still is . . .'

Birch curled her free hand into a fist.

'Yeah, that sounds like classic Grant Lockley,' she said. 'Hire a PI, dig up shit on people, and spread it as far as you can.'

There was a pause on the other end of the line.

'Hire a PI?'

Birch glanced over at the takeaway counter, but could see no one.

'I've had some personal experience of this,' she said, lowering her voice. 'Lockley had his claws in my family for a while, too.'

She looked down again at the newspaper, its grainy photo of Ryan Summers. She remembered a particular photo of Charlie that Lockley had repeatedly run under his byline: her smiling brother with his arms round his uni halls flatmates. Lockley's picture editor had cropped it so the two other men were just flanking shoulders and arms. Without the wider context of the rest of the photo, Charlie looked drunk, propped up, unstable. The memory stirred an old anger in Birch that she knew she had to tamp down fast, or it might spread, engulfing everything. She remembered Rehan, breathing quietly at the other end of the phone.

'But that's old news,' she added, a little too quickly. 'More than ten years ago.'

Rehan was quiet. Birch wondered if he was reading something, or watching TV – somehow distracted.

'He didn't use a PI,' he said, finally. 'This is all coming from Jack Egan.'

'The boy who lived?' Birch knew she shouldn't be joining in with this not-even-a-funny-joke name that her colleagues had started using, but she was too tired to stop herself.

'Yeah. It looks like he sold his story to Lockley.'

Birch let out a long sigh. Clearly Lockley had more cash at his disposal these days.

'Okay, two questions,' she said. 'One, have you seen the text of this piece?'

'Yes,' Rehan said. 'He sent it to me so he could get a comment. Called it *doing the decent thing*, if you can believe it.'

Birch took a moment to count to ten. *Do not say something unprofessional over the phone, Helen.*

'Yeah, he's a real role model for positive values,' she managed. She remembered Lockley's catchphrase – *I'm just doing my job* – and passed a hand across her weary eyes. 'Second question: have the Hodgekisses seen the piece?'

Another pause: this time it was longer.

'Aidan has.'

'You showed it to him?' Birch was trying to calculate the

potential fall-out of all this, but, in her tired and hungry state, was largely failing. 'Lockley didn't send it to him direct?'

'No,' Rehan said. 'I showed it to him. I wanted to see if the claims about him were true, so we could decide what to do about them.'

Birch closed her eyes.

'And they are, aren't they?'

Rehan's reply was almost a whisper, but Birch caught it.

'I'm afraid so.'

For a while, there was silence. Birch imagined Rehan trying to do the same mental arithmetic as her – hopefully, he was doing a little better.

'I don't know what to do about Ishbel,' he said eventually. 'She's . . . very fragile.'

Somewhere near Birch's head, a brown paper bag landed on the counter with a thud. Steam trailed out of it in a graceful arc.

'Black bean tofu, spring rolls.' The old woman spoke quietly, and Birch threw her a grateful smile.

'Okay, Rehan,' she said into the phone. 'I'm afraid you're going to have to tell her, and you're going to have to do it tonight. I know Grant Lockley, and I know he'll publish this article with or without a Hodgekiss quote – and it should be without one, I assume you know that.'

'Yes. Aidan's already agreed we won't comment.'

'Okay. So it's coming out tomorrow, whether we like it or not. He's an absolute scumbag for doing this on the same day as Abigail's cremation, but then – well, he's an absolute scumbag. He's timed it that way deliberately for maximum clickbait. And trust me, once the rest of the press get hold of this, it'll be the bandwagon they all want to leap on. You can't let Ishbel find out that way. You have to forewarn her as well as you possibly can.'

'I'll do my best.' His voice was small, far-off sounding.

'I'm so sorry, Rehan.' Birch stood up, and lifted the warm weight of her takeaway bag by its gummy paper handles. 'I've been waiting for the other shoe to drop with Lockley, but I was assuming his real bombshell would be about the Summers family.'

On the other end, she thought she heard Rehan sigh.

'I wouldn't be surprised,' he said, 'if that's what he's lined up next. Because ... there's something else, though it hasn't come from Lockley. Something else about Aidan Hodgekiss.'

Birch clicked along the promenade quickly. *Fucking Grant Lockley.* She decided, for about the thousandth time that fortnight, that she hated journalists – him in particular, of course, but all of them. She'd been watching the news constantly, keeping an eye on the media's – and by extension, the public's – perception of her investigation. When such a senseless thing happens, everyone wants to see a bad guy in the dock, wants someone to blame. Order restored, some measure of justice done. But what happens when the bad guy neatly takes himself out of the equation? *Grant Lockley*, she thought. *Grant Lockley happens. He inserts himself into the vacuum, and instigates a trial by Twitter for anyone unlucky enough to be involved.* For all she knew, Birch realised, she herself might be next.

Tired and hungry as she was, it was tempting to linger outside her front gate. A haar had been hanging over the city all day: it was pouring off the sea, smudging the white orbs of the streetlights, blurring the edges off everything. At this hour, it was quiet, but two late-night dog-walkers were still out on the sand in the dark, the beams of their torches zipping back and forth in the foggy air. Birch took her takeaway bag in both arms and pressed it to her chest to warm herself against the wet chill of the mist, and the bag's steam twirled around her. It smelled too good for her to stand there more than a few seconds. She dug her keys from her handbag and slammed into the house.

She didn't usually sit in the living room – it was still full of unpacked boxes, tat of the old man's that she'd hauled down from the loft and not yet taken to the charity shop. But the living room was where the TV was, so she cleared a space on the dust-sheeted couch and hunted among the debris until she found the remote. The newsreader had just begun speaking. Birch unwrapped her chopsticks and began to scoop fried rice – which tasted miraculous after a day of police station canteen food and coffee – into her mouth.

'Tomorrow,' the newsreader said, 'Three Rivers shooting victim Abigail Hodgekiss will be laid to rest, at a private cremation service in an undisclosed location in Edinburgh.'

Abigail's portrait appeared on the screen: the coral sweater, the matchy-matchy lipstick. Birch had seen that photo so many times now, it felt etched on her memory.

'Abigail's funeral will be the first of the Three Rivers victims',' the newsreader was saying. 'But it is believed that more will follow in the next few days, as each set of remains is released back to the victim's loved ones. Police Scotland have issued an apology for the delay, but questions are already being raised about their investigation into the shooting two weeks ago.'

Birch tried not to cringe.

'We're doing the best we can, you bastards,' she hissed.

'Plans are under way,' the newsreader said, 'for a public memorial service to honour the memory of the thirteen young women who died at the hand of gunman Ryan Summers.' On cue, the screen cut to Summers' scowling face.

'The service,' the newsreader went on, 'is likely to be televised, and the First Minister has already confirmed her attendance.'

Birch rolled her eyes. *Great. So we'll have to drop everything and trail around after* her *all day – and that'll be wrong, too.*

'We just can't win, can we?' Birch asked the TV. But the newsreader had disappeared, and the now-familiar slideshow of victims' photos was being flicked through once again. *Christ only knows what they'll be saying tomorrow*, she thought. Grant Lockley's face materialised in her mind.

'Fucking arsehole,' she said.

After what felt like a long time, the newsreader finally uttered the words, 'in other news,' and Birch allowed herself to relax. She flipped the TV off, crunched through her last spring roll, and thought about the other thing Rehan had told her.

'It's not much more than a hunch at this point,' he'd said, 'but . . . those death threats that were sent to Moira Summers?'

'They're *still* being sent,' Birch had replied. Once people got their hooks in someone, they really didn't let up – especially with the press practically cheerleading for them.

'Okay. Well, I have reason to believe that at least one of those threats might have – and as I say, it's only a *might have* right now – been sent by Aidan Hodgekiss.'

Birch had needed to stop walking, and close her eyes for a moment to take stock of this. *That would make sense,* she told herself, thinking of Marcello's analysis report. *Yes. It would explain a few things.*

But it would also be utterly terrible.

'Rehan.' Birch had stood rod-straight in the hazy yellow cloud under a streetlight. 'You're saying *might have . . .*'

On the other end of the line, Rehan had cleared his throat.

'Look, I know,' he said. 'I know it seems completely insane. I know it would basically lob a huge grenade into this investigation, and if you think I want this shit to deal with on my first FLO gig then you'd be dead wrong . . .'

Birch had blinked in surprise, but didn't check his tone. Foreboding was swirling inside her like the fog falling in curtains across the promenade. That frayed edge she could hear in his voice was more convincing right now than any evidence he could have produced. *He* believed Aidan Hodgekiss had done this thing, and that, really, was what she was asking.

'It's okay, Reh,' she said, and though she'd felt a little silly using the shortened name she'd heard around the station, it did quiet him. 'You're not on your own with this.'

No, Helen, she thought, *but that doesn't help much, does it? Shit.*

After a moment, Rehan spoke again.

'I think I've built up a pretty good rapport,' he said. 'He seems to trust me. He's letting his guard down a little. And it's just . . . there've just been a couple of things he's let slip, you know?'

Birch had tried to relax her shoulders at this, tried to exhale. There was a knot in her chest. *That's nothing,* she tried to convince herself. *A couple of things? This could yet turn out to all be nothing.*

'A couple of things like *what?*'

On the other end of the line she could hear Rehan shifting, thinking – choosing his words.

'Okay . . . I'm worried this is going to sound nuts when I say it aloud.'

Birch had gritted her teeth, and remembered Marcello making his *cut to the chase* comment to her a few days ago. Rehan needed to learn how to *just say a thing.*

'Try me,' she said, keeping her tone even.

'Well . . . Aidan is keeping strange hours – he's routinely not there when I go round, and doesn't answer his phone. Which is fine, I guess . . . but he also has a bad case of Moira Summers mentionitis.'

In spite of herself, Birch had smiled at her colleague, a grown man, using a term she'd only heard teenage girls use up until now.

'I understand he's angry,' he was saying, 'but he mentions her just a little more often than really seems normal. Whatever normal *is* under these circumstances. And when I say he's angry, I mean . . . he seems really angry. He talks about her, and at times there's real rage. And – yeah, this *does* sound nuts when I say it aloud, but . . . it's like he's conflicted. It's like he's trying to swallow how angry he is, but also *show* me it, at the same time.'

Birch said nothing for a moment. She was nodding again, as though Rehan could see her.

'I know this isn't *evidence* . . .' Rehan spoke into her silence, his tone defensive, as if he'd assumed her not talking was a sign of disdain. 'But I just have this awful nagging feeling, you know? Something's just *off* with him.'

Birch struggled to mobilise words. In the pause, Rehan said, 'I'm sorry I don't have anything more for you right now. But it's not nothing. It's not in my head.'

'No, I know – you're doing well,' she'd said to Rehan. Her stomach felt as though a rock had settled in it: that *something's off* feeling he described was catching. 'Just keep at it for now, please. And come back to me when it's more than just a hunch.'

Birch shivered. It was getting chilly in the living room, and she needed to start thinking about bed. She began to stack the empty takeaway cartons one inside the other. On top of the still-parcel-taped box she'd been using as a coffee table, her phone buzzed. *Amy Kato*, the lit screen informed her. Birch hesitated, but then whispered a curse, and picked up.

'Hey, Amy,' she said. 'Everything okay?'

'He*llo*,' Amy said, her usual cheeriness apparently undimmed by the late hour. 'Yes, everything's fine. I was just looking for you, and you're nowhere to be seen.'

Birch blinked.

'You're still at the station?'

She could practically hear Amy's mouth fall open.

'You're not? Oh God, Helen, I'm sorry. Are you at home? I'm so sorry, I'll go—'

'No, don't. It's fine. You're where I *ought* to be. I just couldn't hack it any more. I got to the point where I'd read the same interview transcript five times and I still couldn't remember who was being interviewed. I had to ditch out. You're a better woman than me.'

Amy laughed.

'Not really,' she said. 'I've been in the canteen for the last hour, mainlining coffee and trying to work myself up to ... well, anything.'

'Get yourself home,' Birch said. 'I'm not sure *that* coffee should be ingested in large quantities, and I need you alive.'

Something about the joke landed awkwardly, and they were both silent for a moment.

'I did want to have a quick chat with you, though,' Amy said. 'I mean, since you're on the line. It'll only take a minute.'

Birch dabbed her napkin at a spot of soy sauce that had dropped onto her thigh.

'Sure.'

'I just – I'm a bit worried about Moira. I'm probably being silly, I think, but – I could just do with a bit of reassurance.'

'It's okay, Amy. None of us has done this before.'

Amy sighed.

'I know. I just wonder . . . I felt like she was largely fine while she was here at the station. Someone was almost always with her – me, or you, or Anjan, you know? But now she's on her own in that house. And the SOCOs really did a number on the place. I had a look around and Ryan's room is totally trashed. I told her not to go in there for now, but I'm pretty sure it's the first thing she does every time I walk out that door.'

Birch shrugged, as though Amy was in the room with her, and then felt stupid.

'She's mourning the loss of her only son,' she said. 'I think some erratic behaviour is to be expected. You're doing all the right things.'

'Okay,' Amy said. 'But what I want to know is, is she *safe*? Am I doing all I can to keep her safe? To protect her? I don't think I am.'

Now Birch was glad she and Amy weren't in the same room. In her sleep-deprived state, she felt a powerful urge to give the younger woman a hug.

'Amy,' she said. 'You're not on your own here. I mean, you're right to be worried about the scale of the public's . . . *response,* for want of a better word, towards Moira. I've seen some of those threats, and they're pretty damn credible.' Birch's mind flitted back to Aidan Hodgekiss – the press conference he'd held in the front garden, his grieving-father demeanour just a little . . . what? Practised, almost.

'But . . .' She forced herself to tune back in to Amy. 'That's why we have scene guards at the door. That's why she has a panic button. And apart from anything else, there are about fifty paparazzi outside her house right now if the ten o'clock news is to be believed. For all that they're a nuisance, they're part of her security team, too. No one's going to get to her in that house, I promise. She's in less danger there than she would be in a police safe house, in my humble opinion.'

Amy stifled an exasperated noise, but Birch heard it.

'But I don't *mean* she's in danger from other people. I'm worried she might be a danger to herself.'

Birch said nothing. She was getting so tired that thoughts were taking a long time to form themselves fully. The words *suicide watch* moved through her brain, and she wondered how something like that worked with a person who was guilty of nothing, but who was essentially under house arrest.

'I keep wondering,' Amy was saying, 'should I be there? You know, at the house. More – permanently.'

'If you're asking to move in with her,' Birch said, 'the answer is *that's not your job.* To be totally frank, if Moira Summers is planning to try and kill herself, what makes you think that you sleeping in her spare room for a few nights would make any difference?'

The line was quiet. *You're being cruel,* Birch thought. *You're not thinking straight.*

'I know,' Amy said. 'You're saying things I've already said to myself. You're right. But I do think we need to get her some more support. I know she's not a victim, but – well, she kind of *is*, you know?'

'I do know,' Birch said. 'This sort of crime . . . a crime with no bad guy? Victims are all there is.'

Birch looked up then. The house around her was dark – she hadn't switched the lights on, and without the glow of the TV, the room was lit dim and ghostly by the streetlight on the promenade outside. On the wall opposite the shrouded sofa, the old mantelpiece was visible above the hearth, with its jumbled stack of boxes. The only thing sitting on it was a photo of Birch's mother, its silver-plated frame caught in what little light there was. The photo itself was invisible, a dark square – but Birch could see that photo's wan face in detail if she closed her eyes.

'Victims are all there is,' she said again, more quietly this time.

'You're tired,' Amy said. 'I'm sorry I bothered you at home. I'll let you get some sleep. I need to get out of here myself.'

'You do,' Birch said, trying to inject a smile into her voice. 'I'll be in early tomorrow, and we'll talk more. We'll make a plan for Moira, and then you can go and see her and get her feedback. How does that sound?'

'Good,' Amy said, after a moment's pause. 'That sounds good. Thanks, Helen.'

Birch nodded, her eyes closed. Her mother's pale face still hung, spectreish, behind her eyelids.

'Oh,' Amy said. 'Sorry – before I go, I should tell you. I've been getting a load of missed calls from that Grant Lockley guy.'

Him again. Birch heaved out a sigh.

'I know,' she said. 'Will we never be free?'

'I've been ignoring him,' Amy said, 'but – he was calling about ten times a day. I'd just got used to hanging up, you know? And then all of a sudden, the calls stopped.'

'When?'

'Two days ago,' Amy said. 'Absolutely nothing for two days.'

'Well, lucky you.'

'No.' Amy's voice was once again creased with worry. 'I don't believe it's luck. I don't think a guy like that just gives up because you ignore him.'

Birch glanced up again at her mother's picture.

'No, you're right,' she said. 'He doesn't.'

'So something's going on, then,' Amy said. 'He'd only stop if he'd got whatever it was he wanted, right? I'm worried it means he's got something on Moira, and he's getting ready to publish it.'

Birch hesitated.

'Or,' she said eventually, 'it means he's moved on to a new target.' She thought of Ishbel Hodgekiss, the conversation she must be having with Rehan right now.

'Like who?'

Birch closed her eyes again. Her tiredness felt like deep, warm water, and she was beginning to give in to its undertow.

'You'll find out tomorrow,' she said.

Amy made a little sound on the other end, but then obviously decided not to push.

'It's just . . . I think you were right,' Amy said. 'What you were saying a couple of weeks ago, when we were interviewing her. There *is* something Moira's not telling us. I'm trying to get to the bottom of it, but . . . what if Lockley got there before me?'

Amy was right. There *was* something about Moira Summers' testimony that just wasn't quite right, it had been bothering her too: spattering in the background like a fly against glass. Moira had seemed genuine enough: her grief and shock were real. Birch was sure she hadn't known her son was going to die. She probably hadn't known he was going to go on a murder spree, either – surely, *surely*. But what she might know was *why*. Why her son might hate women enough to remove thirteen of them from this world. What spark might have lit the touchpaper of his anger and allowed it to detonate that day in the Three Rivers refectory. If Moira Summers did know, she seemed intent on silence.

'If he has,' Birch said, too tired to verbalise those thoughts to Amy, 'there'd probably be nothing we could do about it.'

There was a long silence on the line. Birch heard Amy yawn, though she was obviously trying to do it quietly.

'You think he ever, like . . . goes home?'

Birch blinked – her eyelids had begun to flutter.

'Who?'

'That Lockley guy,' Amy said. 'He left me a voicemail at midnight the other night. I mean, don't these people have *lives*?'

Birch thought for a moment. She'd asked that question herself, before, but only ever in the abstract, as a sort of sideways insult. She supposed she'd always thought about Lockley and his ilk – those particularly persistent tabloid columnists who saw provocation as part of their 'personal brand' – as not quite human, not really fully part of society. She realised she'd never thought about whether Lockley went home at night to a wife and kids, or a boyfriend, for that matter, or an adorable collection of cats. Although her tired brain wouldn't allow her to imagine it, she guessed he *did* go home to something. Everyone had something they cared about, didn't they? Even people like him. But having to consider Lockley as a fully rounded person irritated her – she couldn't dwell on it.

'Hey,' she said, forcing brightness into her voice. 'We ought to go and grab a beer sometime. After work. After things quieten down a bit, obviously. Thanks to Ryan Summers, I've rather missed out on the whole get-to-know-your-new-colleagues thing.'

Amy laughed a small laugh – as much to rally herself as anything, Birch could tell.

'That sounds great,' she said, then added, '*guv*.'

Again, Birch felt an upsurge of good, sisterly feeling towards this woman.

'Listen, you call me any time,' she said. 'Okay? With a case like this, there's no such thing as home time. Not for me, anyway. You need me? You phone. Got it?'

'Thanks, Helen.'

Amy hung up. Against her own better judgement, Birch kicked the takeaway boxes and half-unpacked clutter off the sofa, swung her feet up onto the dust-sheets, and lay down.

28 May, 8.45 a.m.

Ishbel had been staring at Abigail's prom dress for about fifteen minutes. It was hanging on the front of the wardrobe in Abigail's bedroom, its watermark-patterned taffeta distorted through its clear plastic dry-cleaning bag. She was trying to conjure the memory of going to buy it – she and Abigail spending a giggly afternoon in the dress shop's plush fitting room, coming home with the dress in one of the shop's shiny, rope-handed totes. Did they go out for dinner afterwards, maybe? Did they buy the shoes that day, too, or some other time? Ishbel felt like she was digging through sticky tar, trying desperately to dredge up the memory. But all she could remember was that night, two weeks ago, when she and Abigail had argued in the car. Her daughter's last words to her: 'Mother, you're on fucking crack.'

At the time, Ishbel had balked at the way she'd been spoken to. But the retort was also a drugs reference. Ishbel closed her eyes and tried – as she had several times since Grant Lockley's revelations – to imagine her daughter taking drugs. Carrying drugs; taking money for them in risky, unwholesome exchanges. She tried to imagine Abigail high: messy and throwing up. The images refused to be summoned. She couldn't believe it – *wouldn't* believe it. The realisation of Aidan's infidelity had hit her like a train she'd already heard coming: there was shock, and pain, but there was no surprise. *I should have known*, she thought. But Abigail? *No*. It simply couldn't be true.

Ishbel had smoothed out some space on the still-unmade bed, and placed a holdall there. Then, as calmly as she could, she'd packed as many of her daughter's things as the bag would fit. She'd found the coral sweater in the wardrobe, drooping lopsided on its hanger. Without any real idea why, Ishbel had unhooked it, folded it into a fat square, and placed it into the holdall. Then she'd rifled through the rest of the wardrobe. She found Abigail's old school tie – navy with diagonal white stripes – and, having stood for a moment with it coiled loosely around her hand, Ishbel had folded that too, and placed it on top of the sweater.

Hanging on the back of the wardrobe door was Abigail's satin dressing gown. It was powder blue with a pattern of tiny pink and red flowers. When Abigail had bought it, Ishbel had frowned at how adult it was – how like *lingerie* it seemed. But now she balled up the slippery fabric and added that, too, to the bag.

It became systematic. Ishbel had looked through every drawer. She'd found Abigail's jewellery box and winkled a few things out, and dropped them into her own cardigan pocket. She'd pulled out the under-bed boxes, held their sheets and towels up to her face – though of course they were clean, and smelled only of lavender fabric softener. Shaking out one towel, Ishbel had heard a thud, and looked down to find a thick book lying at her feet. When she picked it up it felt surprisingly weighty. The cover was bouncy padded leather in baby pink, and the covers were clasped tightly together by a brass catch, a tiny padlock dangling from it. Ishbel hadn't even hesitated before pressing on the little unlocking mechanism, but no luck. Locked. She'd packed it into the holdall anyway.

The prom dress wouldn't fit in the bag – not with everything else already packed – she knew that. But it felt suddenly important. She'd found it crushed into the back of the wardrobe, and had cried as she peeled it out into the open air, the dry-cleaning bag making slippery creaks. She was still crying now.

Her first realisation upon stepping into Abigail's room had been that she, Ishbel, hadn't set foot in there in weeks. It was a mess of spilled laundry and unmade bedclothes. Her second realisation was that there must be some mistake – her daughter could not possibly be dead, not with this room the same as it always was. The scent of spiced cake hung in the air. Abigail loved scented candles, and bought a particular brand that came in thick glass jars. But underneath was the smell of *Abigail herself*: the hair and skin and human girl of her. Ishbel's third realisation was that yes, it was true, her daughter was dead. The room was cold and quiet and no one was going to live here ever again.

Crying was what Ishbel did now – her default setting. She was getting used to seeing everything through a thick veil of tears: the world blurred and dragging. The only moment of not-crying she'd had in two weeks had come the previous night, when Rehan and Aidan had cornered her in the kitchen, and Aidan wordlessly handed her a crumpled print-out of the journalist's article.

'This is disgusting,' she'd said, tears pulling their tracks over her face's dusty skin. 'How does he sleep at night, this man? How does someone even come *up* with these lies?'

She'd watched Rehan and Aidan exchange looks. For a while, the kitchen echoed with her quiet sobs.

'I'm afraid,' Aidan said at last, 'he isn't lying. I know this is the worst time for you to find out about this, Bel, and I never would have said anything . . .'

Ishbel had looked back down at the print-out, now dappled with the tiny, damp circles of her tears, her fingerprints.

'Which part,' she said, 'is true, Aidan?'

'The affair.' Rehan had said it, as it seemed Aidan could not.

'That's not how I'd categorise it—' Aidan said, but Ishbel had cut him off.

'With who?'

That was when the tears had stopped – then, in that long yawn of silence while she waited for him to speak.

'Netta,' he said, quietly.

Ishbel had cast around for the name, realised he meant Annetta, one of the dental nurses at his practice.

'*Netta*,' she repeated. 'But she's – what, twenty-five?'

Aidan's face was pale. Ishbel's vision had suddenly become clear and sharp enough to see the fine stubble that misted his jaw: more grey in it than she remembered.

'Twenty-eight,' he said.

There had been an empty wine bottle on the counter, Ishbel remembered that. She remembered wondering, in that moment, how it had got there – who had drunk the wine? She made a mental note to put it into the recycling box in the hall. Then she had reached for it, and then—

There was a noise in the garden below that shook her back to the present. Rehan was outside, wrangling the crowd of paparazzi away from the street, so the funeral cars could pull up. In front of Ishbel, the prom dress swam back into focus. *I could wear it*, Ishbel thought. *To the cremation.* She glanced down at the black pencil skirt and jacket she was already wearing, then back up at the deep turquoise fabric of the dress. She reached out for the zip of the dry-cleaning bag, and her fingertips registered the strange dry-wet feeling of the plastic. She slipped the dress off its chunky hanger and rustled it out of the bag's opening, leaving the bag hanging on the wardrobe like some emptied chrysalis, mildly obscene-looking. She pinned the dress against her own body with one forearm. She'd hoped it would smell like Abigail, but it didn't – it smelled like the plastic of the bag, like the cedar balls dropped in the bottom to keep away moths. With her free hand she scrabbled at the side of the bodice for the zip.

'Bel?'

Aidan was standing in the doorway. Ishbel spun to face him, and as she did, the wide taffeta skirt swung out. *Give us a twirl*, she remembered him saying, Abigail standing in front of him, breathless, waiting for the prom limousine to arrive.

'Bel, what are you doing?' he said.

'I was thinking about wearing this.' She had no energy in her to make up a lie. 'To the cremation.'

She watched Aidan look her up and down. There was a bruise on his left cheekbone, purpling like a stormcloud under his eye. A cut oozing in the bruise's centre. She remembered last night – remembered putting it there – and her face flushed.

'Bel,' he said, quietly, 'you have to keep it together, okay? Just for today. Just for this *morning*.'

He put out one hand, palm down, as though she were a skittish dog he wanted to pet.

'Just keep it together for a few hours, and then we can talk.'

He began to advance across the bedroom towards her, and her hand reached out for the holdall, as though it were some protective talisman. The prom dress fell to the floor in one ragged movement, its fabric shushing down around Ishbel's feet.

'I won't talk,' she said. She swung the holdall, heavy now, around in front of her, dangling it in the air between them. 'Not to you.'

Aidan reached down and hooked the prom dress up in one hand. He rolled it into a fat, crumpled bandage around one arm – his idea of how to fold a thing. A noise leaked out of Ishbel like she'd been squeezed.

'Come on, Bel,' he said. 'We can move past this.'

'Hang that up,' she instructed. 'In its bag, like it's supposed to be.'

She gestured at the empty bag, still hanging like a spectre on the wardrobe's front.

'And no,' she added, after a moment. 'We can't.'

Aidan looked back up at her, the dress half wrestled into its plastic.

'Move past it. We can't. I can't.' Ishbel brandished the holdall. 'I'm going to the cremation, and then I'm moving out. I'm taking the car – I'm not getting in one of those hearse cars, not with you. I don't want to breathe the same air as you ever again.'

Her pulse stuttered in her ears, loud and irregular. The thought *this is right* came to her: *this is what you should be doing. You should have split up long ago – why didn't you?* Was it her daughter's voice she was hearing? No, surely not. Abigail was the very reason she and Aidan had lasted as long as they had – wasn't she? And if she wasn't, then why *had* they kept this charade going for so long? Hadn't she, Ishbel, known there was something going on with Aidan lately – something sinister that had invaded their marriage, a pin-thin beam of light she didn't want to look directly at? She heard Abigail's words again: *Mother, you're on fucking crack –* meaning, you're crazy, you're delusional. *Perhaps I have been those things*, Ishbel thought. But then her scattergun anger coughed into life again. How could Aidan have done this? How could those have been the last words Abigail had spoken to her own mother? It was as if those words had started a chain reaction: from that moment, everything in Ishbel's world had begun to fall apart. She half expected, as she walked out of the room – leaving Aidan standing open-mouthed with his hands full of taffeta – that the floor beneath her feet would split, and she'd be pulled down through the falling wreckage of that house, down through the air, and into the earth.

The crematorium was a low, flat slab of a building, made from breezeblocks, and surrounded by a breezeblock wall that could be seen between the surrounding trees in any direction. The wall was high, and topped with barbed wire in places. As she drove in, Ishbel thought about prison, about the sort of place Ryan Summers might have been put if he hadn't killed himself, the sort of punishment he might have been given. It shocked her, his sudden presence in her thoughts – she realised she hadn't really thought of him all that much since Abigail died. What had she been thinking of, all this time? She found she didn't really know. She'd mainly been crying, and recalling old memories of Abigail, playing them again and again, like a worn-out old VHS tape.

'You've been so busy crying and rending your garments,' Aidan had said to her – shouted at her – the night before, 'that you haven't done anything *useful* in two whole weeks! What about me? What about supporting me? What about supporting *each other*? You should be *glad* I had someone to turn to.'

You should be glad I've been keeping a mistress. That was when she'd flown at him, fists first. Rehan had peeled her away.

She stood in the crematorium car park for a while. Because she'd come in her own car, she was there first, not obliged to travel at the plodding speed of the funeral cars. At one end of the car park there was a huge skip, filled to the top with flowers. White lilies with petals browned, spilling their dark red pollen into the air; frilly roses whose blooms were too far out now, showing their frayed yellow stamens.

With a jolt, Ishbel realised that only days ago, families had agonised over these flowers. She imagined the careful conversations in florists' shops: *He always loved pink roses.We must have lilies; it's tradition.* Now each floral fetish was rotting in a rusted blue skip. Ishbel had chosen no flowers – this service was the cremation only, brought on by the sudden release of Abigail's remains. There'd be a nice memorial service later, Aidan had promised her – when the press lost interest and there didn't need to be a police escort, or any of that. They'd scatter the ashes and have flowers and songs and everyone could come. Today it would just be Aidan, Aidan's mother Pauline, and a few other people – she couldn't remember who. Aidan had said their names to her and she had nodded without really hearing. She'd been crying at the time. She put a hand to her face and found that sure enough, she was crying now, too. The skin felt like it had been pulled off and stitched back on wrong – surely this wan, wet thing was not her own?

It began to rain, and Ishbel went inside. There were pews, like in a real church, and off to one side there was a raised wooden platform with mechanical rollers embedded into its top. A cheap velvet curtain hung beside it: this was where the coffin would sit. Ishbel took the seat nearest that platform, at the extreme front left of the chapel space. She wanted to be able to reach up, if she had to, and put her hand against the coffin's varnished side.

She sat for a while, wondering if she ought to try and pray – but no, she thought. *Nothing lives here.* The jewelled cross on the altar was made of plastic, she could see that from fifteen feet away. The space smelled like Febreze and radiator singe. Whatever god there might be, it didn't live here. Abigail wouldn't be bundled up out of the flames, and taken to some better realm – not from this place. Here, she was just dead. Ishbel chugged up thick, ugly sobs.

People began to shuffle in. Pauline came first, sat down next to Ishbel, and took her hand.

'Aidan told me everything, hen,' she said. Ishbel looked down at her mother-in-law's hand: grey, and roped with veins. 'I'm so sorry. You poor lass. And that reporter, how it's all come out today – that man should be locked up, the things he's writing.'

Pauline was looking earnestly into Ishbel's face – seeing, Ishbel presumed, how pale it was, the blueish puffed skin around the eyes. Seeing the unwashed, unbrushed hair, the unironed jacket dragged from the back of the wardrobe. Ishbel could think of nothing to say, so she turned her head to look back up the chapel's aisle at the handful of people who'd gathered.

The first person she saw was Greg – he'd placed himself in an empty pew about halfway back, as though he'd ranked himself in order of importance. As though lots more people might arrive, who'd need to be seated closer to the front. He raised a hand in greeting and smiled a serious kind of smile. Ishbel felt surprise open in her like a bloom, and realised no one had smiled at her in two whole weeks. For some reason, she found herself thinking of Greg's late wife, Lisa, and imagining their life together, from the first time Lisa saw that smile to the last, at the end of her long illness. Ishbel shook herself, summoned a watery, mechanical smile back, and then let her eyes move on. But now she was remembering that day a fortnight ago, Greg leading her down one hospital corridor, then another, the whole building ringing with shouts and footsteps. Into a little room they went, a little room with sofas and scatter cushions and a box of tissues – a room intended to be cosy, but everything was still stripped and clinical somehow. In that room he told her, *Abigail is dead. She died at the scene. There was nothing anyone could do.* And Ishbel remembered thinking, *Why are you telling me this? What about* my *daughter?* And Greg had taken hold of her by the shoulders and said, *Ishbel, sweetheart, do you understand what I am telling you?* Ishbel frowned. How long had it been since Lisa had died? How long since she'd even thought of her? *I'll ask Aidan later,* she thought, *what year it was.* But then she realised that no, she wouldn't. Thinking of Aidan felt like stepping into deep shade, a place the sun never touched.

A few pews in front of Greg were a trio of staff members from Three Rivers College – Ishbel recognised the college principal, having seen her speaking on TV news. There were also some young women – five or six, sitting together, talking quietly. A few of them Ishbel recognised, though she couldn't dredge up their names. Friends of Abigail's. From college, or from the football club. *I ought to remember them*, Ishbel thought, but she couldn't.

Near to the girls sat a few people Ishbel also vaguely knew from somewhere, but couldn't initially place. She allowed herself to stare, eyebrows knitted, until she realised – it was the Kesson family. They'd been at the gathering that night at Fettes police station. Their daughter was Evie Kesson, another of the girls killed. Ishbel realised she ought to feel grateful to them for coming, but instead she felt a twang of anxiety. When was *their* daughter's funeral? Had she missed it? If not, would she be required to go to it, now? She turned her face away.

Rehan had seated himself in the pew behind Ishbel, over at the opposite end, nearest the aisle. He looked tired, she thought, and for the first time, she wondered about his life. Did he have children at home? What was he missing, working these long hours, babying her and Aidan through their grief?

Pauline was also looking backwards, and she gave Ishbel's hand a hard squeeze.

'Here she is,' she whispered.

The coffin was being carried into the chapel, led by a man in a plain black and white church robe. The doors had been propped open and Ishbel could hear the rain outside, spattering down now onto the flat perspex roof that the hearse was parked under. She turned away, not wanting to see the expensive box as it plodded aloft up the aisle. But all too soon it arrived at the front of the chapel, and she was forced to look. Two undertakers carried the coffin's front end: one of them was a woman around Ishbel's age, her salt-and-pepper hair pulled into a tight, streaked bun. At the back corner nearest Ishbel, Aidan stooped his large frame to keep the coffin level. He seemed to be shuddering; the single small flower wreath, provided by the undertakers, shivered on the coffin's lid. Ishbel realised he was crying, and beside her, Pauline was crying too. She felt a spike of anger that she couldn't explain. Aidan was almost within touching distance, the bruise on his cheek as damning as a Grant Lockley headline.

The robed man – *vicar? Minister?* Aidan had told her, but she couldn't remember – stopped at one corner of the altar with its tacky plastic cross, and turned to face the room. The coffin bearers manoeuvred the box onto the platform, and stood back. *It's so small,* Ishbel thought. *Surely she can't actually be in there.* For the first time, Ishbel could clearly see the fourth person who'd steadied her daughter's body down the aisle. Without thinking, she rose to her feet: one long, involuntary movement.

'*You.*'

Her voice was loud in the chapel's emptiness. She was dimly aware that everyone was looking at her, then at the man in front of her, then back, like a crowd at a tennis game, collective breath held, waiting for the mistake.

'How *dare* you come here?'

Ishbel felt Pauline stand up, and put a hand on her arm. Aidan had raised his hands, and now dragged them down his damp, haggard face and said, 'Bel.'

'What is he doing here, Aidan? What is this . . .'

The young man stepped forward, closing the gap between them to a foot. Ishbel blinked. He was tall – almost as tall as Aidan – slim, with dark curly hair that had been recently cut, and trendy glasses with tortoiseshell frames. He held out a hand.

'Mrs Hodgekiss,' he said. 'I'm Jack Egan.'

His hand was elegant, long-fingered, groomed. When she didn't take it, he tried a smile.

'I know who you are.' Her voice was the snarl of a cornered animal. 'You're the one who spoke to that reporter. You're the one who made up lies about Abigail, and let him print them. You're the one who took his money. How *dare* you. How *dare* you show up here?'

Ishbel heard her own vowel sounds echo off the chapel's walls. Everyone was on their feet now: Pauline was clinging with both hands to Ishbel's arm, making shushing sounds, trying to drag her back down into her seat. Rehan, she was dimly aware, had moved along the pew and was behind her now, saying her name like a chant: *Ish-*bel. *Ish-*bel. *Ish-*bel. Greg and the others were huddled in the aisle, speaking in low voices.

Aidan stepped into her line of sight.

'Bel,' he said. 'You knew Jack was coming. I told you. When we talked about the list of names.'

Ishbel stared up at her husband.

'How can you be okay with this?' She was shouting, and her face was hot.

Aidan put his face close to hers.

'Bel. I asked you to keep it together, for *one* morning. Can't you even do that? Can't you just, for *once*, do what you're asked?'

Ishbel looked past Aidan's face – so close that she couldn't quite focus on it – at the boy standing behind him. The navy suit he was wearing looked made for him. The smile he'd flashed her was like a bright light turning on. *So this is my daughter's boyfriend.* He looked like a male model, blinking his long-lashed eyes at her now. She could see how Abigail had been taken in.

'You have to leave,' she said, over Aidan's shoulder. 'Aidan. He has to leave.'

The boy's beautiful face hardened, his mouth a sudden, thin line. Ishbel recalled the only other time she'd ever seen him – stretched out, gasping, on a hospital gurney. She remembered his white torso daubed with blood, his shirt cut away by paramedics. She remembered Grant Lockley, materialising in the waiting room and leaning over the prone, bloodied body to take a photograph. How could this boy possibly collude with a man who did such a thing, in such a moment?

'Abi was right about you.' Jack Egan was speaking, his good teeth bared now. 'You *are* an uptight bitch.'

A collective gasp went through the room. Aidan put a hand out towards the boy.

'Hey,' he said. 'That's out of order, sunshine.'

Jack looked Aidan up and down, as though sizing up his chances in a fight.

'Fuck that,' he spat. 'You two need to take a look at yourselves.'

Ishbel could feel tears on her face again.

'Please,' she said, and the word was a hoarse whisper. 'Please leave now. Don't be a monster.'

But the boy was still talking.

'You two were the ones making her miserable. You need to look a*round*. I didn't kill her! I got shot too, remember? Instead of raging on me, maybe you should rage on Ryan Summers! Or *his* fucking mother, now he's dead.'

Ishbel thought she saw something happen in Aidan's face – a flinch, like a shadow had passed over him – as the boy mentioned Summers' mother. But she didn't have time to really register it: Jack had stepped sideways, into the aisle, and was now looking right at her.

'Ask yourself,' he said, throwing a small nod backwards – at the coffin? At her? She couldn't tell. 'Who's the *real* monster?'

There was a pause: the people around her seemed enraptured, as though this were a play.

'That's enough, now.'

Ishbel jumped. It wasn't Aidan who'd spoken, but someone standing behind her. She turned, aware that her movements were mirrored by Jack Egan's as he also looked in the direction of the voice. Barry Kesson had stepped forward and was standing in the middle of the aisle, both his fists balled.

'You should be ashamed of yourself,' he said, 'speaking to this poor lady that way.'

He was looking Jack up and down. Not as though sizing him up for a fight, Ishbel realised later – Jack was by far the taller man – but as though appraising his glossy exterior, and finding it wanting.

Behind her, Ishbel felt Aidan flinch: a movement in the air around him that probably only she noticed. She felt his anger before he spoke, like the crackle in the atmosphere before thunder.

'I'll deal with this,' Aidan said, after the slightest pause. Ishbel knew him well enough to know that he'd caught himself just in time: said a moderated version of what he might have liked to say. Beside her, Pauline made a deflating noise, her hand now slack on Ishbel's arm.

Barry Kesson's face hardened. *Something to prove*, Ishbel wondered, *from the last time he and Aidan had tangled?*

'Your wife is right,' he said. His own wife – Ishbel realised she didn't know Mrs Kesson's first name – wore no expression on her face. She was the woman who, at the police gathering, had stared evenly ahead at the same spot while others talked around her, as if she were a statue. She was, Ishbel realised now, likely medicated.

Barry Kesson was still speaking, whether to Aidan or to Jack, it wasn't clear. It didn't really matter.

'This intrusion is totally inappropriate. I don't know what you were thinking.'

Ishbel braced every muscle in her body. She was grateful to this man for his support, but now she was also frightened. Barry Kesson didn't know Aidan, didn't know how readily a hot flame could leap out of the smouldering coals of his anger. Jack's presence in the room stung like a brand. She hadn't realised it was possible to feel so many sharp, urgent things at once. She felt Pauline waiting, too, waiting for her son's outburst.

But the outburst, when it came, was from Jack.

'*Fuck* all you people.' The last of his slick exterior slid off. Underneath, Ishbel glimpsed Jack's years-ago self: a picked-on little boy building the slow, vibrating hive of a grudge against the whole world. 'I loved Abi. More than any of *you* ever did. She *belonged* to me.'

In the hideous quiet that followed, the boy fixed his gaze on the open doors at the back of the chapel. Ishbel twisted around, slowly, painfully, so she could watch him stride back down the aisle, under the clattering perspex porch, and out into the rain.

28 May, 10.00 a.m.

She was following her son through a deserted car park. She was close to him: close enough to see that his hair needed a cut, the back of it grown out into a chewy line. The stray thought *This is wrong* came to her – *it shouldn't be deserted, there ought to be lots of cars, and people.* But Ryan walked out across empty tarmac, striding over the white checkerboard lines, and she followed.

In, through a grey swing door that was heavy – she watched him put the full weight of his torso against it. The long corridor inside was lit only by what light came in through windows of the rooms off it. It was colourless light, like very early dawn. In the gloom, she followed the back of Ryan's neck: one white flash visible between black cloth and that jagged edge of hair.

Halfway along he stopped, as though listening, as though he knew she was there. But instead of turning to face her, he elbowed open a door to his right. A strip-light guttered on. In the wall of mirrors, she saw his face – the face that had sold a million tabloid papers. She couldn't see herself.

She watched him assemble his act. He didn't look at his own hands; instead, he watched the mirror version of himself, the way he'd clearly practised. The bathroom had mirrors on both sides. If she angled herself right, she could see him reflected back and back and back into nothing, each copy a little smaller than the last. Thousands of him, all about to step out of this bleached room with its dripping sinks, and do the exact same thing.

He walked the rest of the corridor slowly. His hearing was muffled now, she knew, so he had to be careful. He walked in the upright pose of a person trying to remain calm.

Get in front of him, someone said. *Do something.* But she did nothing. In his back pocket, she could see the outline of his mobile phone. In the secret pouch behind his ear, the gold-plated back of a stud earring glinted. He stopped at the end of the corridor, at a double fire door with a porthole window in either side. For a moment he stood, looking through at the bright scene beyond, and she thought that anyone on the other side would be able to see his strange, white face, criss-crossed by the tiny threads in the reinforced glass. He pressed one palm against the door, ready to shove his way in, and she saw the shredded cuticle on his thumb, the nail bitten down. She realised his breath was fast and shaggy, like he'd run here from a long way away. Or was he laughing? Or crying? *Touch him,* the voice said. But he already had one shoulder through the door.

Moira woke up. Someone was ringing the doorbell – had been ringing the doorbell for a while, something told her. She sat up. In the corner, the TV was still on. Her room was still in that thrown-back-together state of disarray, still as she'd found it nearly two weeks ago. She was still dressed in yesterday's clothes, her skirt twisted partly around. On the bedside table was an empty wine bottle. She'd gone downstairs to get a drink in the middle of the night, having woken up filled with a terror she couldn't shake. The thick ache behind her eyes reminded her. This was becoming a habit.

As she tottered down the stairs, the ringing became a banging against the glass partition of the front door. Beyond its frosted pattern, she could see three vague figures: the neon-coated police-man, and two others, with dark clothing and hair. She pressed herself against the wall, not wanting to see anyone, and not wanting to be seen. There was something at the back of her mind, like a forgotten name, something she didn't want to think about. As she reached the bottom step, she remembered, the way she remembered every morning, and her knees almost gave way: *Ryan is dead.*

The people on the other side of the door were speaking in hushed tones, but now she was in the hall, she could hear them.

'She's in there,' a man's voice said – the neon man. He banged once again on the door with a closed fist. 'She can't have left without being seen. It's not possible.'

'In that case, I need you to break down the door.' That was Amy. Moira felt a surge of relief. It was only Amy, and her uniformed friend.

The scene guard in the neon get-up snorted.

'We can't just go breaking down doors,' he said. 'What about those vultures out there? You want a photo of me breaking this door down on the front page of all the rags tomorrow?'

Amy hesitated.

'Look,' she said. 'I need to get into this house. She's not answering her phone, she's not answering the door, and if she's on the brink of death in there and you stood in the way of vital first aid—'

Moira lunged for the security chain. At the sound of its rattle, Amy fell silent. With some difficulty, Moira undid the various locks, and pulled open the door.

'What,' she said, looking into Amy's horrified face, 'makes you think I'd be lying dead in here?'

Beyond the garden wall, the reporters started up their repetitive, gull-like cries. The two policemen manoeuvred themselves into a kind of protective wall behind Amy. The one in the plain black uniform leaned forward, and spoke close to Amy's ear.

'Let's take this inside, shall we?'

Moira still hadn't dealt with the broken window. As she wandered into the living room, she vaguely registered the darkness thrown by the hoarding, but kept walking. Behind her, Amy let out a shriek.

'Moira, your feet!'

She looked down. She was wearing yesterday's tights, but no shoes, and the nude Lycra fabric of one foot had begun to turn a dull, iron red.

Amy was beside her then, gripping her arm with both hands and part guiding, part lifting her over the flecks and shards to the couch.

'You should have let me clean this up,' Amy said. 'Now look what's happened.' She squatted beside Moira and lifted her foot.

Behind her, her male colleague hovered, his face pale. Amy looked back at him and gestured towards the kitchen door.

'Go find me a pair of scissors, will you? I'm going to need to cut these tights and get to the problem. And run some water over a clean cloth.'

The man disappeared through the swing door.

Moira pressed a hand to her forehead. Her skull seemed to pulse against the palm.

'Amy,' she said, 'why did you say you thought I was dead?'

There was no answer. Amy had her face up close to the sole of Moira's foot.

'Have you people got me on suicide watch? Is that why you're here?'

Amy's fiddling around had loosened the piece of glass from her flesh. She could feel it now, prickling between her skin and the wet netting of the tights.

'I'm sorry, Moira,' Amy said. 'There have just been a few things, this past week, that made me think . . .'

Moira remembered the balled-up letter in the kitchen bin, how she'd had the thought herself while she was writing it.

'Well, you needn't worry,' she said. 'I'm not going to kill myself. I've decided I'm not.'

Amy looked up at her.

'How could I?' Moira said. 'How could I end my life after all those girls lost theirs? And because of my son.'

Amy was still looking at her, steadily, not speaking.

'No.' Moira looked away. 'I couldn't do that. I couldn't be that selfish.'

Amy's colleague came back into the room, his hands bundled with items.

'Scissors,' he said, and handed Amy a long pair with grey handles. They were the ones Moira used to cut meat: to snip apart strings of sausages, slice the skins off things. She didn't say anything. Amy began snipping at the tights fabric.

'I saw on the news,' Moira said, 'that it's Abigail Hodgekiss's funeral today.'

Amy and the policeman exchanged looks.

'Cremation,' the man corrected, and when Moira's brow furrowed, he added, 'too much public scrutiny for a big funeral right now. They'll do that part later, I expect.'

Moira closed her eyes. Ryan's body had not yet been released to her, though she guessed it wouldn't be long before Amy sat her down for that particular talk. She tried to imagine herself organis-ing Ryan's funeral. It felt like only an eye-blink ago that she'd stumbled through Jackie's – Ryan beside her in an ill-fitting suit, his teeth chattering slightly in the cold chapel with its meagre congregation of relatives. She tried to remember the order in which she'd done things: coffin? Flowers? Readings? But the very thought of it hurt – physically, a hot pain in the side of her head. She remembered now why she'd gone downstairs in the middle of the night for the wine.

'They're talking about this big, public memorial service, of course,' the policeman was saying. Moira could see Amy gritting her teeth. 'Televised live, they're saying.'

'Oh,' Amy said – a little too quickly, too brightly, dabbing at Moira's foot – 'this isn't so bad. The blood just made it look worse than it was.'

The policeman had also brought a damp J-cloth, a tube of Savlon he must have rifled out of a drawer, and a box of plasters. Moira was impressed. She was fairly sure that if she'd ever sent Jackie to find first aid supplies in that kitchen he'd have come back with nothing but a hangdog expression. She considered making a comment about it, but then remembered: *no. No jokes. People are dead.*

Instead, she avoided the policeman's eyes, and none of them spoke as Amy daubed cold cream onto the wound, and then gingerly placed a large plaster over it.

'Steve?' Amy eventually said. 'Can you nip upstairs and fetch a pair of shoes for Moira?'

She waggled an index finger.

'This isn't to happen again, all right? I'm going to get this cleaned up for you.'

Moira smiled a thin smile and thought of the wine bottle. She wasn't sure she could guarantee the not-happening-again part.

Amy stood, and brushed down her pencil skirt. She crunched back across the glass, into the hallway, and then reappeared, carrying a laptop bag, which she placed on the sofa next to Moira. It took Moira a moment to realise that the bag was hers. The laptop she'd bought herself when she started her OU degree – she'd forgotten about all of that, and now tried to care. No emotion came.

'We're finished with it,' Amy said. 'Turns out, it's clean – we don't think Ryan ever used it. You can have it back.'

Moira waited until Amy and the policeman named Steve had closed the front door behind them, waited until she heard the baying of the paparazzi outside dwindle, and then stop. Then she unzipped the bag, removed the laptop and booted it up.

Things were a little different. Her desktop display picture had disappeared: now, the little file icons floated on a background of plain black. The photo had been one of Jackie and Ryan, taken a few family holidays ago. It showed Ryan in teenager mode, looking sulkily at the camera, his grinning father's arm thrown around his shoulders, a white beach in the background. Moira wondered if it had been removed in order to spare her the painful moment of opening the laptop and seeing it there.

After only a moment's deliberation, Moira did exactly what Amy had told her not to do. She clicked on the little icon in the task bar at the bottom of the screen, and opened a new browser window. *I just want to look*, she thought, *and see if the graffiti is still there*. With shaking hands, she typed 'Ryan Summers family home' into the search bar.

Naturally, there were plenty of photos of her house. She peered at the little rectangular thumbnails. It was disorientating, seeing the house she'd lived in for decades through the lenses of the pack of men outside. Some of the photos had people in them: various different scene guards, some of them women. Amy, walking down the garden path towards the road, her hand held up to shield her face. The graffiti was visible in all of them.

Moira wasn't satisfied. She'd known as soon as she'd opened the computer that she wouldn't be, that photos of her house weren't really what she was looking for. She clicked out of the *images* tab and into the *web* one, and began to read. It felt as though all the air in the room – in the house – was being sucked out. Like she was suffocating.

Her son's name was everywhere, and it appeared alongside words like *monster, crazed, loner* and even *beast. Is serial murderer Ryan Summers,* one bright blue line of text read, *the ultimate product of toxic masculinity?* Another: *Three Rivers killer Ryan Summers practised his massacre via first-person shooters.* And another: *Murderer's mother released from custody – they say she's innocent, but there's blood on her hands.*

Moira was pitched headlong back into a memory: it happened so fast she felt physically jolted, as though she'd hit an unseen pothole while driving at speed. It was a scene she'd tried not to think about these twenty years or more, and she'd done okay – yet here it was. The memory of looking down at her own hand and finding it smeared and filmed with blood – her own blood, blood that smelled like her. Terror flooding her heart's engine. Twitching back the sheets and finding the bed filled with it, that same rusty blood. The sound that rose out of her, waking Jackie – how young he was, in the memory, how alive! – not a scream, but a sort of low animal drone. They'd agreed, later, on the day of Ryan's careful, miraculous birth, not to tell him about the older brother or sister he never did get to have. But since Jackie's death Moira had considered it, more than once. She had thought that perhaps it might pull them closer, might call her son back from whatever distant place he seemed to have drifted to since his father passed away. Now he was gone, and Jackie was gone, and the baby that never became a baby had been gone for so very long, and it was as though the secrets that had never been shared inside the four walls of this house were the problem, the reason, for it all.

Moira felt a hot spurt of rage rise up inside her: it started behind her breastbone and built until it spilled out of her mouth in that same droning growl she'd only ever made once before. Her body lurched: she gripped the front corner of the laptop and flipped it off her lap as though it had scalded her. It thudded onto the carpet. Moira bent over double, put her head between her knees, and howled. The sound was like a drowning machine: its big guttural rev ebbing, flecking her face with strings of snot and spit as she sobbed. She felt as though everything she'd ever loved had been lost, and it was her fault – somehow, every time, *she'd* done it. *Her.* *You deserve this*, she thought, over and over. *You. deserve. this.*

But after a while the noise she couldn't quite believe was coming out of her began to dim. She blinked fast, and waited until quiet fell. This was it: she was still here. She really was going to have to keep on living.

Moira straightened up, and wiped the gunk from her face with a yanked-down sleeve. Feeling empty and absurd, she lifted the laptop from the carpet and righted it across her knees once more. The lit screen still showed the returned search page, and as though the past quarter-hour hadn't happened at all, she resumed her mechanical downward scroll. Moira didn't click on any of the links – merely marvelled at the sheer number of them. As she moved backwards through the many pages of search results, the website names became less and less familiar. The results started with BBC News, the Guardian, Huffington Post, and various websites belonging to tabloid newspapers. By page 8 or so, the article sources began to change: personal blogs and forum threads called things like *opencases, operationjustice* and *unsungheroes* began to appear. Moira shuddered. The world was making its mind up about her son.

Out of habit, she clicked open her emails. The inbox was chock-full of unread messages, some with subject lines like *So sorry for your loss* and *Are you okay?* and *Thinking of you.* But near the top, in the newest messages, there were also a few with subject lines like *Rot in hell* and *You will pay for what you've done.* Some were prefaced with *Re: Re: Re: Re:*, and Moira realised that there must have been many more of these – the police must have been removing them while the laptop was in their care. Her vision swam. A bubble of panic began to swell in her mind. People hated her. What did they know about her? What *might* they know about her?

Then, as she began ticking the little 'select' boxes that would allow her to delete the hateful emails, her eyes alighted on a subject line that caused her to sob, just once, out loud into the still of the house. *Is Ryan still alive?* it read.

She opened the message up almost instinctively, without even looking at the sender's address.

```
Dear Moira,
    My name is Grant Lockley. I'm a freelance journal-
ist. We spoke briefly on the phone the night you were
released from police custody, but it seems you were a
little too fragile to really talk then. That is
totally understandable. However, I'd like to take this
opportunity to reach out to you again, and offer you
some information I have come across that I thought
might be of interest to you.
    I've been tracking the chat threads on a website
named Truth Unifies. The community there is, like many
members of the public, very keen to know why Ryan
might have done what he did at Three Rivers, and they
have been conducting their own investigations. What
they're discussing at the moment is the possibility
that there's more to the shooting than the police or
media are telling us. You can see that discussion at
http://truthunifies.com/110355
```

Moira paused, and stared at the glowing blue text of the hyperlink.

'I really wouldn't go on the internet right now,' Amy had said, not for the first time, as she left the house. 'I'm sure I don't need to tell you that people out there are grieving, and one of the stages of grief is anger. People are angry. That's why we've got uniformed officers outside your door.'

Moira's face must have looked sceptical – or perhaps she just hadn't responded fast enough – because Amy added, 'I strongly suggest that you just take my word for it. Trust me. The internet is not a healthy place for you to be right now.'

Moira let Amy's words drift through her head once again. Then she took a sharp, deep breath, and clicked on the link.

truthunifies.com

the freedom to think is the freedom to think differently

HOME | FORUMS | DONATE | SEND INTEL

truthunifies: FORUMS: POPULAR: Three Rivers College Ryan Summers is still alive?

Submitted by | **FoolBritannia**
Moderators | **LastManPandering f1ypaper 86vintage born_ yesterday iamthatgirl** | Report thread

FoolBritannia *View profile* *11 posts*
Posted at 22:34:07

Hey truthers,

I've started this O/T because I've seen various claims and/or theories floating around on here relating to Three Rivers College and I'd like to get to the bottom of them. I'm talking specifically about the posts here and here. Both threads have already been compromised by false flag deniers and as a result all attempts at discussion are being derailed. The questions I have are being ignored or used as an opportunity to attack me (this has been reported to the mods but I'm guessing nothing will come of it). So here are my questions:

Why so little panic? From what I have seen on TV news coverage, witnesses appear calm and unfazed. Aerial shots of the campus show very little movement with all police and other emergency vehicles appearing to be stationary and a long way back from the main entrances to the college buildings. Once they'd

ascertained Summers was down, wouldn't the ambulances
be right up there?

Where are the students? This is the main campus of a
college that serves several local authorities (I guess
what you in the US would call 'counties'?) and according to the Three Rivers Wikipedia page, there are over
7,000 students in attendance at Tweed Campus alone
(though this includes part-time and distance-learning
students who may or may not have been there that day).
Again, on the aerial shots I've seen, there are suspiciously few people milling around, and many appear to
be first responders/emergency personnel. Where are all
those students?

If this event was in fact a false flag or some kind
of drill, what possible reason could there be? I get
that in the US false flags are used all the time as
excuses to tighten gun legislation, but the fact
Summers got hold of any kind of gun in this country is
already pretty incredible (trust me, I have tried
myself. It sucks). Is this about surveillance?

Again, if this event was a false flag, who is Ryan
Summers? Does anyone out there have any intel on him?

[Reply]

Moira blinked: once, twice. She could understand only parts of
what she was reading, but the words *some kind of drill* made her
heart clang like a bell. She thought back to the morning of the
shooting – was it really two whole weeks ago? – standing on her
own front lawn. As the black-clad, flak-jacketed policemen had
beetled back and forth around her; as her neighbours had appeared
in increasing numbers to gawk from the opposite pavement; as
she'd watched possessions of hers and Jackie's and Ryan's being
carried out of the house and placed into the vans outside, she'd
had the very same thought. *Maybe this is just some kind of drill.*

She forced her eyes to refocus, and CTRL + clicked on the link
where the text said *aerial shots*. It took her to a blog that may have

been the commenter, FoolBritannia's, own. The aerial photos had been taken from a news helicopter: some were stills from rolling footage and snippets from the live ticker were visible along their bottom edge. Someone had circled the clusters of emergency vehicles in shaky, MS-Paint-red. Captions explained to Moira what she was seeing: the drop-off point outside the college entrance was empty, the ambulances parked a good hundred yards away. She clicked back to the first tab, read on.

underthejail *View profile* *2341 posts*
Posted at 22:41:55

Well first off welcome <u>FoolBritannia</u> thanks for your insight from Britain
   Hows the mood over there rn?
   So I also have been monitoring the situation closely and watching news coverage which here in the US has been less full than I would like but even so I have noticed same things as you
   Lack of panic and where are the students
   Strange position of emergency vehicles and also low numbers for this kind of incident
   I am convinced this event was a live drill perhaps an active shooter drill in which case Ryan Summers probably a paid actor or member of the military trained for this purpose
   My guess is as with the many US hoax shootings he is alive and well and picking up a new id and big paycheck right now
   You ask why the British govt would do this
   Pretty obvious they have followed in the footsteps of USA and seen how Democrats have benefitted from many hoax shootings here
   Could be that US govt brought pressure to bear on Britain and actually this is a US false flag just done on British soil

```
We know there have been other US false flags abroad
just look at Ukraine
   However as you say there may also be a surveillance
agenda you are better placed probably to speak about
the agenda of British govt
   Keep asking questions
```
[Reply]

Moira had the feeling of being unstitched, of splitting into two distinct halves. One half of her thought, *No, these people are wrong. Ryan is dead. I saw him.* That half of her remembered watching, as if in slow motion, as the morgue APT lifted the cover off what had been her son's face.

'Why does he . . . look like that?' she'd asked. The young police-man – Gibbie, they'd called him – put a comforting hand on her shoulder.

'Comminuted skull fracture,' the APT had said. 'The bullet entered just above his right eye, and . . .' Pausing, the man had looked at Moira and mistaken her distress for misunderstanding. 'He shot himself in the temple, like this,' he said, and pressed two fingers to the side of his head. 'Like you see them do in the movies.'

That half of Moira had broken down and was led away, bent over almost double, sobbing and retching, by Gibbie.

But now there was another Moira: another voice in her head which sounded like her own, but which was arguing with that memory, was shouting over it, yelling and kicking. *But what if he's not dead?* the voice insisted. *Here's someone saying he's not dead. What if he's not? What if he's not? What if he's not?*

Moira read the post again.

```
Ryan Summers probably a paid actor or member of the
military trained for this purpose
   My guess is as with the many US hoax shootings he is
alive and well and picking up a new id and big
paycheck right now
```

She didn't know how such things might work, or if they even really happened: the two halves of her fought as she wondered at the scenario's absurdity. But she knew that if someone *had* approached Ryan and asked him if he wanted to be involved in a covert government operation – apparently what this commenter was describing – he'd certainly have thrilled at the possibility. As a child, while other boys charged around the primary school playground being firefighters, policemen or cowboys, Ryan had usually gone off on his own. Had gone off to watch from a corner, to collect small items and stuff them in his pockets, or to scribble nonsensical lines and symbols in the back of his exercise book.

'I'm being a spy,' he'd say to her, when she asked him about it. 'Go away, Mummy. I'm being in disguise.'

Was he in disguise now? Did she dare believe what these people – these internet strangers – were saying?

She read on.

ElectRICK *View profile*   *554 posts*
Posted at 00:47:21

Hey truthers,

I would like to talk about the guns, because I call bullshit. We're expected to believe that this kid went in with three modified starting pistols and eighteen rounds and managed to kill thirteen people and himself? He supposedly fired all eighteen rounds and we know that some of the so-called victims got shot twice. Do the maths, something's up.

If Summers really did only have 18 rounds at his disposal, and if he really did kill all thirteen girls AND hit some of them more than once, then he is a super-skilled marksman. You're telling me there were no stray bullets, no ricochets, EVERY SINGLE BULLET hit a person? That guy's a serious marksman, and I'm not just talking down the shooting range on Saturdays.

He's a trained killer, and he's been training for this
live shooter false flag drill for years.

Let's hear your thoughts truthers. I'm pretty sure
no one can tell me I'm wrong.

Moira's head buzzed. She felt drunk, or faint, or some combination of the two. She cast her mind back to all the times that her son had been out of the house and she hadn't really known where. She'd always tried to give him a little free rein, especially in recent years, telling herself, *after all, he's a man now.* Those unknown hours – was her son in some government facility somewhere, being trained?

This is science fiction, one half of her said.

But what if he's alive? said the other.

She clicked back to Grant Lockley's email.

I might be able to supply further information to you, he'd written. *But as you can imagine this is all very sensitive. If you'd like to speak more about this then I'd recommend that we meet in person.*

At the bottom of the email was a mobile phone number, and it was signed, *With deepest sympathy, Grant.*

Moira read the online comment thread again, and then again. She read the email again. She closed her browser window, then re-opened it. She sat, looking at the black words on the white screen until her vision blurred. Outside, one of the journalists landed the punchline of a joke, and a chorus of braying laughter went up beyond the shattered window's chipboard. Moira's thoughts drifted back – the way they always did now, like metal filings drawn to a magnet – to her final conversation with Ryan, over the kitchen table the night before the shooting. She wanted to time-travel back to that moment so badly that her whole ribcage ached with the wanting. If she could have him back again, in front of her, and speak to him, just for a minute . . .

Again Moira read the email, and again. Her two arguing halves had gone quiet – in her head there were only this man's words, expanding like the smoky fall-out from an explosion.

What if? one of the two halves whispered. Moira reached for the phone.

BREAKING! THREE RIVERS SHOOTING VICTIM TO BE CHARGED WITH DRUG OFFENCES, AS POLICE INSIST THEY HAVE NOTHING TO HIDE

By GRANT LOCKLEY
PUBLISHED: 08:45 29 May

Three Rivers shooting victim Jack Egan is to be charged by police after confessing to dealing drugs at the college's Tweed Campus. Egan, who is 21 years old, made his confession in an explosive two-part interview with this columnist, <u>the full text of which you can read here</u>. In it, he said he used the money from his exploits – securing Class B drugs and peddling them to his classmates – to support his mum, who is reliant on disability benefits.

<u>Three Rivers gunshot victim Jack Egan tells all: read the exclusive interview in full here!</u>

Egan's girlfriend, Abigail Hodgekiss, was also caught up in the criminal activities, which, Egan claims, 'everyone at college knew about.' Hodgekiss was one of the thirteen young women murdered by gunman Ryan Summers when he rampaged through the Tweed Campus on the morning of 14 May. Yesterday, Abigail's loved ones, including Jack Egan, gathered at an undisclosed location in the city of Edinburgh for her cremation.

But this morning police have taken Jack into custody, and it's likely he'll face charges relating to the possession and supply of illegal drugs. His legal representative was approached yesterday, but declined to comment. (As always, you can keep up with developments on this story by following me on Twitter @thegrantlockley.)

In pictures: with affair rumours swirling, Abigail Hodgekiss's parents leave for her cremation in separate cars – read more here!

In related news, there is increased speculation over Police Scotland's ongoing investigation into the Three Rivers shooting. One online group – known as Truth Unifies – have been carrying out their own investigations into the murder spree and, like many of us, are questioning the official version of events. They are particularly interested in the ballistics report released by Police Scotland, claiming that it paints an inaccurate picture.

We've put together our own detailed ballistics report: read more here

Ryan Summers, says one Truth Unifies member, was, 'a serious marksman, and I'm not just talking down the shooting range on Saturdays'. According to Truth Unifies ballistics experts, modifying a gun is no mean feat – yet, according to police, Summers successfully modified three. 'He's a trained killer,' our source goes on, 'and [it's likely] he's been training for this . . . for years.' Truth Unifies is a conspiracy theorist website, of course, but what we've been told about ballistics thus far *does* seem fishy, and points once again to my theory that the police are telling us only a fraction of what they really know about this case.

Meanwhile, Police Scotland continues to provide costly round-the-clock protection for Ryan Summers' mother, Moira. 'We currently have reason to monitor a handful of threats made toward Mrs Summers,' an official statement said. 'While credible threats are being circulated, we have a duty of care towards the victim.' The police were invited to comment more specifically, but declined. Personally, I continue to raise a sceptical eyebrow at this paranoid, protective treatment of Mrs Summers. One cannot help but ask, once again – does she deserve it?

See more from Grant Lockley

Share or comment on this article

TOP COMMENTS

kirsten_i Personally I don't think it's right that this poor boy should be arrested – he is 21 for goodness' sake!!!! Who did not do silly things at that age? Read his interview yesterday and he seems to have been through so much! Give him a chance?

^ 797 people liked this

miKomiKo the police owe us the truth!!!a govt inquiry into this shooting is coming & senior officers should all be sacked!!!

^ 561 people liked this

stonej86 I had a look at Truth Unifies and a lot of the people there seem to be unhinged conspiracy theorists. However, they are right that it takes a lot of skill to modify a weapon. We haven't had much in the way of information released about this, probably to prevent copycat killings. But here's my speculative take. I believe Summers most likely replaced the barrel, or part of the barrel, in order to remove the 'pinch' that prevents a blank-firing pistol from firing a live round. This would be the best way to do things in order to avoid ammunition jamming inside the gun, and subsequent shots causing the gun to then explode. Either that, or he made custom ammunition in some way. It's very hard to modify a blanks gun but it isn't impossible. People have done it and maybe Ryan Summers is one of them. I speak as a former target shooter who sadly had to give up most of my collection to amnesty.

^ 423 people liked this

1357924 how is cannabis even an illegal drug? Jack Egan 'dealing' something millions of people use every day wake up!

^ 310 people liked this

29 May, 9.15 a.m.

'I am so fucking sick of this Lockley character.'

Birch winced. She'd arrived at work nearly two hours ago, had a meeting with Rehan, been briefed on the events at Abigail Hodgekiss's cremation, and chipped away at the avalanche of emails in her inbox (anything unrelated to Three Rivers, she was ignoring). McLeod had been in the building only ten minutes, and already word was spreading through the team that he was in a foul mood, to be avoided at all costs. She hadn't been quick enough off the mark, and he'd cornered her.

'We must have grounds to arrest him, surely.'

McLeod looked as put-together as he ever did – all the way up to his perfectly Windsored tie – but his eyes were bulging. Birch scooted crumbs along the coffee-room worktop with the blade of her finger, to avoid looking at him.

'Well,' she said. 'Personally, I've long suspected him of obtaining data illegally. He fits the same profile as other journalists who've gone down for it, especially his hiring of PIs.'

'You're talking about hacking.'

'Yes – emails, I reckon, and other things, too. There've been times where he's said things and I've speculated that the only way he could have known them was by hacking into the Police National Computer.'

McLeod threw her a *go on I'm interested* look, and she added, 'But of course, I've been dealing with him for a long time. Some of what I'm talking about is years ago.'

'Your brother's case.'

'Yes.' Birch winced. *Please, let's not talk about that this morning,* she thought. McLeod didn't pick up the signal.

'How are you handling that, Helen?'

She stared down at the crumbs on the sticky work surface, now corralled into a ragged line. McLeod cocked one ear almost to his shoulder, trying to hook her gaze.

'I know enough about you and Lockley,' he said, 'to know that anything to do with him must feel . . . *personal*.'

It's not personal at all, Birch thought. That was Lockley. That was why he'd got so good at this shit. *He bloody believes his 'I'm just doing my job' mantra.* But there was no way to explain this to McLeod. There was no way to explain the very specific way in which anything to do with Lockley just sort of *hurt*.

'It's fine, sir.' Birch drew herself up into a straight line, and looked her boss in the eye. 'I'm not going to let my personal history with this man get in the way of my work, I absolutely promise you.'

McLeod studied her for a moment, in silence. She forced herself to hold still in the blue tractor-beam of his glare.

'Okay,' he said, eventually. 'So you think Lockley got this stuff on the Hodgekisses from poking his nose where it shouldn't have been?'

Birch finally flinched her eyes away.

'Unlikely,' she said. 'I'm afraid it looks like the poison he's spewing at the moment really has come from this Jack Egan character.'

'The boy who lived.'

'The very same,' Birch said. 'Lived to tell the tale.'

McLeod huffed through his nose.

'And what a tawdry little tale it was. What exactly did the little scrote *think* was going to happen when he announced to the fucking world at large that he'd been dealing drugs? Did he not know he was on the record? I mean, really, Birch.'

Birch shrugged.

'I think it's a case of pretty, but not very bright. That, and he maybe thought that the outpouring of sympathy over having been shot might offer some protection from the long arm of the law.'

McLeod's jaw was working. Birch tried to ignore it.

'I feel sorry for the boy, to be honest,' she said. 'Miniature drug empire aside – he *is* only twenty-one, just lost his girlfriend . . .'

McLeod snorted. 'You mean his drug mule.'

Birch paused, to think.

'I suppose,' she said, speaking slowly. 'But if you read the interview with Lockley, the kid talks about her as if she's the great love of his life. Were it not for the circumstances you could almost find him adorable. Or maybe that's just the way he's been advised to play it, but he seems too daft to be acting. I'm afraid I think Jack Egan has been a victim of his own naivety.'

'Well, poor bastard,' McLeod said, his voice thick with sarcasm. 'At least we'll likely get to lock him up. What about this Lockley character? Every time I open a paper I see some fucking awful byline of his. He's laid out the bait and now every journo in town is crawling all over the Hodgekiss house, and this is a family we were already worried might sue us. He's injected this Egan kid into an investigation that was already too fucking hot to handle – I know I don't need to tell *you*, Birch. He's phoning every single one of the victims' families at all hours of the day and giving all our FLOs the most tremendous fucking headache. And you yourself said he's threatened to keep going after us once he's finished with his little human interest stories about the families. And they're all at it – every unscrupulous bastard in the business is standing on the doorstep of a Three Rivers family member right now. They're out there, getting their tell-alls off the college kitchen staff or the lucky kids who bunked off that day and cheated death, or blah blah blah. Clickbait vultures, and Lockley's their patron fucking saint. He's got to be stopped.'

McLeod flailed an arm out, punching the thin plasterboard of the wall beside him.

'How the *fuck* do we stop him, Birch?'

Birch had been only half listening. The coffee room they were in was high up on the building's corner, and had a little slice of window that looked out toward the grounds of Fettes School. Birch had been watching the speck of a man driving a ride-on mower up and down the huge lawns, weaving under the cover of beech trees that had to be a hundred years old. Their leaves were still a pale, new green, and hazy at this distance. If she leaned left a little, Birch knew she could also look down at the Astroturfed playing fields of Broughton High School. The school's high fence and wind-swayed floodlights looked vaguely penal in comparison to Fettes' sweeping driveway and leaded turrets. She knew from reading the Hodgekiss file that Abigail Hodgekiss had attended a football club that met on those playing fields.

McLeod's question shook her.

'Sorry, sir,' she said, having spent a moment too long under his piercing blue glare. 'I thought that was a rhetorical question.'

McLeod gave her a look that – in spite of his sharp suit and the tie-knot so large it was almost distasteful – was pure *schoolmarm*.

'It very much was not,' he said. 'I'm wondering if perhaps . . . I mean, you've known Lockley since he first signed up for his NUJ card, so if you might have any intel we could use on him. You know. From the bad old days of your brother, and all that.'

Birch closed her eyes for a moment. She thought back to the day when her mother had received the official police phone call to say that Charlie's case was henceforth considered cold. Her mother had folded down into a sort of N-shape, and had sat like that on the floor for several hours while Birch clucked and fussed around her.

'Charlie's put you through so much,' Birch remembered saying. 'If it turns out he's still alive, I'll kill him myself.'

Her mother had raised her head from her bent knees then, and looked up at her. Birch remembered her gaunt, white face – how thin she looked, after months of not eating properly, not sleeping properly.

'He's still alive, Helen,' she'd said, with an icy certainty that had made her daughter's heart clutch. Birch had put in her application to police recruitment the following week. *If he's still alive*, she'd thought, *I'll find him*. Now, she realised, she'd given up thinking that years ago.

'I miss the old days,' McLeod was saying. 'Once upon a time I'd've arrested him first and just figured out why later.'

Birch shuddered at the thought. She could imagine Lockley's legions of commenters, the stink they could kick up – *would* kick up – at the slightest provocation. She decided to change the subject.

'To move away from Lockley for a minute,' she said, 'I'm afraid I have more bad news to deliver.'

She waited, stalling for time. McLeod blinked a slow, *how bad can it be* blink. *Oh God*, she thought.

'Rehan Ibrahiim tells me that there's reason to suspect Aidan Hodgekiss is involved with the Moira Summers death threats.' She said it as fast as she could, as though swallowing foul-tasting medicine.

McLeod said nothing, but she watched as several emotions appeared to pass across his face, one after the other.

'He's saying it's a hunch at the moment,' Birch added, 'but it would explain a lot.'

McLeod put his half-empty coffee cup down on the worktop. There was more than a little force in the gesture, and the thin dark liquid leapt out in a small wave, soaking Birch's neat line of crumbs.

'Fucksake,' he said.

'I know.' Birch found she couldn't think of anything else to say. 'I know, sir.'

'Well,' McLeod said, 'the Hodgekiss family certainly have the motive.' Then, after a pause, 'Oh, for fuck's sake, Birch.'

She realised she was nodding mechanically, and made herself stop.

'I think it's just Aidan Hodgekiss we're looking at,' she said. She felt an odd urge to protect his wife, having read Lockley's recent revelations. 'And it could be nothing, of course. Rehan could have got entirely the wrong end of the stick.'

McLeod had put one hand over his eyes.

'I don't need to tell you,' he said, 'what an absolute unmitigated disaster it would be if we had to arrest the father of one of these victims . . . *for anything*. The press, Birch. You can imagine.'

She felt her lip curl, in spite of herself.

'It would be somewhat more of a disaster if Aidan Hodgekiss succeeded in hurting Moira Summers,' she said, then instantly regretted it. She braced for the impact of McLeod's comeback, but it didn't come. He was thinking, she could tell – he was playing out all the various shit scenarios that now had the potential to come about. He was worrying about his job; Birch could see it in his face, clear as day.

'Sir,' she said, aiming for a warmer tone than before. 'There's really nothing to be done for now until we have the evidence to either confirm Rehan's hunch, or put Hodgekiss in the clear. But I promise you, I am on it. It's a priority, as of now.'

Just saying it – just adding yet another priority to her to-do list, made her feel tired, right down to her bones. McLeod didn't reply immediately: she could see the stormclouds were still gathering in his mind's eye.

'I'll keep you updated,' she added.

'Do, please,' he said.

Birch opened her mouth to speak again, but her phone rang. She let loose a silent prayer of thanks for the opportunity to escape from McLeod and his brooding. She knew it was Amy before she'd even pulled the phone from her pocket; she'd asked her to report back on the previous day's meeting with Moira.

'How's it going, Amy?'

On the other end, coarse breathing, and the clip of high heels: it sounded like Amy was running.

'Oh God, Helen,' she said. 'I think we've got a situation here.'

Birch's face immediately rearranged itself into a smile, which she fired haphazardly at McLeod.

'Right,' she said, a sick feeling rising in her. 'Let me just nip back to the office so I can check that for you.' Still smiling, she backed out of the coffee room, and – once the door had swung shut on McLeod – swivelled round and began walking.

'Okay, what's happened?' Birch's free hand flew to her other jacket pocket. Her immediate reaction to most things these days was *How fast can I get there?* and right now she wanted the faint, reassuring clink of the Mondeo's keys. But the pocket was empty.

Shit. The keys must be on her desk somewhere. 'Has Moira hurt herself?'

She heard the slam of a door, and when Amy spoke again it was from inside the sealed quiet of a car.

'No – physically, she's fine. She's in rude health, in fact. But she's threatening to do something really stupid, and I don't think I can stop her.'

Birch's mind raced. She made it to the wall at the end of the corridor and rattled the lift's 'call' button.

'What, Amy? What is it?'

The sound on the other end of the call changed: Amy had put her on speakerphone.

'She phoned me first thing this morning,' she said, her voice now tinny and thick. 'She's been online. And guess what? She's got mail.'

Birch groaned. She didn't know what was coming next, but she knew it couldn't possibly be good.

'It's Grant Lockley,' Amy went on, 'saying that he thinks Ryan Summers is still alive. He's found some conspiracy theorist group that claims they know the truth about what happened with the shooting. And he says that—'

'Let me guess,' said Birch. 'He says that *we're* all covering it up.'

Amy sounded frantic, her breath loud.

'Yeah,' she said.

The lift pinged, and the doors shuddered open.

'I'm getting in a lift,' Birch said, 'so I might lose you, but – I should have seen this coming, what with Lockley's latest hot take on the ballistics. I should have known he wasn't just after *us*.'

'He's told Moira that the shooting was a false flag,' Amy said. 'Do you know what that means?'

The lift doors closed. Birch passed her free hand over her eyes. The palm was damp.

'A false flag,' she said, 'is a term these conspiracy nutters came up with to describe an event they think was faked. Like, the CIA shot Kennedy. 9/11 was an inside job. That sort of thing. They call those false flags.'

'Oh.'

The lift trundled downwards.

'Wait,' Birch said. 'My brain just caught up with my ears. Did you just say Lockley *told* Moira the shooting was a false flag?'

There was a pause. The lift clunked to a halt and the doors opened.

'I'm afraid so,' Amy said. 'They've spoken on the phone. Moira was apparently leaving messages on his voicemail all of yesterday . . .'

Recorded evidence, Birch thought. *Fucking great.*

'. . . and they spoke last night. He's telling her that Ryan might still be alive.'

Birch stepped out onto the ground floor. Along the hall, Anjan was sitting on a plastic chair, a briefcase across his knees. He spotted her, and raised one palm in greeting.

'I see,' she said. She needed to zero back in on Amy. 'You're right: we've got a situation here.'

'*That's* not the situation, Helen. There's more.'

Birch closed her eyes, in the hope that when she opened them again she'd find it was all a dream, as though this were some sort of terrible, runaway fairytale. Instead, when she re-opened her eyes she saw Anjan had stood up, and was walking towards her.

'Tell me,' she said.

'They're going to meet.' Amy's tone had gone from frantic to defeated, like she'd realised there was no solution Birch could give her. 'Moira's going to meet Lockley. In a cafe. In public.'

'Oh Jesus,' Birch said.

Anjan stopped, still a few feet away. His *hello*-face disappeared, like a candle being blown out. Amy was still talking.

'I've tried to talk her out of it,' Amy said. 'Over the phone, I mean. Steve and I are about to drive over there, but she says there's nothing I can say that will stop her. She was giving me *I'm a private citizen of a free country*, and all that. It's like Lockley's inside her head.'

Birch held up the index finger of her free hand, gesturing to Anjan that he should wait – she might need him, she realised.

'I mean,' Amy was saying, her voice dialling back up towards panic again, 'how do we know that these conspiracy theorists aren't the same people as the death-threat suspects? They could have made up this whole internet forum, made up this whole thing, to lure Moira out of the house . . . right?'

Anjan wasn't even trying to hide the fact that he was listening. Birch shot for a glare, but wasn't sure she'd managed it.

'That's possible,' Birch said. She thought of Aidan Hodgekiss, and for the first time, hoped it *was* him behind the death threats. *He* at least – Birch was sure – would never actually act on them. 'But it doesn't really matter either way, Amy. We just need to stop this meeting from happening if we possibly can, okay? How soon can you be there?'

In the background, there was the swish of a seatbelt.

'We're nearly there,' Amy said. 'We've stopped for petrol at the garage in Canonmills. But she's talking about going today. She's got it all arranged.'

'Okay,' Birch said. 'Get back to Moira's and keep her there. I've got Anjan standing right in front of me, as luck would have it.'

Anjan's worried look flickered, and he flashed Birch a quick, winning smile. *You think you're a good lawyer,* she thought. *Okay then, get me out of* this *little mess.*

'Tell Moira,' she went on, 'that I want her to speak with Anjan before she goes ahead with this. Hopefully that'll slow her down. And then, hopefully, Anjan has the powers of persuasion to put a stop to it altogether.'

Amy was quiet for a long time. Birch heard the car engine start up.

'If you say so, guv,' Amy said. 'But she's pretty adamant. We might need a plan B.'

Birch waved Anjan towards her office.

'I'm on it,' she said. 'Just keep Moira indoors.'

She hung up. Anjan opened the office door, and held it open for her to walk through.

'I've been called for a meeting with your boss,' he said, once they were both inside. 'I hate it when that happens.'

Birch cast her eyes across the clutter of her desk, searching for her car keys.

'I can't joke around with you today,' she said. 'Close the door.'

He did, but he was still smiling.

'I didn't just say that stuff to get you out from under McLeod,' she said. 'There really is a problem.'

That smile made the inside of Birch's head itch.

'I know, Helen,' he said. 'You're not that good an actress.'

She had to look away. She spotted the keys glinting in the midst of a stack of folders, and sent the top folder flying as she darted for them.

'So.' Anjan set his briefcase on the floor and reached down to hand her the spilled papers. 'What's happening with Moira? How can I be of service?'

Birch flushed. He was getting to her, and she wasn't quite sure why. The thought crossed her mind that people who charged as much per hour as he did shouldn't be allowed to say things like 'How can I be of service?' She watched him beginning to clear paperwork off a chair, and threw up her hands. The car keys jingled.

'Don't start making yourself comfortable,' she said. 'I have to move. I'll explain on the way down to the car.'

Birch sat in the Mondeo, halfway up Moira's street. It was an unremarkable street, built in the fifties: all window-boxes and pebbledash. Between the houses, Birch could see into back gardens full of plastic kiddie slides and sheets inflating on their whirligigs. The Summers house was at the end, where things got a little more expensive: theirs was double-fronted, though only detached from next door by a vennel with a panelled fence. Birch had managed to arrive and park without fanfare, though from here she could see the pack of paparazzi scuffing around, vaping, leaning against the bonnets of Moira's neighbours' cars. Had the gaggle shrunk a little in number? Perhaps. There hadn't been anything to photo-graph for a full week except a Tesco groceries delivery Amy had organised, and Amy herself, coming and going – but regular FLO visits were to be expected. Birch could see from here that the scene guard on the front step looked bored. Amy's car was half parked, half dumped outside the house, two tyres propped up on the kerb. She tutted.

'What would *you* do?' Anjan had said. They'd got as far as the car park. Birch had given a garbled account of the unfolding situation on the way down in the lift. Anjan's cologne smelled of something familiar, and in trying to place the scent, she'd struggled to get her words in the right order.

'I mean it.' He was giving her that look he had, the one that made her feel like he could see right into the workings of her head. 'If you'd just lost a loved one, and then someone phoned you up and said, I think that person is still alive and this has all been some sort of hoax, what would *you* do?'

She'd said nothing. He was describing a scenario she'd imagined herself, many times, especially in the wake of her mother's death. But that was different – wasn't it? Imagining it was different. Everyone daydreamed that sort of thing. It didn't actually *happen*.

'But Ryan Summers *is* dead,' Birch said. 'I've seen the autopsy report. He shot himself in the head.'

'That's academic,' Anjan said. He seemed to be always on the verge of smiling, even when discussing something extremely grave. She could see how it must unnerve people in court. 'You know that, and I know that, and I'm sure somewhere deep down, Moira Summers knows that, too. She saw his body, in fact, which is more than you or I have done. But it's not about what you *know*. It's about what you *do* when presented with this scenario. Do you ignore the person who seems to be offering you a way to walk back your own grief? *Can* you? Or do you simply have to go and find out more, in spite of your own better judgement? Because what if that person – magically – is right? Could you really go on with your life without ever making sure? I think you know the answer, Helen. I certainly know what *I'd* do.'

'But – the death threats. It's not safe for her to be running off to meet Lockley, or anyone.'

'So escort her.' Anjan had pointed to the radio clipped on Birch's lapel. 'Get on that thing and say you want a police escort, for – what? An hour? It won't take long. I doubt this man actually has anything of substance to say.'

Birch had pressed her hands over her eyes.

'That's my whole *point*.' She was aware that her voice, filtered through her fingers, had come out petulant, child-like. She threw her hands down again, which didn't help the effect. 'I can't justify putting any more manpower into what I know is a wild-goose chase. I need you to help me stop her from *going*.'

Anjan had drawn himself up a little taller.

'Is my client a suspect in your investigation?' he asked.

Birch had closed her eyes.

'No.'

'Do you suspect that she may be going to commit a criminal offence?'

Great, Birch thought. *It's come to this.*

'No, but—'

'Do you have any grounds to take my client into police custody?'

'No. I don't.'

'Well. In that case, you cannot *stop her* from doing anything.' He'd mimicked Birch's tone almost perfectly, and for just a second, her palm itched with the desire to slap him. 'She's a free agent, and if she wants to go and have coffee with a madman, then she's completely within her rights to do so.'

Birch dithered. Not only was he clearly not going to help her, he was also entirely right.

'But . . .' She decided to try a final time, but her voice came out small, chastened. 'The press are going to have a field day. McLeod'll *sack* me if I let her go. You know we're walking on eggshells with this investigation.'

'Helen,' he said, letting loose the smile he'd been threatening her with all along. 'I'm a solicitor. I don't deal with PR problems.'

With that, he'd turned and begun walking back towards the building, leaving her beside the car, its keys hanging uselessly in her hand.

'Where are you going?' she called after him.

'I'm late for a meeting with your boss, remember?' He'd half turned back, stopping mid-step, and seeming to float there. 'Good luck with Moira. If she looks like she's about to commit a crime, you may call me.'

Birch swore, and then hoped he hadn't heard.

Now, a fine mist of rain began to fall across the Mondeo's windscreen. Birch thought of all the washing she'd seen in all the back gardens on this street, thought of washing out on lines all over the city, and the people rushing out right now to bring it in. *Star anise.* The answer came to her, unbidden: *that was the smell, in Anjan's cologne. Star anise.* Charlie had been obsessed with anything that smelled or tasted like aniseed – as a wee boy, and even more as an adult. She'd visited him in his uni halls at Warrender Park Road, and found a bowl of star anise in the middle of the kitchen table, set there fussily, like pot pourri. He'd made curries so full of anise that they were barely edible. He drank absinthe when he could afford it, and Pernod when he couldn't. He'd've loved that cologne of Anjan's. It probably cost hundreds of pounds a bottle.

Birch shook herself. *Stop thinking about Anjan,* she commanded her brain. *And definitely stop thinking about Charlie.*

She picked up her phone, scrolled to Amy's number, and dialled.

'Amy? I'm outside,' she said. 'I've had a think, and here's what we're going to do.'

Moira unfolded herself from the car into a cloud of police radio static. Four large men in dark-coloured plain clothes loomed around her like trees. Beyond them, a few feet away, DI Birch hovered under the tree-line, chewing her bottom lip. The last time Moira had seen the DI was the day she'd been allowed to go home. Birch had opened the door of that car with the tinted windows, had held it open while Moira got in, and had batted a hand off the roof once, twice, the way policemen do in movies. Moira had noted at the time how tired Birch looked, and she looked fifty times worse now. Moira wondered if DI Birch was having the same thought about her.

She put a shaking hand on the car roof to steady herself. She pulled a long, cold drink of real-world, outdoors air into her lungs. It smelled like wet conifer and grass clippings. Moira counted slowly in her head: she hadn't been outside in eight days, not since that car ride, and Amy hustling her up the garden path under her own coat with the journalists baying.

Now she looked around. They'd backed the car as far into the little footpath as they could, before it got too narrow. On one side, the rain-streaked back walls of garages hemmed the path to its vanishing point. On the other, those wet conifers with their peeling branches snagged plastic bags that the breeze was trying to wrench free.

'That's a go,' one of the men said.

They'd sent a scout up the path a little – he'd walked a few dozen yards and looked around, then stopped and turned to face them. Now he put up one hand and beckoned to Moira. She had the urge to hold up her thumb and snuff out the tiny, dim figure of him, a thing she suddenly remembered doing with Ryan when he was a small child – a thing she hadn't thought about for years. She remembered sitting on the top deck of the bus, headed into town: pulling up at the traffic lights and teaching a delighted Ryan that, thanks to this trick of perspective, he could make people disappear. She shivered, and bit her lip. *Don't cry*, she chanted inside her head. *Don't cry, don't cry, don't cry.*

'Mrs Summers?'

One of the men placed a paw-like hand on the small of her back, and she flinched into action. Adrenaline had pushed her to keep arguing with Amy, to insist to DI Birch that she had to go, had to do this. Adrenaline had got her out of the door, and she'd even showered and changed her clothes – another first, since she'd come home. But during the drive here in yet another tinted police car, that adrenaline had seeped away. Now she walked slowly. She felt like one of those rattling plastic bags – washed out, thin and empty. Like she too could easily let go, and blow away into the white afternoon sky.

She reached the distant policeman. Now he was as overlarge and imposing as his colleagues. He walked ahead of her down a fork off the footpath: a narrower gap, hidden by the garages. Here, there were bottles and graffiti, a bad smell. The backs of sheds. Fence panels. Moira felt like she was floating, rather than walking. She was hungry. A headache buzzed in her eye-sockets. The little path bent and twisted. She had no idea where she was in relation to the black car, or the road they'd driven here on, or her own house with its shattered front window. When the policeman in front of her stopped, she almost cannoned into him.

'Here we are, then,' he said. He sounded so cheery that she almost smiled. He unlatched a scruffy wooden gate, set into a scruffy wooden fence, and Moira stepped into a little grey concrete yard.

'Where am I?'

The yard was loud with the whir of an industrial extractor fan. Against the fences were stacks of sun-faded bread delivery trays, recycling bins spilling over with cardboard. Above her, the back of a tenement loomed, boot-blacked with hundred-year-old soot.

'You said Muffins Cafe, right?' The policeman was wearing a lopsided smile, as if he believed this might all be some sort of trick she was playing. 'This is the tradesman's entrance.'

He stepped up to the building's back door, a plain, chipboard-covered job that had a steel grille screwed onto it. He knocked, loudly and urgently, and the door was opened, though Moira couldn't see the person on the other side.

The policeman flipped his badge, and said his name. Behind her, beyond the scruffy fencing, Moira could hear the radio static of the other men, gathered now, and waiting.

'We called ahead,' the policeman said, with that same half-smile.

The door opened a little wider.

'On you go, then.' Moira's queasy feeling must have shown on her face, because he added, 'You'll be grand. Amy and Steve are already in there, panic button at the ready.'

He stepped back into the yard, and put an arm around her. She shivered.

'Besides,' he said, steering her towards the door, 'he's no match for you, that Lockley guy. A puff of wind'd knock him over.'

He didn't remove his arm until she was standing on the threshold, looking into the cramped strip-lit kitchen inside, at the sticky shine of its stainless-steel units and hoods. She knew what he was thinking. *We're all in too deep for you to back out now.* His job was to deliver her to this place, and he'd see that job done.

'You coming in, or whit?'

Moira stepped forward. She now saw that the door had been opened by a young woman, who was maybe twenty or so. Her hair was pulled into two braids that had been clipped up around her head. Each braid had a pink streak in it, Moira noticed. She was wearing an apron that looked like it needed a wash.

'Well come *oan* then,' the girl said. 'I'm on my ane today. Dinnae need this, frankly.'

The door swung shut with a clang.

Moira felt she ought to say something.

'I . . . appreciate this,' she said, her voice hoarse. 'Thank you.'

The girl pulled her mouth into a tiny bud, and looked Moira up and down.

'Save yer thanks,' she said. 'I ken who you are. Cannae believe they're letting you walk free after whit you did.'

Moira felt her eyes glaze with tears.

'It wasn't me,' she whispered, though she didn't know what she was denying – didn't know whether she had a right to deny it. The girl only rolled her eyes.

'Yer man's through there,' she said, gesturing towards a swing door with a small square window set into it. 'I've got a hundred things oan, so go dae whitever it is you're here for.'

Moira staggered through the swing door, which was lighter than she'd expected and gave way too readily under her weight. The cafe seemed dim after the industrial lighting of the kitchen, though it had floor-to-ceiling plate-glass windows on two sides. It wasn't especially busy, but every single face whipped round to look at Moira as she barrelled into the room. It felt like one of those moments you see sometimes in movies, where everyone's frozen but the hero, and the camera swings round to show all three hundred and sixty degrees of that frozen scene. The afternoon light was coming in refracted through the twee net pelmets on the windows, through the barrelled glass cake cabinet, and it sparkled on the tabletops with their wipe-clean gingham PVC cloths. Moira noticed that everything was green: green flocked wallpaper, green patterned coffee cups, green artwork hanging in clip-frames on the walls. There was a little moulded vase on every table, and a green plastic flower in every vase.

Moira straightened up. *Look normal*, she told herself, though she didn't really know what that meant any more. She tried to avoid catching anyone's eye as she cast about the room for Lockley, but her gaze did alight for a moment on Amy, who was holding a coffee cup in mid-air, looking more worried than Moira had ever seen her. She didn't want to look at her too long, so – *yes*, there he was. Lockley had settled himself at a table right by the window, so Moira could be seen by any passer-by who happened to look in.

She felt her annoyance flare up and then go out, like a thrown match. She didn't have the energy to keep it alight.

'Mrs Summers,' Lockley said as she sank into the chair opposite him. 'May I call you Moira?'

Moira looked, blinking, into Lockley's face. He'd emailed her a photo of himself so she'd know him when she arrived, and though it had helped her to pick him out, it wasn't a true image of him. He was smiling at her, but only with his mouth. He had small, neat teeth, with a gap in between every one – like a child's teeth, she thought. His eyes were remarkably pale, and a little strange, almost expressionless. Moira felt cold. She didn't know what she was doing here.

'Yes,' she said, after what felt like a long time. 'I suppose so.'

'I *so* appreciate you coming here,' Lockley said, but as he said it, he rattled the teaspoon in its saucer against his empty cup, to show her he'd been waiting. 'Allow me to say before we begin that I am so terribly sorry for . . . what happened.'

Moira swallowed hard, but said nothing.

'Right,' Lockley said, after waiting a moment, watching her with his pale eyes. He fished behind him, amongst the folds of the coat he'd thrown over the chair-back. Moira wanted to turn and look over at Amy, but she didn't want him to see her do it.

Lockley pulled out a mobile phone that, to Moira, looked huge. He fiddled with the screen for a moment, and then placed the phone face up on the table between them.

'You're recording this?' Moira asked. Her voice came out like a squawk. She could feel people's eyes on her.

Lockley smiled his mouth-only smile again.

'I record everything,' he said. 'You've got to be whiter than white in my line of work, Moira.'

Moira shook her head. A faint tinnitus was troubling her hearing, making her feel like somewhere behind her, someone was whispering something she couldn't quite catch.

'I don't think I'm okay with that.'

'The recording?' Lockley spread his hands, palms up. 'No problem, but I can't tell you what I know unless you agree to my terms.'

Moira looked down at the table, felt him watching her.

'Fine,' she said, after a long moment. 'Let's talk.'

This time, Lockley's eyes smiled too, but the smile had an edge to it – a glint, like moonlight on a knife.

'Great,' he said. 'First, Moira, I'd like to ask you: why do you think Ryan did what he did at Three Rivers College that day?'

Moira blinked.

'I'm not here to talk about that,' she said.

'Did you have any idea – any idea at all, Moira – that he might have been planning something?' Lockley didn't acknowledge that she'd spoken; he barely paused. 'Even if you didn't at the time, do you now, with hindsight? Maybe there was something he said. Maybe the two of you had a conversation that looks different now, in the cold light of day?'

His words seemed to echo around her. *A conversation that looks different now. Now, with hindsight.*

Lockley watched her.

'Tell me what you know, Moira,' he said. 'Tell me what you *knew* about this crime.'

Moira passed a hand over her mouth. She was trying not to cry.

'I'm here to – you said you would—'

She stopped, closed her eyes, and pulled air in through her nose.

'You said I was coming here,' she said, a little more steadily, 'to hear about this . . . theory.'

Outside, a pedestrian slowed down to look into the cafe. Moira met the man's eye, and watched as he struggled to place her. She saw it happen, a light going out in his eyes as he realised who she was. His face darkened and he hurried on, out of sight.

'I'm right, aren't I?'

Lockley was still watching her – with those weird eyes he seemed to be looking right through her skull.

'I'm right,' he said. 'You knew something, didn't you? Something you still haven't told anyone. You talked to him, and something he said made you suspicious. Or maybe you found a diary entry he wrote, and you couldn't help but read it. You dismissed it at the time, but then – what? A week later? A month later? All those young girls were killed. Thirteen deaths you could have prevented if you'd spoken up.' He leaned forward over the table. 'You could have been the hero here, Moira. You could have saved those women. But you didn't, did you? You let them die. You did that. *You.* When all along you could have—'

Moira flicked a hand out from under the table, and smacked her palm against the tabletop, just once.

'*Stop.*'

The sound was louder than she'd intended – a *slap* against the shiny plastic tablecloth. The cafe fell silent around them.

'Is there something you'd like to say?' Lockley nudged the phone a little closer to her.

Moira closed her eyes, waited for the gradual ebb of background noise to return.

'Tell me,' she said, 'about these people.'

Lockley widened his eyes. 'People?'

'The internet people,' she said. 'The truth – truth unifies? Those people. They think Ryan is . . . they think this was all some sort of hoax?'

'Is that what you hope happened, Moira?'

Looking back, Moira would realise that the reality of the situation had already begun to dawn on her then. Hopelessness was rising in her, a column of smoke through cold air. But still, she answered him.

'Of course,' she said. 'Of course I want to hope . . . that it isn't true. That none of this really happened.'

'You wish Ryan were still alive – that these Truth Unifies folks are right?'

She was crying now, she realised; she'd forgotten that she was trying not to.

'Of course I do,' she said. 'I wish that more than anything.'

'More than anything,' he echoed, 'you wish the Truth Unifies folks are right.'

He smirked, avoiding her eyes for perhaps the first time since she'd sat down.

'Interesting,' he said.

Moira's heart chugged. '*What*'s interesting?'

Lockley's eyes snapped back up to her face, and she had to glance away.

'Well,' he said. 'First, Truth Unifies is generally considered to be the online equivalent of the padded room at the loony bin. These people are certifiably nuts, Moira. They believe in *chemtrails*, for goodness' sake. If you think that *I* was taken in by their garbage for even one minute then you're out of your mind. But second – you wish what they were saying were true? Really? Because what they're saying is that your son was recruited by the military, trained for years as a licensed-to-kill marksman, and was then sent to test out his hard-earned skills on a bunch of innocent girls. They're saying that in the immediate confusion that followed this blood-bath, he walked away, was given a golden handshake and a new passport and he's now living the high life on the Riviera or some-where. So tell me, Moira – *do you* wish that were true?'

Nausea rose through her body. Moira leapt to her feet, looking down at Lockley as though he'd administered an electric shock.

'I didn't say that,' she said. 'I didn't say that. I didn't.'

Lockley picked up the mobile phone and waved it at her. He shrugged.

Moira stood there, looking down at the table, for what seemed like an hour. The gingham pattern of the tablecloth flashed and swam. She felt her hands and arms go cold, prickles of static running up and down the skin, but her torso was hot and loose, as though her ribcage were suddenly molten. Rage – it took her a couple of seconds to recognise it but yes, here it was. Rage at this snide man whose desire for clicks and comments outweighed all else. Rage at her own stupidity for coming here – for demanding to come here, no less. Rage at Amy and DI Birch and Anjan and all the supposedly responsible people who'd allowed her to walk out of the house. But mostly rage at her son, at Ryan. In that moment, she felt so angry with her dead son that she thought she might throw up all over this man in his shabby grey clothes, all over the bright green disinfected *everything* around him. Her hand still stung from when she'd slapped the tabletop, and the sting felt good. She felt like she wanted to hit out at more things, wanted to overturn every crockery-laden table in the whole place.

'I can't,' she eventually said. She had no idea what the rest of the sentence might be.

'Moira.' Lockley flung her name like a rock as she turned her back on him. 'You should really sit back down and tell me what it is you knew. You *want* to tell someone. That's not going to go away.'

Moira closed her eyes and began to walk. She had a vague idea of where Amy was, and began to head there. The hot-ribcage feeling was almost too much to bear.

'The guilt's going to keep eating at you, Moira.' Lockley had raised his voice, so it seemed to fill the room, seemed to gently shudder the artwork in its clip-frames, the plastic flowers in their vases. 'It'd do you good to share the load. I'd be doing you a favour – that's why I contacted you. Let me do my job.'

Two hands took hold of Moira's arms, above the elbows. She opened her eyes, and it was Amy; Amy had her. Behind Amy, Steve was already halfway through the kitchen's swing door, holding it open for them to escape. But it was too late.

'You owe it to the public, Moira.' Behind her, Lockley was shouting. 'And I won't wait forever.'

Everyone was staring. Moira didn't need to be able to see them to know. Amy's face was the same washed-out green as the cafe's walls – in her eyes, Moira could see real fear.

'I'm sorry,' she whispered, as Amy began to guide her out into the too-bright kitchen.

'You know I'll print something either way,' Lockley yelled from the other room. The pink-streaked girl had pulled open the back door, a *serves you right* expression all over her face.

Moira fled.

29 May, 3.45 p.m.

Ishbel had walked out immediately after the cremation. She'd had no desire to huddle under that plastic carport roof, exchanging platitudes. She didn't want to talk about what had happened – any of it. Not the scene Jack Egan had caused, not Abigail's relationship with him, not Aidan's now-public indiscretions, not Barry Kesson's taking her side. And her daughter's death, in all its horrible violence . . . that she wanted to talk about least of all. So she'd simply walked past those things, out into a day that seemed to be built from rain.

She'd found Greg, standing in the thin lee of the huge blue skip, smoking under its overhang of rotting flowers. It wasn't until she recognised the angular line of his turned back that she realised she'd been looking for him.

'I didn't know you smoked,' she said.

He hadn't heard her approaching, and he jumped.

'Sorry,' she said. And then, again, 'I didn't know you smoked.'

Greg shrugged.

'I'm a doctor,' he said. 'Doesn't go down well.'

Ishbel had stood there, feeling the rain pushing her clothes against her, making them heavier and heavier, plastering them to her skin.

'People have so many secrets,' she said.

Greg threw his cigarette on the ground. She heard it fizzle as the lit end hit the wet tarmac. He took a step towards her, then stopped. She felt the same strange ache she'd felt that night in the hospital: she wanted him to take hold of her and tell her everything was going to be okay.

'Look,' he said, now standing next to her in the full pelt of the weather. 'I didn't really know Abigail. But I've known plenty of men like that kid. That Jack kid. They're so smooth, so plausible. She was tricked. Men like that make having secrets seem exciting.'

Ishbel had watched as the shoulders of his jacket began to darken with rain.

'Whereas in fact,' he added, 'secrets are nothing but a pain. You regret ever making them.'

Ishbel glanced back at the small huddle of bodies under the carport. Aidan was shaking hands with the grey-streaked female undertaker, but his mouth was a hard line. Barry Kesson had bundled his family quickly away before Aidan had had the chance for a face-off that Ishbel knew he'd dearly have loved. Jack Egan's parting words bounced around inside Ishbel's skull: *she belonged to me. She belonged to me.*

'She would have come back to you,' Greg said, as though he'd been thinking of those words, too. 'In time. I didn't really know her, but I know she was smart. She'd've seen through him eventually. She would have come back to you.'

Greg reached out through the rain and put one hand on Ishbel's shoulder. She flinched a little at his touch, but forced herself to hold his gaze. Water oozed in the fabric of her coat.

'You have to believe that,' he said.

Behind her, Pauline had called her name across the car park. She ignored it.

'In time.' She echoed Greg, but her own voice was nowhere near as strident.

'Yes,' he said. The way he glanced behind her told her that Pauline was beginning to advance towards them. 'I'm so sorry that Ryan Summers took that away. That opportunity for her to see her mistake. To learn.'

Ishbel turned her face upwards a little, let the rain hit it more squarely, to hide her tears.

'He's just so awful.' Ishbel realised she wasn't sure who she was talking about. Jack? Or Aidan? Perhaps she was talking about Ryan Summers. She didn't know.

'He's twenty-one,' Greg said, choosing Jack from the unspoken list. 'Twenty-one-year-old men *are* awful. Having been one, I apologise. He'll be sorry, mark my words. He's playing the tragic boyfriend now, but just wait until he gets typecast in that role. Wait till he's forty and it's still all anyone ever talks to him about.' He paused for a moment, and then added, 'And you know, he probably did love Abigail. Not like *you* love her, but . . . in his own awful twenty-one-year-old sort of way, he probably did.'

Ishbel looked directly at her friend. She felt like this was the first attempt anyone had made to say something meaningful – truly meaningful – to her in two full weeks.

'I'm sorry about everything,' Greg said. He dropped his hand from her shoulder. It's absence held the sleeve of her jacket against the skin.

Pauline was almost upon them.

'I have to go,' Ishbel had said then. And then, because she felt there were other things to say but no way to ever begin saying them, she added, 'Thank you, Greg.'

She'd pulled out her keys and dashed towards the car.

As she'd sat in the queue of traffic at the roundabout at Elm Row, the anger she'd felt towards Aidan had begun to solidify. She realised she wasn't crying any more.

'This roundabout has never worked,' she hissed, as though talking to an invisible passenger. 'People turning right out of Broughton Street just queue up all the way round.'

She'd looked out of her passenger-side window at the Theatre Royal bar, its tall upstairs windows and gaudy painted jester figurines. She'd always found them quite charming – their primary colours defiant in the face of even the worst Edinburgh weather – but now they looked cheap, fake.

'I've left my husband,' Ishbel said, aloud. Then, louder, 'I've left my husband. I've left my husband and my only daughter is dead.'

She'd crawled up Elm Row in the wake of a number 8 bus. The traffic had stopped her outside the bridal shop where they'd bought Abigail's prom dress, the one she'd thought about wearing that day, before Aidan had stopped her. It was a bridesmaid's dress, really, but then, what was the difference? Ishbel had glanced back at the holdall in the back seat and wished, again, that she'd packed that dress. Ahead of her, above the roof of the bus, the clock tower of the Balmoral Hotel loomed in the low cloud. Ishbel had allowed herself a moment to daydream: she could check in there, hand her car keys to the kilted valet, walk upstairs and lie down on a fancier and more comfortable bed than she and Aidan could ever have justified buying. No one would ever find her. When she ran out of money, she could live in the clock tower like Hallam Foe. But no, of course not. When the bus had finally moved, she'd driven right past the front of the Balmoral with its beautiful balustrades and old-fashioned revolving door, and turned left onto Waverley Bridge, then left again onto Market Street.

She'd checked into the Premier Inn using her mother's maiden name. Aidan could still find her, of course – Rehan had asked her to text him and let him know where she was, and as he was technically a policeman, she'd felt like she had to. But no one else could reach her for now. When she opened the door to the poky room, with its cookie-cutter artwork, its regulation teabags and bland-smelling shampoo, relief had carried her inside like a wave. That was twenty-four hours ago now.

She wasn't quite sure where those hours had gone – the holdall was still sitting at the foot of the bed. All she'd taken from it was one change of clothes: she'd peeled off her outfit from the cremation and dumped it in the bath. For a while she'd stood there in her underwear and watched streaks of grey rainwater run out of the pile of cloth and into the plughole. For a while, and then a while longer. It had begun to get dark.

She'd closed the curtains and lain down on top of the spotlessly made bed, still dressed. She must have slept, though she didn't feel like she had. When she opened the curtains again – heavy on the rail thanks to their matte blackout lining – a pillar of spring sunshine had streamed into the room. To the east, beyond the

Calton Hill observatory and the shoulder of Leith, she'd watched a black stripe of weather moving landward. A rainbow trailed behind it like the tail of a kite. *One of those Edinburgh days*, she thought. Right out of the old local joke: 'Don't like the weather? Just wait five minutes.'

She hadn't eaten for a full day, and she didn't really care. *I've left my husband and my only daughter is dead,* she reminded herself, every so often. The TV – which had been switched on and waiting for her when she first walked in the room – flashed and glowed. Sometime during her fitful sleep, she'd woken to find that TV showing an extended episode of *Newsnight*, devoted to, what else, the Three Rivers shooting.

'. . . so to what extent,' the *Newsnight* presenter had asked, 'can there really *be* an investigation in a case like this? Can there ever be justice for these families?'

The camera panned to a member of the panel who, according to the bar below his face, was a retired deputy chief of police from somewhere in Colorado.

'Well, you know,' he said, 'you're right. A case like this, it's hard to think about it in terms of justice. Because what justice can there be for these families, when the gunman can't be held accountable? Right now there's a lot of anger, a lot of resentment, we've seen that in the community already. And I think that's understandable. But at the end of the day, it's a fairly open-and-shut case. We know who did it, we know all the details of how he did it – the only thing we'll never know is *why* he did it. And although that's a question that may torture us all for the rest of our lives, it's not the business of law enforcement to answer that question.'

Ishbel had cast around, sleepily, for the remote, and hit *mute*.

Ishbel's blood felt fizzy. She'd lost a whole day to the suck of grief, to this bland room – she needed to do something. She crawled on all-fours to the end of the bed, hauled the unzipped holdall up onto the duvet, and tipped the contents out in one quick jerk. The pink diary bounced out, settled itself atop the haphazard pile of cloth.

Ishbel sat on the hard hotel mattress, looking down at it. She hadn't noticed before, but now she saw that the cover had lettering embossed onto the leather, and picked out in screen-printed gold. *Be so good they can't ignore you*, it read. It was the sort of sentiment that, three weeks ago, she'd have scoffed at.

'People can always ignore you,' she imagined saying, Abigail's heart-shaped face frowning back at her.

She cast her eyes around the hotel room, looking for something that might help her break the little padlock. The lock on her daughter's secret diary. *Your dead daughter*, she reminded herself. *Your only daughter. Your daughter who is dead.*

Her eyes came to rest on the tea tray with its two clean cups, its saucers and sugar packets. The knives the hotel provided were blunt, bendy plastic, but the teaspoons were stainless steel. Ishbel stood, grabbed one, jammed its handle into the loop of the little padlock, then braced the diary against the table. For ten or so agonising seconds, she levered the spoon against the padlock's hasp and thought nothing was going to happen. Then suddenly, there was a metallic pop, and the padlock broke free. It cracked against Ishbel's kneecap, and she let out a cry – a mingling of pain, shock and triumph – as it fell to the floor.

The diary opened with a delicious crackling sound: the cheap glue binding splitting in a million tiny ways. The first entry was from Abigail's first day at college: over eight months ago, the previous September:

First day of college today. Was late – mortifying. Didn't realise the 21 bus was so fucking slow. Still, it was only Freshers stuff today so I guess it didn't matter too much.

Met some other folk off my course. Mostly girls. Almost all younger than me, most of them are straight out of high school. Lots of pretentious bitches who want to be Meryl Streep or something. There are only three guys on the whole course. Chatted to one of them, Jack. He's the oldest person on the course, about eighteen months older than me or so. He's pretty hot. But guys who do drama are basically always gay, so I need to not get my hopes up.

Ishbel almost bailed here, as the short entry gave way to plain white page. The sensation of reading Abigail's most private thoughts – with the knowledge that Abigail was dead chilling her like the shadow of some terrible obelisk – was almost too strange to bear. But she knew that she couldn't *not* turn the page.

There were a few entries about the drama course, vague vignettes of days spent signing up for classes and chatting with course-mates in the canteen. Various complaints about the number 21 bus and having to get up early. Then, about two weeks in:

Got paired up with Jack in class. Think I might be a bit in love with him now, which is SUPER AWKWARD as I am still worried he might be gay. The way he dresses is so cute – he always wears a button-down shirt with a cardigan over it. His favourite shirt is this Ben Sherman one that's a pink check – pink shirt = gay, right??? I know it's his favourite cause he wears it basically every other day. And then he wears this dark grey lambswool cardigan all the time. And these thick-framed glasses with tortoiseshell frames. He ought to look like someone's grandpa but actually it looks pretty cool. He looks like a poet – no wait, he looks like an actor. He totally looks like he's an actor already. Dark curly hair and this big smile. His teeth are so white that I try not to smile with teeth when I'm around him in case he notices mine are yellow. But he's gay, right? I mean he's into drama and he's well dressed and he's SO NICE. No way he's not gay.

Ishbel felt a spike of anger, trying to match this tender description to the man who only the previous day had yelled at her in the cold crematorium. She was determined that, at twenty-one years old, he was a *man*, though diary-Abigail breathlessly referred to him as a *boy*. As she read on, the anger rattled her. She remembered what Greg had said about secrets and tricks.

OK, so Jack is definitely not gay. (I guess he might still be bi.) We were chatting and he mentioned his girlfriend. I guess I must have had some kind of look on my face because he looked at me and then he said, 'I mean, she's my ex-girlfriend now.' So, great, he's not gay. GREAT! But also, nice work Abi, you totally failed at playing it cool. But also also also, he wanted me to know that he doesn't have a girlfriend

RIGHT NOW, so ... does that mean he's interested? It would be basically the best thing that ever happened to me if he is. I am so totally over being a nineteen-year-old virgin and having to fucking LIE all the time.

Ishbel didn't have the stomach to read the next few entries in any detail. She'd found herself skipping whole pages, because she could tell from the first sentence that they'd be too painful to read. She could feel her little girl slipping away from her – being *pulled* away from her by this young woman, this adult woman who seemed to have snuck up on Ishbel from some shadowy alternative world. She thought of Abigail aged four, pulling on her powder blue tutu to perform in her first ever ballet recital. She thought of her aged seven, trying on Ishbel's lipstick for the first time at her birthday party. She thought of the time they'd chatted, awkwardly and in low voices, about the coming of Abigail's first period, when she was twelve. Each of those moments had come with a pang of horror at how rapidly time was rushing by. But those small flashes of pain were nothing compared with the agony of sitting in a hotel room, realising that time had stopped now, and there would be no more growing up, no more moments to record, no more firsts or lasts. The agony of reading Abigail's account of losing her virginity: *It's okay, I knew it would hurt and I don't think Jack noticed. I had a little cry in the bathroom and then I was fine. When I got back he was asleep.* Ishbel cried then, too.

But there were stranger things to come. An entry in December read:

So you know I've been wondering how Jack has so much money always? Well today I found out he's basically a drug dealer. That little creeper Ryan Summers came and told me during the SU meeting. I didn't believe him at first but it bothered me, so I decided to just ask Jack and he fessed up. I guess that explains why he has so many nice clothes and always looks so great. That explains his car and everything. We had a big fight about it and he told me I was naive and sheltered and I should run home to Mummy and Daddy's big house. He's a fucking asshole and I want to hate him but I'm sitting here missing him so much. I'm an idiot.

For a few moments, Ishbel struggled to breathe. There, in her daughter's own handwriting, was the name of her murderer. They knew each other. They had spoken. *SU*, Ishbel realised slowly, was the students' union. Abigail had been a fair-weather member. Ryan Summers must have been involved in it, too. For the life of her, Ishbel couldn't imagine him wanting to be part of such a thing – it didn't fit with the shadowy picture she'd built in her mind.

A few days later:

So happy Jack and I are back together. I missed him so much it hurt. And I can live with the job – that's what he calls it, 'the job', which is kind of funny. Whatever. I can live with it if I ignore it. It's none of anyone's business, anyway. Definitely none of Ryan's business. Little freak came to find me again and told me he thought it was a bad idea that I was back together with Jack. Like anyone asked him! I don't even know him. Don't even want to know him.

Then, in late March, a short one:

Long time no see, diary. I guess I've been busy. In the end I cracked and agreed to help Jack with the job. I've got pretty involved. Guess that explains the absence, right?

Ishbel had felt a sensation like kicking up through water. She'd become completely submerged in the diary – in the weird, adult voice of her daughter – that coming back to the hotel room, with the TV showing *Neighbours* on mute and the window's quiet smatter of rain, felt like surfacing from the depths of a choppy sea. It was true, then, what Grant Lockley had said about Abigail and the drugs. She could no longer pretend that it wasn't. Ishbel's face burned.

'Baby,' she said, aloud, into the stale quiet of the hotel room. 'You silly, silly, silly girl.'

She blinked: once again, there were tears. On the crumpled duvet, Abigail's diary sat open to the most recent entries. They'd grown so perfunctory that each double page held ten or so:

Drop-off today after college. J got us stuck in traffic on the way back and I had to make up some shit about where I was. Disapproving mother–daughter chat. Wish I had money to move out.

Ishbel remembered that evening. She'd accepted her daughter's version of events – something about the bus, that same number 21 bus, being diverted down some strange new route. Abigail had been late for dinner, and hadn't sent a text or called to say where she was, hence the *disapproving mother–daughter chat*. Ishbel felt stupid now. There must have been signs, and she must have ignored every last one.

Missed all my classes today but got cornered by Mr Welsh in reception. SU meeting was just starting and I couldn't think of an excuse. Hadn't been for weeks. Ryan Summers was there and made some gross joke about Jack and me. I'm so fucking sick of him creeping around me. After everyone had gone I told Mr Welsh Ryan's been making me uncomfortable. Mr Welsh is going to log it as a formal complaint and talk to him. I made it sound way worse than it was. Serves the little freak right. Jack thinks he's in love with me but I think he's just a pathetic loser who likes other people's business. He ought to get high sometime, that'd sort him out.

Ishbel closed her eyes. Her head felt like it was full of noise: blood shuttling in her ears and this voice, the voice of this awful, abrasive woman that her daughter had apparently turned into. There was also Greg's voice – *She was tricked. This wasn't who she really was* – and Jack Egan's words from the crematorium, as though he were arguing with Greg. *Take a look at yourself. Who's the real monster?* But as Ishbel re-read the page, the voices faded. She felt like she'd been digging for a long time, digging at frozen earth with her bare hands: she was hungry and tired and had cried so much over the past fortnight that she wasn't sure she could ever bring herself to cry again, about anything. But now she'd reached what might be, possibly, the thing she'd been digging for all along, and it felt like a moment of calm, a fleeting white space where she could think clearly.

That could be why he killed her, she thought. *That might be why she was first.*

The final entry was from that Monday, the night before the shooting. *The night before she died*: the thought formed itself before Ishbel could push it away. The night they had fought.

The night Ishbel wished she could go back and do again, more than she wished for anything – perhaps more, even, than she wished for Abigail to be still alive. She remembered standing on the stairs, carrying on the fight with Aidan because Abigail had removed herself to her room. Then she'd stomped past her daughter's bedroom door like a teenager, hoping Abigail could hear her petulance, her rage. She'd gone to bed in the spare room and lain awake in the dark, thinking of all the righteous and punishing things she should have said. She'd even thought about marching back to Abigail's room, waking her up and saying them. Now, she sat on her hotel bed and thought, *It's me. Me. I'm the monster.* She realised she hadn't once thought to wake Abigail and ask her what was really wrong. To tell her daughter she was sorry. To say she loved her. To do these things in case the next day her daughter ended up dead.

The diary entry from that night read:

Got a lift to the pick-up from Mum. Ha, just joking. She drove me as far as football practice and I went on from there. Jack bailed on me though, just never showed up. Jamie was fucking raging, scared the shit out of me. AND no lift back, so I had to get the bus. Timed it wrong and Mother Dearest saw that I hadn't been at football. Had to basically run out of the car and lock myself in here to avoid the twenty questions. Last thing I need is her sniffing around.

To top it all off I had to rearrange with Jamie to go back on Friday with Jack. So that's another morning of classes missed. I'm fucking failing my course. I'm freaked. I've got to get out. Especially if Jack's going to bail on me anyway. I love him but it isn't worth this. I've got to get out.

Ishbel's phone rang, vibrating off the bedside table with a noise so loud that her pulse gunned. She snatched it up: for just a moment it was Abigail, phoning to tell her she was sorry, she'd made a mistake, but she was coming home now. *I'll see you at home, Mum.*

But on the other end of the line was a man's voice. A voice Ishbel recognised: that only-very-slight Scottish accent.

'Ishbel Hodgekiss?'

She wanted to hiss, like a cat does when it's cornered.

'How did you get this number, Lockley?'

There was a pause, but when he spoke again it was as though she'd said, *How can I help?*

'I was phoning to see if you'd like to make a comment on a new piece I'm writing. It's to coincide with the public memorial service next week.'

'Tell me,' Ishbel said, feeling every muscle in her body tense, 'how you got this number.'

'Will you be at the memorial, Ishbel?' He had a true talent, she found herself thinking, for persistence. 'Or are tensions between you and your husband just running too high?'

She found that she couldn't speak. She heard her own incredulous breath crackle in the phone's speaker.

'I know,' Lockley said, 'that the rumour mill is a terrible thing. Why don't you set the record straight, hmm? Tell your side of the story. You and I could sit down, somewhere private, no one else around, and you could just say absolutely everything you've been wanting to say to the world. About Abigail, about Jack Egan, about Ryan Summers. You could reach out to the families of the other victims, all those other people who are hurting. You could tell the world what a wonderful young woman Abigail really was. I can help you do that. That's how I like to see my role – I can be your mouthpiece to the world.'

Ishbel's mouth hung slack at the sheer gall of this man, but a small part of her pulled and twisted in his direction. If it came without strings, his proposition would be attractive indeed. She could see how Jack Egan had fallen for it. But she'd also seen, thanks to the hotel TV, that Jack Egan was now in police custody.

'I had a talk with Moira Summers today,' Lockley said. 'You know *she's* got opinions on everything that happened. Should the mother of your daughter's killer be allowed a platform, if you don't have one? Don't you want to be able to counter anything she might say?'

Ishbel did feel a spike of anger, then – but she forced herself to push it down. *He's getting to you.* Ryan Summers' mother might think she had something to gain by speaking to the press, but she was wrong. Anything that came out of her mouth would be shot down. Under the anger, Ishbel was surprised to find herself feeling sorry for the woman.

'I can make you a generous financial offer,' Lockley tried.

Ishbel opened her mouth to speak, and still could not. Clearly tired of her silence, he changed tack.

'You know,' he said, his tone darkening, 'it would be a good idea for you take this opportunity, and get into the clear while you can. There's damaging information out there about everyone, and it doesn't take much to dig it up.'

Ishbel found her voice.

'Are you *threatening* me?'

Lockley blustered loudly into the phone.

'Not at all,' he said. She could practically hear him throwing up his hands. 'I'm just doing my job, writing what comes to me. Writing the news. It's not me you have to worry about. It's people like the Telford family.'

Ishbel blinked in surprise. She knew exactly who he was talking about, because the case had been on her mind a lot lately. She'd begun to think of it as the starting point of something – the wheels coming off her marriage, really, if she was honest. Three years ago, she'd had a case at work that involved accusations of embezzlement at a privately owned care home. With the help of another agency, she'd uncovered a years-long paper trail of profit-skimming by the business's founders: a couple named Stuart and Annie Telford. She'd handed her evidence over to the police, but not before the Telfords had hit back at her with an official complaint that they took all the way to the ombudsman. She'd been cleared, but it had been a long, hard year and had impacted on her other cases, her relationship with Aidan, and even her health.

'Don't you want to get your name cleared,' Lockley was saying, 'before Stuart Telford hits the papers saying you had him unfairly sent to jail?'

The line went quiet. Ishbel listened to the dim swish of Lockley's breath as her mind raced.

'Just think about it, Ishbel,' he said, at last. 'And call me when you'd like to talk.'

29 May, 6.45 p.m.

'I'm sorry, Helen.'

McLeod didn't look the least bit sorry. He'd gone home two hours earlier, but someone had called him back in. Lockley had finished his write-up of the meeting with Moira, including a detailed paragraph about police manpower being used to set it all up, and had emailed in wanting a quote. Some complete bastard somewhere in the building had forwarded the email to McLeod, and he'd *actually come back to the office* in order to play hell with every single officer who'd been even vaguely involved.

Birch and Amy he'd saved for last.

'I just do not know what possessed you.'

Amy was fighting tears. Birch was trying not to look at her.

'DI Birch thought that—'

McLeod's head snapped round towards Amy, who made a kind of choked sound to silence herself.

'I'll get to you in just a minute, Kato,' he said. 'DI Birch can bullshit me all by herself, I think you'll find.'

Birch began to count, in her head. *Stay calm, Helen.* She got as far as six before McLeod's angry blue silence became too much to bear.

'As I said, sir, my first priority was always Mrs Summers' safety. I spoke with Mr Chaudhry, and—'

'You see, Birch.' McLeod pressed one palm against his forehead. 'Those were your first two mistakes. One: you dragged that fucking greasy lawyer into things. Two: you forgot that your first priority ought always to have been *the success of this fucking investigation.*'

Birch tried to make herself count again. She failed.

'With all due respect, sir, I don't think we need to resort to that sort of language about Anjan Chaudhry.' She felt her cheeks turning red, but realised there was nothing she could do to stop it. 'I went to him because I *wanted* to find an easy solution to this problem. I thought he could talk Moira out of it.'

McLeod snorted. He'd noticed the blushing. *Don't let him fluster you* – the voice in her head was a yell, but it wasn't working.

'And how did that work out for you, Helen?'

'It didn't.' Birch set her teeth. 'Mr Chaudhry pointed out to me that Moira Summers was free to do what she liked. It became apparent that she *would* do what she liked. So then I had to make a call about her safety.'

'Bollocks to her safety.' McLeod banged a hand against the desk beside him, so hard that Birch found herself thinking, *That had to hurt.* 'What about how this looks? We'd *just* been talking about this fucking Lockley problem. You went and made it ten times worse!'

I still think what I did was right, she wanted to say. *If I'd let Moira go out alone and she'd been attacked, we'd all look a whole lot worse in the press right now.* But there was no point. McLeod was raging from a place of fear that she couldn't assuage. Come the inquiry, he'd be the one getting photographed walking in and out of court. If a scapegoat were required, he'd be it. As if he'd read her thoughts, he leaned in close to her, and said:

'If I get taken down by this, Helen, I swear to God I will be taking you with me.'

She felt the words brush against her ear as they left his lips. A shiver ran through her.

'Yes, sir,' was all she could manage to say.

McLeod straightened up.

'I'm reining you in, Birch,' he said. His voice was back at full volume, as though he were saying this for the benefit of someone sitting outside the room. 'From now on, I want to hear about everything. Every decision you make, you run it by me first. Every penny that's spent on this investigation, I want to approve it first. Consider your wings mightily fucking clipped, do you understand me?'

'Yes, sir.'

'You do?'

'*Yes*, sir.'

'Fucking *good*.'

He turned on Amy.

'As for you, Kato,' he said, 'what I am about to say should come as absolutely no surprise to you whatsoever. I'm taking you off this case, and I'll tell you right now, I think it was the wrong call to put you on it in the first place.'

He glanced back at Birch, who decided not to meet his eye.

'You'll hand over to another FLO of my choice,' he said. 'I'll have a think about it and let you know who in the morning.'

'Yes, sir.' Birch didn't look at Amy, either, but from the crack in her voice she knew that the younger woman had now lost the battle with her tears.

'Right.' McLeod straightened up, and knocked his hands together as if shaking off dirt. 'Both of you get the fuck out of this office. I should have been home an hour ago.'

Birch held open the door for Amy.

'Chin up,' she whispered, as Amy passed in front of her. Straight away, Amy snapped her face upwards, and screwed her tearful face into a hard line.

'Good girl,' Birch said. She closed the door on McLeod, already climbing back into his overcoat.

She took Amy gently by the elbow, and steered her down the corridor, away from ground zero.

'Don't let them see you bleed,' she said, as two male officers rounded the corner and began to approach.

'Lads.' Birch nodded as they passed, and they nodded back. When she glanced at Amy, she saw she was just about holding it together.

They made it to the ladies', which was mercifully empty. Birch hoisted herself up onto the bank of sinks and perched there, biting her bottom lip, while Amy collapsed into a stall and sobbed. Birch passed the time trying to think and re-think the events of the day – was there some other call she could have made? Was McLeod right? Did the PR stuff come first? But she kept thinking about Anjan's star-anise smell, then thinking about Charlie, and *then* thinking how much she hated Grant Lockley and how she wished that, just for once, karma really would be the bitch everyone said it was, because that man was due one hell of a karmic kicking. The thoughts chased one another in a circle, over and over, and Birch realised her brain was done for the day.

In the cubicle, Amy's sobs were easing.

'I'm sorry I got you into this, Amy,' Birch said. 'Maybe McLeod was right: I shouldn't have put you on this case. I should've seen it would turn to shit. It couldn't *not*, with a crime like this.'

There was a clunk as Amy unlatched the cubicle door. She emerged looking younger than usual – her makeup mostly smeared away, and her face a little puffy.

'Remember you said we could go for a drink sometime, guv?'

Birch blinked. 'I do.'

'Well.' Amy gestured at her own reflection in the mirror behind Birch. 'I think now is as good a time as any, right?'

They ended up in a Stockbridge wine bar, a few doors down from Amy's flat. The place made Birch feel old, and the lighting was too dim. But she watched with some admiration as Amy ordered a steak burger with sweet potato fries, and then when it arrived, practically inhaled the stack of food. Birch ordered a salad and silently wished she had Amy's metabolism.

'I'm so sorry this happened.' She could no longer keep from saying it, even though Amy had explicitly forbidden her from apologising any more. 'The more I think about it, the more I think McLeod was right about some of this. We should have just let Moira go out and meet Lockley. She knew the risks. Probably nothing would have happened to her, and you'd still be her FLO right now.'

Amy was shaking her head.

'No,' she said, quietly. 'I'm glad you – we – did what we did. If nothing else, it showed Moira that we care about her. That we value her life as much as the lives of the victims' families . . . even if no one else does.'

'I guess so. But I'd be lying if I said I did it out of concern for Moira. You know, I look down my nose at McLeod's preferred mode of police-work, but I could do to learn a thing or two there. He's aggressive sometimes, but he never gets personal. He never takes it home with him, have you noticed? He clocks in at nine and clocks out at five and that's the only time he gives it. He doesn't get emotionally attached, ever.'

Amy swilled the wine in her glass and then watched the mini-tornado she'd created as it whirled and subsided.

'You think that's a good thing?'

Birch was quiet for a second.

'Before this case,' she said, slowly, 'I would have said no. But now I think . . . yeah, he's maybe got the right idea.'

Amy wrinkled her nose.

'It's easy for him, though. I mean, emotional attachments or not, I'd love to just put everything down at five o'clock and walk out the door. And you know you're being generous to him there, guv. Four thirty's nearer the mark most days.'

Birch laughed. She could feel the wine starting to muddy her thoughts.

'Okay, you're right about that. And *maybe* he can only do his tidy little leave-it-at-the-office thing because he hands so much work down to the rest of us.'

'That'll be you one day,' Amy said, raising an eyebrow.

Birch clapped one hand against her chest in mock-horror, reminding herself of Lockley.

'God forbid,' she said. 'To be honest, after this case? If they asked me to give my pips back tomorrow I wouldn't fight them.'

Amy seemed to be watching as Birch polished off the wine in her glass.

'I think you're doing the best job you can,' she said.

'You're a kind woman, but you're wrong. This is what I mean about not getting too involved. I think I made the wrong call with Moira today because I let it get to me.'

Birch looked over at the bar and cocked her head slightly: *more wine required.* She hadn't drunk this much for a long time.

'Specifically, I've let Lockley get to me.'

Saying it out loud felt significant: not a relief, exactly, but something close. Like feeling the rock you've been trying to push aside shift, just slightly.

'Yeah, what *is* that? I mean, if you don't mind me asking.'

Birch looked at Amy. She knew what she meant, but said:

'What is . . . what?'

A waiter delivered two new glasses of wine to the table. Birch thought he looked about twelve, and then immediately thought, *Great, I've got to that age where I think all young people look twelve.* She watched the waiter look at Amy's legs as she thanked him.

'You and Lockley,' Amy said, oblivious. 'There's a rumour doing the rounds that you two have previous.'

Birch shrugged.

'Anyone who's been around long enough has previous with Lockley,' she said. 'He's been a champion cop-baiter since he was still in short trousers.'

Amy smiled, clearly disappointed. *Oh, what the hell,* Birch thought.

'But yeah,' she added, 'it's true. I've got more beef with him than most. And it's not professional, in my case. It's personal.'

Both women took a long drink. Birch watched Amy settle back, waiting for the story.

'Okay,' she said. Somewhere in the ragged landscape of her mind one mast was still upright, transmitting a vague warning against going any further. But she was fuzzy with wine, and didn't know if she could keep thinking about Charlie all the time without going mad.

'The reason I went into police-work,' she said, 'was my little brother. His name was Charlie. You might not remember it, but thirteen years ago he was at the centre of a big missing-person case.'

Amy's eyes widened.

'Charlie Birch,' she said. 'That was your *brother*?'

Birch winced. It was usually better when people hadn't heard of Charlie, hadn't read the articles, hadn't formed an opinion.

'Yes,' she said. 'For better or worse, Charlie Birch was my wee kid brother.'

'Wow, Charlie Birch . . . the teenage gangster,' Amy said. And then, 'I'm sorry.'

Birch shrugged. 'One of Lockley's finest headlines, that,' she said. 'Never proven, of course, but that didn't stop him from printing it. When someone goes missing I guess it's Christmas – you can say what you want, if they're not around to defend themselves. I've just about got it in perspective, now. But at the time I was determined something more could be done – to find Charlie, I mean, or most likely find his body. Confirm or deny those rumours once and for all. That's why I joined the force. I thought I could succeed where everyone before me had failed. I thought I could find him.' She laughed, short and bitterly, into her wine glass. 'Goes to show what thinking does for you.'

Amy was frowning.

'So, Lockley . . .?'

Birch nodded.

'Lockley was brand new, then,' she said. 'He can't even have been twenty. He was interning at one of the major rags – they weren't paying him, and he wanted to get a place at the big boys' table, so he latched on to Charlie. Or rather, he latched on to *us*, the family. Decided he'd dig up the scoop that would make his name. So all those articles you remember, with family skeletons being kicked out of closets? Perps of old being paid to say they'd seen Charlie involved in every shady job since god knows when? Those hit-pieces were all written by Lockley. Those photos of the haggard-looking woman that ran beside them? That was my mother.'

Amy's eyes were wide now, her hand over her mouth.

'He hounded us for bloody months,' Birch said. 'Showed up at the house. Went through the bins. Phoned us up at all hours of the day. He got in touch with people I'd forgotten we knew, offered them their fifteen minutes of fame, then misquoted them left, right and centre. Mum moved house, and he hired a PI to find out where it was. We were his apprenticeship. My family is why he's now a much-loved daily columnist . . . although much-loved by *whom*, I have no idea.'

'I guess he *doesn't* have a life,' Amy said, and Birch remembered their conversation on the phone.

'Yeah . . .' Birch heard her own voice come out dreamy, far-off sounding. 'You got me wondering about that. He's a real piece of work, but to what extent is that just a public face? A *brand*, you know? He might – I don't know – volunteer at a soup kitchen in his spare time, or . . . something.'

Amy grinned. 'You believe that?'

'Not so much,' Birch admitted.

'Me neither.'

Okay, enough about Lockley, Birch thought. She took another long mouthful of wine.

'Sorry,' she said, 'if that was all a bit TMI.'

Amy was blinking a little sleepily.

'Not at all,' she said. 'You know, I always wondered – at the time, I mean – how much of that stuff was really true.'

Birch bit her lip. 'Honestly? We'd have to ask Charlie to find out. And the case has been cold these twelve years. More, even. Not just cold, closed.'

'I'm sorry,' Amy said again. 'How's your mum doing these days?'

Birch closed her eyes, just briefly. That photograph of her mother was there, clear as day in her mind's eye, as soon as she thought of it.

'She died last year. Bowel cancer. It was very quick, which I suppose might have been a blessing. During the whole thing with Charlie, she stopped eating right, had all sorts of digestive problems from the anxiety. She never did get back to health with that, I don't think. There's no proven link, but I'm sure the cancer was connected to . . . well, all of that. That anxiety that never really went away.'

'Jesus,' Amy said. 'I really am sorry.'

'It's okay,' Birch said. 'She went to her grave still convinced that Charlie was alive. That he's out there somewhere. Which I guess was good, in a way; she never grieved for him, never had to. But it drove a bit of a wedge between her and me. I'm a realist. After a while, I accepted that if he ever did turn up, it'd be in a box. And she always wanted to know what progress I'd made, what leads I was following. I kept having to tell her there weren't any, it was over.'

'Oh God, that's heartbreaking.'

Birch shrugged.

'Yeah, but it became just like anyone else's family politics after a while. Daughter fails to live up to mother's expectations. It happens all the time, we weren't special.'

Amy was frowning again.

'Still,' she said, 'you deserve a medal for not . . . I don't know, *doing something* to Lockley.'

Birch laughed. Everything was blurry at the edges, and she felt a strange kind of elation, having shared her story with Amy. Elation, but with a bitter tang to it, too. She felt like she might start to cry, if she didn't navigate through the next few moments carefully.

'You never know,' she said, cranking out a smile. 'At this rate, I won't have to *do* anything. It looks like McLeod is on the verge of doing it for me.'

Three weeks and four days later

FIRST MINISTER AMONG HIGH-PROFILE ATTENDEES AT TODAY'S LONG-AWAITED THREE RIVERS PUBLIC MEMORIAL

By GRANT LOCKLEY
PUBLISHED: 08:02 8 June

The thirteen girls who were brutally killed in the mass shooting at Three Rivers College last month will be remembered at a public memorial service, to be held in Edinburgh's St Giles Cathedral later today. The memorial service will be televised live by STV, and numerous high-profile guests are expected to attend, including the First Minister – who, as we know, never wastes any photo opportunity – the Deputy First Minister, and MSPs from all of the major political parties.

In pictures: our tribute to the Three Rivers College shooting victims

The memorial service will pay tribute to the thirteen young women who lost their lives when their classmate – deranged 20-year-old Engineering student Ryan Summers – burst into the canteen area of the college's Tweed Campus armed with three modified handguns on the morning of 14 May. Tragically, all of the victims were under 30 years old. Among them were Abigail Hodgekiss who, it has been revealed, was involved in a drug-dealing operation at the college; and Liz Gill, the brave 17-year-old who died while trying to disarm Summers. It was announced last week that Gill will be awarded a posthumous medal for her actions – which feels like a silver lining, however slim, among the dark clouds surrounding the Three Rivers investigation.

Brave Three Rivers teen Liz Gill to be awarded George Cross: read more here

Today's memorial service will begin with a public vigil outside the Scottish Parliament buildings. It is expected that staff and students from Three Rivers College will then lead a procession up the Royal Mile to St Giles Cathedral, where the official service is due to begin at 11 a.m. Thousands of people will gather to attend the vigil and church service: STV have erected large screens in West Parliament Square so that those who cannot fit into the cathedral can watch from outside its doors. Millions more will be able to watch via terrestrial TV and online, as the service is live-streamed across the world.

Local communities pay tribute to Three Rivers victims as families bury their loved ones: read more here

The content of the church service hasn't been confirmed, but it is expected that the First Minister will pay tribute to the shooting victims, and that their families will be given the chance to speak to the assembled congregation and viewers at home. Police Scotland have scrambled to support the event, perhaps in a bid to quash the growing public discontent over their handling of the Three Rivers investigation. That's right, folks: they still haven't revealed what really went on that day, *and* there is more and more speculation that things were mishandled at the scene of the shooting. Did this cost vital seconds in which lives could have been saved? The fact that they don't want to tell us speaks volumes.

The police are also supplying hundreds of personnel to staff the vigil, the procession and the outdoor part of the service. Some senior officers at work on the Three Rivers investigation will be in attendance, though others are refusing to confirm whether or not they will be there. Looks like certain people would prefer to avoid the media spotlight. Good thing I'm planning to be there, camera phone in hand.

Grant Lockley live at the Three Rivers memorial: sign up here to follow our reporting throughout the day

Yes, this columnist will be reporting live from today's memorial events: you can sign up at the link above in order to get a full picture of what's happening on the ground, as it happens. You can also follow the hashtag #TRCmemorial to see official tweets, as well as social media reactions from around the world. As always, you'll find my personal take on Twitter @thegrantlockley. See you there?

See more from Grant Lockley

Share or comment on this article
TOP COMMENTS

JohnEnglish Thinking of those girls today. Planning to light a candle and observe a minute's silence at 11am because they deserve their own remembrance day.
^ *894 people liked this*

moongurl7 Do we kno if Ryan Summer's mother is going to be there? Hope for her own sake she stays @ home – no one wants u there Moira! Personally Im still waiting for her public apology
^ *690 people liked this*

keith00 @moongurl7 Personally I am still waiting for her to be locked up! Police Scotland have failed these poor girls and their families in so many ways. No justice. RIP beautiful girls.
^ *599 people liked this*

stacey_xo Still want to know what makes someone commit an act like this. Thank you Grant Lockley for always striving to get to the truth. My theory is that Ryan Summers was taking drugs as we know drugs were in the college. But I know that if that is the truth then Grant will find it. Love this column. Will be there at W Parliament Sq today too. See you there Grant.
^ *409 people liked this*

8 June, 9.15 a.m.

'I really don't want this.'

Moira was very aware of her unkempt state. She'd got tired of being aware of it, after nearly a month – tired of other people showing up at the house and *making* her aware of it. Right now she was standing in the poky hall with two uniformed officers and Callum, her new FLO. She was still in her dressing gown, which – she felt, on a day like today – she had every right to be. But somehow Callum made her feel ashamed of her grief, her guilt, and their physical manifestations – something Amy had never done.

'It's not a question of *want*, Moira,' Callum said. 'It's a question of *need*.'

In the close confines of the hall, Moira tried to square up to Callum. She was determined not to let him get comfy today, and she was certainly not about to let these two strange new officers into her living room. Callum stood at around six foot four, and sported a beard so thick that Moira was amazed his superiors didn't ask him to shave. She may as well try and square up to a polar bear.

'We'd rather not take any chances,' he was saying. 'Tensions will be running high today, because of the memorial.'

Of course because of the memorial, Moira thought. *I'm not stupid, I know why you're suggesting this.*

'I know I was worried,' she said, 'when you first reduced the rotation. But I've had a full week now with no daytime scene guard at all and I see that you were right. I feel fine. And those – those *journalists* have been gone, most days, until this morning.'

Callum hadn't been idle: the first thing he'd done after coming into the job was to insist that Moira have her front window fixed.

She'd got rather used to the hoarding, and still felt exposed: though she kept the curtains closed at all times their barrier felt useless, flimsy. Callum's second task had been to reduce her protective police presence, no doubt a ruling from somewhere on high. Moira had seen the news just like everyone else – knew a lot of people out there were of the opinion that her continued safety didn't merit a single penny of taxpayers' money.

'The night rotation will go eventually, too,' Callum reminded her. He used a paternal tone with her that she really didn't care for, especially as he couldn't yet be forty. 'The threats have largely petered out, but for that one persistent bastard . . . and we think we're close to an arrest, there. Plus, this isn't a reinstatement, it's a one-off. It would just be for today.'

Moira hesitated, and then decided to tell the truth.

'Okay, listen. I don't care if I get a visit from this death threat . . . *person*. You said it yourself – only last week, if I remember rightly – *we can't guard you forever*. You're right, you can't. And you shouldn't. And I'm telling you now that I don't want you to, either. Perhaps if people think that I ought to die in order to avenge those girls, then I ought to. Do you have any idea how many times I've thought about dying, this past month?'

Callum blinked. She could see she'd surprised him.

'In fact,' she went on, 'I've started to think that it might have been better if Ryan had started with me – shot *me* first. Or better yet, shot me *instead*.'

The three policemen exchanged looks.

'Oh, don't you worry,' she said. 'I'm not going to do myself a mischief. Amy and I already had that particular heart-to-heart. And I'll tell you what I told her: me killing myself would be utterly craven, given everything that's happened. I couldn't do it – I won't do it. But a person that Ryan hurt, coming to kill me because they thought they could find some measure of solace in that? I've thought about it a lot – about what I might be able to do, to make those families feel better. So . . . I don't think it would be any bad thing.'

'Except,' Callum said, 'it would be murder.'

Moira rolled her eyes.

'Of course,' she said. 'That *would* be how *you*'d see it.'

There was a pause. Moira watched Callum trying to decide how to play things next, and chose to cut him off.

'I don't want scene guards today,' she said. 'I don't see why today should be different to any other day. And apart from anything else' – she waved vaguely in the direction of the front garden – 'the pack of vultures has come back. So if anyone *does* come to murder me, you'll have plenty of photographic evidence.'

The men were looking at each other again. For a moment, Moira imagined how they must speak about her when they were not in her presence. *Fucking Summers woman, bloody pain in the arse. She's right, she deserves whatever she gets.*

'I'd like you to leave now,' she said. 'This is me officially refusing the offer of a scene guard.'

She went upstairs to watch the three of them file down the garden and across the road, while the paparazzi photographed them and shouted questions. She watched Callum fold his large frame into the passenger seat of the panda car, and pull out his mobile phone to report her unruliness. She waited until the car was out of sight, and then she walked out onto the landing, plugged in the phone extension, and dialled the number she had now committed to memory. Amy answered after only two rings.

'I hate Callum,' Moira said, by way of a greeting. 'He talks to me like I'm a child.'

There was a pause on the line: Amy stifling a sigh, Moira could tell.

'You have to stop phoning me, Moira. I'm not your FLO any more. I'm not even working on the investigation any more.'

'I know,' Moira said, 'and I still don't get it. I'm sure Callum is a very good policeman, but . . . I hate him. I *liked* you. You didn't treat me like – like . . .'

Moira waited for Amy to finish the sentence, though she didn't really know what she was trying to say. *Like I did something wrong? But you did, Moira. You did do something wrong.*

'You didn't treat me like he does.'

Amy still didn't say anything.

'I felt like I could *talk* to you,' Moira said. Something flickered in her chest, a warning that she was skirting close to danger. 'What if I needed to ... talk about something? To tell someone something?'

'Moira, you can tell Callum anything, I promise you. He's extremely professional. In fact, he has much more experience at the job than I do. If anything, it's better that you have him as your FLO.' Amy was trying to inject a smile into her voice. 'You should think of this as an upgrade.'

She's trying to fob you off, Moira. See? They're all sick of you.

Moira took a long breath.

'What if I wanted to talk to a woman? I'm allowed that right, aren't I?'

Amy made a kind of deflating noise, which Moira assumed she hadn't been meant to hear.

'I'm really sorry,' she said, 'but you can't talk to me any more. We shouldn't even be having *this* conversation.'

In the beat that followed, something seemed to occur to Amy.

'I'm standing quite close to DI Birch right now, though, and I can put her on the phone.' After a pause, Amy added, '*She's* a woman.'

Moira almost laughed. She pictured DI Helen Birch – remembered her standing on the scruffy footpath round the back of Muffins Cafe, chewing on her bottom lip, looking like she hadn't slept in weeks. Remembered Amy saying that Birch had fought their corner and lost: that the order to install Callum had been made above her.

'Okay,' she said.

There was a sort of rummaging noise on the phone line – Amy's hand over the receiver, no doubt, as she explained to DI Birch that the unhinged Summers woman was on the phone and making an annoyance of herself. Moira looked around at the dingy landing, her vision blurring and sharpening in the gloom. Without really thinking, she reached out and pushed open the bedroom door nearest to her, to let a little light into the windowless space. The bedroom nearest to her was Ryan's bedroom. The light that came in bounced off the ruined divan bed – set right side down again by Callum, but still slashed – and the upended drawers. The mounds of clothes looked chewed and spat out. For the millionth time, Moira remembered: who she was. Who her son was. What he did. What she had failed to prevent him doing.

'Mrs Summers.' DI Birch's voice on the phone jolted Moira, pulled her gaze away from the wrecked room with its empty bed. 'Amy tells me you're in need of a warm ear.'

Moira hesitated. She'd anticipated a very different sort of tone.

'In need of – a what?'

DI Birch laughed, and inside that laugh Moira could hear a month of weariness.

'Sorry,' she said, 'it's something my mother used to say. You'd like to talk to someone, Amy says. Is that right?'

Moira's mind raced. *Would I? Really?*

'I – did say that, yes.'

'You're struggling with the new arrangement we've come to?'

Something about the way Birch said 'we've' confirmed what Amy had mentioned about the decision being taken over her head.

'Yes.'

'Okay.' Moira imagined DI Birch looking at her watch – remembered her frazzled hair. 'Today's going to be a hard one, I don't have to tell you that.'

'No.'

'But if it's all right with you, I'd like to come and talk to you myself, once the memorial service is over.' DI Birch waited a moment, and then added, 'Would that be okay?'

Moira thought for a moment.

'Yes,' she said. 'It would.'

'You're sure you don't need to talk to someone sooner than that? I know at your handover meeting with Amy and Callum you had . . . something of a heated discussion. About today.'

Moira closed her eyes.

'We did,' she said. 'But I was in the wrong, then. I see now where they were coming from.'

'It's not that we don't think you deserve to be there,' Birch said. 'Personally, I think what you said is right. This memorial service *should* be recognising Ryan, too. After all, he died too.'

'That's not what I said.' Moira was wincing now – wishing she'd had the sense at that handover meeting to focus on trying to save Amy, and fend off Callum – but also wincing at DI Birch's words. *He died too. He died.*

'I'm sorry,' Birch said, and sounded like she meant it. 'I might have got the wrong end of the stick. But Amy told me you wanted to be at the service today, and she and Callum – well, they had to explain why . . .'

'. . . why it's not a good idea,' Moira said. 'Yes. And they were right. That's not what . . . it's not why I said I wanted to talk to someone.'

'Okay. And Callum's been to see you this morning?'

Moira sniffed.

'He has.'

'So you're going to be okay until later today, when I can come and see you?'

In spite of herself, Moira twisted round a little, to look again at Ryan's room. It was going to be a beautiful day: she could tell from the long, pale yellow light slanting in through that room, past the half-opened curtains. Dust danced in the sunbeam: tiny little pieces of hair and skin. *Tiny little pieces of Ryan*, she thought, and shivered.

'I think so.'

'Great.'

Moira looked at the clock on the wall of Ryan's room, marvelled at the fact that it was still there, on its nail, though the SOCOs must have examined it. One of them must have set it back there, and Moira wondered what had prompted that action.

'DI Birch,' she said, hurrying to hold Birch's attention before she hung up. 'I didn't want to cause a scene, or anything. At the memorial, I mean. I didn't want to suggest that it should be made about Ryan . . . or about me, for that matter. That's the last thing I want. I just . . .'

The line between them crackled.

'I've had a lot of time to think,' Moira said. 'About what I want. About whether there is anything I can ever do to . . . fix things. Make things better. And I sometimes think, if I could just . . .'

Go on, just say it. For God's sake, woman.

'I don't know. If I could just . . . talk to some of the families. The families of the victims. If I could just explain . . .'

DI Birch was quiet. *Explain what?* Moira thought. She wasn't sure she knew.

'I understand.' DI Birch's reply was so quiet, Moira almost didn't catch it. 'I know it sounds unlikely, but I actually do. I understand exactly what that feels like.'

Moira blinked. The line between them stretched and ebbed.

'Perhaps I can tell you what I mean,' Birch said, 'when I see you later.'

For a moment, Moira said nothing. Then she said, 'Yes. Thank you.'

'I don't know when I'll be there.' DI Birch's voice had lost its softness: she sounded as if she'd physically shaken something off. 'It's going to be an unpredictable sort of day.'

'That's fine.' Moira glanced again at the clock in Ryan's room. 9.45 a.m. 'I'm not planning on going anywhere.'

Moira stood on the landing for a few minutes after putting the phone down. Inside Ryan's room, the dust motes danced and swam. The sunbeam had crept over the threshold now: she found she was standing inside the golden square it had thrown. The air felt warm. Outside her grey house, beyond the constantly drawn curtains, it was summer. Moira took a moment to marvel at this: the world kept on with its routine, in spite of whatever horror human beings dreamed up. The same was true of the smaller world of her own body. Most days, Moira wanted to do nothing, or as close to nothing as was possible: to lie in bed in the dim light and turn her grief over and over like a dark grey stone. Yet, in the month since Ryan had died – since all those girls had died – her body had kept interrupting. Insisting that she stand up. Hydrate herself, eat what little she could manage without vomiting. These days, it was also telling her to wash, sometimes, and put on clean clothes. And somehow, impossibly, summer was here.

Moira stood in the doorway of Ryan's room. Since Callum had righted the bed base, she'd taken to creeping in sometimes and lying down on it – no mattress, just the flimsy board that bowed a little under her weight. She'd never lain on that bed while Ryan was alive. Now, she'd taken to staring at the ceiling with its Anaglypta wallpaper, a throwback to a bygone era of décor that Jackie had always talked about replacing but never had. She imagined Ryan lying there every night, in that exact place, reading the wallpaper's swoops and curves like a child reads clouds. *That part looks like an elephant. That part like a swan with an S-shaped neck.* The divan base must have bowed under his weight, too – perhaps she was lying in a groove he'd already made, over many years. Lying there comforted her, and she also hated every second of it. It made her feel weak. Getting up from that bed again to go and get into her own, or to go and feed her nagging body, was the hardest part of any day. And days were hard. Moira realised she'd never done anything this hard, never endured any pain this cold, this unrelenting.

She leaned down and put the phone back into its cradle. Then she bent down further and unplugged the cable, just to be on the safe side. When she straightened up, the room was still there, full of sun, the cloth-covered top of the divan white and flat as an embalmer's table. She'd been awake only an hour, yet the desire to lie down again was almost overwhelming. But for the first time, a small voice in her head said, *Don't.*

Moira stood very still, and listened. There was nothing: only the scuffing voices of the photographers outside and some distant, far-off traffic. But that '*Don't*' hung in the air like the clean peal of a bell.

Don't go in there. Go and do something else.

The only thing Moira had come to appreciate about Callum was the fact that he gave her commands. *Show me where you keep the mugs. Just stay here for a minute while I make a call. Let me get this window fixed for pity's sake.* They were similar to her body's commands – *You're thirsty*, or *You have to eat* – she didn't have to think too much. She realised she'd barely made a single decision in almost a month; even the disastrous meeting with Lockley had been *his* decision, not hers. Until today, when she'd refused the scene guard. And right now. Right now she was deciding not to go and lie on her dead son's bed and spend the rest of the day there, crying. She took a long breath in. The air felt warm.

Results for **#TRCmemorial**

Spr G Gulbraith @SapperGeo   45m
Setting off for the **#TRCmemorial**. Important to assemble and reveal
what truly happened. http://www.truthunifi . . .

Grant Lockley @thegrantlockley   42m
First Minister among high-profile attendees at today's long-awaited
Three Rivers public memorial **#TRCmemorial** http://bit.ly/grantlo . . .

Grant Lockley @thegrantlockley   41m
I'll be there live-tweeting from set up, the vigil, and the memorial
service itself. Follow **#TRCmemorial** for updates throughout the day.

Alison Ross @alibalyalibalyb   38m
I was there at Three Rivers College. Sad & proud to be going to the
#TRCmemorial for my classmates :'(

Marianne Egan @maeg21657   35m
So pleased that my boy Jack will be by my side for the
#TRCmemorial today. We won't stop fighting for #justice.

Edinburgh Watcher @ALookAtEdin   33m
#Edinburgh residents remember today is the **#TRCmemorial** so
expect road closures and other disruption in city centre #travel
#travelsafe

Grant Lockley @thegrantlockley   31m
Poll: should gunman's mother Moira Summers be allowed to attend
#TRCmemorial today? Have your say here: http://bit.ly/poll983 . . .

Logic Ninja @___logical   30m
@thegrantlockley No way!!!!! That woman has blood on her hands! **#TRCmemorial**

MG @moongurl7   30m
@thegrantlockley Like I said on yr column Grant – no one wants u there Moira! Personally Im still waiting for her public apology **#TRCmemorial**

MG @moongurl7   29m
@thegrantlockley @___logical U r right, srsly she better not turn up to **#TRCmemorial**!

#ThreeRivers newsbot @threeriversbot   28m
#TRCmemorial is today: 438 tweeting about this #threerivers #three-riverscollege #threeriversbot

#ThreeRivers newsbot @threeriversbot   28m
RT @thegrantlockley Poll: should gunman's mother Moira Summers be allowed to attend **#TRCmemorial** today? Have your say here: http://bit.ly/poll983 . . .

Spr G Gulbraith @SapperGeo   25m
I may be in the minority but I think Mrs Summers has every right to be at **#TRCmemorial** @thegrantlockley @___logical @moongurl7

Logic Ninja @___logical   23m
@sappergeo delete your account troll @thegrantlockley @moongurl7 **#TRCmemorial**

MG @moongurl7   22m
Haha um yea this!!!! RT @___logical @sappergeo delete your account troll @thegrantlockley **#TRCmemorial**!

8 June, 10.00 a.m.

Ishbel had woken at 5 a.m., and felt a stab of fear: what was this strange room, dimly outlined by the green glow of an emergency fire escape light? It didn't smell like her house in Primrose Bank, didn't sound like it. She could hear too much traffic noise: delivery lorries on cobbles, and somehow, the clunk-clunk of trains. And then she remembered, the way she did every morning, now. After a few moments of blissful oblivion, memory rushed in: *She's dead. My old life is gone. I've left my husband. And my only daughter is dead.*

She'd been here for ten days, though it felt like one long blur of sedated sleep, with periods of waking to cry. Ishbel had, a couple of times, made herself go outside and walk around the block. She'd gone to the little newsagent's on the corner of St Mary's Street and bought a few things: apples, bottled water. She'd cried as she paid for them. Tourists on the Royal Mile had stared at her as she walked back.

Her phone was filled with voicemails from Aidan and Pauline. She'd listened to them – Aidan trying a different emotional tack in each one: angry, pleading, sulky – but had not called back. She only answered the phone when Rehan called her. He was a policeman, after all. They spoke awkwardly and in short bursts. He told her he thought it would be a good idea if she and Aidan met to talk. She told him thank you, but he was not a marriage counsellor and she felt he ought to do the job he was being paid for. She knew that was unfair, but it worked – Rehan hadn't mentioned it again after that.

Now, Ishbel dressed in the little enclave of the hotel en-suite, the holdall propped on the counter, miniature shampoo bottles cannoned over like ninepins. She had nothing left of her own that hadn't been worn, now, and Aidan wasn't here to tell her what to do. Since she'd arrived at the strange halfway house of the Premier Inn, she'd taken Abigail's belongings out of the bag many times – just to touch them. Unfold them, shake them out and then fold them again. Just to put her face against them and breathe in.

Now she began to put them on. First, a pair of tights she'd found in the chest of drawers in Abigail's room. They were good quality, expensive; they had none of the raspy static about them that Ishbel's own workaday ones had. They also had a black seam running up the back of each leg, like wartime stockings, or the kind that burlesque performers wore. *Mutton dressed as lamb*, Ishbel thought, looking at them on her own legs.

Over them, Ishbel put on the plain black skirt she'd worn to the crematorium. Then, Abigail's coral top, which was pretty, but altogether the wrong colour for a memorial. The school tie came out of the bag in a kind of snarl, and as Ishbel unwove it, she wondered at the way some things can do that – knot themselves up without any human hand touching them. For a moment, she considered wearing the tie as a sort of headband, but then changed her mind and looped it twice around her neck, as though it were a very thin scarf. Among the jewellery Ishbel had pilfered were two different pairs of earrings. She couldn't decide which to wear, and so opted for one of each, a different one in each ear. She clipped on the gold locket, and snapped into her hair two glittery hairclips she'd found alongside the jewellery. Abigail had used them a lot, to keep her unruly, pale hair out of her face. But Abigail had been blessed with Aidan's hair: Ishbel's own was dark, and cut severely. The hairclips bunched it into two clumps that looked like tiny shaving brushes. But Ishbel reached up and touched the hairclips gently, in turn. It didn't matter what they looked like. *These are Abigail's.* She corrected herself: *were Abigail's.*

There wasn't much left besides the silky dressing gown, and though she was sorely tempted, Ishbel realised she was going to a holy place, and couldn't stoop to the disrespect of nightwear in church, whatever the occasion. She pulled on the black jacket she'd worn to the cremation – stiff and a little warped now from being left for days on the hotel radiator. In the mirror, she looked unhinged: like a mother who'd agreed to let her small child pick out clothes for her. *But I am unhinged,* Ishbel thought. *Uncoupled from everything that made me who I was.* That blank room had been her home long enough now that she felt stateless, like she was no one. *And nobody,* she thought, buttoning the outfit in behind her too-warm overcoat, *notices a no one.*

She'd walked up towards the Canongate, and found neon-vested stewards placing cordons at the line where the pavement met the cobbled road. They were doing so all along the length of the street. Traffic was still rolling up and down the Royal Mile, but police vehicles were beginning to gather, and soon the whole thing would be closed to allow the procession from the vigil site to the cathedral to pass through. Ishbel dithered at the corner of Cranston Street, trying to decide whether or not to turn left, downhill, to the vigil. She was distracted by the slant of yellow light along the fascia of the tenement in front of her: the sandstone block was lit up like a paper bag with a candle inside it. As she stood there, a flock of pigeons took off from one of the high slate roofs and barrelled, clattering, through the blue air to the other side of the street. The chimney stack they settled around had one fine feather of smoke drifting up out of it: somewhere in the maze of the building, a fire was lit, in spite of the June morning's early warmth. Ishbel turned her head right, to look up the hill for the Tron Church clock tower and St Giles beyond it, and as she did, she caught the good, bread-like smell of the Caledonian brewery. The vigil would be crowded. There'd be TV cameras. Aidan was going. Rehan had phoned up to tell her, to ask if she'd like to meet there, maybe say a few words? If she looked up the hill, the sun was behind her, throwing her own shadow long and gunmetal grey onto the pavement. If she walked that way, that shadow would always be ahead of her. Ishbel put her hands into the pockets of the overcoat, and made for the crossing.

She'd expected to find St Giles Cathedral as it usually was: a cool, dark cavern in the midst of the city, hushed but for the occasional squeak of a tourist's shoe against the stone floor, the occasional whispers of its visitors. But when she rounded the cathedral's shoulder, she found West Parliament Square was full of activity: cordons erected, trucks chugging in and out between the chain-link barriers, men in hard hats removing scaffolding from the fronts of giant erected screens. A few news crews were already there, their anchors standing at various points around the Queensberry Memorial, cameramen vying for the best angle of the cathedral's exhaust-blacked face. Though there were official-looking personnel everywhere – people in hi-vis or wearing fleeces with the STV logo stitched into them; people talking into headsets or brandishing walkie-talkies – no one tried to stop Ishbel as she climbed the few steps to the cathedral's entrance and made her way inside. And inside, things were even busier: the central nave was rigged with a steel climbing frame of lights. Around her, people rushed and chattered: men in polo shirts with STAFF screen-printed across the back hoisted camera equipment and taped cables to the floor. Above it all the Great West Window blazed its refracted colours.

Someone tapped Ishbel on the shoulder.

'Mrs Hodgekiss?'

She turned, and found herself facing a young woman whose hair was pulled into two long, straw-coloured braids. The girl was wearing a headset with a curved antenna that pushed a little microphone up under her chin. She was carrying a clipboard. Ishbel flinched, and then tried to steel herself for a fight: *She's about to throw me out.*

'Yes?' she said.

The girl huffed out air.

'Oh, it *is* you. I thought I recognised you ... from seeing your picture. In the paper. But you know how it is, when you go up to someone? Like, is this actually them? Or did I just make an idiot of myself?'

The girl pushed out a squeaky giggle. Ishbel blinked.

'My picture's in the paper?'

'Oh.' The girl shifted her weight, and as the clipboard shifted with her, Ishbel caught a glimpse of the ID hanging on a lanyard around her neck. *Poppy* something.

'Yes – sorry. Yes, it has been. Just – paparazzi-type photos, you know. I saw one of you getting into your car, I think.'

Ishbel couldn't think of anything to say. The photographers camped outside the house had bothered her, but more because of their unwanted presence than anything else – their constant watching. Ishbel realised she hadn't at any point done the simple mental arithmetic that would have told her that where there are photographers, there would also be photographs. Of her.

'I've been very . . . distracted,' she said, explaining to herself, really, not Poppy. 'And I've been trying not to look at the papers.'

'That's probably sensible,' Poppy said, and then, as though she had only just realised who it was she was talking to, 'Oh, I really am so very sorry about . . . everything.'

Possible responses flickered through Ishbel's mind: *Thank you. You're very kind. I appreciate it.* Or *So you should be. But you don't mean it. No one means it. They think they do, but they don't.* She decided to stay silent.

'You're rather early,' Poppy said, either not sensing Ishbel's unease, or sensing it and deciding to ignore it. 'You're not going to the vigil first?'

'No,' Ishbel said. That didn't seem to suffice, and she heard herself add, 'My husband will be there.'

Poppy tilted her head slightly.

'I don't mean – that's not the reason why I'm not going . . .' Under the glare of the TV lights, Ishbel felt hot. Flustered. *Except it is. It's exactly the reason.*

'It's okay, Mrs Hodgekiss.' To her surprise, Poppy reached out and touched her arm, just once, and lightly. 'I've seen what they're saying in the papers, what Grant Lockley's writing about . . . well, about it all. It's enough to put strain on any relationship.'

The girl's face was suddenly serious.

'Thank you,' Ishbel said, 'for saying you were sorry, just then. For saying you were sorry about everything. I appreciate it.'

Poppy gave her a watery smile.

'Some of those girls were the same age as me,' she said. 'It makes you realise, something like that. Life is short. It really was awful.'

Ishbel swallowed hard. *Don't cry. You can't cry just because some-one is kind to you. You can't cry at every small thing for the rest of your life.* But it was too late: a watery smear was forming on her vision.

'Let me take you to your seat,' Poppy said, and laid a small hand on Ishbel's elbow. Ishbel allowed herself to be guided along the central aisle, right to the front of the cathedral. The chairs in the first few rows had pieces of paper laid across them, bearing the STV logo, and the word 'Reserved'.

'This is you,' Poppy said, glancing at the clipboard and then pointing at a chair about one third of the way along the front row. Ishbel swallowed hard.

'I'm on the front row?'

'Yes,' Poppy said. 'We've put all the, erm – all the parents along here. Parents and siblings. And then other family members will be behind you, and Three Rivers staff have also been reserved seat-ing. General mourners can sit wherever they like behind that. Press are at the back.'

Ishbel recognised Poppy's tone: some official document had clearly been memorised.

Poppy bent down and removed the 'Reserved' sign from the seat she had pointed to, and Ishbel sank onto it, realising she hadn't the energy to argue.

'You've put Aidan next to me, I suppose?' she said.

'Oh yes,' Poppy replied, but then seemed to remember some-thing. 'Wait – is that bad? Would you prefer . . .' She began looking around rather desperately, as though seeking a superior to confer with.

'It's all right,' Ishbel said, waving a hand. 'I just wondered.'

Poppy's face relaxed. She smiled.

'I'm afraid I need to leave you,' she said. 'I'm needed elsewhere. I'm needed *everywhere*, this morning. But if you need anything, just give a shout, and any one of us will be happy to help. I really am sorry, again. Sorry you need to be here . . . that any of us need to be doing this today.'

Ishbel felt the threat of tears once again, and could only smile.

Poppy had half turned away, but then spun back on her heel.

'Oh,' she said, touching two fingertips to her throat. 'The school tie?'

Ishbel's hand flew to her own neck. Above her coat's collar, she could feel the silky polyester with its raised white cotton stripe. She'd forgotten about it.

'Nice touch,' Poppy said. Then she righted herself, and strode away along the aisle.

Ishbel sat very still, looking up at the Great West Window. She watched as the light that fell through it ebbed and changed as clouds passed, or as the TV lamps behind her were adjusted. The wooden seat was hard, uncomfortable. Ishbel's gaze drifted to the altar, which stood below the huge window, and which had been adorned with a white embroidered cloth and two simple vases of white lilies, white roses and baby's breath. Between the vases, the huge brass altar cross, so much more *real* than its plastic counterpart in the crematorium, flashed and darkened with the movements of the TV crew, their lamps and monitors.

Again, as she had in that weird crematorium, Ishbel wondered if she ought to pray. She'd been raised in the Church of Scotland, and guessed she would probably still know when to stand and when to sit in the standard Sunday service. She knew St Giles well enough, too, because she and Aidan attended the Christmas Eve Watchnight service most years. Abigail had come along as well, of course, when she was small. Ishbel liked church for its muted voices and musty smells, and at Christmas she loved the candlelight and some of the more hopeful carols. But she'd stopped attending Sunday services as a young woman. She'd never been able to understand – if there was a God who saw and knew everything anyway – why she needed to get up when it was still dark, and give up her ever-more-precious Sunday mornings to go and sit in a cold barn and get a telling-off from some elderly minister. Surely she could just pray at home? And she had done, for a while, until praying fell down her list of priorities, and then eventually off the bottom of it altogether. That was years ago, now.

And what God, she wondered, what so-called *loving God*, could allow things like Ryan Summers to happen? *It's not just the shooting,* she found herself thinking, *it's what's happened since. Photographers on the doorstep. Harassment. Aidan, sleeping with his dental nurse, behaving like some stranger. The papers and their rumour mill. Grant Lockley threatening people over the phone. Jack Egan. Abigail – we can't even celebrate Abigail's life, thanks to the press.* Ishbel realised that she was praying, in a way, but it was a strangled, bitter prayer.

What sense can there be in any of this? The thought seemed to grow in her mind, like a ripple on the surface of a deep pool. What sense was there in Abigail's death? *Why* had she been first – the drugs? The student union complaint? Something else Ishbel had no way of ever guessing? Or had it all just been one great mess of noise and blood and rage? '*Why?*' was the only question left, but it was the only question that had no answer.

She looked up again at the polished altar cross.

'That's it,' she hissed. 'I'm done with you. I refuse to believe you exist.'

She waited, as though some response might come. But there was only the clang of scaffolding, and the background scuffle of feet and voices.

'How could you, anyway?' Ishbel looked away from the altar, its white cloth dappled with patches of stained-glass light. 'How could you exist when such senseless things happen?'

Ishbel realised someone was standing near to her: one of the men with STAFF printed across his back, carefully avoiding eye contact. He was setting up a large TV monitor under the pulpit – doing as his colleagues had done throughout the church, gaffer-taping cables to the stone-flagged floor. He flicked the monitor on, and raised a walkie-talkie close to his face.

'Check live feed on six,' he said.

A picture appeared on the monitor. It was a few feet away, but Ishbel recognised the backdrop of the Scottish Parliament: the white stone, and the weird bamboo-cane bars across the doors.

She realised she was looking at the vigil, watching it happen live at the far end of the Canongate. She couldn't see the entire crowd, but she could guess at the scale of it from the way people seemed bunched together, jostled. A lot of people held candles: the thin, white kind that came with a cardboard skirt to keep hot wax off the hands. The feed began to show cutaways of individual faces, some of them crying. They must be listening, Ishbel realised, to a speech of some kind. The monitor gave out no sound.

'Six is a go,' the man said into his walkie-talkie. He lifted his gaze and threw a thumbs-up sign, apparently at someone or something high up in the cathedral's roof space. But Ishbel didn't turn to look. As the man walked away, a new picture appeared on the monitor. The camera had panned round to show the speech-giver, the person whose words were drawing tears from the amassed crowd. Ishbel felt her own mouth fall open: it was Aidan, standing at a white podium, holding one of those same white candles, and talking, with his head bowed. Behind him were some of the other Three Rivers relatives. Barry Kesson's eyes were turned to the floor, and he was shaking his head, as though despairing of the words Aidan was saying. A little further back, but still clearly in shot, was Annetta. *Netta*, Ishbel thought, remembering the pet name Aidan had used. *His mistress. He asked his mistress to be at the vigil. The vigil for our daughter.*

Ishbel put a hand over her mouth. Her stomach flipped and swam: she struggled to place the feeling that churned inside her, and she worried that she might vomit, right there on the scrubbed stone of the cathedral floor. She swung her head around, casting about for Poppy, though she wasn't sure what she wanted her for. She was aware of someone behind her, someone shuffling around in the aisle not far away. She turned, thinking maybe she could ask for the awful monitor to be shut off, or at the very least moved. But the figure in the aisle wasn't Poppy, or anyone else who could help her. Once again Ishbel's mouth fell open.

'*You.*'

Grant Lockley was standing about five rows behind her, his mobile phone raised in his hand as if to take her picture.

'Oh, Ishbel,' he said, loudly enough that his voice rang the nave with harmonics. 'That was going to be a lovely shot – just you, on your own, contemplating. I had the window in the background and everything. I wish you hadn't turned around.'

Ishbel jumped up from her seat, and felt herself sway. The ground seemed not quite level, and not quite still, as though she were somehow afloat.

'Don't you *dare* take my picture without my permission,' she said.

Lockley made his trademark shrug.

'Don't worry,' he said. 'I didn't get the chance. But if I could just . . .'

He took a step towards her.

'Don't you come near me.' Ishbel held up one hand, like a policeman stopping traffic. To her surprise, Lockley did stop moving. 'What are you *doing* here? Is there really no space you people won't grub your noses into? Is nothing sacred?'

At the back of the church, a few faces had flicked anxiously up to look at them, and Ishbel realised that her voice had been raised.

Lockley held up both hands – in his right, his phone was wedged between thumb and palm, its screen glowing. He was smiling a serpentine smile.

'I don't know *what* you mean,' he said, speaking quietly, now he knew people were watching. 'There are a lot of folk can't be here today – I'm simply reporting what's happening for the people at home.' He brandished the phone, and added, 'All thanks to the wonders of Twitter.'

Ishbel wanted to spit. She might even have done it, had she not been in a church, and surrounded by cameras.

'Does *anyone* fall for you when you play stupid like that?'

Lockley only shrugged again, his face still split in a lopsided smile.

'And if you really are reporting,' Ishbel was thinking aloud, 'why aren't you at the vigil right now?'

Lockley smirked.

'I could ask you the same thing.' He nodded at something just beyond her, and she remembered the monitor. 'Though I could take an educated guess.'

Ishbel turned. The vigil seemed to be breaking up: the camera showed a vague line beginning to form, as people prepared to walk up the street towards the cathedral. A close-up: Aidan shaking hands with the First Minister. Then Ishbel watched as her husband turned away from the podium, and stretched out a hand to Annetta, who stepped forward, smiling, to take it.

'That's got to hurt,' Lockley said.

Ishbel rounded on him, but found she couldn't speak. She could barely breathe: she pulled in a single mouthful of musty church air, and made a sound that was something like a sob, though for once, there were no tears in her eyes.

'I'm sorry,' Lockley said. Had Ishbel not known better, she might have said that he meant it.

He waited for a moment before speaking again.

'I was going to ask you if you'd had any more time to think about my suggestion. My offer still stands, even after today.' He nodded at the monitor again. 'Especially after today, perhaps. Wouldn't you like to be able to talk about all this, Ishbel? Wouldn't you like people to know how you feel?'

Behind her, on the monitor, Aidan and Annetta were leading a slow march of mourners up the hill of the Canongate: part of a front row that also included the First Minister, the parents of Liz Gill, the Three Rivers principal, and – Ishbel's throat tightened – Jack Egan. They were flanked by neon-coated police officers and sinister-looking men in black suits who had little spirals of clear wire tucked behind their ears. Lockley was watching, and Ishbel was watching him watch. She didn't want to look at him, but she couldn't turn back to the screen.

'I wouldn't sell my story to you,' she said, slowly, 'if you were the last man on earth.'

Lockley smiled again.

'You know,' he said, 'I've heard that before. It's amazing how often people change their minds once they see the size of the cheque.'

Ishbel closed her eyes.

'Get away from me,' she hissed. 'This is a *church*. I'm here to think about my daughter, and remember her.' She opened her eyes, and looked Lockley up and down. '*You're* here to do business deals. You ought to be ashamed.'

Again, the trademark shrug.

'Okay,' he said. 'Can I ask what you're thinking about Moira Summers right now? There's a rumour she may turn up today.'

Ishbel blinked, once, twice. She was still learning about Lockley's tenacity, his batter-and-blindside approach to communication.

'*What?*' she said, in spite of herself.

'Shocking, isn't it?' Lockley said. 'That the police – well, that *anyone* – would think it was appropriate for her to be here.'

'Why wouldn't it be?' Ishbel wasn't sure where the thought had come from, but as soon as it had come she'd said it aloud, and the echoes hung in the air between her and Lockley. It was the same thought she'd had at the family meeting that DI Birch had invited them to at the police station, when she'd asked Rehan whose FLO Amy was. 'Why wouldn't it be appropriate for her to be here? We're remembering the people who . . .' she paused, but then went on, '. . . the people who died, that day at Three Rivers College. That includes her son as well as my daughter, doesn't it?'

Lockley's smile widened.

'Oh Ishbel,' he said, 'you really should think about calling me, after today is over. I think we could do so much together. I mean, imagine you and Moira Summers in conversation. Two women who've been so differently affected by this tragedy, working out their differences in print. It could be a beautiful thing.'

Behind Lockley, a young man was moving between the chairs, counting out pieces of paper and placing one on each seat. An order of service, Ishbel guessed: at fifty paces, she could clearly recognise her daughter's smiling portrait, shrunk into a small square on the front cover, alongside twelve others.

Lockley turned his head, following her gaze. The TV people had begun to scatter, and seemed to be taking up strategic positions around the cathedral.

'Showtime,' Lockley said, looking back at her. 'I'd better get to my allotted square foot of space.' He threw her a hammy eye-roll. She pretended not to see it.

'Ishbel,' he said, and in spite of herself, she looked back up at him. In a seamless movement, he flicked something out of the inside breast pocket of his scruffy grey jacket, and tossed it towards her. Instinct made her stumble forward to try and catch it, but it skittered onto the stone floor under her chair: Lockley's business card.

'You can call me any time,' he said.

Ignoring the card, Ishbel sat back down on her hard wooden chair, and thought about crying. But instead, after a moment, she took out her mobile phone.

8 June, 11.45 a.m.

Birch wasn't listening to the service: had stopped listening a while ago. She hadn't heard a word of the First Minister's over-long address; hadn't paid attention to the various relatives or members of college staff who got up to speak about each of the victims in turn. She didn't even tune in to Aidan Hodgekiss – now a person of interest in her investigation, though he didn't know it. She was thinking about that morning's phone call with Moira Summers.

It was exactly as she had always thought, right from that first interview at Fettes, right after the shooting: Moira clearly *did* have something she was holding back, something she wanted to talk about. Would she be willing to reveal it to a senior officer she'd only spoken to a handful of times? Amy had spent so long building up their rapport, whereas Birch was almost a stranger. McLeod was a bloody fool, far too concerned with what the press might think of him. People like Lockley needed to be ignored, not worried about, however hard it may be; she of all people knew that. Now Amy was no longer on the case – *and it's all down to me. And I'm frazzled. I'm struggling. What if I make a bad call?* This was the tumbleweed of Birch's thoughts, blowing about in her brain.

Liz Gill's twin sister, Valerie, was speaking now, or trying to, between long pauses in which she put her hand over her mouth and closed her eyes, and the congregation made mumbled, encouraging noises. She was talking about her sister's brave but fatal decision to tackle Ryan Summers in the Three Rivers cafeteria.

'That was just the way Liz was. If she could see a way to help, then she would just do it.'

Birch's attention drifted once more.

She sneaked a look around. She'd almost arrived late, as she'd been needed to help coordinate things outside when the vigil attendees arrived in Parliament Square, bringing with them half of the Scottish government, and most – or so it seemed – of the world's press. As a result, she'd had to squeeze onto the end of a row as the service started. Amy had saved the seat for her. McLeod was a few chairs along, and although he was looking intently at Valerie Gill as she struggled through her speech, his eyes looked glazed. Birch would bet any money that he was trying to figure out how to surreptitiously check his phone.

If she turned her head in the other direction, she could see Jack Egan. He was sitting directly across the aisle from her, flanked by one of her colleagues on one side, and a custody officer on the other. *That* investigation was ongoing, but Egan had been granted permission to attend the service. He sat with his elbows on his knees, resting his chin on his hands, a wholly inappropriate pose for church, Birch thought. But he didn't look bored – rather, as though he were deep in thought about something wholly uncon-nected to Valerie Gill or the memorial or Three Rivers. When he moved, light from the stained-glass windows swam on the lenses of his thick-rimmed hipster specs.

Also across the aisle, and a couple of rows in front of Egan, Birch could see the back of Anjan's head, and his shirt collar, and the impeccably cut shoulders of his black suit jacket. She'd picked him out in the throng as the attendees began to file into the build-ing, and then realised she'd been trying to. Now she was telling herself not to look at him, and then ignoring the command.

There was a shuffling noise behind her: the quick scrape of a chair-leg against the cathedral's stone floor. In spite of herself, she looked round. In the press area towards the back, Grant Lockley had stood up and was now apologising his way out of his row.

'The hell is *he* going?' Birch said it through her teeth, but just loudly enough that Amy turned her head and whispered, 'What's up?'

'Lockley's about to go AWOL,' she hissed back. 'I'm just going to go and keep an eye.' Amy threw her a warning look, but Birch ignored it. Yes, this was personal. She didn't trust that man an inch, especially not on a day like today.

As swiftly and quietly as she could, Birch stood, thanking her lucky stars that, pre-coffee that morning, she'd chosen flats not heels, and padded up the aisle after Lockley, and out of the cathedral into the sun.

She'd been expecting to emerge into the usual hustle and bustle of the Royal Mile: bagpiping buskers, traffic rumbling across the cobbles. Instead, everything was weirdly quiet. The road was closed, of course, and West Parliament Square had filled with hundreds of people. Most of them stood with faces upturned, watching Valerie Gill as she struggled through a thank you to her brave twin sister, her face projected dozens of feet high onto STV's huge outdoor screen.

Birch paused at the top of the steps outside the cathedral door. From here, she had a decent vantage point from which to look out over the crowd, and she watched as Lockley began picking his way around the edge of it, glancing around and behind him as he went. Once, he stopped, and raised his mobile phone to snap a photograph that must have taken in most of the crowd's wide sweep, the big screen a bright backdrop. *I'll be in that photo*, Birch realised, though at that distance she'd be too small to be recognised.

'Guv?' Amy was at her elbow. 'You okay?'

Birch didn't look round: her eye was fixed on Lockley as he shimmied along the ragged line at the very back of the crowd.

'I'm fine,' she said, and nodded towards the journalist's slow-moving figure. 'I just wanted to see what the hell he's up to. Why's he leaving early, when the action's inside?'

Amy grimaced.

'He's been writing all sorts on the internet this morning,' she said. 'Live-tweeting, he calls it. I was watching him as we came in, taking photos of people – seconds later they go up on Twitter with some caption or other. He's all over the hashtag.'

'Hashtag?'

Amy smiled.

'Get with it, guv. #TRCMemorial. People at the vigil were even posting selfies. There really is nothing sacred on social media.'

Birch squinted. The sun was strong now, flashing up off the shiny cobbles and glancing off the windows of the High Court and the Signet Library. Lockley had come to a stop, and was talking to a man who looked vaguely familiar.

'You can have a look, later,' Amy was saying. 'Though there are a lot of Lockley fans on there, so it might make you sick. All these people tweeting to thank him for being brave and pursuing the truth, and—'

'Who's that he's talking to?'

Amy blinked, and then, following Birch's gaze, squinted out over the crowd herself. A small gaggle of men had now gathered around Lockley: they watched as he shook hands with a couple of them.

'They might be fans,' Amy said, rolling her eyes. 'Like I said, there were plenty of people on this hashtag who love Lockley. A couple of them were saying that if they saw him in the crowd, they'd come over and say hello.'

Birch patted herself down: no phone. It must be in the car. She cursed.

'Can you get on that hashtag now?' she said. 'See who's been in touch with him lately?'

Amy fished out her phone and jabbed at it.

'It'd be so like him,' she said, 'to get up and leave an event like that because someone outside wanted his autograph. Ah, right – okay, here we are. Grant Lockley, tweets and replies.'

Birch watched the men on the other side of the square as she waited for Amy to speak again. In the crowd, people were starting to fidget, to come out of their big-screen stupor just a little. Clearly, they sensed the service was drawing to a close.

'The last person he tweeted at was – oh, surprise surprise.'

'What?'

Some of the men were holding – something. Concealing something, it looked like . . .

'Four minutes ago, he tweeted someone called @SapperGeo to say, "I'll be out in a minute, stay put". Guv?'

Birch was already halfway down the steps. Placards. They were hiding placards. There was about to be some sort of unauthorised demonstration, Birch realised, led by a known scumbag named George Gulbraith, online alias SapperGeo. Gulbraith was a member of the SDL, a fascist protest organisation that seemed to consist of about thirty middle-aged men and a few daft teenage lads. George had other causes, too: in fact, it seemed his hobby was to show up on the vexatious side of just about any rally or picket publicly held in Scotland. Now he had a captive audience of hundreds, not to mention the thousands of others who might be active on Lockley's hashtag. Following roughly the path that Lockley had taken, Birch began to fight her way towards the gaggle, aware that Amy was struggling along in her wake.

When she was about halfway over to the group, she saw that Gulbraith had organised them into a rough line, and that Lockley was poised a few feet away, phone raised, ready to take their photograph. Typical Lockley: never mind a respectful write-up of the memorial. This was the picture that would grace the top of his column come tomorrow: *Fascists air grievances as Three Rivers crowd look on.*

Birch came to a clear patch at the fringe of the crowd, and signalled to a uniform whose name she knew, but couldn't, right then, remember.

'Come here, sunshine,' she called over. 'You're needed.'

Too late: Gulbraith's gang had now uncovered their placards and arranged them in a scruffy row, grinning for Lockley's photo. Or some of them were grinning, at least – others wore scarves across their noses and mouths. People in the crowd near them began to jostle one another, and point.

Birch was only about twenty feet away when Gulbraith lifted his placard high above his head, and barked out the words daubed on it over the heads of the still-quiet crowd.

'Ryan Summers is an anti-feminist hero!'

The echoes rang off every wall.

'Shit!' Birch nudged the uniformed officer. 'Get some more bodies over here, would you? Like, *yesterday*.'

The neon-coated officer began speaking rapidly into his radio, though Birch could already see some of her colleagues moving in their direction.

She lunged towards Gulbraith, elbowing Lockley aside.

'Come on now, George,' she said, loudly enough that the whole group turned to look at her. 'This is a bit farcical, isn't it? Even for you.'

Gulbraith looked at her for a moment, his arms still raised above his head, the placard waving in the air.

'We're protesting against discrimination, Sergeant Birch,' he said, his voice still raised. 'There are feminist agents preaching a radical agenda of hate in this country. They say Ryan Summers committed murder because he was a white man. They say white men are the cause of all violence. They say they want to eradicate us all. Isn't that hate speech?'

Birch forced herself not to roll her eyes, but she knew Amy had done so behind her – a couple of the men threw angry looks in her direction.

'Ryan Summers,' Gulbraith was saying, 'was a victim of this feminist agenda. He was trapped. He felt like his only solution was to try to overthrow the feminist state.'

Birch closed her eyes for a moment. *Count to ten, Helen.* Around them, the crowd was becoming fractious, as more and more people became aware of Gulbraith's sign. A few had begun to shout back at him.

'And you know that how, exactly?' She was stalling for time: out of the corner of her eye she could see a flank of flak-jacketed officers approaching Gulbraith's gaggle from the back. 'You been going to see some dodgy medium, or something?'

'Those women died because they had signed up to the radical feminist agenda,' Gulbraith shouted. Something hit his still-waving placard with a *thwack*, and then landed at his feet. A white candle with a white cardboard skirt, thrown from somewhere in the crowd.

'Keep order, please!' The neon-coated officer Birch had collared to help was doing his best to keep a gap between the now-angry vigil attendees and Gulbraith, and he began to yell those three words over and over at the crowd. The tang of panic was in the air as people stomped and elbowed around. The back-up was nearly upon them, but Birch needed to do something.

'All right, George,' she said. 'You're under arrest.'

She reached up and clamped one hand around his forearm. The men around him seemed to rear up like angry dogs, but Birch was unmoved: she guessed that they all had records, and none of them would particularly fancy a stretch for assaulting a police officer.

Gulbraith lowered the placard, but flinched his arm out of Birch's grip.

'On what grounds?'

Birch took hold of his arm again, digging her fingertips in this time. McLeod's face drifted across her mind, and she remembered what he had said about Lockley.

'I'll figure it out later,' she said.

The flak-jackets were upon them. A few began to seize hold of Gulbraith's companions, while the rest formed a line between the protesters and the crowd.

'This is a violation of my freedom of speech,' Gulbraith spluttered. 'And our freedom of assembly! We have a *right* to protest!'

Birch spun Gulbraith around easily, though he attempted a struggle.

'Now George,' she said, 'you're not resisting, I hope?'

His body went limp. Birch snapped her fingers at the neon-coated officer, who took over, latching Gulbraith into handcuffs.

'I'll write this up,' she said to him, in a low voice. Then, to Gulbraith, 'Oh, George?'

The man squinted over his shoulder.

'It's *Inspector* Birch, these days.'

She turned her back on Gulbraith as he was led away. Amy was grinning, and as Birch approached, she held the flat of her hand up in the air. Birch hesitated for less than a second before reaching up and high-fiving Amy, and both women laughed.

'Nice work, guv,' Amy said. 'McLeod, eat your heart out.'

Birch snorted.

'More like "McLeod will eat my heart for dinner",' Birch said, 'once he finds out about that little stunt.'

'Detective Inspector Helen Birch, there.' It was a man's voice, and it came so close and so unexpectedly that Birch physically jumped. 'Arresting a peaceful protester without legitimate grounds.'

Lockley was standing only an arm's length away, holding up his camera phone. He was filming them. With a sickening jolt, Birch realised he had not only filmed the short-lived protest, and Gulbraith's arrest, but he had also filmed her high-fiving Amy.

For a moment, the two female officers stood motionless. Birch wanted to yell at Lockley, wanted to smack the phone from his hand – she wanted to ream off every name she'd ever called him privately, to tell him all the ways in which he'd messed with her life, and her dead mother's life, and yes, her long-missing brother's life, too. But whatever she said or did next would be captured on film, and uploaded to the internet. Behind her, the memorial attendees had begun to file out of the cathedral. They might be visible too, in the background of Lockley's shot. Birch stood frozen, with no idea what to do next.

'Mr Lockley?'

They all looked round: Amy, Birch and Lockley, at Ishbel Hodgekiss. She was standing about a metre away. Lockley immediately turned the camera phone away from Birch, and towards her.

'No, thank you,' Ishbel said, passing one hand over her face as though shielding it from the glare of some bright light. 'I don't give my permission to be filmed.'

Lockley hesitated, but then lowered the phone.

'Thank you,' Ishbel said. She looked over at Birch for a moment. *How long has she been standing there?* Birch thought.

'Mr Lockley,' Ishbel said again. 'I've been thinking some more about what you said. About your offer. Of an article, or . . . something. With me . . . telling my story. I think I'd like to do that, please.'

Lockley's face broke into a grin. It seemed Birch's moment of indiscretion was, for the time being, forgotten.

'Ishbel,' he said. 'I'm so pleased you've changed your mind. When can we arrange a time to speak?'

Birch threw Amy a look, but Amy only shrugged.

'Mrs Hodgekiss,' Birch said. 'Do you think perhaps you should talk this over with Rehan before you . . . commit to anything?'

Ishbel's expression was cold.

'I don't think so,' she said. 'Between you and me, DI Birch, I don't have a huge amount of time for Rehan. I don't think he's given me very good counsel, these past few weeks.'

Birch thought about Reh, her spy in the Hodgekiss house, and all the ways it must have seemed to Ishbel like he was cosying up to the husband who'd betrayed her. She could think of no response, but Lockley was quick to fill the silence.

'The sooner the better, really,' he said. He was fully facing Ishbel now, having turned his back on Birch and Amy. 'I know this must have been a difficult morning for you, but if you had time just now, we could—'

'No,' Ishbel said. 'I don't have time now. I need to . . . talk to someone else, first.'

Your husband, no doubt, Birch thought. *And I'd want to do more than talk to him, if he was mine.*

'I dare say you have to go and do some . . . *reporting*, too.' The way Ishbel said it seemed to betray something seething under the surface. *Why is she selling her story to him when she clearly knows he's hateful?* Birch threw Amy another look, and Amy shook her head: *No idea.*

'This evening, perhaps,' Ishbel was saying. 'I need to go and have a bit of a rest, and a think. But we could meet this evening.'

'That sounds *great*.' Birch rolled her eyes – Lockley was practically slavering.

'I have one condition,' Ishbel said.

Lockley's body language shifted, but he said, 'Name it.'

Ishbel nodded at the phone, still hanging in his hand.

'That video you've just filmed,' she said. 'It is not to become public before we have spoken.'

At this, Lockley glanced back at Birch and Amy. Birch tried to make her face as impassive as possible.

'If you don't mind me asking,' he said, 'why? The video isn't of you, but of DI Birch here, and some protesters who were here a moment ago. You only appear at the very end there, and I would happily edit that part out.'

Ishbel's face hardened.

'I saw the protesters, Mr Lockley,' she said. She nodded at Amy. 'I followed this lady through the crowd. I saw that whole little spectacle.'

In spite of herself, Birch blushed.

'Then surely,' Lockley said, 'you'll agree with me that the public needs to *see* what just happened!'

Birch looked again at Amy, who mouthed *Sorry* back. Around them, the crowd had begun to disperse properly. Across the square, Birch spotted McLeod emerging onto the sunny cathedral steps, blinking as though he'd been asleep. *Shit*, she thought. *He's going to have my head.*

'Be that as it may,' Ishbel was saying. 'I'd rather we spoke first before that video was put into the public domain.'

She seemed to think for a moment, and then added, 'After all, if I'm going to tell my story, I don't want everyone paying attention to some other item from your column.'

Slowly, Lockley began to nod. She'd spoken his language.

'That,' he said, 'is fair enough. Though I can assure you that your personal testimony – that might be what we call it, if you're in agreement – will dwarf anything else in the news, once we release it.'

Birch couldn't see his face, but she imagined pound signs popping up in his eyes.

Ishbel stepped towards Lockley and put out her hand.

'You say you're a man of integrity,' she said. 'So shake my hand. Give me your word that I won't see that video on the internet today.'

Lockley paused for just a fraction of a second before grasping Ishbel's hand. Birch looked at Amy, but Amy was watching them, bemused.

'Thank you,' Ishbel said. 'I'll be in touch later today.' She brandished a piece of card between finger and thumb. 'I have your number.'

'Fantastic,' Lockley fawned. 'That's just great. Phone me any time, I'll be waiting to hear from you. And I can meet you anywhere you like. Anywhere you feel comfortable to talk.'

For the first time, Ishbel smiled at him – but the smile was cold.

'I'll be in touch,' she said.

At the cathedral steps, the rest of the press gaggle had gathered to hear the First Minister give a short, scheduled press conference. Lockley glanced over at their little company, and then looked back at Birch and Amy.

'Duty calls,' he said. He looked back at Ishbel. 'I mean it. Call me any time.'

He sprang away and began weaving through the remaining clumps of people, short-cutting across the square and back to the cathedral doors.

For a moment, the three women did not move, and did not speak. Ishbel eyed Birch with an expression that wasn't easy to read. Finally, Birch broke the silence.

'Mrs Hodgekiss, I'm so sorry for—'

Ishbel held up a hand.

'Helen,' she said. 'It's Helen, isn't it? You have absolutely nothing to apologise for. If you hadn't had that man arrested, right now I would be asking you why the hell not.'

Birch tilted her head. Ishbel Hodgekiss was dressed a little strangely: her black formal suit was crumpled, and hung lopsided. Under the jacket, she was wearing an orange polyester top that appeared to be a couple of sizes too small. Her hair stuck up in odd clumps, and around her neck she seemed to be wearing a man's tie, loosely snaked. Yet in her bearing she seemed lucid enough: there was no quiver in her voice, and though her eyes were red and puffy, she seemed emotionless – businesslike.

'He seemed to be suggesting that the man who murdered my

daughter was some sort of hero,' Ishbel was saying. 'To be honest, it's a good job you got hold of him before I did.'

'I'm afraid it's unlikely he'll be charged with anything,' Birch said. 'I didn't give him enough time to cause a breach of the peace, though it was touch and go there for a minute. He didn't use hate speech or threaten anyone. I'm afraid he was right about grounds for arrest. I . . . wasn't thinking straight. It's going to be my head when I get back to the office.'

Ishbel frowned. Amy, who was standing closer to her, leaned into her line of sight.

'Mrs Hodgekiss,' Amy said, 'please. Don't sell your story to Grant Lockley. I know he might have made you think that it's a good idea, but it really isn't. Whatever you say to him he'll twist for his own ends. Moira—'

Amy stopped, realising too late who she was talking to. But Ishbel looked sharply at her.

'Moira,' she echoed. 'You mean Moira Summers? What were you about to say?'

Amy seemed to shrink before Birch's eyes.

'I'm . . . I *was* Mrs Summers' family liaison officer,' she said. 'Lockley convinced her to meet with him, a bit like he's trying to do with you. Against all our advice, she went.'

Ishbel looked thoughtful for a moment. Amy glanced again at Birch, a desperate look in her eyes. Birch shook her head: *You're in too deep now.*

'It was a disaster,' Amy said. 'She realised she'd walked into a trap. The first thing that came out of her mouth, he twisted it. He made it sound like she was a conspiracy theorist, who wanted to believe her son was *trained* to . . . do what he did. Trained by the government. He made her sound completely unhinged.'

Ishbel nodded. 'I've looked at a couple of his columns. I just don't get why people *believe* these things.'

Amy shrugged.

'We've discovered that a lot of people want to believe the worst of Moira Summers,' Birch said. 'But in truth, she's just a parent in mourning . . . like a lot of people here today.'

Quiet fell again. Something flickered across Ishbel's face that might have been anger, and Birch cursed inwardly: *That was stupid, Helen.* Across the square, the First Minister was speaking to the cameras, McLeod edging around behind her as though trying to make sure he was in shot. Lockley was looking down at his phone. Birch felt a quick gust of fear, remembering the video of her and Amy.

'Why did you do that?' she said, turning to Ishbel. When the other woman looked blank, Birch went on, 'Why did you ask Lockley not to post that video?'

'For the reason I gave him,' Ishbel replied. 'I don't want people to be distracted from what I have to say to him.'

Amy and Birch looked at one another, but Ishbel added, 'I'm just not going to say what he thinks I'm going to say.'

The First Minister had finished her remarks – the assembled journalists began baying out questions.

'Also,' Ishbel said, 'it gives me some handy leverage with you, DI Birch. I need help with something. You're not going to like it, but now . . . well, you owe me a favour, don't you?'

8 June, 6.00 p.m.

Moira had been watching coverage of the memorial all day. She'd watched the breakfast news presenters speculate about what the First Minister might say. She'd watched the live feed of the vigil outside the parliament, and then the service itself. She'd looked on the internet, and found shaky mobile phone videos filmed by people in the crowd at Parliament Square. There had been one – short, and shot from far away – of a man with a placard that said her son was a hero. She'd watched as the placard was pulled from his grip, and he was led away by police. She felt sick.

By now, she knew everything that had happened at the memorial. She knew what Twitter was chattering about, what had piqued the interest of the crowd. Less was being said about the placard man than about Aidan Hodgekiss, and his decision to appear at the vigil with his very young-looking mistress. At the service itself, he'd sat next to his wife – the camera had lingered on them a few times – and she'd looked vulnerable, curled in on herself, and her outfit was bizarre. Moira felt sorry for her, but then thought, *No: you don't get to feel sorry for people any more. People don't want your feelings.*

But she *had* feelings. Though she tried to push it away, she felt an anger that twisted and grew as the day lengthened. Where was her son's memorial? Would his death ever be marked by anything other than venom and vengefulness? What would happen when *she* died? Who then would remember him as the little boy who loved seeing how things worked, the little boy in the white hula-hoop in the back garden? Who would remember that he made glittery Mother's Day cards at school and brought them home to hide under her pillow? Who would remember that he was afraid of the dark, or that his favourite colour was green? When she was gone from the earth, no one would remember him as anything other than the freak boy who snapped and killed a bunch of people. His name would only ever be mentioned alongside other young men of his kind: Elliot Rodger. Adam Lanza. Ryan Summers.

The pack of journalists had hung around outside the house all day, their hopeful looks turning mournful as it became clear that she was not planning to walk out in mourning dress to gatecrash the memorial. The light had turned a little pinkish: a column of midges hung in the sunlight over Moira's front lawn. The gaggle had dwindled – she could see its dark, shifting shape through the flimsy living-room curtains, and that shape was smaller now than it had been that morning. It was 6 p.m. Out of habit, Moira flicked on the TV to watch the news, and saw that one station at least had sent a correspondent to speak live from outside her garden gate. They had nothing to say, of course: *Though we hoped Moira Summers might show up today and make a scene, she never left this house. Shame.*

Once again Moira sat and watched the footage she'd been seeing all day. The wide, white pavement in front of the parliament building thronged with people. Close-ups of tear-stained faces and hands holding fluttering white candles. A snippet of the First Minister's speech at the vigil, and then that ten-second clip of Aidan Hodgekiss turning from the podium and taking the hand of a pretty young blonde woman. The collective sigh of interest that went up from the crowd. Then, footage of the vigil moving up the Royal Mile: a few placards, people holding A4 print-outs of the victims' photographs. The First Minister looking sombre, but still waving to the people crowding the pavements as she passed. Finally, inside the cathedral: Valerie Gill crying at the lectern. Close-ups of pillar candles with artistic lens-flare effects added. At last, the footage ran out, and the newsreader reappeared on the screen.

'With me in the studio now . . .' he said, and Moira flicked the TV off. She had no desire to hear pundits' analysis of the memorial. Though there seemed to have been an unspoken agreement not to mention Ryan over the course of the day's events, those events were over now, and it would be open season on him – and, by extension, Moira herself – once again.

Moira sat on the sofa, staring at the blank TV screen for what felt like a long time. The room began to dim. Beyond the curtains, the last of the journalists made their farewells to each other and sloped away. For the first time in about a week, she felt a thread of worry run through her. She had no scene guard any more, and in a few hours, it would be dark.

There was a knock at the front door, and she jumped. Her heart began to race: *Who could this possibly be?* She pulled her hands into fists and sat, frozen, listening. Then, from behind the door, a muffled voice.

'Mrs Summers?' Another knock.

Moira exhaled. Of course: DI Birch. She'd forgotten all about her. She stood, shivering off the apparition of some axe-murderer on the doorstep – *because of course an axe-murderer would knock, Moira, you idiot* – and moved towards the door. In the hallway, she quickly checked her hair in the mirror, and then felt absurd.

'DI Birch,' she said, opening the door and trying for a smile. But the smile soon faded on her lips.

'Oh,' she said.

There was a silence that felt fragile and sparkling, like one of those mercury glass Christmas ornaments, so easily crushed in the hand. Standing behind DI Birch on the garden path, only about three steps away from Moira, was Ishbel Hodgekiss. The woman whose daughter Ryan had killed first.

'Mrs Summers,' DI Birch said again. Moira made herself pull her eyes from Ishbel. The DI looked miserable: tired, and something else. Was she frightened?

'Could we possibly come in?' Birch asked. She glanced around her, and Moira remembered the journalists. Clearly, they'd gone home too early. Whatever this was, any photo taken right now would make one hell of a front-page story.

'Yes,' Moira said, though a quiver in her voice betrayed her uncertainty. 'Of course.'

'I assume I don't need to tell you who this is,' DI Birch said to Moira, once they had gathered in the relative safety of her living room. Moira had backed away towards the kitchen door, making as much space for Ishbel Hodgekiss as she possibly could. This woman couldn't possibly want to be near her, Moira, could she? What on earth was she doing here? Moira realised that now *she* was frightened: the space she'd created was an attempt at protection.

'No,' Moira said. She tried to think of what to say next. The obvious thing – the word that, for almost a month, she'd wanted to shout and keep shouting again and again and again until she was hoarse – seemed totally inadequate, now. But Moira forced herself to look Ishbel Hodgekiss in the eye and whisper it, just once.

'Sorry.' She dissolved into tears.

Ishbel watched her.

'Did you know?' she said.

A look of panic crossed DI Birch's face. 'Mrs Hodgekiss,' she said, 'we're not here to—'

'Did you,' Ishbel said, louder this time, 'have any idea? Any suspicion?'

Moira folded over, as though a great wave of something had risen up at her back and crashed over her.

Between sobs, she hauled in a breath.

'Yes,' she whispered.

DI Birch's eyes widened, but then she turned to Ishbel and said, 'There are ways to do this.'

Ishbel Hodgekiss ignored her.

'Right,' she said, in a voice that sounded hollow. She looked at Moira – waited for her to straighten up a little and meet her eye.

'Go upstairs, please.'

'What?' Birch took a step towards Ishbel.

'DI Birch,' Ishbel replied. 'We discussed this. I promised to do no harm to this woman, and I will keep that promise. But I don't think I can be in the same room with her right now.' She turned to Moira. 'And although she might not understand why, I think Mrs

Summers will be willing to do what I ask, in light of – everything. Isn't that right, Moira?'

Moira straightened up, and sniffed in a long breath of air. After a moment she wiped a hand over her face, and then said, 'Yes.'

'You too, DI Birch,' Ishbel said. 'I'd like you to go upstairs for a moment too, please. When I call Moira down you can come down with her.'

Birch's brow creased.

'I'm sorry,' she said, 'but this is *not* what we discussed. You said you were coming here to—'

'DI Birch.' Moira stepped over to Birch and put a hand on her arm. 'If this poor lady needs a moment alone, I don't think that's asking too much.' She heard her own voice crack and buckle, but she forced herself to keep it together. 'I can only imagine how hard it must be, to be here. To be in this room . . . with me.'

Ishbel's face twisted, and then smoothed again. Moira noticed now that she was wearing the same strange outfit from the memorial, though the tie was gone from her neck. Like Birch, she looked tired.

Without saying anything more, Ishbel stood to one side, and allowed Moira and Birch to file past her out of the room, into the hall, and then up the stairs. Moira heard her close the living-room door behind them.

On the landing, Moira began to walk towards her own bedroom. It was the largest in the house, and was not directly above where Ishbel was standing. But DI Birch paused behind her, her head turned by something.

'Was this Ryan's room?' she asked. Moira turned back, and watched DI Birch step over the threshold and disappear. She didn't need to answer: the state of the room made it obvious.

'Jesus.' Birch was standing in the middle of the carpet, turning slowly around and around, taking in the destruction. 'I am so sorry – the SOCOs did a number on you.' After a pause, she added, 'Amy and Callum really should have got on with getting this sorted out.'

Moira stepped into the room.

'They tried,' she said. 'But I wasn't ready. It would have meant . . . getting rid of things. Of Ryan's. I've only just got to the point where I can look at them, really. I haven't picked anything up yet. I can't imagine sorting through them, disposing of them.'

Without warning, DI Birch sank into the computer chair, as though she had suddenly reached the limits of all her energy, and could no longer hold herself up.

'I'm so sorry,' she said, 'about this. It was a huge mistake to bring Mrs Hodgekiss here, and I knew it from the start. But she was insistent. She said she wanted to talk to you. And I knew you'd said you wanted to talk to some of the . . . the families. So I thought, *Well, okay*. And . . . she kind of had me over a barrel.'

Moira picked her way through the room, skirting around Birch, to the divan. She sat down. The urge to lie down, in the way that had now become normal to her, was almost overwhelming, but she stayed upright.

'I don't know what this is,' Birch said. 'I don't know what she's doing down there. She might be setting the house on fire for all I know. Sorry – I shouldn't have said that.'

Moira was quiet for a moment.

'I don't really care if she is,' she said. 'It might be the best end to this place. You know I've only been outside once, in nearly a month? And *that* was for that disastrous meeting with Lockley. I've had Amy sorting out my food deliveries; I've been sitting watching awful news footage day in and day out. This house is a prison. I might actually be glad if it burned down.'

They sat in silence for a while. Downstairs, they could hear Ishbel's voice, too muffled for them to pick out words, but she was definitely talking to someone. Or to herself.

'Oh God,' Birch said. 'I've done a lot of things badly wrong lately. I've totally let this investigation get to me.'

Moira said nothing. The rise and fall of Ishbel's voice on the ground floor stopped. There was quiet.

'So,' Birch said, seeming to straighten up a little, 'I heard what you said downstairs, when she asked you if you knew. I think I know what she was asking. Amy said she had an inkling that you knew something, too.'

Moira said nothing, but let Birch watch as her face crumpled, and tears came once again.

'Amy was right,' she said, quietly. She covered her eyes with her hand, and began to rock back and forth – not sobbing, but shuddering, silently, as though being shaken by angry, invisible hands.

DI Birch's voice was gentle when she spoke again.

'Why didn't you tell us, Moira? All those days you were at Fettes, at the station. Why didn't you tell me? Or Anjan – you could have told Anjan.'

Moira spluttered, but she was nodding.

'I *could* have told Anjan,' she said. 'I *could* have told him; he seemed trustworthy. But you know . . . it's silly, but I kept thinking about these crime TV shows, where the lawyers are always slippery. They seem plausible but they're slippery. So in the end I said nothing.'

'Moira.' There was the edge of a smile in Birch's voice. 'Those TV shows get it so wrong – *so* wrong, trust me. Anjan is the most straight-up bloke I know.'

After another period of quiet, Birch went on.

'And you know . . . you would have been providing information about a crime committed *by somebody else*, not by you. I know from talking to Amy that you've been struggling with this, but you have to understand. *You are not Ryan*. It wasn't *you* who did this. You could have told us just about anything, and you wouldn't have been punished – you, personally, are just a very valuable witness.'

Moira looked up at Birch.

'You are *not Ryan*,' Birch said again. 'Plus, this investigation is basically over. Between taking you to see Lockley, and now this, I've fairly ballsed it up. So it's likely that whatever you know will make absolutely no difference whatsoever, not now. Why don't you just tell me?'

You're lying to me, Moira thought. But Lockley had been right: keeping things secret *was* hard. It *did* just make everything worse.

Once again, Moira straightened up. She took a long breath in, and then let it slowly out again.

'It was the night before ... the shooting,' she said. DI Birch leaned forward, resting her elbows on her knees, and lacing her fingers together. She looked, Moira thought, like a prize-fighter, waiting in her corner for a big fight to start. Moira closed her eyes, and told herself she was talking to no one – just Ryan's quiet room. Just empty air.

'I'd been up in the town,' she said. 'I was supposed to be working on my essay at the library for the OU degree I'm doing. *Was* doing. But ... I don't know, it was like something was off. I just didn't want to, so instead I spent the day just really ... well, walking around the Old Town. With hindsight, I've wondered if I had some sort of – this sounds silly, but – some sort of psychic sense, that something bad was coming. That I should spend one last day being outside, just enjoying life. Anyway. For some reason that day I was thinking about Ryan a lot. I was thinking about how moody he'd been lately, how he'd come in from college and just go straight up to his room and not come out again, not even to eat meals. How little I'd seen of him. It was worrying me. I knew it was my fault. After his father – after Jackie died, I sort of tunnelled down into my own little cocoon of grief, and didn't come out for perhaps eighteen months. I neglected Ryan during that time – I ignored him. I was so focused on myself, my hurt. I felt like I was rebuilding myself, slowly, by being still and just looking inwards. I'd assumed he'd been doing the same, but now I think he must have needed me, during that time, and I let him down. I'd begun to feel so guilty, these past – well, for a few months now. But because of that guilt I hadn't been doing much about it, hadn't really said anything to him. But that day I started to think that it had gone on long enough, and I needed to speak to him.'

Moira took another long breath. Her eyes were still closed.

'Then there was this boy,' she went on. 'That afternoon, something made me want to walk to the Royal. That is, the old Royal, the hospital – or where the old Royal used to be. I worked there, you know, as a young woman, before I met Jackie. I was a staff nurse. Anyway, for some reason I decided to go and look at it, see what they're doing with the new buildings there. And . . . there was an accident. A young man was hurt. He . . . got impaled on something.'

Birch spoke, making Moira jump.

'I remember that,' Birch said. 'Jesus, it just goes to show. That day, I'd heard about that accident and was praying that it wouldn't come across my desk. Then, the next day – well, you know.'

Moira's face creased.

'So you don't know – was the boy okay, or not?'

Birch's eyes flicked up.

'Oh,' she said. 'Yes, he was fine, apparently. I mean, as fine as you *can* be after an accident like that. There's going to be a big legal stink about it, though, I think. Anjan's firm are representing the guy.'

Birch looked panicked, for a moment.

'At least, I think that's been announced. Maybe keep that to yourself, Moira, sorry. But yes – the boy's fine. He's fine.'

Moira could tell by the look on Birch's face that this was something of a platitude, designed to get her to keep talking. *Well, all right*, she thought, and closed her eyes again.

'Anyway,' she said. 'That boy . . . seeing that, it really shook me up. He was about Ryan's age, and – well, it was like he made up my mind for me. I decided I *had* to go home and have a talk with Ryan, *that night*. Whatever was going on with him needed to stop. I was worried he'd been badly affected by his dad's death and then my reaction to it. Now, of course, I know he must have been . . . oh God. Planning. Planning to kill people.'

She heard DI Birch shift her weight: a squeak in the fake leather of the computer chair.

'What did you say to him that night, Moira?'

There was a silence. Moira screwed up her face. *If only I could remember properly*, she thought.

Ryan had come in from college: Moira listened to the familiar scatter-click of his key in the front door, the front door's slam, and then the fast, heavy tread as he made his way up the stairs.

'Sweetheart?'

He would have been able to hear her. She was in the kitchen, her hands immersed in grimy water at the kitchen sink. Ryan's room was directly overhead: she heard the familiar thud as he dumped his backpack in the middle of the floor. She waited until the water in the sink stilled: there was a pan that the dishwasher just wasn't cleaning right. She had greasy gunk under her nails, from scraping it off. Ryan had made no reply.

She found herself climbing the stairs quietly, as though she didn't want him to hear her approach. She wondered why. What was she afraid of? On the landing, she paused outside her son's bedroom door – closed of course – and listened to the muted staccato beat of a first-person shooter, playing out on the other side.

Good, she thought, *he doesn't have headphones in. He can hear me*. 'Ryan?' she said. She sort of called it, the way someone might shout up a ladder to a man on a high roof. No answer.

'You're going to come down and eat with me tonight, Ryan.'

Moira stood on the landing, thinking for about the thousandth time what a weak spot it was in this house: so gloomy with its absence of windows. Jackie had talked about having a skylight put in but never had. *I'll never do that now*, she realised.

No answer came from her son's room: no sound of acknowledgement, but also no dissent. *The food isn't even cooked yet*, Moira thought. *There's time*.

'Did you hear me, Ryan?' she said, and this time, there was an almost immediate response: a muffled 'Yes'. Just that – 'Yes.' Flat, but certain.

Moira smiled. She rattled back down the stairs, into the hall's well of light, and back into the kitchen to ready herself.

She'd expected to have to call him, but just as she bent to pull the roasted veg from the oven, she found he was standing over her – the shock of his height, which she'd never quite got used to. *He's all limbs*, she thought, as she straightened up, smiling. He had shoulders like a crow: hooked in as though to minimise his ranginess, but the effect was more like drawing a black line around it, making it sharper.

'What's cooking?' he asked, standing there. He made no move to help her, but she flicked away that little irritation. He was here – she'd asked him, and he'd come.

'Pasta,' Moira said. 'With chicken and roast veg. I'm back on my health kick.'

Ryan rolled his eyes.

'If you deign to eat with me more often' – she'd said it teasingly, sarcasm sweetening her voice – 'then I'll be more inclined to cook steak and chips, okay?'

He'd smiled then, and Moira had smiled back. Sometimes, when Ryan smiled, she could feel herself falling backwards through a kind of vortex, into the past where Jackie was still alive and Ryan was maybe eleven or so, rushing out to the shed to work on some invention he'd dreamed up. She could see that little eleven-year-old when he smiled – could see him now.

They sat opposite each other. For a while, Moira watched her son wolf down the food she'd made, in huge bites. It had always alarmed her, the way men ate: like they were in a rush to fill themselves with fuel for whatever the next thing was that they needed to do. Jackie had been like that, too – full of energy and ravenous.

'It's good?' she asked.

'Yeah,' Ryan said, his mouth half full. He peeked up at her from under his dark, sawn-off hair. 'For health food, I guess it's okay.'

This was the moment, Moira realised. *Quick, before he finishes up.*

'I haven't seen much of you, lately,' she said. She tried not to sound pleading, and thought she'd done all right. 'You've been busy, I guess? With college?'

Ryan's eyes darted back down to his food.

'I guess,' he echoed.

'I . . . haven't really asked you much about your course lately,' Moira said. 'I'm sorry about that, sweetheart. What are you working on at the moment?'

She watched him swirl linguine onto his fork.

'Just stuff,' he said – the response she'd been so certain was coming that she could have chimed in with him exactly as he spoke.

'Practical stuff?' *Tone it down, Moira*, she thought. She sounded just a little too sunny. 'Or are you writing essays, or something?'

Ryan had looked up at her again, then – actually lifted his face and made eye contact, his jaw working on the food.

'No offence, Mum,' he said, 'but you don't exactly know much about engineering. You always space out when I talk about my course stuff.'

Moira felt her face colour. *He's right*, she thought.

'I'm sorry, sweetheart. I know I haven't been very attentive lately. But I think I'm finally getting back on my feet, you know? After Dad – I think I might finally be back to normal.'

Ryan said nothing. He lifted another forkful of food.

'How about you?' Moira tried. 'How are you doing, these days . . . post-Dad, I mean?'

She waited for an answer, but none came. As he chewed, her son breathed out hard through his nose.

'You seem . . .' Moira clawed for the words. She had to get this right, or he'd clam up entirely. 'Not yourself, right now. Are you doing okay? Can I do anything?'

Something was happening in her son's eyes. She watched him choosing what to say to her.

'Okay, Mum,' he said. 'Hypothetical. Imagine you and Dad, when you first met.'

Moira blinked in surprise, but said, 'All right.'

Ryan looked down at the table.

'When you first met Dad,' he said, his voice gappy and faltering, 'did you like him?'

Moira smiled. She was surprised by the question, but it kicked up a memory so vivid that she found herself easily sucked into this hypothetical scenario of her son's.

'I thought he was pretty gallus,' she replied, laughing. 'You know how your dad was – such swagger. But yes, I couldn't help but like him. That was part of *why* I liked him.'

Her son's face fell. She'd said the wrong thing.

'I don't have that,' he said, quietly. 'Do I? I don't have swagger.'

'Oh honey,' Moira said. Ryan had stopped eating. He was bouncing his fork between his thumb and the side of his forefinger, as though it were a drumstick. 'Tell me what this is about. What's bothering you?'

Moira stopped. Her throat felt dry, and she was fighting tears once again. She didn't know if she could go on, but she also knew it was too late to go back.

'It's okay, Moira,' DI Birch said. 'You're doing great.'

Moira opened her eyes and threw a grateful look at Birch. Then she closed them again.

'He said it was private; it was none of my business – that sort of sulky teenage boy stuff. I said, "I assume it's not a college-work thing?" And he laughed a sort of strange laugh. There was just something about his manner that made me feel uneasy. He had this look in his eye that I've only ever seen a couple of times before, when he was younger. There was this one time – he was about fifteen then, I think, and already tall – he got into an argument with his father. Jackie could be . . . well, pedantic about things. And Ryan was stubborn, perhaps even more stubborn than your average teenage boy. So this argument, I can't even remember what it was about now, it escalated, and it escalated, and then I saw this awful dark look come across Ryan's face. And then . . . then he hit his father. Just once. But he hit him hard. Felled him, right onto the carpet in that living room. Jackie and I were just stunned. I've never forgotten that look, and he was wearing it again, that night, talking about *swagger*.'

DI Birch was nodding. Moira tried to picture her son's face.

'Ryan.' The food on her own plate was cold. Moira had no stomach for it now; she wanted only to get to the bottom of whatever had come over her son. Anxiety bubbled in her gut. 'Ryan, you know that if you're in any kind of trouble, you really should tell me.'

That black look again – that, and Ryan gave a strange sort of half-smile. Hairs stood up on Moira's arms.

'What kind of trouble do you *think* I might be in?'

He was holding her gaze now. *What if something's really wrong?* Moira thought. But she had to press on. She thought of the worst possible thing that she could imagine it might be – perhaps they could work backwards from there.

'I've been worried,' she said, 'that you might be taking drugs.'

This was a lie, Moira realised. She hadn't been worried about anything so specific. But now that it had dawned on her she felt gripped in the fear of that eventuality.

'Have you heard,' he said, surprise softening the hardness in his eyes, just slightly, 'about what's going on at college?'

Moira shook her head.

'There *is* a drug thing.' Ryan dropped his eyes once more, began to swirl the tines of his fork lazily around in the discarded pasta on his plate. 'I'm not into it. But yeah, the college is full of drugs. I wondered if the word had started to get out.'

Moira felt the blood draining from her face.

'This is the first I've heard of it,' she said, 'but – what are the staff doing?'

Her son made a snorting sound, short but loud.

'Fuck all,' he said. 'That's what.'

Ordinarily she'd have pulled him up on the language – and he knew that – but she didn't want to stop him from talking.

'What does this have to do with me and your dad?' she asked. 'Why did you ask me to think about him just then?'

There was a long silence, broken only by the sound of Ryan's fork skriking across the glazed surface of the plate. Then, just when she thought he wasn't going to speak again, Ryan looked back up at her.

'Mum . . . you remember Abigail Hodgekiss, right?'

DI Birch had sat bolt upright.

'I'm sorry.' Moira passed a hand over her eyes. 'I know I should have told you . . . I should have told you that Ryan . . . that there's a bit of a history, there. With Abigail. They were in high school together, you know.'

DI Birch stared at her.

'Yes, I knew *that*, but – you're saying there was something more significant than that?'

Moira's face crumpled, like paper being palmed into a ball.

'I'm so sorry,' she said. 'I should have told you. But I decided that . . . well, no one else ever knew, I don't think. Not even Abigail, she never realised. I thought maybe it wasn't important, or it was a coincidence that she was one of the . . . the women. The women killed.' Moira was hiccupping sobs now. 'And then . . . every time I didn't mention it, it became harder. Harder to say, *oh, actually . . .*' Moira let her head fall into her opened palms.

'To say oh actually, *what?*'

The sharpness in DI Birch's voice made Moira flick her face up again, the room swimming beyond her tears.

'To say, oh, actually . . . Ryan was desperately in love with Abigail. All through high school, he had the most powerful crush on her.'

DI Birch's mouth fell open.

'She never had any idea,' Moira said, her voice a thin squeak now. 'She barely knew he existed.'

'She still barely knows I exist.' Ryan clattered the fork onto the side of the plate, and it glanced off onto the table, making a red smatter of sauce on Moira's tablecloth.

Moira smiled. She knew she shouldn't – she'd spent enough thir- teen- and fourteen- and fifteen-year-old evenings with Ryan, cajol- ing him into thinking that Abigail *would* notice him eventually and even if she didn't, there would be other girls – but she was relieved. *Girl trouble*, she thought. *After all that, it's only girl trouble.*

'In fact,' Ryan said, 'it's worse. She knows I exist, but she hates me. And she has this fucking dumbass of a boyfriend.'

Again, Moira flinched at the language, but again, she decided to let it slide.

'He's a total asshole,' Ryan was saying. 'He's right in the middle of all this drug stuff that's going on and Abigail just loves him. Just like women always love asshole guys – even you, Mum! Even my own mother.'

Annoyance flared across Moira's vision.

'Hey, young man,' she said, hearing the words come out sharper than she'd intended. 'You don't speak that way about your father. Not in this house. Not anywhere.'

Ryan's voice went low and sulky.

'O*kay*,' he said. 'It's just . . . I try to do the right thing, and she doesn't give a fuck. None of them do.'

'Who?'

'Just . . . all of them. Girls. Women. It's like I'm invisible.'

Moira looked at her son. He sat, hunched over the table with his head pulled low into his crow's shoulders, and looked at the plate in front of him, its congealing swirl of food.

'Ryan,' Moira said, after a while. 'I really think it's time that you put Abigail Hodgekiss behind you.'

He looked up at her then. In his eyes was that same dark look she didn't like, his pupils enlarged, the brown rings of his irises shadowed somehow.

'Yeah?' he said. 'Me too.'

Moira tried for a smile.

'She's a person from your past,' she said. 'Think of her that way, maybe. Put her in the past, and leave her there. Move on.'

Ryan was looking into the middle distance, nodding steadily.

'Put her in the past,' he echoed. And then, 'I could put them all in the past.'

Something flickered in Moira – there was a strangeness sitting over her son that she couldn't quite fathom.

'Sure,' she said, the word quivering between them.

Ryan pulled his gaze back into focus, and met her eye.

'Okay, Mum,' he said. 'You're right. I'm going to do it – put them in the past. I'm going to do it tomorrow, okay? I have your blessing now.'

He made to stand up. The conversation, it seemed, was over.

'You do,' Moira said. 'I want you to do whatever you think you need to.'

Moira opened her eyes. The words she'd just pulled out of the memory seemed to reverberate against the empty, faded walls of her son's room.

'Do you see now why I didn't tell anyone, DI Birch? How could I have *said* that? What if the press got hold of the fact that I'd said that? People like Lockley would have had a field day. I was worried you might think I'd encouraged him, might think I was an accomplice – once it had happened, of course, and I realised what he'd been alluding to. I promise you at the time, I had no idea. Not a clue.'

DI Birch was nodding.

'Then what happened?'

Moira closed her eyes again – it was helping her remember.

'Then he said, "Thanks for the last supper," and walked out of the room. I heard him go up the stairs, back to his room. I shouted after him, because I didn't think he'd eaten enough, and then because I didn't like the way he'd left. I was worried, by that "last supper" comment mainly, and I wanted him to come back and explain what he meant. I thought perhaps he might kill himself, I think. It's hard, now, trying to remember what I really thought, trying to think anything other than *I must have known*. Or *I should have known*, at least. I called him back, again and again. I yelled. But he didn't come. I tried going back up to his door but I got no answer, though I could hear him moving around in there. In the end I gave up. It had shaken me, but I went to bed trying to console myself, thinking, *Well, at least we spoke. I've started a dialogue*. And then ... everything that happened, happened. I feel so stupid, now.'

She stopped speaking. Her breath felt ragged. The room had grown darker. There was no sound from downstairs – Moira suddenly remembered why she was sitting there, on Ryan's bed, with DI Birch listening. Birch's brow was creased. She looked to be deep in thought.

'I think,' she said slowly, and after a long silence, 'that what you've just told me makes very little difference, in the grand scheme of things. I don't think you ought to feel stupid. There were too few dots to join, there. Personally, I don't think you could possibly have added together the remarks he made and got to a place where you felt you ought to raise the alarm with the police; not before the shooting happened, anyway. But you should have told someone – me, Anjan, Amy – from the start of the interview process, about this conversation. And we'd have wanted to know more, we'd have talked about it a lot, those first few days when you were at the station, I dare say. But I don't think anyone would have said you should have done anything differently. You told Ishbel downstairs that you *knew*, but you didn't know. Not really.'

Moira was crying again – loudly now, her sobs fluttering the tattered fabric of the divan.

'It's amazing,' Birch said, 'the secrets that can be kept from you, by the people you love. The people you think you know absolutely everything about. Like I said on the phone earlier, I know how you feel. I know what a shock you must have had, that day.'

Moira looked up at her, her own brow furrowed now.

'*Do* you?' she said. '*Really?*'

But DI Birch was distracted. Her phone had buzzed, and she drew it out to look at it. After a moment, her eyes widened.

'Oh,' she said. 'Well. Okay then.'

Moira craned her neck, as though she had any chance of reading the tiny words on the screen in Birch's hand.

'What?' she said.

Birch looked up at her.

'The death threats,' she said. 'Our suspect . . .' She trailed off.

'What? *What* about the death threats?'

But Birch had gone stiff, and was listening. Downstairs, there was a knock at the front door.

8 June, 8.00 p.m.

Ishbel had stood for a while, looking around Moira Summers'
living room. It was a little old-fashioned, décor-wise: textured
wallpaper, thick with many layers of paint, and a gas fire set in an
ugly, mock-stone fireplace. The mantelpiece was dusty, and along
its top there were clear marks – gaps in the dust, where picture
frames had stood, but had been taken away. Ishbel felt a pang of
something. She was glad she didn't have to look at pictures of this
woman's son . . . but she was also sad that his mother had been
forced to banish him.

She knew what she needed to do, what she had come to this
place to do. She just had to summon the courage to do it. She
wasn't sure how long DI Birch would be content to stay upstairs
and out of the way, so she ought to get things in motion.
Nevertheless, she was afraid. Stalling for time, she drifted to the
kitchen door and opened it, quietly. Poking her head around the
door, she registered a line of empty wine bottles on the worktop
– they reminded her of the bottle she'd thrown at Aidan, that night
in her own kitchen, and the cut she'd made on his cheek. She felt
a tiny spark of pride now, remembering. It warmed her – it felt like
something inside her was coming back to life. But as soon as she'd
registered the feeling, she folded it away again. Moira's kitchen
had a bad smell, she realised: the bin, slowly ripening. There was
more than a day's worth of dirty dishes piled up in the sink, and
beside it.

Come on, Ishbel thought, backing away and returning to the
living room. She took out her phone, and from a different pocket,
Grant Lockley's business card. The word *entrapment* drifted
through her mind as she thumbed in the number. Was what she

was about to do illegal? She didn't know. At the sound of Lockley's voice on the other end, she found she didn't care.

'You've reached Grant Lockley,' he said. And then, 'Ishbel, is that you?'

She swallowed hard.

'It is,' she said.

She fancied she could hear him punching the air.

'Oh, fan*tas*tic,' he said. 'I'm *so* glad you felt able to call. Is now a good time to talk?'

Ishbel took advantage of the fact that he couldn't see her, and rolled her eyes.

'Yes,' she said. 'You're able to come to me?'

'I can come wher*ever* you like,' he said. *You're overegging it*, she thought. *If we were really doing what you think we're doing, you ought to be more careful.* But perhaps, she thought, the successful manipulation of Jack Egan had made him complacent.

'Are you at home?' he asked.

Ishbel blinked. Surely if anyone knew she'd moved out of the matrimonial nest, it was him. *It's a test*, she thought. *Don't tell him.*

'Not just now,' she said, trying to sound breezy. 'Actually . . .'

Just say it. Make it sound normal.

'I'm at Moira Summers' house.'

In the stunned pause that followed, Ishbel allowed herself to imagine a particularly contorted expression on Lockley's face.

'Oh,' she said, before he could respond, 'didn't you know? Moira and I . . . we've been in touch.' She closed her eyes, to see if that might make it easier to lie. 'For a little while now, actually. She . . . offered me an olive branch. We're . . . building bridges.'

Never mix your metaphors, she thought. But these euphemisms, she hoped, would keep her from wading too far into the swamp of untruth.

'I had no idea,' Lockley said, and his voice was rueful.

'No one can know *everything*, Mr Lockley.' Ishbel couldn't resist it. But she went on, 'Anyway, you know now. And after I saw you this afternoon, I had a chat with DI Birch.' That part was true, at least. 'Then I had a chat with Moira.' Also true, technically, if their cold exchange of a few words could be called a *chat*. But now came the big lie. 'And we've decided, we'd like to talk to you . . . together. Both of us. Moira and I, in conversation, like you suggested. We both want to . . .' Ishbel swallowed, her nose wrinkling with distaste. '. . . To sell you our stories.'

There was another long pause on the line, and within it, a scuffling sound: Lockley was getting his coat.

'Mrs Summers is there with you now?' he asked. Ishbel closed her eyes, and let loose a silent *thank you*. He'd bought it.

'Yes,' she said. 'She's . . . not keen to speak on the phone, but she's here. You can come, now?'

There was a pause on the line.

'Wait,' Lockley said. He sounded uneasy. *Come on*, Ishbel thought, *you're a shark, and I'm laying a trail of blood.* 'I don't want to be seen. Are there photographers outside? If I'm going to do this, I want it to be an exclusive, obviously.'

Ishbel quickly shuffled to the window, and twitched the curtains aside, just a little.

'No,' she said, 'there's no one outside. I was able to arrive unseen, after all. I'm sure you'd have got a call from someone otherwise, wouldn't you? To say I was here, and . . . and there was a story?'

Ishbel felt out of her depth. Her bargaining skills were failing her. Her head felt like a faulty lightbulb, fizzing in and out. She listened to Lockley considering things.

After a long while, she could hear that curiosity had got the better of him.

'Okay,' he said. She heard the zip of his coat.

'And you know the address?'

Of course he does. And plenty more besides.

'I do.'

'Great,' Ishbel said. Her heart smattered like hard rain. 'We'll see you shortly?'

'You will,' Lockley said. He began to say something more, in his fawning voice, but Ishbel had already hung up.

The light went out of the room. Ishbel sat on Moira Summers' sofa, still wearing her coat until she realised that would look weird to Lockley and stood up and took it off. She tried to run through in her mind what she wanted to say to him, how she wanted to present the information – tried to anticipate how he might react. But that train of thought kept slipping away from her. Instead, she thought about Ryan Summers. This wasn't just his mother's house: it had been *his* house, too. He'd sat here, in this very spot, on this very sofa. He'd breathed this air. In this house, he'd hidden his guns. He'd plotted to kill her daughter, because she'd complained about him at the student union.

In the quiet gloom, Ishbel tried to imagine how such an action might begin, what thought might spark it. *It's unimaginable*, a lot of people had said to her, since the event. *Since Abigail died* – she forced herself to think those words, to mouth them silently. *It's unimaginable*: Greg had said it at the hospital. Rehan had said it to her, and to Aidan, more than once. Pauline had said it to her, on the phone. It was a phrase she'd heard a hundred times on the news.

But now, she found it wasn't unimaginable at all. She allowed herself to sit there, on the same couch that her daughter's murderer had sat upon, and imagine it all. He was a lonely boy, maybe – a weird kid that people steered clear of, if Abigail's journal was any indication. His dad had died not long ago. He was sad. Ishbel didn't remember much about being twenty, not really, but she remembered that it had been hard work. She imagined adding sadness, frustration and loneliness into the mix. And she tried to imagine being a man – Aidan was always telling her that things were harder for young men, growing up. *Baby's got it easy*, he used to say of the teenage Abigail, whenever she got whiny about something. *She doesn't know the half of it.*

Then Ishbel imagined that sad, frustrated, lonely young man hearing that one of his classmates had complained about him – 'creeping around me', those were Abigail's words. Yet really, all Ryan Summers had done to Abigail was try to protect her from the influence of Jack Egan. Had things not ended as they did, Ishbel might have thanked him.

I'll kill her, she imagined him thinking. *I could kill her.* That was it: *that* was the thought that sparked the action. They were words Ishbel had thought, too: plenty of times, about all sorts of people. She'd thought them about Abigail herself – regularly, in fact. And she'd said them, aloud, to Aidan. At times, she'd been frightened by how close she'd come to *meaning* them. *I could kill her. I could kill her with my own bare hands.*

Ishbel shook her head: her face was wet. She wiped her eyes with her sleeve.

Upstairs, she could hear Moira and DI Birch, talking quietly, though she couldn't hear what they were saying. She felt loneliness settle over her, cold and hard as frost. She wanted to walk up the stairs and join them, to tell them the things she was thinking, and hear what they had to say. *I should be angry*, she thought. *I shouldn't be trying to understand Ryan Summers, I should just be angry with him.* But she felt only that loneliness, and a strong desire to lie down and sleep.

There was the sound of a car drawing up outside, and then – after a period of quiet, during which Ishbel tried to steel herself – a knock at the door. The voices upstairs fell silent.

'Don't come down, DI Birch,' Ishbel whispered, standing and moving towards the door. 'Just give me one minute with him.'

Lockley was standing on the doorstep. He'd abandoned his small, gunmetal grey car halfway up the pavement outside.

'You found us,' Ishbel said.

He blinked, as though sensing a challenge.

'I'm afraid *everyone* knows this address,' he said, stepping up and into the hall without waiting to be asked. 'This house was on the news every single night, for a while there.'

She stepped back, and he walked past her into the living room. She followed him in, and watched him as he looked around for Moira.

'Where's Moi— Mrs Summers?' he said.

'Upstairs.' Ishbel indicated that he ought to sit down. 'She's just . . . gathering herself.'

Stop pausing right before you lie, she thought. *It makes it obvious.* But Lockley sank down onto the sofa, apparently content with that explanation.

'I'll just let her know you're here,' Ishbel said, and walked out into the hall.

At the bottom of the stairs, she looked up, and listened for a moment. The two women above her were obviously doing the same, for she couldn't hear their voices. *Good.* Lockley shouldn't know that Birch was here. Ishbel laid a hand on the newel post and tried to summon the correct voice for hailing Moira – a stranger she ought to hate, but was pretending to be friends with. She felt a déjà vu so strong that she swayed on her feet for a moment, and she had to shake herself: she'd almost called out her daughter's name.

'Moira?' she tried, in a sing-song voice. 'Mr Lockley's here now.'

She waited. DI Birch appeared at the top of the stairs, her eyes narrowed. Ishbel put her fingers to her lips, and then mouthed, *Trust me.* Birch's frown deepened, but she nodded, slowly: once, twice.

Behind her, Moira's face appeared.

'There you are,' Ishbel said, loudly. She pointed at Moira, and then held her hand up, flat against the air. *Stay there*, she mouthed. Moira looked confused, but stayed still. Ishbel then pointed at Birch, and mouthed, *You. Come here.* She beckoned, before putting her finger to her lips again. Birch began to creep slowly down the stairs, her face a mask of confusion.

'Oh, it's okay, Moira,' Ishbel said, trying not to sound too theatrical. 'If you're not ready, you just stay up there a little longer. Come down when you're ready, all right?'

DI Birch had reached the foot of the stairs. Ishbel glanced behind her at the living-room door, which was slightly ajar. She risked a very quiet whisper.

'Stay here,' she said to Birch, 'and just *listen*.'

Birch shook her head, sadly. She looked very tired. She held up a spread palm.

Five minutes, Birch mouthed.

Ishbel walked back into the living room, leaving the door half open.

'Right, Mr Lockley,' she said. 'Let's not beat around the bush, shall we? Are you ready to hear what I have to say?'

Lockley blinked in surprise.

'Of course,' he said. 'Just give me a sec.'

He fumbled in the pocket of his grey coat, and pulled out his phone. Ishbel watched as he fidgeted with it, and then, with a flourish, laid it on the arm of the sofa. She sat down in the armchair opposite him.

'You're recording?' she said.

'I'm afraid I need to. You're okay with it?'

'Oh, I'm okay with it,' Ishbel said, 'if you're okay with it.'

'Why wouldn't I be?' he said. 'I always record this sort of thing.' He settled back on the sofa, a satisfied smile on his face. *He thinks he's made it*, Ishbel thought. *He thinks he's finally bagged his story. Jack Egan was just a rehearsal for what he thinks he's about to do.*

'You just start whenever you're ready,' Lockley said. 'If you don't mind, I'll leap in with questions as you go.'

Ishbel smiled. Inside her chest, she felt that little spark again: *I'm going to enjoy this.*

'Okay,' she said. 'I'd like to start by talking about Stuart Telford.'

Lockley frowned.

'Sorry?'

'Oh.' Ishbel let her eyes widen in mock-surprise. 'Don't you remember? When you first called me, asking to do this . . . story. You know? You mentioned Stuart and Annie Telford. That couple, with the care home.'

Lockley straightened up a little.

'Why do you want to talk about *that*?' he asked.

Ishbel shrugged.

'You brought it up, on the phone that day. In fact, if I were a hysterical sort of person, I could say you threatened me. You seemed to be suggesting that if I didn't talk to you, you'd do an interview with Stuart Telford instead . . . right?'

Lockley spread his hands, and forced his lips into a smile, though his eyes remained cold.

'*Ish*bel,' he said, 'that was never my intention. I was never actually in *touch* with the Telfords. I just thought you needed a little push, to get you to a place where you could open up. And now that you're here, and we're doing this, can you blame me?'

'I can question your journalistic ethics. Do you deny that you were making a threat?'

Lockley kept smiling.

'I don't think it's uncommon for people in my line of work to … push the boundaries. Just every now and again, it's necessary.'

'Will you at least apologise?' Ishbel kept her voice level, even pleasant. 'Whatever your end goal, you phoned me up when you knew I had just lost my only daughter, in a terrible act of violence, and you threatened me. Can I ask for an apology?'

'Ishbel, I'm *so* upset that you've formed such a negative opinion of me—'

Ishbel stood up quickly, cutting him off.

'I guess that's a no, then,' she said. 'Okay.'

She walked across the room, past Lockley, and over to the window, turning her back on him. She stood there a moment, and then reached out and flicked the curtain aside slightly, as though she wanted to look out at the street. But instead she snuck a glance through the slightly open door at Birch, who was still there, standing in the shadow of the hallway. She'd drawn close to the door, to listen. Ishbel raised an eyebrow at her: *Watch this.*

'So,' Ishbel turned back to look at Lockley, 'tell me. Where did you find your information, exactly? About the Telfords. That was all … what? Three years ago? It's ancient history, isn't it?'

For the first time since he'd walked through the door, Lockley looked uncomfortable.

'I don't see why this is relevant,' he said. 'Maybe we should try more of a question-and-answer format?'

'Maybe in a minute,' Ishbel said. 'I would just really like to know where you heard about that whole Telford case.'

Lockley shifted a little in his seat.

'It's a matter of public record,' he said. 'Stuart Telford went to trial, and was convicted. It was in the papers. I think I even reported on it a little, at the time.'

'Of course.' Ishbel allowed herself to smile a rather nasty smile. 'How silly of me. But, see . . . the thing is this: I can't figure out for the *life* of me how you found out that I was the lead regulator on that case. My understanding was that those case files were anonymised. In fact, it was a condition of my testimony at Mr Telford's trial. So it's been bothering me, these ten days since we spoke on the phone. If you *haven't* been in touch with the Telfords, then how on earth did you manage to follow a trail to me?'

Lockley glanced at the mobile phone at his elbow, still recording.

'You know,' he said, 'there are some questions I'd like to ask you while we're alone, before Mrs Summers joins us. Maybe I could get on with those, and we could come back to this later?'

'Oh,' Ishbel said, 'won't you just put me out of my misery? It's been niggling at me all this time.'

'For example,' Lockley said, waving her words away with a flick of his hand, 'I'd like to ask you the question that absolutely *every-one* would like an answer to. Why do you think Ryan Summers did what he did? What do you think could have led him to murder your daughter, and all those other poor girls, in such an unspeakable way?'

Ishbel batted her eyelashes.

'Oh!' She'd been right: she *was* enjoying herself. 'I know exactly why. Abigail wrote about it in her journal. But if we can just go back, just for a second . . .'

Lockley leaned forward in his chair.

'Did you just say . . . you *know* why Abigail was killed?'

'Oh yes,' Ishbel said. She took a couple of steps back across the room, and stopped in front of Lockley. 'But I'm not going to tell you about it until you answer my question.'

Lockley leaned back again, clearly unnerved by her standing over him.

'Okay, look,' he said, 'you were right . . . about my conduct on the phone, when we spoke ten days ago. It was unprofessional.' He glanced again at his mobile phone, its red blinking light. 'You're right. I used a threat. And . . . I'm sorry. Okay? Can we move on now?'

Ishbel rearranged her features for a moment, making it look as though she were deep in thought.

'Well, I accept your apology – thank you.' She paused to watch Lockley relax a little, but then added, 'However, I really do want you to explain to me how you knew I was connected to the Telfords.'

Lockley stared up at her, apparently at a rare loss for words. She couldn't help but smile.

'I'm not going to let this go,' she said.

Suddenly, Lockley was on his feet, his face very close to hers.

'What is this?' he hissed.

Ishbel stiffened. This was it – this was the moment.

'This,' she said, 'is me accusing you of hacking into my private correspondence. All the official documents from the Telford case were sealed, as a condition of the trial. I've been thinking about it, and this afternoon I've made some calls. And I know now that the only possible way for anyone to find out about my involvement would be . . . what? Can you tell me, Mr Lockley?'

She waited, holding his gaze. Lockley faltered, and looked at his feet.

'Would be to read my personal emails,' she finished. 'Emails where I poured my heart out to friends, or to my mother-in-law. Emails that have absolutely no place in the public domain.'

Lockley's eyes snapped back to look at her.

'You couldn't prove that.' His voice had become a snarl. 'You couldn't prove that I ever *mentioned* Stuart Telford to you. If you pursue this, I'll deny even knowing that name.'

His thin, pale face was colouring: two scarlet patches had appeared high up on his cheekbones, and his eyes were bulging. Ishbel held her nerve.

'Would you admit that you did it,' she said, 'if I promised I would hand over Abigail's journals to you?' She paused for effect. 'Just . . . for me. Just admit it for *me*.'

Lockley was quiet. Behind his eyes, Ishbel could see a fight starting up.

'Just to set my mind at rest,' she said. 'I've been so strung up lately, with everything that's gone on. If I could just know I was right . . . that my detective work was right. You'd make me feel so much better.'

She watched him.

'And,' she went on, 'just think what you could do with those journals. If I gave you permission to excerpt from them, everyone would get to know the truth, at last. Isn't that what you strive for? That's what you always say, isn't it? You just want to get to the truth? That's your *job*, isn't it?'

Lockley's blood was up. Their faces were close enough that Ishbel could feel the heat of his breath, a little ragged now. He smelled strange: musty, and somehow medicinal. Fear battered at her like a high wind – they were roughly the same size, but he was wiry, and coiled tight as a spring. If he decided to attack her she'd have to scream for DI Birch, and this spell she'd got him under would be broken. She forced herself to look calm, and meet his eyes. The fight in them went on, and then, suddenly, was lost.

'Okay, *fine*,' he hissed. It was barely more than a whisper, and Ishbel prayed that DI Birch could hear it. 'You've got me. *Yes*, I went in your emails, okay? I wasn't looking for Stuart Telford's name . . . I was just looking for something I could use, to get you to talk. If you'd have just come quietly I would never have mentioned him. But you were being so *difficult*.'

Ishbel was silent. It had worked. She couldn't believe it had worked. A strange, warm feeling surged through her, and for the first time since she'd run out of her office on that awful day – her heart shuddering and her car keys in her hand – she felt like laughing. *Control yourself*, she thought. She knew that her time with Lockley was running out. *Let's see what else we can do.*

'Was it terribly hard?' She widened her eyes. 'I can't imagine the skill it must take, to break into someone else's email.'

A vein was pulsing in Lockley's neck.

'Oh, don't be silly,' he said. 'It's fucking child's play, once you know how. I've done it a million times.'

Ishbel nodded.

'You got into Aidan's, too, didn't you?' she said. 'That's another thing that's been bothering me . . . the idea that Abigail knew about Aidan having an affair, and kept it secret from me. That really cut me up, for a while, that she would do that. It seemed so unlike her. And I didn't see it mentioned anywhere in her journal. But then . . . when you mentioned the Telfords. I started to think, *Well, maybe he didn't get that information from Jack Egan.* You didn't, did you? Jack didn't tell you Aidan was having an affair – he didn't know that. Abigail didn't know that. You got it from Aidan's emails, didn't you?'

Lockley reached round behind him, and snatched up the mobile phone from the sofa arm. He punched at it with a stiffened index finger, switching off the recording and then, as Ishbel watched, deleting the file.

'Yes,' he said, 'I did. Are you satisfied? Because you shouldn't be. I didn't make any of it up, so I'm afraid it doesn't make your situation any better. Your daughter really *was* dealing drugs all round Three Rivers College, and beyond – Jack Egan did tell me that, and trust me, that kid's too stupid to lie. Your husband really *is* having an affair, no matter how I found out . . . he's been carrying on for years, in fact.' He paused, to look Ishbel up and down, his breath fast. 'And of course, none of this changes the fact that your daughter is dead – *murdered*. So . . . does it really matter, how the information came out?'

Out of the corner of her eye, Ishbel caught a movement in the corner of the room. DI Birch had slipped silently in through the door, and was watching them. Ishbel looked back at Lockley, and smiled.

'Not to me,' she said, 'no.'

She watched Lockley relax. He'd drawn himself up to his full height, she realised, and now he seemed to shrink two or three inches, back into the slightly hunched shoulders of his threadbare grey jacket.

'Good,' he said. 'I'm glad I could set your mind at rest. Now, can we pick up where we left off? I'd like to hear more about these journals.'

'I fucking bet you would.'

For a split second, Lockley looked confused, as if he'd just seen Ishbel speak without moving her lips. But his face was a white mask of panic: he'd recognised the voice. As he spun around to face her, DI Birch cleared the three paces over to him and closed a hand around his wrist.

'Grant Lockley,' she said, 'I'm delighted to tell you that you're under arrest.'

Lockley spluttered. To Ishbel, he looked like a drowning man, gasping for the air that might save him, but finding none.

'You do not have to say anything,' DI Birch was saying, 'but it may harm your defence if you do not mention, when questioned, something which you later rely on in court. Anything you do say may be given in evidence.' She grinned at Ishbel, then looked back at Lockley. 'Why don't you sit down, until my colleagues arrive?'

Lockley wrenched his arm free of Birch's grip. He finally found some air.

'You can't arrest me! What have I done?'

Birch rolled her eyes.

'You just confessed to illegally acquiring confidential information,' she said.

Lockley laughed a warped laugh.

'Yeah?' he spat. 'Prove it!'

Birch looked at Ishbel, and Lockley followed her gaze. Ishbel allowed herself a pantomime flourish as she drew her own mobile phone from the breast pocket of her jacket.

Lockley threw up his arms.

'This is *entrapment*, Birch! I'll have you fucking *struck off* for this!'

'Oh, shut up.' Ishbel heard her own voice, the force in it, and was shocked. 'Will you for once just shut up? Sit down, like DI Birch has asked, and stop your blustering. It isn't entrapment. You agreed to being recorded right at the start of our conversation.'

Lockley's eyes boggled.

'I did no such thing!'

Ishbel felt a strange calm, though her heart was racing.

'You did,' she said. 'You remember? I said, "I'm okay with it if you're okay with it." And you said that you were. So when I got a chance, I stood up, I went over to the window' – Ishbel pointed, as though Lockley might not remember – 'and I started recording.'

Lockley opened his mouth and tilted slightly towards Ishbel, as if he intended to counter her. But then he seemed to have another thought that cut off the words before they formed. In the quiet that followed, he sank down onto the sofa.

'That's my boy,' Birch said, still grinning.

Lockley scowled up at her.

'I'll fight you on this, Birch,' he growled. 'There's no way you can make this stick.'

Ishbel watched Birch: she was beaming, and some of the fatigue and worry that had been there seemed to fall away.

'D'you fancy a bet on that, Grant?' she said.

Lockley looked sullenly up at her for a moment.

'No comment,' he said.

Birch glanced at Ishbel, who smiled back at her: a tired smile, but a genuine one.

'I thought so,' Birch said.

In the corner of the room, the door was pushed open, and Moira Summers shuffled in, her movements almost apologetic. She looked down at Lockley sitting on her sofa – at first in surprise, and then as though he were some slimy invertebrate creature that had found its way in from the dirt outside.

'Moira,' Birch said, her face like Christmas morning, 'can you dig out your panic button for me, please? Let's call up the cavalry.'

8 June, 9.00 p.m.

Birch watched from Moira's front doorstep as Lockley was led out of the garden gate and put into the back of the panda car. It was a strange sensation: this was a fantasy film-reel she'd allowed to play out in her mind so many times in the past. Lockley in handcuffs, walking towards an adequate punishment for the hurts he'd inflicted. Of course, there was still work to be done to ensure that happened. But seeing him fold himself into the back of the police car, and be driven away, prompted a deep, warm feeling of calm. For a moment, she was alone on that front doorstep: the summer twilight was deepening around her, and beyond the roof-tops of Moira's street she could hear the general hush of the city's traffic, a distant siren somewhere, like always. Moira had flicked on the outside light, and in its beam, little moths and midges danced like dust motes. Birch felt her mother's presence with her then: a pillar of warm air beside her, so seemingly real that she almost spoke to it aloud. But two uniformed colleagues were advancing back up the path towards her, so she said the words inwardly: *It's over, Mum. He can't hurt us any more.*

'Marm?' One of the uniforms was standing in front of her now. Birch gave herself a little shake, and the spell was broken.

McLeod was on the phone.

'Helen,' he said, 'you've made my night.'

She blinked. She'd told him as many of the details as she dared, but still, he sounded pleased.

'Don't congratulate me just yet, sir,' she said. 'Lockley's lawyer will have some fun and games with the way we got that confession.'

McLeod seemed unperturbed.

'Oh, whatever,' he said. 'The point is, we can build a case here. I bet my bottom dollar that if he's been in the Hodgekiss emails, he'll have been messing with the other families, too. And I doubt that "learn how to spy on people" was one of his new year's resolutions: he'll have been doing this stuff for donkey's.'

Birch took a deep breath.

'Before you go out and celebrate, sir,' she said, 'you should perhaps also know that Lockley does have at least one damning story left up his sleeve.'

McLeod's snort buzzed in the speaker at Birch's ear.

'I assume you mean Lockley's mobile phone footage of you arresting a peaceful protester and then openly gloating about it with a colleague?'

Birch squeezed her eyes closed, and braced herself.

'Yes, sir,' she said. And then, 'You heard about that?'

McLeod laughed a mirthless laugh. 'Oh yes,' he said. 'Your young drinking buddy ... Ms Kato? She came to me in something of a flap about it this afternoon, and told me everything. Not your best police-work, Birch, I have to say.'

Birch sighed.

'I know, sir. I'm so sorry. I don't know what came over me.'

'I do,' McLeod said. 'Grant Lockley came over you. This investigation can't have been easy for you, Birch – I *can* see that.'

He's right, she thought. *Dammit.*

'So you decided to set up your own little meet-and-greet at Moira Summers' house? I can tell you that neither of the respective FLOs are huge fans of that decision ... Reh Ibrahiim especially.'

Birch's eyes were still squeezed shut. She was glad McLeod couldn't see her wincing.

'And, for the record, I am not a huge fan of you going into vigilante mode and deciding you can fix everything on your own, either.'

'Sir—'

'However.' There was an edge of something in McLeod's voice, as though he were on the verge of laughter. He certainly seemed to be enjoying himself. 'If I'm speaking off the record? I'm rather pleasantly surprised at you setting fire to the rule book and reverting back to some old-school policing. It isn't like you at *all*, but I'm enjoying it. You'll be beating up bad guys down dark alleyways next.'

Birch flinched.

'Sir,' she said. 'Please don't joke about it. I'm looking at a potential misconduct hearing here, and rightly so.'

McLeod huffed into the receiver again.

'You're a good girl, Helen,' he said. 'And you did good today – in the end, anyway. It'll all come out in the wash, don't you worry.'

Birch grimaced. She could hear McLeod's wagons beginning to circle already, and wondered, for a moment, what Anjan might make of it all. She felt her heartbeat speed up, just a little.

'I've decided,' McLeod was saying, 'that it's important we keep you around.'

Birch sagged. *He's going to smooth it all over, isn't he?* she thought. *He's going to try and make it all go away.*

'Sir, I really don't think that—'

But fatigue had risen up around her like flood water, as she stood there: she felt every moment of the last three and a half weeks, as though the weight of them had been dumped onto her shoulders, all at once.

'Quiet, Helen,' McLeod said. 'For once, I strongly suggest that you do not argue.'

He wants this, she thought. *It'll end up with me owing him the most almighty favour, and then he'll be able to lord it over me forever.*

'Sir—'

'You just leave it with me,' McLeod said. 'And don't worry about a thing.'

'I've thought a lot about this,' Moira Summers said. Ishbel was sitting across the room from her, on the sofa where Lockley had been until DI Birch led him out into the hall. A young uniformed officer had come inside, and Moira had instructed him to make them both a cup of tea. He complied without a word, and only once he'd gone into the kitchen did Ishbel realise the oddness of everything, and she'd begun to laugh, quietly, surprising herself. Now, she and Moira both sat with a steaming mug on their knees. The young policeman had retreated into the hall, and DI Birch was in the front garden, on the phone. They could hear the quiet rise and fall of her voice outside the front window.

'I've thought about what I might say,' Moira went on, 'to you, or one of the other . . . relatives. I thought there were so many things. But now . . . I can't think of anything. Except to say again how sorry I am. And that just doesn't cut it, does it?'

Ishbel took a sip of her tea. They both sat in silence.

'I know,' Ishbel said, eventually, 'what you mean, in a way. I've thought about meeting you, too. And I've thought about meeting your son, though I know that's impossible. I've thought about everything I might say – and assumed I'd be angry, that I'd lash out. But it's odd now, sitting here. It's the oddest thing. I don't feel like I expected to at all.'

Beyond the living-room curtains, they caught a snatch of DI Birch's talk: *Sir, I really don't think that—*

Moira frowned.

'I hope they won't be too hard on her.'

Ishbel nodded. DI Birch sounded agitated. They probably shouldn't be listening in.

'You . . .' She'd begun speaking before she really knew what to say. 'You don't have any other children?'

Opposite her, Moira blinked. Something passed across her face – an expression Ishbel couldn't identify.

'No.' It was almost a whisper. 'For a while we thought we couldn't – have children, I mean. At all. But things find a way of happening, don't they?'

Ishbel said nothing. She found herself wondering what the past month might have been like, had *she* had another child to care for – a brother or sister of Abigail's. Ishbel had been so keen to get back to work after her daughter was born, to get back to the slowly ascending career she loved and then came to loathe, that it had just never happened. Might they have helped, this past month, that ghost sibling? Or might they just have been another thing that

Ishbel found herself neglecting, in favour of sleeping all day on the hard-sprung spare-room bed? Was it better to just be left alone, completely alone? She wanted to ask Moira Summers this question, but didn't know if she could.

Around them, the house began to settle into evening: floorboards clacked as they cooled. From the kitchen, the distant buzz of the fridge.

'He warned me,' Moira said into the silence. 'The night before the shooting, we talked, and . . . I said to you before that I *knew*, but I didn't really, not exactly. I didn't know what he was talking about. He didn't tell me. But he said some things that . . . now, when I think about it, I think he *wanted* to tell me. I'd like to think, anyway, that really, he wanted me to stop him. But I was too stupid to catch on.'

Ishbel looked up. Tears glinted on Moira's face.

'I'm so sorry,' she said, again. 'I'm so sorry I couldn't save your little girl.'

Ishbel looked down. In the cup on her lap, the dark tea reflected a flickery version of her own pale face. *Right now*, she thought, *you have a choice. You can accept this apology, or not. Move on, or not.* She thought about what Aidan would do, if he were here – something ugly, probably, she realised. Then, out of nowhere, she found herself wondering what Greg might do – what he'd advise her to do. Ishbel blinked several times, as though waking from a long sleep. Yes, she *could* choose. She looked up at Moira, whose head was curled over into her chest, and considered her options.

'I thought,' Ishbel said, slowly, 'that I could save her. That morning, when I heard what was happening . . . I thought, if I could just drive fast enough, just get to her quickly enough, I'd be able to save her.'

Moira had looked up, her crying paused by surprise.

'But now,' Ishbel was saying, 'I know that even before I got to my car, she was already lost. I'd lost her.'

Quiet fell again. Outside, DI Birch was ending her phone call.

'She upset him, you know. They were in the student union together, and . . . oh God.' Ishbel had begun to cry, too, and her words became spitty and slurred. She pushed on. 'She had this awful boyfriend. Jack Egan, you might have seen him in the papers. He sold his story to Lockley, told him they'd got into drugs together – he got my Abigail into *drugs*. I had no idea. And in the midst of all this, your – *Ryan* . . .' Ishbel stopped. Saying his name in front of his mother felt strange, like she'd realised for the first time that this name belonged to an actual human man – not just a shadow, not just a bad act that could never be taken back.

'Ryan tried to help her,' Ishbel said, her voice wet and rasping. 'He tried to tell her that Jack was no good. But she didn't listen. She reported him to the student union – said that Ryan Summers was being creepy around her. I guess . . . that must have made him angry enough, to . . .' She couldn't finish the sentence. From the look on Moira's face, she didn't want to hear it, either.

Moira opened her mouth as if to speak, but then sat that way for a while, as though thinking carefully. Ishbel watched her face: it was a white mask of weariness.

'I think,' Moira said, at last, 'that probably wasn't the reason – *the* reason. Or, it wasn't the *only* reason. It wouldn't explain . . .' She faltered, but rallied again. 'It wouldn't explain all the other girls. I've read about these online posts, people's theories about, what? MRA activity? I don't know what's true any more, and it's the most frustrating feeling. But . . . you telling me that, it's like . . .'

For a moment, Moira seemed to want to stop talking. But then, carefully, she went on.

'It's like I'm fumbling around in this terrible darkness. I'm trying to find a lever, or a switch – something I can press that will flood everything with light, and make it all seem all right again. If I can just find that switch, I'll find myself in a brightly lit room, and on the floor in the middle of it will be written the reason – *the* reason – why my son . . .' Moira swallowed hard. 'Why my son killed those thirteen women. The darkness is that question: *why, why, why?* And the light switch would give me the answer – an answer that I know for sure is true. But I don't think I'll ever find it. I think I'll be staggering around in that darkness for . . . well, for the rest of my life.'

Ishbel was nodding, slowly.

'But you telling me that,' Moira said, 'it's as if the darkness doesn't feel quite so dense as it did just before.'

For a moment, the two women held each other's gaze. Something passed between them, like electric current.

'So – thank you.'

Ishbel tried for a small smile, and found it came more easily than she'd expected.

'You're welcome,' she said.

Moira sank back into her chair. With a shuffle of feet, DI Birch walked back into the room.

'I owe you both an apology.'

Birch's throat hurt. She felt hot. *I'm coming down with something*, she thought, and then tried to put out of her mind everything that she'd have to deal with in the near future. George Gulbraith, Lockley's case, the endless Three Rivers paperwork. Misconduct hearings. Probably a public inquiry. Her vision swam, just thinking about it.

She tried to anchor herself in the room again: Moira's living room. Ishbel was sitting on the couch beside her. Moira sat in the armchair opposite. They'd been talking, though Birch couldn't think for the life of her what they might have said to each other while she was outside.

'I need to apologise,' she said, 'for not having done things properly this evening. If you two wanted to talk, I should have set up proper mediation. There are channels for this kind of thing to be facilitated.'

Moira looked at Ishbel, and when she knew she'd caught the other woman's gaze, shook her head slightly. Ishbel smiled.

'You don't have to apologise, DI Birch,' Ishbel said. 'I essentially blackmailed you into coming here, what with the video and everything. And I'm glad I did, and I'd do it again. What's more, I'll say that in front of any disciplinary panel that you have to face.'

Birch felt her face colour.

'That's kind,' she said, 'but probably not really appropriate.'

Ishbel looked down at her cup of tea, now cold, but still hugged between her hands.

'I wasn't really planning it,' she said, almost to herself, 'but I kept thinking of it at odd moments. That thing he'd said – Lockley – about the Telfords. My brain kept reminding me that he'd said it. It got to be quite annoying – I'd be trying to focus on something, and the thought would pop up again. I didn't *want* to be thinking about him. He ruined everything, really. Lockley, I mean.'

Birch nodded.

'If it wasn't for him,' Ishbel went on, 'I would never have known about Abigail and the drugs. I would never have known she was in an awful relationship with that boy. I'd have been able to remember her the way I thought she was . . . the way I *knew* her. Now I feel like whenever I think of her, I'll think of that, first.'

Birch put a hand on Ishbel's arm.

'You won't,' she said. 'It feels like that. Right now you feel like you're always going to be angry at her for those things she did that were weak, or wrong, or criminal. But after a while, that anger does fade. I promise you.' Birch paused and took a deep breath, then added, 'Mine did.'

Both women looked up at her. Moira's head was cocked to one side, as though she were listening for a very faint, far-away sound.

'What do you mean?' Ishbel asked.

Birch took a deep breath.

'My little brother,' she said, 'was Charlie Birch.'

She waited for a reaction. Ishbel's face told her that she'd heard of Charlie, but Moira's brow furrowed.

'Charlie was a big missing-person case,' Birch said. 'Thirteen years ago, he went missing, and it was all over the news.' She waited, to see if anything dawned on Moira.

'Thirteen years ago,' Moira said, slowly. 'Ryan would have been seven. I don't remember much from that time that wasn't . . . well, Jackie was always busy with work. I was very wrapped up in motherhood, back then.'

'Okay,' Birch said. 'Well, Charlie went missing, and at first he was just another missing young man. He was twenty.' She paused, and then decided to say what she was thinking – what she'd been thinking endlessly, unbidden, these past three and a half weeks. 'He was Ryan's age.'

The two women nodded, as though this had helped them understand.

'Then . . .' Birch pulled herself up a little straighter. 'We started hearing these rumours. This was before I joined the force, so we were just *the family*. There were no FLOs back then, and we weren't kept in the loop all too well. But we learned that some local ex-cons were making noises about Charlie. It was implied that he'd been mixed up in some . . . illegal activities.'

Birch frowned, remembering.

'At some point,' she went on, 'Lockley picked up the trail. He was just a kid reporter then, just an intern. But for some reason he really latched on to this idea that Charlie was a bad apple. He started to dig up dirt on him that I had no idea about, my mother had no idea about. He hired a PI, and found all this damning information, apparently out of nowhere.'

Ishbel raised an eyebrow, and Birch nodded.

'Yeah . . . I guess now we know how he might have done that. Anyway, it turned out that Charlie had – well, fallen in with some really bad guys. I mean, I hesitate to use this word, but *gangsters*, basically. And – this is my theory, anyway – he'd got out of his depth. He owed people money, or favours, or something . . . and he couldn't make good. So he disappeared, or more likely, he *got* disappeared. Lockley wrote some really lurid stuff at the time, all these theories about it. He linked Charlie to every unsolved crime that he possibly could. He turned my brother from a missing man into a wanted man. It nearly killed my mum.'

All three women were quiet for a moment.

'I remember that,' Ishbel said. 'I remember reading some of those things. They were suggesting all sorts of . . . gangland-type things, weren't they?'

Birch nodded, her mouth a hard line.

'Some of the evidence pointed to an organised crime connection in Glasgow, yes,' she said. 'As you can imagine, Lockley had a field day.'

Moira's eyes were very wide.

'What happened?' she asked. 'Did they ever find him?'

Birch shook her head.

'The trail went cold,' she said. 'I went into the force because I wanted to look for my wee brother. If I'd found him, I might have ended up putting him behind bars – or worse, putting him in the ground. But . . . that would have been worth it, just to get closure. Thirteen years on, and he's still lost. It looks like he'll always be lost.'

Moira let out a small sigh: a soft, deflating sound.

'And your mother?'

Birch's eyes stung.

'She died,' she said. 'Cancer. Last year.'

'I'm sorry,' Moira whispered.

Birch straightened up, and turned back to Ishbel.

'So you see,' she said, pushing brightness back into her voice, 'for a while, whenever I thought about Charlie, I could only think about those allegations. I could only think about the things he'd done, or been accused of. But these days, I remember things like . . .' Birch laughed, surprising herself. 'Well, just recently I've been thinking about these curries he used to make. He loved star anise – you know, the spice? He made these curries with so much of the stuff in that they were almost inedible. I've been . . . smelling them, just recently, in my mind, and thinking of him. So . . . the good memories do come back.'

Moira looked doubtful. Birch nodded at her.

'It might take a while,' she said, 'but I truly believe – even for someone like you – they do.'

Ishbel climbed into the passenger seat of Birch's big black car. It was getting dark now, and rain had begun to fall. In the distance, she could hear the endless *shush* of cars moving through the slick, wet streets. Through the car window, the dim outside light on the front of Moira Summers' house refracted into a thousand raindrop sparks. The house's open front door threw a long stripe of orange light along the wet garden path. In that stripe, DI Birch stood silhouetted, shivering slightly, saying things to Moira that Ishbel couldn't hear.

While she waited, she watched the ghostly film-reel of Aidan – turning from his place at the vigil podium to take Netta's hand – playing out again and again in her mind, as though projected weakly onto the inside of the filmy windscreen. The more she let herself think about it, the less it stung. *Of course he had a mistress*: the thought was so obvious to her now that she wondered how she'd never let it occur to her before. Ishbel realised that the reasons she was bothered by it were nothing to do with loving Aidan. She'd stopped doing that a long time ago. They were more to do with the secret kept, with the fact that they'd carried on living inside the collapsed lung of their marriage for as long as they had. There had been so many angry words, and for nothing. Had they split, might Abigail still be alive? Ishbel could have moved west, could have taken Abigail with her, so she'd have attended a completely different campus – she'd have come home shocked and pale but safe, that May afternoon. That thought hurt too much to be borne – it dwarfed the pain of Netta, the pain of Aidan's long and pointless lie. *Think about something else*, Ishbel thought. *Anything.*

DI Birch's words drifted through her mind then, as though bidden: *the good memories do come back.* She tried to think of a good memory of Abigail. It was tricky: she wanted a memory that didn't also contain Aidan. In the end, she settled once again on the day they'd spent shopping for Abigail's prom dress. Though some of that day was hazy – key details feeling just out of reach – Ishbel remembered the pride she had taken in marking what felt like a milestone. Abigail was officially becoming an adult woman, with her own thoughts and secrets and hurts and joys. She had made sure they did grown-up things: going out for brunch before they walked to the shop, accepting the offer of free champagne to drink in the huge boudoir of the changing room. She'd been complacent, she realised. She'd assumed that this milestone was just one of many, stretching out into a future that eventually would no longer contain her, Ishbel. A future that

Abigail would walk on into alone, grown, and growing old herself. Ishbel remembered – watching Abigail preen and twirl in the changing room that day – imagining that one day they'd return there, this time for a wedding dress. And then later, that the wedding dress they bought together might be re-worn by Abigail's own daughter, while Ishbel looked on proudly, bent and old though she may be. She had eyed this future lazily, never once considering all the million tiny things that would need to happen *just so* in order to make it come true. Now it was a fiction: one so painful that Ishbel found herself breathing hard thinking about it, as though she'd been kicked.

'What are you thinking about, Mum?' Abigail had said to her. She'd walked out of the satin-curtained cubicle in a swishy taffeta dress that would, eventually, be the one Ishbel paid for.

'Time,' Ishbel had replied. 'I was thinking about time. It only feels like two minutes since your father and I were buying your first school uniform. Now suddenly you're this terrible adult. How did that happen?'

Abigail had laughed, showing the good, white teeth she was proud of, her smile very like Ishbel's own.

'I'm only seventeen,' she'd said, rolling her eyes. 'Don't condemn me to adulthood just yet.'

Ishbel blinked the memory away – the pain was too hot, too sharp. DI Birch was probably right: *it might take a while.*

Birch opened the driver's-side door of the car and sank down into her seat. Moira was still standing in the doorway of her house, watching them: a black figure in that orange column of light. The house looked big and empty, Ishbel thought: no other lights on anywhere, and curtains pulled across all the windows like grey shrouds. It looked sad – haunted, even. Against the side of the house the hoarding from the now-mended bay window was stacked: the words *Death is too good* still daubed there in red paint. As DI Birch started the engine and began to edge the Mondeo out into the road, Ishbel raised a hand and held it up close to the steamy glass of the car window. She saw Moira raise her own hand in farewell – and in the rear-view mirror, Ishbel watched her small form dwindle in the lit doorway, until they turned a corner and Moira Summers, and her house, disappeared.

They drove through the rain-lit streets in silence for a while, the car thick with unspoken things, each woman busy with her own thoughts.

'Okay,' Birch said, and Ishbel turned to look at her. 'I'm afraid I have to tell you something. Something not-great.'

Ishbel slumped in her seat. *Something else?* she thought. *Really?* 'What?'

Birch had her tongue slightly out: she was negotiating a roundabout.

'It's about Aidan,' she said. 'He's been taken in for questioning. I just had an email about it, while you were . . . dealing with Lockley.'

'Questioning about *what?*' Ishbel's head swam. Birch looked pained.

'You might have seen in the papers that Moira . . . she's been receiving death threats.'

'Yes.'

'Well,' Birch paused at a junction, and risked a glance at Ishbel. 'At first there were a *lot* of threats. I mean hundreds. Not all of them were credible, but . . . several were. That's why we've been . . . keeping an eye – on the house, and on Moira herself. As the weeks have gone on, they've thinned out pretty drastically, and we've been sifting through them, monitoring them all. We've ended up with only one source that we consider particularly credible, and . . . my guys have been working to find out who that source is.'

Ishbel let Birch see she'd figured it out.

'And . . . *your guys*. They think it's Aidan?'

There was a pause.

'He hasn't been arrested yet,' Birch said, and Ishbel could tell she was trying to tread carefully. 'We're very aware of how the press might report it, so at the moment he's just talking to us, and they're not being told what it's about.'

Ishbel kept her eyes fixed on the side of Birch's face, and stayed silent: a trick she'd learned for when people were dodging a question. Birch got the message.

'They're pretty sure,' Birch said, 'yes.'

Ishbel pressed one hand to her forehead.

'DI Birch,' she said, 'I cannot *believe* I married someone that stupid.'

They drove on in silence again. Ishbel closed her eyes, and listened to the hiss and ebb of the rain-soaked city.

'Anyway,' Birch said at last, as though the quiet had become too much for her, 'it's been quite the day. You must be exhausted.'

Ishbel thought for a moment.

'I am,' she said. 'But I feel like I did something good today. I haven't felt like that in a really long time.'

Birch smiled.

'You did something that a lot of people have wished they could,' she said. 'You've neutralised Grant Lockley, even if only temporarily. Many have tried . . . but in the end, it took a very smart woman.'

Ishbel was quiet.

'Not smart,' she said. 'Just desperate. It felt like he was never going to leave me – leave *us* – alone. And I don't think I could have survived another Lockley grenade being lobbed into my life.'

Birch was nodding, her eyes on the road.

'But I didn't mean Lockley,' Ishbel went on. 'Just then, when I said "something good"; I meant . . . well, just talking about it. About what happened. With Moira.'

Birch stopped at a crossing. A young woman walked into the street in front of them, bundled under an umbrella and looking down at her phone, her face illuminated by a little updraft of light.

'You know,' Ishbel said, 'I haven't talked with many people, since that day. Aidan of course, and my mother-in-law, and Rehan. I talked a little bit with a friend of ours – a friend of *mine*, Greg – at Abigail's cremation. I kept expecting people to understand, to *really* understand, you know? But I felt like no one did. Especially not Aidan, though she was his daughter, too. And . . . it's odd. It's really odd, but . . . tonight, I feel like I finally talked with someone who got it. When she said she was sorry for my loss, I really believed it. Isn't that strange? Of all the people . . .'

Both women were quiet for a moment. The light changed, and the Mondeo chugged on.

'These are strange times,' Birch said, into the quiet. 'I think we've all been navigating a world that none of us really recognises.'

The black car slid on through the streets. Whenever it slowed or paused, Ishbel looked out at pedestrians hurrying home through the weather, and in at lit windows softened by condensation, beyond which glasses and silverware and faces vaguely gleamed.

'I've just realised,' Birch said, 'I'm driving you home. To Trinity. But . . . is that where you want to go?'

Ishbel said nothing for a long time. The car idled at a cross-roads, floodlit by the high windows of a steamed-up city bus.

'You can't stay in a Travelodge forever.' DI Birch's voice was gentle. 'Don't you have somewhere else you could go? Perhaps . . . the friend you mentioned?'

Ishbel frowned: no, that was no good. She realised it wasn't the first time she'd considered calling Greg, asking if he could help her. He would want to, she knew. Taking care of people was what Greg did. But he wouldn't understand, not properly. Moira Summers understood, but it turned out even she couldn't help, even if she had shone a small and temporary light into the darkness. The darkness was still huge, and loud: things moved around inside it that Ishbel couldn't see, and it frightened her. The darkness was called *my only daughter is dead* and she knew she would have to navigate it alone, for as long as it took. For as long as its terrible terrain stretched out in front of her.

'You're right,' Ishbel said. She sniffed back a sudden headful of tears. 'But it'll do for now.'

She straightened her shoulders and looked up through the windscreen, at the yellow lights of the Old Town, aware of DI Birch watching her.

'I can tell you how to get there,' she said. 'We're already going in the right direction.'

ALLEGATIONS OF EMAIL HACKING: OUR OFFICIAL STATEMENT OF 10 JUNE

It has come to our attention that several allegations of email hacking – and of the dissemination of confidential information obtained illegally – have been made against Grant Lockley. Mr Lockley has for three years been one of our staff columnists, and prior to that worked as a freelancer, with some articles commissioned by our parent group and published here.

We want to assure our readers that we take such allegations very seriously, and that we do not condone any kind of exploitative or illegal behaviour conducted in the pursuit of news stories. We will always seek to work with regulatory and legal bodies to ensure that any such behaviour is thoroughly and fairly investigated, and we support appropriate sanctions – legal and other – for any individual who is found guilty of conduct that breaches our code of practice.

We are currently working with Police Scotland to assist their investigation into Mr Lockley's activities, both historical and more recent. We are unable to comment on the specifics of this investigation at this time, for legal reasons. However, we can confirm that Mr Lockley has been suspended from his post, pending the outcome of this investigation. Until such time as this matter is concluded, Mr Lockley's column will be authored by a series of guest writers.

Richmond Sheridan
Editor-in-Chief

Grant Lockley is away.
Comments are disabled on this article.

That day

14 May, 7.45 a.m.

Abigail stepped down off the bus, blinking fast. It had been stuffy in there: too many people crowded together, swaying sleepily in their seats and in the aisles. She'd been nodding off herself, and almost slept past her stop; the inrush of cold air from the folding doors, and the chatter of her fellow students as they jostled to disembark had roused her. She'd been weirded out by a dream – could still feel the shadow of it clinging to her like a chill cloud, like the shadow of a stranger standing a little too close. She'd been dreaming about her mother. They'd fought, last night – they'd been sniping at each other a lot lately, and in her more honest moments Abigail knew that it was her own fault, and that she was making her mother sad.

In the dream, Abigail was floating, like she had no body, or as though she were weightless: able to hover above the world without effort, and watch it go by. She was watching her mother from a great distance – though of course, because it was a dream and dreams are strange, she was also able to see every detail of her mother's movements, right down to the expression on her face. And her face was frantic. Her mother was convinced that something had happened to Abigail, something bad, that Abigail was lost, somewhere, and needed her. Her mother was running, running, running – her feet slapping on concrete, her possessions scattering around her – trying to get to Abigail, trying to reach her. Above her, Abigail could feel herself floating, bodyless, motionless, and she was calling out, *Mummy, it's okay, I'm fine. I'm fine – I'm here. Look up! Mummy, I'm here!* But her mother couldn't hear her: she only got more and more frantic. She only kept on running, and running.

Abigail did her best to shake off the dream. She had other, bigger things to think about today. As she climbed the sloped pavement, the outline of the campus buildings began to appear on the rise above her. The sun, not long above the roofs, lit up their topmost windows with soft bands of pink and orange light. All around her, fellow students were plodding towards the campus gateway: backpacks slung low on their shoulders, and white wires, exactly the same as her own earbuds, hanging from their ears. Among them, Abigail tried to pick out Jack – the long, slim curve of him in his good wool coat – or to smell on the air the fragranced smoke from his cherry-flavoured vape. But Jack wasn't in yet. She'd planned to come in early, and she'd actually managed to do it. She had a little time left, to think, before he arrived.

She made it to the campus gates. In front of her, the great expanse of the car park stretched – almost full already. The weather forecast had said it would be warm today, but the air still felt cool and damp: little curls of steam were rising from the shiny bonnets of recently arrived cars. Along the side of the car park, there was a row of sycamore trees, with picnic benches dotted around underneath them. They were still young trees: out of nowhere, Abigail remembered the day they'd been brought on a huge truck and planted, their roots wrapped in some weird, pale-coloured felt. Between them, the watery sun was shining now, throwing bars of light–dark, light–dark across the grass. As everyone else funnelled towards the college buildings, Abigail peeled off from the pack and crossed to the nearest picnic bench, which, though cold to the touch, was fairly dry. She swung one foot into the bench's well, and then the other. Around her, the foggy strands of her dream still hung.

This is it, she thought. *Today is the day.* She felt strangely excited: today would be like all those scenes in movies, where the heroine makes a decision to leave her old, terrible life behind and walk forward out of its smouldering ruins. The movie versions usually involved some sort of radical makeover, too: Abigail toyed with the idea of shaving her head, or ditching her patterns and colours in favour of rock 'n' roll black and red lipstick, like Sandy in *Grease*, her secret favourite film. But no – she mainly just needed to *do the thing*. And *the thing* was get rid of Jack. Abigail didn't like the word *dump* – it was so teenage, and felt like too trivial a description for her scenario. But yes, she was going to dump him. She expected it would nearly kill her, but she felt like she was dying anyway. Dying of anxiety at being caught with enough gear on her to make an intent-to-supply charge stick. Dying of jealousy whenever Jack talked about another girl, or looked at another girl, or made a disparaging comment about her, or forgot to text back. Dying of embarrassment about the meet last night, which Jack had failed to show up for. Dying of fear over what Jamie might do to her if the next meet didn't go perfectly to plan. And dying of shame, because her parents were paying for her to do a college course that she wasn't really doing, paying for her to pursue a career and a future that she was rapidly losing sight of. She was failing. She was dying of failure. So, though it was going to hurt probably worse than any hurt she'd felt before, she had to do it. She had to get out.

Abigail rummaged in her backpack, and took out the brand new journal that she'd bought just a couple of days before. Last night, having fought with her mother, and having locked herself in her room to cry, she'd got up in the middle of the night and written a stern letter to herself, on the first two pages of this crisp new book. *A fresh start.* This journal didn't have a lock, like her old one – that also seemed too teenage – and she was worried that someone might steal it, and find out what was inside her head. But now she flipped the front cover and quickly skim-read the bullet points she'd made, the action plan that, any minute now, she'd need to follow. When she got to the letter's final paragraph she slowed down, and read more carefully, letting the words sink in.

This is it, girl. This is enough. Haven't you had enough? This is NOT how love is supposed to feel. This is NOT the person you really are. I mean, who have you become? Who IS this girl who's blowing off all her friends to hang out with a guy? Who is this girl who's being a total dick to her parents? Who is this girl who's throwing away her dream career so she can hang about in cemeteries and do pathetic drug deals with pathetic men? That girl is not me, that's not who I want to

*be. I want to be able to think my own thoughts, without Jack constantly
hijacking them. I want to be able to put my phone away and not look
at it for an hour, or a day, or however long I like! I want to be able to
walk down the corridor at college and not have everyone staring at me
and whispering. I want to give Mum a big hug and tell her I'm sorry
for all these times lately that we've fought, and I'm sorry for all the
things I've said that were terrible. I want to be better. I really do. I love
Jack, but I love my family more. I love myself more. It's time to let go
and GET OUT! Tomorrow, okay? NO BACKING OUT. This is IT.
This is it, Abigail. GO GET IT.*

Abigail sat looking at those final lines for what felt like a long
time. Around her, she could hear birds singing. She could hear the
low rumble of buses pulling up at the stop down the hill, and the
chatter of students as they wandered onto campus, still rubbing
the sleep from their eyes. She felt cold, and she shivered, and the
shiver felt like a bolt of electricity running through her, galvanis-
ing her for the task. *Yes.* She was going to do it. She was going to
do this thing.

The smell of cherries on the air made her look up. Jack was
standing on the other side of the car park, vaping and looking
down at his phone, a fat plume of smoke hanging beside him in
the chill morning air. He wasn't wearing his wool coat today –
instead, that pink checked shirt that was his favourite, with the
grey lambswool cardigan buttoned over the top. *His uniform,*
Abigail thought. He hadn't spotted her, and she let herself luxuri-
ate in a last, long look at him: the last few minutes of being his
girlfriend, before she did the painful deed. She looked at his fancy
brown brogues as they tapped – one toe and then the other, a
nervous tic – against the tarmac. She looked at his fine face with
its high cheekbones: his grey eyes held captive by the big glasses
in their tortoiseshell frames. He'd seen something on his phone
that made him smile, and she felt a final snap of jealousy, wondering who might have sent him a text, who might be flirting with
him. His smile was what she'd always loved most about him, she
thought, but lately, he'd weaponised it. He brought it out whenever he wanted something from her, and withheld it when she

didn't comply. It had become the smile of a tiger: beautiful, but also a warning. It always came before a snarl.

She looked down again at the journal in her hands, and let her eyes flick over the words one final time. *I'm sorry for all the things I've said that were terrible. I want to be better. I really do.* She almost laughed. She didn't need this any more: the path into her future was solid now, she was sure. She took a quick look around her, then ripped out the two scrawled pages from the front of the book. She kept her eyes on Jack as she tore the pages first into two, then into four, and then started shredding them, erasing and erasing her words until they were nothing more than marks on little bits of confetti. As she pushed the now-empty journal back into her bag, she balled the scraps and tatters into one fist, then raised it, to glance at her watch. 8.10 a.m. *Time to face the music,* she thought. Time to do the first good thing in a new, good life. *Yes.*

She stood up, opening her hands, and walked out across the sun-striped tarmac towards Jack. Behind her, a flutter of white petals, scattering into the grass, and over the car park, and into the air.

Acknowledgements

I cannot express enough gratitude to Nelle Andrew: Nelle, before you came along this book was less a novel, more a giant knot, and I couldn't have untied it without your help. I am deeply grateful to the other Lucy Cavendish College Fiction Prize judges and organisers, too, and to former Lucy Cavendish winner Catherine Chanter. Catherine, your wise words are in my head every time I sit down to write.

A huge, huge thank you to my gorgeous agent Cathryn Summerhayes, for everything, but in particular for always being happy to sit down and explain things to me in words of one syllable. Thanks also to Irene and everyone else at Curtis Brown.

I have been incredibly lucky to have the brilliant Ruth Tross as my editor. Ruth, thank you so much for just *getting* this book, and for being my champion every step of the way. Thanks too to Louise, Cicely and everyone at Hodder: you've made me feel so welcome.

I want to hug all of the staff at Moniack Mhor Creative Writing Centre: folks, I was with you during one of the most difficult times of my life, and you took incredibly good care of me. Special mention to Heather Clyne, who rescued me from peril more times than I care to mention.

To everyone at Scottish Book Trust, but especially to Koren, Philippa, Caitrin, Lynsey and Kay. Thank you, ladies, for everything.

Thank you to the people who helped with technical bits and pieces for this book: Emma Hack, for being my unofficial DI Birch;

JH Campbell, who advised me on ballistics; @ConstableChaos for schooling me on shift rotations for scene guards; @MsAshleyDavies for giving insider info on tabloid papers, and Michael O'Byrne for writing *The Crime Writer's Guide to Police Practice and Procedure*. Any errors in this book are mine, and not theirs.

Thank you to the two greatest beta-readers (and, coincidentally, the two greatest friends) in the world: Leon Crosby and Stella Hervey Birrell. I love you two.

A thousand thank yous to the gang of incredible women writers who have offered unstinting support throughout the writing of this novel: my coven Julie Danskin, Sasha de Buyl and Alice Tarbuck; the brilliant Natalie Fergie and all of the Write Like A Grrrl! and #GrrrlCon gang; Jane Bradley and Kerry Ryan, who give the best pep talks; and Marjorie Lotfi Gill, who bakes the best flapjacks. An extra-special mention to Helen Sedgwick: Helen, I can't even begin to thank you. Without you, this novel would be gathering dust in a drawer.

So much love and thanks to my mum and dad, and to Nick Askew: brother, housemate and personal Samaritan. Without you three, I wouldn't be a writer. You never ever stop cheering me on: thank you. The same love and thanks to Stephen Welsh: Steve, your patience and kindness meant so much to me, and always will.

Finally: there is not enough love or thanks in the world for Dominic Stevenson, without whom this book would never have seen the light of day. Dom, with every fibre in my being: thank you. #Stevenskew for the epic win!